TRIALS FOR THE HAUNTED

TRIALS FOR THE HAUNTED

J.J. KĪMMORIST

BOW'S
BOOKSHELF

EBook ISBN: 979-8-88716-030-6

Trade Paperback ISBN: 979-8-88716-028-3

Hardcover ISBN: 979-8-88716-029-0

Cover design and artwork by Justin Scott

Published by Bow's Bookshelf, Inc.

Anna Stileski, Publisher

Join our Bow's Bookshelf Reader's Club for new projects, deals, and giveaways. Sign up at Bowsbookshelf.com.

For Jenna
For all the nights you read to me past our bedtime.

PART ONE
GARON

1

THE ALTAR

Syn's hand trembled on the dagger she held at the sacrifice's neck. The metal blade pressed against the woman's skin, drawing a single droplet of blood.

"Come on, Syn. Kill her," she said to herself.

Syn didn't dare look the sacrifice in the eye. Instead, she focused on a chipped board on the altar beneath her. "It'll be worse if she's left alive when the Scalers come for her," she said to the board.

Instead of bringing the killing strike, she sat on the frozen structure protruding into the morning air. The village called the wooden slab atop of the Ancestral Hill "the altar," but Syn recognized it for what it was: a butchering block. What had she expected? A feathered bed for the soon-to-be-dead sacrifice? The altar contained no ceremonial carvings or decorations, it simply served its function: a trap for the Scalers.

And today was Syn's turn to bait the trap.

Her hand hesitated on the blade. A cold gust of wind pierced through the thick hide of her fur cloak and a creak sounded above her. She looked up, seeing the domed trap dangling from thick ropes attached to the crossbeams at each corner of the altar. Through the metal bars of the cage suspended above her, she could see the sky promised snow. The cage loomed with assurance to fall and imprison any Scalers who might enter the Surface world in search of blood. With the trap cranked and set, all that remained was for Syn to perform the sacrifice.

Syn cursed the Season and turned back to the altar. On the final day of the Season of Slaughter, and at the age of nineteen, Syn had delayed her initiation long enough. Her last chance to prove herself a Legionite citizen laid before her.

Still, she hesitated.

It is the greatest honor to give your life as a sacrifice. Memories of the Elders' voices echoed back to her. As a child, Syn would sit cross-legged on the floor of the community lodge and listen to the teachings of the Elders. *A life surrendered for the protection of the village will be blessed by the Legion in the next life.*

The teachings of sacrifice always made Syn's stomach churn. She preferred when the Elders would move on to the legends of Nighterrian warriors battling the beasts on the other side of the portal.

A shimmer at the corner of her vision snatched her attention, and she glanced over her shoulder toward the lip of the hill just a few paces away. Bones from generations of human sacrifices littered the sloping ground and poked out from the snow like sprouting flowers of death. Beyond the skeletal remains, the portal glimmered like the surface of a puddle at midnight. The presence of the gateway called out to her like the prickly feeling of eyes at her back. Syn's mind swirled with images of deadly creatures clawing their way out of the portal.

"The Nighterrian defenses could be enough." She spoke again to the splintered plank beneath her knees to avoid eye contact with the sacrifice. "The Scalers might not break through. I would end up killing this woman for no reason." She attempted to convince herself but found no true conviction. The beasts were tenacious and the protection of the Nighterrians only extended so far.

Trapped by indecision, she turned her attention away again and peered over the edge of the altar built atop the mountain of bones. Though she couldn't see them, she knew a small crowd gathered at the base of the hill. The crowd would contain the village Elders—along with her parents. She could feel their expectant stares pointed at her like nocked arrows.

The village of Garon spread out around her in the distance. Rings of homes circled the Ancestral Hill in a series of concentric circles that broke up the white vastness of the snow. Smoke rose from chimneys and firepits and, if she listened past the clatter of daily life, she could pick out children laughing.

"I need to protect them."

Syn fought back a pounding headache and wrestled her focus back to the blade in her hand. Despite the freezing weather and the piercing wind, sweat pooled beneath her furs. With her free hand, she pushed the hood of her fox pelt cloak off her head and tucked a stray braid behind her ear.

It's time.

She sensed the sacrifice—a stranger from another village—staring up at her. Syn let her sight wander over the pitiful woman without reaching her eyes. She had the tanned skin and dark hair of Legionite heritage. Syn assumed her eyes—if she looked into them—would be teardrop shaped just like Syn's and the rest of her people. The sacrifice's body looked tiny and fragile against the bloodstained wood. The woman— no, *girl*—was young, perhaps even younger than Syn, maybe around sixteen or seventeen.

She must be freezing. The girl wore only a flimsy cotton shift with no shoes. Her lips were a bright shade of blue. The blue, however, seemed too unnatural to be from the cold. Syn attributed it to whatever disease she appeared to be dying from. If it weren't for the rise and fall of her chest and the wisps of condensed air escaping her lips, she might appear already dead. The sacrifice didn't fight or protest the dagger Syn held to her neck. The Elders hadn't even bothered to tie her feet or ankles when they placed her on the altar. Either the girl was truly devoted, or a complete invalid.

"You'll die soon no matter what I do. The Legion has decided your fate." Syn's breath came out in shallow puffs. "They deemed you terminally ill. I'd just be putting an end to your suffering."

The sacrifice did not respond. Perhaps she couldn't speak.

Clenching her jaw, Syn imagined herself running the blade across the girl's throat. Her upbringing as a butchers' daughter taught her how to sever the arteries of various animals without unnecessary suffering. She tried to picture the sacrifice as a goat or a wolf. A single, clean slice would end the girl's life quickly; yet her hand remained frozen in place.

She fought the desire to look into the girl's eyes. She didn't want to see into her soul, yet part of her felt the urge to behold the life she was about to take. *No, don't look.* Her grip on the knife trembled, leaving shallow cuts along the girl's bare throat.

Without warning, a sharp stab of fear clawed up Syn's spine and dumped its weight into her chest in a smothering heap.

"No, not now..." Signs of her curse began to shove their way into her mind. Dark shadows crept at the edge of her vision. Her headache flared to life inside her skull. "Not here, not today!"

Syn begged the visions to leave her be, but they remained perched inside her mind, gathering strength. She could feel them bearing down. Soon she would drown beneath their presence.

No more time to think. She needed to act fast and get off the Ancestral Hill before the ghosts converged. Distracted by the haunting visions, Syn glanced carelessly down at the sacrifice. They locked eyes.

The simple mistake was all it took for Syn to know it was over.

The girl had gray eyes—the same color Syn saw staring back at her from her own reflection in the blade of the dagger. In an instant, Syn understood the girl's terror. The transference of her pleading stare reverberated through Syn's chest and crippled her resolve. The sacrifice did not want to die, and Syn knew she could not take her life so much as she could melt the glaciers or leap across the ice gorge.

Syn yanked the knife away from the girl's neck, but blood still needed to be spilt to attract the Scalers' scent. Syn untied the leather bracer on her left wrist and rolled up her sleeve. Wincing, she ran a long slice along the back of her forearm.

"I'm sorry, I'm so sorry."

Syn dripped the blood from her wound over the dying girl's neck. The girl didn't respond; she didn't move or protest. She just continued to stare at Syn with those familiar gray eyes filled with fear and betrayal.

Dark images began to flit across Syn's vision. Fighting against the arrival of her curse, she spilled as much blood as she dared. She prayed it would be enough to bait the trap and pull the Scaler's attention away from the hundreds of innocent lives below.

When the deed was done, she pulled her sleeve back down and tied the leather bracer tight to halt the flow of blood. Half muttered prayers tumbled from her lips as she implored the

Legion for forgiveness. All the while, seeds of fear blossomed in her chest.

Syn jumped to her feet and nearly collapsed from the sharp movement and loss of blood. Once she gained her composure, she left the slab of the altar and gave the cage's lever two extra cranks for good measure. She then raced for retreat down the slippery stairs built into the steep hill.

Guilt halted her on the first step.

She stopped, squinting past the shadows writhing in her peripheral vision to regard the blue-lipped girl. The poor stranger would meet a slow, horrifying end once the trap sprung and caged the Scalers in with her. No one would be there to offer her a swift death when the beasts tore their way through her guts to eat her alive. Or worse, if she was bitten and survived, she would lose her soul forever.

No, she'll freeze to death first. Syn held on to that rationale, her only defense in the face of her disaster.

Remorse settled around her shoulders. She turned away and held back tears as she ran down the steps of the bone-filled mountain to greet her family as a liar, a weakling, and a failure.

2

HAUNTING

Snow crunched beneath Syn's feet as she stepped off the last step of the Ancestral Hill and onto flat ground. She took a deep breath hoping to banish the dark shapes coalescing around her. It bore no use. Fear welled up in her throat and she swallowed hard as her parents jogged up to her.

"Did you do it?" asked her mother, Vertah.

On the outside, Vertah appeared as the older rendition of Syn. Her hair flung around her heart-shaped face in a multitude of tiny braids. She grabbed Syn's hands to examine the blood. The disbelief in her expression stung.

Her father beamed his wide, honest smile. "I knew she could." Predon patted Syn's shoulder.

Syn glanced beyond her father's proud expression and spied the Gravers making their slow retreat away from the base of the Ancestral Hill. With the sacrifice delivered and the job now done, they would be moving on to deliver offerings and sacrifices to the next village. Tiny tendrils of shadows wormed their way into the edge of her vision as she watched the three red-hooded figures exit the palisade.

A shiver trickled down her back at the sight of them. The holy transients wandered the land and practiced secret rituals for the dead. During the Season of Slaughter, the Gravers scoured the region for appropriate sacrifices. They collected people dying of disease or crippled victims of animal attacks. Anyone deemed unfit to fight might find their way upon the altar.

Syn had met three of them earlier that morning when her mother stitched up a wound on one of the men's arms. The Gravers were strange but harmless. Syn feared them, nonetheless. Their presence reminded her she might only be a broken leg away from becoming a sacrifice herself.

Syn shifted her focus away from them as Chief Groth and six Nameless Elders stepped forward. Groth wore his typical serious expression lined with age and displeasure. His ceremonial wolf headdress made it look as if the jaws of the white beast swallowed his face.

"You have the blade?" Chief Groth asked.

Syn surrendered her dagger. She hoped no one would notice the blood weeping from the wound beneath her sleeve or spy evidence of her haunting spreading over her expression.

The Chief nodded to Syn, and she knelt before him. The Divine Creedence would come next. Syn had prepared for this moment all her life. Over the past five years she had watched with bruised pride as each one of her snickering peers gained their citizenship before her. She grappled with the desire to seize her place among her people all while choking back utter shame at the undeserved honor. The deception, she was certain, must be as visible on her face as the blood on her hands.

Chief Groth eyed her with wary suspicion.

He knows I didn't do the sacrifice! Syn felt she might be sick and fought back the burning taste of bile as she tried her best to imitate bravery. Fear thundered through her veins and shadows shot across her vision like bats taking flight.

Groth broke the stare and motioned to the Elder on his right. The Elder dragged his finger up the side of Syn's blade to collect the blood while Chief Groth commenced without preamble.

"We are Legionite," he began. "We are the keepers of the portals."

Syn tried to voice the response carved into her since she learned to speak. She had rehearsed the words a thousand times—she could say them in her sleep—but now she struggled to bring breath to her lungs.

"I-I w-will defend," she said.

The Elder traced a line of blood down her face from her forehead, over her small nose, and down her chin.

"We are the sworn swords of justice," Groth said.

"I will... sacrifice," A blatant lie. She nearly choked on it.

"We are the soldiers at the edge of the world."

"I w-will never surrender." Syn's voice cracked. She bowed her head in embarrassment.

Groth accepted a smoldering bundle of ritual brush from the Elder on his left and circled the red smoke around Syn's head. "May the Legion of the Nameless forever carry you into another life."

The smoke smothered her. It smelled of earth and rust—like the iron tang of blood. Worse, the haunting further solidified its presence around her. The brightness of the snow sent a throbbing ache through her head. She didn't have much time before her curse took over her senses completely.

"Stand, Syndrah Tri-Garon," Groth said, his face smeared with disapproval. "And join your fellow Legionites as a sanctified third-ring soldier."

Syn stood, trying not to cough on the thick stench of

burning sage. She glanced up at the Chief and flinched. Her haunting warped her vision, bringing his wolf headdress to life. It snarled and bared its teeth, its empty eye sockets glaring at her with all the dread of the Abyss. She retracted her focus from the headdress and looked into the Chief's eyes but that only made things worse. His face began to melt. Skin slipped off his bones, revealing bloody muscle and sinew beneath.

It's not real, it's not real! Syn fought the desire to run away screaming.

Groth grunted at her strange behavior and handed the bloodied dagger back to Predon before turning and walking away with the Nameless Elders at his flank. Syn nearly collapsed in relief. It was over, she had done it, but the haunting continued to close in around her. Voices became echoes and background noises roared in her ears.

"I've been waiting to give this to you for many years." Her father's voice sounded far away.

Syn struggled to breathe, but no one else saw how the world was turning dark. Black shadows took on human shapes and glided toward her. Predon placed something in her hands —a sheathed sword, she realized—but she couldn't bring herself to focus on it.

"Syn? Syn, are you well?" Predon asked.

Vertah hushed him and looked over her shoulder at the retreating Elders. She crouched and whispered, "Is it happening again?"

Syn nodded. Vertah gave an annoyed scoff. "Why now of all times?"

"She can't control when the affliction strikes," Predon said.

"Shhh, not so loud!" Vertah scolded.

"I-I have to go." Syn backed away, sword still clutched in her hands.

She saw her mother's disappointed expression just before

it melted from her face in a dripping vision of horror. Her father's face held one of concern before it transformed into that of a beast. Fangs extended from his mouth while his jaw elongated into a snout.

Syn turned and ran.

She dodged the sharpened stakes of the palisade surrounding the Ancestral Hill and passed the first ring of longhouses as the faces of the Prime citizens turned to decayed flesh. The second and third rings of the village fell away behind her as she weaved past homes and jumped over piles of wood and creeping shadows. By the time she sprinted though the fifth ring, silhouettes of long-dead ghosts peered out from behind drying animal hides.

Snow kicked up behind her as she ran past the huts of the Outskirts and plunged into the woods. Tree limbs turned to spindly hands and reached out to grab her. Syn willed her legs to run faster as tears streamed from her eyes.

She followed her well-worn route through the woods, focusing only on her sanctuary. She could see it in the treetop just ahead, but the haunting had reached its zenith. The shadows took on texture as they transformed into blackened apparitions in all shapes and sizes. Onyx fangs, scales, and talons glinted against the snow and lunged out at her from behind the trees. Syn yelped as she jumped away from the swipe of imagined claws.

She reached her destination and threw the sword belt over her shoulder to climb the tree to her hideout. Her practiced limbs carried her up and away from the phantom creatures prowling below. Sobs of fear racked her chest as she grasped for ropes and hauled herself onto the wide hammock strung between two sturdy limbs. Before the branches could turn to clawed hands and seek her throat, she pulled each side of the hammock around her like a bat tucking its wings.

Her cocoon blocked out the visions but offered no protection from the force pressing against her chest. Syn trembled and cried as the haunting squeezed her lungs and strangled her airway. She choked and struggled for air as she fought against the darkness taking over her body.

It's going to kill me this time—her final thought before the fear consumed her and the world went black.

3
THE EMPTY HOUR

The haunting did not bring her death, though it always felt like it would when the darkness clamped its hands around her senses and threatened to steal her breath forever.

Syn untucked her body from the folds of her hammock and peeked out into the dreary calmness of the day. Though she had only been unconscious for a few minutes, the world around her wore a new face. The trees stood natural and intimate, and the shadows kept to themselves. Syn's perception had returned to normal, but she was left feeling hollow and drained. She named the gloomy period following an attack from her haunting "the empty hour."

She sat up with lethargic slowness. Over the years, her hideout increased in necessity and decoration. All around her hung strings of trinkets she had collected since childhood: damaged utensils, half buttons, and discarded toys. All the broken and forgotten things found their way to Syn's hideout.

"Hello everyone," she said to her friends. "It's... it's getting worse." The trinkets didn't speak back of course. She reached out to touch a headless doll named Amy. "Father promised I would grow out of it."

Despondency prevailed as memories of her younger self barged through her unarmored thoughts. She remembered clinging to her father's chest at the age of six. She had shrieked and screamed like a dying animal while her mother tried to pry her free. Syn didn't understand why no one else could see the ghosts she clawed so frantically to get away from. When it ended, she had awoken to the sight of scratch marks left across her mother's arms and her father's face. The fear in her parents' eyes branded her childhood memories with an irrevocable stain.

Syn turned over her shoulder to regard a series of broken pottery named Raymond, Ryan, and Dustin. "Father was wrong." She breathed a heavy sigh. "If anything, it's only getting worse."

Her parents had taken her to every healer in the surrounding villages. She remembered complaining as they trudged through the snow, day after day, seeking answers for her ailment. Eventually, they had met the oldest woman Syn had ever seen.

She remembered shying away from the healer's wrinkled hands and drooping face. The old crone had poked and prodded and made Syn drink a bitter tea while she prayed, and sang, and burned too much sage. By the end, the elderly woman had concluded that Syn was simply an old soul haunted by the ghosts of her past lives.

"The soul is like a tree. The more seasons it has seen, the larger it grows until one day it peaks above the canopy—a force that cannot be contained." She had pressed her crooked finger beneath Syn's chin and tilted her face upward. Syn looked into the healer's milky eyes. *"In a forest of saplings, you are an ancient oak. You must embrace the shadows cast by your branches."*

Syn didn't feel ancient. She was only seven at the time. But even then, she knew what the healer really meant: she was cursed.

"How do we fix her?" Her mother had asked after the diagnosis.

"There is no fixing, only accepting."

"Please, there must be something," her father had insisted. *"She's terrified constantly."*

The healer only shook her head as she continued to stare into Syn's eyes.

Syn now rubbed the dried tears and snot from her face and looked to Miranda, the mangled bone necklace dangling to her right. "How much longer can I keep this secret?"

The image of a boy with a sharp jaw and handsome dark eyes floated into her mind. A son of the black. A boy named Drekton, her betrothed. The only delay to her arranged marriage was her lack of citizenship. Now as an official Legionite citizen, marriage would come within the month.

"Once I marry, there's no way I'll be able to I hide my haunting," she said to Miranda, a mangled bone necklace. Her insides would usually flutter at the thought of Drekton, but now she felt only dread. "Before long, he'll find out the whispers about me are true. He'll know I'm crazy."

Silence answered as she watched her inanimate friends sway in the treetop breeze. She barked a bitter laugh. "Maybe it doesn't matter. I talk to all of you more than anyone else. Perhaps I've already lost my mind."

She shook her head and looked down at the blood staining her hands. The numbness of the empty hour kept the guilt from overwhelming her. She unlaced her bracer and peeled back her wet sleeve to check her wound. Blood surrounded the parted flesh. She'd need to stitch it closed.

Syn collected her emergency supply of needle, thread, and

vinegar from a hollow in the tree and set to work cleaning the cut. She gasped at the sting of the vinegar before threading the needle. Shame volunteered a confession as she stitched her wound closed.

"I couldn't do it," she said to the oppressive silence.

Thoughts of the reptilian beasts surfacing from the portal crawled into her mind. She imagined what the Scaler's bite and the damning power of its venom might feel like. How would it feel to have your soul ripped from your body as you transformed into a beast?

"Don't dwell on it, Syn," she said to herself. "What's done is done."

She blinked hard to cast the image away as she tied off the last stitch. She reached for a scrap of fabric to wrap her arm, but as she shifted to lean against the trunk of the tree, the scabbard of the sword jabbed against her back. With a grunt, she reached back and pulled the sword and belt off her shoulder. She had nearly forgotten about the gift from her father.

Syn recognized the sword before extracting it from its sheath. It was her father's most prized possession.

"I don't deserve this." Syn turned the weapon over in her hands.

The arm length blade glittered with deadly sharpness. The hilt contained antler carved with the skulls of humans, animals, and beasts. The decorative skulls protruded from the hilt in an arrangement of rings that descended into smaller circles around the center of the hilt. They represented the path her ancestors took in ascending through the rings of status in Garon.

Her great-great-grandfather had been a Pen-Garon, a fifth-ring soldier. After generations of feats of bravery and acts of faith, her ancestors had climbed their way up to the third ring of longhouses surrounding the Ancestral Hill and earned the status of Tri-Garon.

She stared down at her vacant reflection in the blade. Wretchedness prickled at her core. The family heirloom did not belong in her lie-stained hands. She returned the sword to its sheath and finished wrapping her arm.

"I suppose I've cowered up here long enough," she said to Marcus, a broken comb. "Mother will still expect me to perform my duties for the day." She slung the sword back over her shoulder and forced herself to crawl from her hammock.

"Goodbye, friends." She climbed down the tree.

Deciding to take the long way home, Syn winded her way through the woods. She felt the numbness of the empty hour fading and guilt began to rush in. She tried to convince herself the Nighterrians who guarded the portal from within Interterra would keep Scalers from surfacing.

"Surely the holy warriors can manage the beasts," she said to the trees. "I mean, that's their job, isn't it?"

The snowy pines accepted her flimsy justification. Sometimes no Scalers arrived from the portal on the ninety days of the Season, the sacrifice rotting without a Scaler's arrival. The decomposing bait would then be replaced with a freshly wasted life the following week. On the final day of the Season of Slaughter, the probability of the beasts' early migration remained in her favor.

"I've made my decision," she said as she trudged on. Consumed by her emotions, she almost didn't notice the dark figure step from behind the trees. "I'll just have to—"

An enormous man lumbered from the trees. He wore no furs—only black trousers and a thin black tunic. With red eyes, pale skin, and a dark beard covering half his face, he held no resemblance to the Legionite men from villages in the surrounding area.

Syn gasped and ducked behind a tree. Too late, she knew he had seen her.

"Who's there?" His voice boomed deep and threatening. His large, leather-booted feet crunched through the snow, closer and closer.

Syn pulled the sword from her back and peeked out from behind the tree. She jumped back as she came nearly face to face with the stranger with red eyes. He raised a three-barrel shooter on his left wrist and aimed it at Syn's face. Blue blood dripped into the snow from a wound to his stomach.

It took Syn the length of a heartbeat to register the color of his blood and the weapon he held. She dropped to snow and bowed on her knees before the Nighterrian.

"Holy warrior, I am at your service." She held her sword out to him in surrender.

When he gave no response, Syn glanced up at the god-like warrior. An odd expression crossed his face, and a gentle groan left his lips. The warrior swayed on his feet, then toppled to the ground.

4

HALLOWED POINT

"Just a little farther, we're almost there."

Syn grunted beneath the weight of the massive Nighterrian. Fortunately, he still had enough strength to get to his feet and half walk, half stumble. They headed toward the village, but their pace remained slow and grueling. Dark, elderberry-colored blood dripped from the wound in the man's gut as they staggered through the forest.

Syn's mind raced. The lore said Nighterrians were nearly indestructible. Yet this one looked as if he were on the brink of death. She stole glances at his left wrist hanging over her shoulder and the dangerous contraption strapped to it. The famous three-barrel weapon contained three sausage-sized cannons in a curving row on the outside of his wrist with a series of skinny metal tubes running down the length of it to a housing of levers at the elbow end of the contraption. Never had Syn been so close to such a sacred and deadly weapon. She worried it might go off as they stumbled along at their lurching pace.

She wanted to ask how he got hurt or where he came from,

but it seemed irreverent to ask such things of the man. Instead, she settled for his name.

"Sacred warrior, may I ask your name?"

"Xedford," he grunted with effort.

Syn knew the proper course of action would be to bring him to the healers, but the healer family only provided elixirs, poultices, and, often, empty prayers to the Legion in a smoky room. Wounds of life-threatening type required help from a profession that dealt with blood.

"Warrior Xedford, I can bring you to the village healers, but I think your injuries are more serious than they're equipped to handle. May I bring you to the village butchers? They often serve as the village surgeons."

Xedford mumbled his assent just as they broke out of the woods and into the scattering of homes that made up the Outskirts of Garon. Gasps surrounded them, followed by whispers and astonished exclamations. The Outskirt Legionites all knelt to their knees and bowed in respect as Syn and Xedford stumbled past. None of the minor citizens dared touch a Nighterrian, so their assistance came in the form of prayers.

Once into the fifth ring of the village, more gasps and bows lined their path. No Pen-Garon citizens volunteered to help as their status also made them unworthy of touching such a holy man. *To the Abyss with their decorum.* Syn's legs felt like a newborn deer. She feared she wouldn't be able to make it home without help.

As if in answer to her prayer, she spotted Drekton passing through with his bow over his shoulder and sweat beading his brow. Based on the angle of the sun in the sky, she assumed he must be returning from morning drills.

Unlike the rest of the outer ring citizens, when Drekton's eyes fell on the Nighterrian he quickly stowed his astonishment and jumped into action. Syn tried not to blush as he approached. Now was hardly the time for bashfulness. He performed a hasty bow and stepped to the other side of Xedford to help support his weight.

"We need get him to the first ring," Drekton said.

Syn stiffed a groan. The healers resided in the first ring, and because of their status as Prime citizens, they presided over all matters dealing with health. "No. He, umm, insisted we take him to someone experienced in surgery." The Legion would forgive her for one tiny stretch of the truth.

Drekton's brow furrowed as he looked over at her from the other side of Xedford. "That would be *your* family."

Exhaustion forced Syn's words out in a rush. "I'm not trying to further my family's status. I'm trying to save his life. Who did you go to when you cut open your head during spear training, the healers, or my father?"

Everyone in the village knew her family's skill at closing wounds. That very morning, the Chief himself had sent Graver with the injured arm straight to her parents to be stitched up.

"We should consult the Elders." Drekton pulled Xedford along at a pace Syn could barely keep up with.

Syn sighed. *Drekton the Dutiful.* As children Syn had often teased him with the name while trying to coax him into breaking the rules.

"There isn't time to go the first ring only for them to send us back to the third."

"Chief Groth would—"

"We can argue, or we can get him the help he needs." She gritted her teeth, hardening her resolve.

Drekton said nothing and Syn took this as a sign of his acquiescence. They pushed toward Syn's home on the eastern side of the third ring. With Drekton's help, they made quick progress through the village. As they entered the third ring, villagers stood from their bows and crowded around Xedford to offer prayers.

"Out of the way!" Drekton yelled as their pace slowed from the hold up of starry-eyed onlookers. Home was close but the increasing crowd of Legionites made progress difficult.

"Move!" Syn demanded, but no one listened to the pair of teenagers. She panted with effort, almost not hearing her name called above the crowd.

"Syn?" came a familiar voice.

Syn looked to her left. Her father's round face and fox pelt emerged from the swarm of people. He stepped forward and Syn let him bear the load of Xedford's weight as he took her place beneath Xedford's arm.

"Let's get him home," Predon said before raising his voice to address the crowd. "Make way! A Nighterrian comes through!"

At his word, the crowd parted. Syn followed behind like a useless tag-a-long. With Predon's respected position and Drekton's assistance, they made it home in a matter of minutes, a tail of curious Legionites following behind.

Syn breathed a sigh of relief as they reached the wooden longhouse and the blood-stained butchering yard. Smoke rose from both the chimney of the family lodge and from the circular hut of the workroom attached to the back of the house.

Roused by the sound of the gathering crowd, Vertah opened the front door and stepped out. Her eyes grew wide as she took in the sight before her. "Predon?"

"Vertah, prep the table. He's hurt bad," Predon said.

Vertah surveyed the crowd of people with narrowed eyes before ducking back inside. Syn slipped ahead of her father and followed her mother inside. The dark warmth of the low-built house invited her in. Leaving behind the comfort of the hearth, she ran to the back door that led to the workroom. She hurriedly helped her mother clear the butchering table at the center of the room.

"Where did he come from?" Vertah swept a vinegar-soaked cloth over the table.

"I don't know. I found him in the woods," Syn said.

Drekton and Predon lifted the Nighterrian onto the table. Xedford growled in pain at the movement but didn't fight them and laid prone on the massive butchering block. Predon turned to Drekton and smiled. "Thank you for your help, Drekton."

Drekton nodded and offered Xedford one last dutiful bow before stepping out the door. Syn hoped Drekton wouldn't begrudge her for insisting they take Xedford straight to her parents before consulting the Elders. The exchange was the most they had spoken to each other in months, and she hated to leave him at the end of a slightly bitter conversation. Yet, she was glad to be rid of the nervousness that seized her in his presence. She focused her attention on the Nighterrian.

"His name is Xedford," she said, standing beside her mother, ready for orders.

Predon patted Syn on the back. "Help your mother. I'll keep the crowd at bay."

Predon closed the hog-hide curtain over the room's single window. The workroom fell into deep shadows, but it was better than having the entire village spy through the window as they tried to save the warrior's life. Syn moved to feed the flames of the small brazier to increase the light in the room. She could hear the muffled voices of the Legionites who followed them through the village. It sounded like there were more now.

Predon bowed to Xedford and slipped out the door to answer hungry questions from the crowd. Although her father was just as skilled as her mother at closing wounds, Syn found it a wise choice for him to deal with the prying villagers. His calm demeanor combined with his charismatic smile would do well in quelling the crowd. Vertah had no such patience.

Vertah leaned over the table. "Warrior Xedford, I'll have to remove your clothes to examine your wound."

Xedford grunted his consent. With a pallid complection and eyes fluttering to remain open, he appeared as if he might pass out at any moment.

"Remove his weapon," Vertah ordered Syn.

Syn pulled the long, heavy sword from the sheath at his right hip and set it on the counter behind her.

"That too." Vertah nodded to the three-barrel on Xedford's left arm. Syn hesitated. It was sacrilege to touch the sacred three-barrel weapons of the Nighterrians. Vertah looked up from removing Xedford's shirt to stare icicles at Syn. "He is in pain, and we don't want any accidental shootings in here. Now take it off."

Syn bent over the table to carry out orders. She undid the three leather straps at the underside of Xedford's left forearm. With delicate hands, she held onto the strange mechanisms at the elbow end of the weapon and pulled the contraption off. The cold press of the metal made her palms sweat. She knew she would never again touch something so sacred in her life.

Making sure to keep the holes of the three metal barrels facing away from her face, she carried it over to the counter and placed it beside the sword. She also freed herself of the burden of the family sword on her back and leaned it against the wall.

When she returned to the table, she found her mother had cut off Xedford's blood-soaked shirt to reveal a mass of criss-crossing slashes and stab marks across his middle. Blue blood seeped from the gashes and ran over his skin to pool onto the table. The sight sent an earie creep of wrongness into the tight workshop. Nighterrians were supposed to be impervious to such wounds.

Syn moved to retrieve a needle and thread, but Vertah stopped her. "It won't do any good to stitch him closed," Vertah said.

"Why not?"

"We need to find the source of the problem." Vertah leaned over Xedford's face. "Warrior, I fear your Hallowed Point has shifted. I need to know where it is so I can put it back in place."

Hallowed Point? What was that?

Xedford grumbled. His crimson-colored eyes looked around in confusion, as if he were seeing the dark room for the first time. "Location's... sacred... never tell..." His eyes rolled back in his head.

Vertah propped his head up with her hands. "Xedford, stay with me now!" She spoke with both urgency and calm resolution. "I swear to the Legion I will keep this knowledge secret, but you must tell me now where it is, or you will bleed out."

Xedford muttered something nearly unintelligible. It sounded like, "My stomach."

"Yes, but I need to know which wound to search in. You have many in your stomach."

"Two... two fingers' width... above... navel," he managed.

Vertah scanned the site of his injuries to find one that looked like a small hole burrowed into the space directly above his belly button. She glanced up at Syn. "Hold him down."

Syn wasn't sure how she was supposed to hold down a man twice her weight—especially a Nighterrian who had the strength of ten men—but she did as she was told and pressed his arms down against the table.

Vertah took a deep breath and pushed her fingers into the laceration.

Xedford let out a war cry and thrashed on the table. He

lifted Syn's feet off the floor with his impossible strength. Syn struggled to keep him from moving as her mother worked. She shuddered as she watched Vertah's fingers disappear beneath his pale flesh. Dark Nighterrian blood squirted forth as she pushed her fingers farther into his stomach.

Xedford writhed in pain.

"Hold him still, I'm almost there!" Vertah ordered. Nearly her entire hand disappeared inside him as she felt around in his gut.

Syn put all her weight and energy into holding him steady. She knew better than to disobey her mother's commands. *Please don't die,* she prayed. Avoiding eye contact with Xedford, she stared at the black material of his torn tunic and noticed a small, round hole in the fabric. Was that a bullet hole?

Xedford cried out and nearly jerked off the table. Syn returned her focus to holding him down. She could hear angered voices from outside. Surely the entire village thought they were torturing him. She knew her father could only do so much peace talking and reasoning before the mob broke in and found her mother wrist deep in the Nighterrian's gut.

"Almost there." Sweat dripped from the tip of Vertah's nose.

Syn held tight and tried her best to reduce Xedford's resistance. The blazing fire behind her wrapped the room in a sweltering circle of bloody stench. Alarmed shouts increased outside the door.

"There! I can feel it." Vertah's eyes gave a far-off look, as if she could see in her mind's eye what she felt in her hand. "I just need to…" She delivered a single shove that made a wet crunch.

Xedford stopped struggling and lay still.

Syn's mouth hung ajar as she watched her mother extract her hand from Xedford's wound. Panic trickled through her.

"Mother, what have you done?"

Verah shot Syn a look that said not to question her. *We've killed him.* She was sure of it. But as she watched through the paralyzing moment, she saw the flow of blood cut off and slowly, his skin melded together before her eyes.

After several minutes of stunned silence, his wounds had healed completely. Not even a scar remained, only smears of blood provided proof of the ordeal. Yet Xedford continued to lie unconscious.

"You can let off him now." Vertah went about wiping her hands with her regular stiff poise, as if she had just finished butchering a boar.

"Oh, of course." Syn leaned away, releasing her grip on Xedford's arms.

The voices outside the hut had fallen to low murmurs. Her father had no doubt succeeded in appeasing them with calm reasoning.

"What, um, what exactly did you do to fix him?" Syn asked.

"Nighterrians have a sacred object imbedded in their bodies."

"The... Hallowed Point? Is that what you called it?"

"Yes. When a Terraborn decides to take on the duties of a Nighterrian, he is imbued with a Hallowed Point. It grants the warriors their strength and healing abilities."

"I thought the Nighterrians were blessed by the Legion."

"They are." Vertah wiped a wet cloth over Xedford's skin to clean away the blood. "And the way they're blessed is with the Hallowed Point."

Syn blushed at the sight of Xedford's strong, immense body. His skin was a pale white canvas interrupted by dark hair across his chest. She had seen many half-naked bodies in her life, but never one so large and muscular.

"What happened to Xedford's Hallowed Point?" she asked to place her attention elsewhere.

"I assume it became dislodged when he was injured. If the Hallowed Point is moved from where it's imbedded in his body, he loses much of his powers. I simply pushed it back into place."

"That's why he didn't want to tell us where it was."

"Exactly. It's a secret every Nighterrian keeps—as you can see why." She motioned to the blood-soaked table. "If an opponent knew where to strike his Hallowed Point, he could be defeated."

"Are the Scalers smart enough to know to strike at their Hallowed Point?"

Vertah smiled with a sad softness Syn did not often see in her mother. "You forget the Nighterrians are warriors of Interterra. There are far worse creatures in the dark realm beneath us that are more dangerous and far more intelligent than the Scalers."

Syn felt grateful for her mother's words. It had been a long time since they were able to talk easily with each other. They argued more and more these days as Syn watched her mother look upon her with growing disproval.

"I always thought the Nighterrians were invincible," Syn said.

"Many do. It's in our nature to worship them after all the stories in our history. But everything in this world can be killed."

Syn mulled this over while she looked at the unconscious warrior. The man didn't appear so threatening anymore. In fact, he could almost look ordinary if it weren't for his size and the short beard he wore. In her nineteen years, Syn had seen a few Nighterrians pass through Garon, but she had never seen one so close before. The sight of him sent thrilling shivers through her body. She wanted to reach out and touch him just to be sure she wasn't dreaming.

"How long will he be asleep?" she asked.

"It's hard to say, perhaps a few hours. He lost a lot of blood."

Syn silently pondered the newfound knowledge of the Nighterrian powers. The secret of their weakness made the warriors far more fragile and human than she imagined. A thought occurred to her. "What if a Nighterrian were imbued with more than one Hallowed point?"

Vertah jerked her head to look at Syn, all softness from moments ago replaced with hot rage. "Blasphemy! What would make you think such an evil thought? Is one blessing from the Legion not enough?"

And just like that, Syn was back to being the disappointing daughter. "No, I didn't mean—"

"There are only three ways to kill a Nighterrian. One is to remove his Hallowed Point, the second is to cut off his head, and the third is to pierce him with another Hallowed Point."

"I-I didn't—"

"I'll watch over him." Vertah turned her back. "You have your duties to complete before nightfall. Your... *episode* earlier today stole much of your time."

Syn made her way to the door in defeat. After the events of the day, she hoped her mother would have offered her a semblance of gratitude. Syn very well could have let Drekton take Xedford to the healers.

Vertah looked at Syn hesitating in the doorway. "Well? What is it? You want to waste more of the daylight? Go!"

Syn stole one last glance at the sleeping Nighterrian and slipped out the back door into the cold air.

5

SECRET

"But did he have red eyes?" Rem asked, his eyes alight with the zeal of youth.

Syn sighed and looked over her shoulder at the eight-year-old boy. "Yes, he had red eyes." She suffered his questions as she sliced through the hide of a dead goat strung up in the butchering yard.

"Wow!" Rem bounced up and down, unable to contain his excitement. "A real Nighterrian warrior here in Garon—and asleep in your house!"

Syn shook her head and turned back to skinning the mountain goat. Rem had refused to leave her alone since she emerged from the workroom. She spent the past hour answering his unending questions about the Nighterrian. She would rather have kept to herself and wallowed in guilt alone. From the center of the Village, the Ancestral Hill of bones imposed its presence out the corner of her eye. It stared its accusation down at her, threatening to whisper her secrets into the wind.

"You promise you'll let me see him when he wakes up?" Rem asked.

Syn rolled her eyes. "For the hundredth time, yes. I promise."

She found Rem's questions exhausting, but she held a special affinity for his excitement. If she had any friends at all, Rem might be a contender. She had long ago grown used to the constant nuisance of his company. The exuberant boy was always filled with wild hopes and vivid imaginations. He reminded her of his older brother, Drekton, back when Syn and Drekton were friends.

The shame of an empty doorstep stalked the back of her mind whenever she thought of her betrothed. Shaking her head, she began cutting the white pelt off the goat while Rem practiced punching invisible opponents. Mother had been right; the work had piled up while she was hiding away in the woods. Syn still had to butcher the goat and deliver the offerings before nightfall. But at least she got out of morning drills. She was thankful she didn't have to suffer the daily whispers and snickers of her peers. At least for today.

"I can't wait to meet him!" Rem twirled on his feet and defended against pretend attacks from the dead goat. "I'm going to ask him about the trials. I've told you about the trials, right?"

"Uh-huh. Now, if you insist on pestering me with questions, the least you could do is help." She motioned Rem over with an impatient nod.

He dropped his fighting stance and hopped over to help her pull the skin off the carcass. Rem yanked as Syn cut, and soon the goat hung naked in the cold air. Syn placed the white hide out on the worktable for Rem to clean.

"You know, the Nighterrian trials for this year are only three days away," Rem said as he set to work on the pelt.

Syn rolled her eyes as she sliced into glistening muscle. "So?"

"So, in exactly five years and three days, I can enter the trials to become a Nighterrian."

"The chances of completing the trials are slim to none, even for Terraborn competitors. What makes you think a little Legionite kid like yourself can make it through to the end?"

"Um, have you *met* me?"

Syn had to chuckle at this. If Rem had nothing else, he had confidence. As much as he annoyed her with his lofty ideas, a part of her wished he would never grow up and gain the dim perspective of responsibility.

At the age of six, Rem had spent nearly a year trying to dig to Interterra despite the repeated advice from family and friends. The dark realm could only be reached through a portal gate. Despite never making it far into the frozen earth, he had continued day after day. However, once he found out about the trials, he abandoned the hole and turned his mind toward training.

"It's all I've ever wanted to be my whole life." Rem continued. "I don't *think* I'll pass the trials, I *know* I will. I'll become a Nighterrian one day."

"How is it you're so certain?"

Rem shrugged. "I'm a son of the black. It's my destiny."

Syn looked from behind the glossy carcass at Rem. Even if he was the half-blooded son of a Nighterrian, he was tiny— even for an eight-year-old. He wore a double layer of brown otter furs over his shoulders to give the impression of a broader frame, but he couldn't hide the skinniness of his arms and legs. The Nighterrian trials were designed as a test to select only those strong enough to survive the process that transformed one into a Nighterrian. If Rem wanted to compete, he had much growing to do before he would be considered fight-worthy.

"Well, it's a good thing you have a few more years to prepare." Syn returned to butchering.

"I'd go right now if they'd let me. It's not fair how you have to be at least thirteen before you can enter."

"I don't think it's fair they only let kids enter the trials. Why is nineteen the cut off? Shouldn't it be reserved for adults?"

"Grandfather says it's because you can't become a Nighterrian after you've outgrown your teenage years. Something about it not working correctly. He never answers my questions about the imbuing of Nighterrians."

"Hmm. Maybe for good reason." Syn assumed it had something to do with the Hallowed Point.

Rem paused his work and looked up at Syn. "What? Do you know something about the imbuing?"

Syn debated whether to divulge what she knew. Her mother hadn't told her the knowledge of the existence of Hallowed Points was an outright secret, but she understood there was a certain unspoken taboo surrounding the sacred object.

"What do the stories say happens after the trials—if you make it to the end that is?" she asked.

"They say the finishers go to the 'Imbuing Hall' where they feast with the Nighterrian captains and receive their blessing from the Legion." A far-off look appeared in Rem's brown eyes as he described the scene with airy admiration. "I always imagined the gods swooping down to infuse the finishers with powers that transform them into warriors."

"Sounds exciting."

Rem continued to talk about the trials and what he thought some of the tasks might be while Syn cut out desirable chunks of meat and set them aside. She tried to work quickly. Her fingers were already beginning to go numb from the cold. She would usually bring the carcass inside to be butchered, but Xedford currently occupied the workroom.

"...and then they probably test you on sword fighting and axe throwing and—"

"I think you're forgetting the most important part," said a voice from behind.

Syn turned to see her father walking up with a wheelbarrow filled with body parts. He offered a kind smile that set Syn at ease.

"What's the most important part?" Rem asked.

"If you're not born in Interterra, you have to be invited into the trials." Predon pulled the wheelbarrow up beside them.

"I have a plan for that!"

"Do you now? Let's hear it." Predon gave a gentle smile.

"Well actually..." Rem shuffled his feet in the snow. "I was hoping you might help me out with it."

"Let me guess, you want to speak to our honored guest?"

Rem nodded, bouncing up and down on his heels. Predon crouched down and looked Rem in the eye. "Remmel Du-Garon, you have my permission to speak to Warrior Xedford."

Rem smiled so wide Syn thought he might faint from excitement. "But"—Predon raised a finger— "you must wait awhile. He is still recovering from his injury."

"Of course. I can wait, I can wait!"

"Good." Predon straightened. "In the meantime, you can help Syn deliver the offerings to the Outskirts. It's their day to perform the ritual."

Syn sighed. She wished Rem wouldn't tag along today. All she wanted was to be alone. "I haven't quite finished the goat." She motioned to the carcass.

"You've had an eventful day. I can finish up for you."

"Thank you, Father." Syn set down the knife and cleaned her hands.

"And don't worry," Predon dropped his voice into a whisper. "I won't tell your mother I helped out." Syn bloomed with gratitude. Her father remained one of the few people who could always make her smile. Though they shared few words, she often felt they weren't needed. "Don't forget this." He took the sword belt off his shoulder and handed it to Syn. "It's yours now, you'll have to look after it."

Before Syn could object, Rem butted in at the sight of the family heirloom. "Wow, a sword! Syn, when were you going to tell me you got a sword?"

Syn accepted the gift and slung it over her back in a hasty maneuver. "We should get going," she said, cutting him off from asking any further questions.

After nodding to her father, she grabbed hold of the wheelbarrow and left the butchering yard. Rem, of course, tagged along beside her. The stench from the tangle of human limbs made Syn wrinkle her nose. Soon, the offerings would be soaked in scented oil and placed at the base of the Ancestral Hill as an offering to the Legion—and as an added layer of baited precaution against the Scalers.

Once into the fourth ring of the village, Syn could no longer resist stealing a glance at the Ancestral Hill retreating behind her. From the village perspective, she knew she wouldn't be able to see the shivering girl she left exposed on the altar. She felt anxiety make itself at home in her bones. Had the frozen air brought the girl's death yet?

"Does it have a name?" Rem asked.

"What?"

"Your sword. I hear all swords have a name."

"That's ridiculous," Syn said. "Why would an inanimate weapon have a name?"

"That's just what grandfather says when he tells stories. Plus, you talk to inanimate things all the time."

Syn cringed. Somehow even an eight-year-old had picked up on her "friends." Though Rem spoke of her odd nature without contempt, it still stung. She knew the village whispered of her eccentricates behind her back. She made a mental note to be more careful in public.

"I think you listen to too many stories." She adjusted the strap of her sword belt. It didn't weigh much—certainly nothing like the axes held by many of the Prime citizens of the first ring—but it hung heavy on her back.

Rem stooped down to pluck up a discarded femur protruding from the icy ground. He swung the bone like a pretend weapon. "I heard you did your first sacrifice today. Is that why your father gave you the sword?"

Ice shot through her at the mention of the sacrifice. "Yes." Syn looked toward the forest beyond the Outskirts, the cut on her forearm throbbing.

"How come you took so long to do your initiation?" Rem sliced the air with his bone and lunged forward with a stab.

"I just... wasn't ready." Syn shook her head and pushed the wheelbarrow faster.

"Wait, where are you going?" Rem hurried to catch up.

"To the East side."

"But that way goes past the Severed man."

Syn smirked. "You want to be a Nighterrian but you're afraid of a Severed one?"

"I'm not afraid." He puffed up his chest. "I just don't like criminals."

"Well, I'm going this way. Feel free to take the long way around." She pushed the wheelbarrow forward.

Rem stepped in front of the wheelbarrow and held out his

bone-sword to stop her. "I'll prove I'm not afraid. I'll go touch the side of his hut!"

"You don't need to—"

Rem broke into a run with his femur held high, heading for the edge of the forest. Syn sighed and followed through the snow, trying not to spill any of the offerings. Beyond the Outskirts, the spread of trees marked the beginning of the forest. Tucked into a crop of trees stood a tiny mud hut with a large X marked over the doorway. A small campfire sent wisps of smoke up through the trees, but the stump beside it sat vacant.

Rem drew to a halt and looked around. "Where is he?"

"He's not here, let's go."

"I need to touch the door." He crept forward.

"Rem, let's go."

Rem continued to tiptoe through the snow with his "weapon" in hand. Syn watched as he stepped around the firepit, reached out a steady hand, and placed it over the X on the door. Keeping his hand in place—as if to demonstrate his level of bravery—he turned to Syn with a victorious grin.

"You proved your worth," Syn said. "Now can we..."

The smile melted from Rem's face. His eyes widened with the warning of a coming threat and focused on something directly behind her. Syn whirled around, slipping on the frozen ground. When she caught her balance, she paused at a pair of large, booted feet. She straightened and cast her sight upward, coming face to face with the Severed man.

The man glared at her with one hazel eye. His other eye stared blindly through a milky-white iris. A pair of scars criss-crossed over his blind eye, forming an X that ran from brow to cheek.

Syn stood frozen in place. The man's working eye burrowed into her, and she felt as she always did when someone looked into her eyes: vulnerable—as if they could see into her soul and spy the weakness that lay within. The Severed man raised a gloved hand into the air and pointed toward the Ancestral Hill in the distance.

He knows.

Syn attempted to step back in retreat, but remained locked in a moment of terrified dread. The silent man continued to point toward the Hill with an ice-cold expression and accusing half-stare. If not for Rem, Syn might have stayed frozen in place —forever absorbing the silent condemnation. Rem ran up and grabbed her by the hand and tugged her away.

Together they scrambled through the snow, pushing the wheelbarrow as fast as they could. Syn glanced over her shoulder as she ran. The Severed man's hand continued to hover in the air, pointing toward the altar on the Hill.

Once they made it back within the Outskirt circle of the village, Rem pulled to a stop behind the cover of huts. He braced himself on his knees and smiled in relief.

"That was close," he said, chuckling between panted breaths.

Syn glanced up at the Hill where her secret lay. She bit her trembling lip and rubbed the cut hidden beneath her sleeve.

6

WEAK

They took the long way home. The extended walk through the cold being well worth avoiding another encounter with the Severed man.

Syn lost herself in a flurry of troubled thoughts on their way back to the center of the village. With the offerings delivered, Rem now occupied the wheelbarrow. She pushed it along at a slow, contemplative pace. She mentally berated herself for running away from the Severed man like a spooked deer. He simply pointed toward the village to indicate they should leave. Yet, her paranoia wouldn't let go the thought of him peering into her soul and seeing her secrets laid bare.

"What do you think his crime was?" Rem asked, turning over his shoulder as he bumped along in the wheelbarrow.

"Hmm?"

"What do you think he did to earn his soul being Severed?"

"I don't know." A part of her felt sorry for the ostracized man, yet the set of scars over his eye proved his true nature. The Severing was a punishment just one step below the death penalty. With his citizenship revoked and his soul withheld from reincarnation, whatever he had done must have been truly unforgivable.

"I heard he ran and hid during a Scaler attack," Rem said, "left his sister to fend for herself. But then I also I heard he lost his nerve during a hunting party and got his friends killed by a bear—oh!" He jumped out of the wheelbarrow to retrieve a stick he fancied. The bone he held before had broken in half when he had smashed it into a chimney a few homes back. He plucked up the stick and examined it. "Either way he's a coward."

A whisper of rage boiled within Syn at the mention of cowardice. "Cowards have no place in Garon." She clenched her jaw to stifle the desire to scream. The blue lips and wide eyes of the sacrifice floated into her memory.

"I wonder what it's like to know this is your last life." Rem twirled his new toy sword around his arm as he walked beside Syn. "To know your soul will never be reborn."

"Perhaps it's peaceful," she said with all the bitterness in her heart. Although she could not remember any of her past lives, carrying the weight of her curse was exhausting. She wondered what it would be like to be free of the burden.

"If this was my last life ever, I think I'd do something better than sit around looking angry all day and scaring kids."

When Syn didn't respond, Rem ran ahead to jab tree stumps and stab mounds of snow. Any other day, Rem's exuberance might have made her laugh. Today, however, she felt the stares of her fellow Legionites.

Passing villagers voiced irritated shouts at Rem when they had to step out of the way of his jabs. Rem paid them no mind. He moved to strike down a snowflake when a fist caught his staff mid arc. Syn looked up to find Drekton holding his little brother's play sword.

"Mother has been looking for you." Drekton wrenched the stick from Rem's grasp.

"I finished my duties hours ago." Rem jumped to grab for his staff.

Drekton held the stick over his head. "Where have you been?"

Rem nodded over to Syn as she parked the wheelbarrow beside the pair. The boys looked similar with their matching brown eyes and straight black hair. Drekton, however, stood a whole head and shoulders over Rem and always had his jaw set in a serious expression. His favorite bow and quiver hung over his shoulder as always.

"Syndrah." Drekton nodded without meeting her eye.

"Call her, Syn, you cumbersome rock." Rem tried to grab for his stick, but Drekton pulled it away and pushed him over. Rem fell into a bank of snow. "Hey!"

Drekton offered his hand and pulled his brother from the ground. "Mother wants you back home."

"But I haven't gotten to meet the Nighterrian yet."

"You're not allowed to meet him, Rem."

"Actually," Syn butted in. "My father gave his permission." Not sure what to do with her hands, she fidgeted with the ends of her braids then stuffed her hands in her pockets.

"See!" Rem crossed his arms in defiance.

Drekton considered for a moment, then sighed. "Be quick."

Rem beamed and looked over to Syn. "Can you see if the Nighterrian is awake?"

Syn agreed and Drekton handed Rem back his stick. "Don't go hitting anyone with this."

Syn finally settled on placing her hands back on the wheelbarrow. She tried to lean on it casually, but she forgot it was empty and nearly tipped it over. She caught herself before she fell and straightened in a rush. Embarrassment crept its way up her cheeks as she nodded her goodbye to Drekton. Drekton nodded back before leaving with long strides through the snow. Syn seethed in frustration at the blundering encounter as she watched him go.

When she looked away, she found Rem staring at her. A teasing smile spread across his face. "Well, that wasn't awkward or anything."

"Shut up." Syn pushed the wheelbarrow onward and welcomed the cold air to cool her burning cheeks. Soon, they rounded the corner to Syn's home with the adjoining workshop and the blood-stained snow of the butchering yard.

"Stay here while I check on him." Syn left the wheelbarrow beside Rem who trembled with excitement at the front door.

She walked around the perimeter of the longhouse to enter through the back door, hoping to avoid her mother's scorn. The less interactions with her mother, the better. Voices drifted toward her as she rounded the corner of the wooden lodge. She stopped in her tracks to listen.

"Do you really think it's wise to trust her with the family sword?" came her mother's voice.

Syn pressed herself against the side of the house. She recognized her father's voice in response. "I was younger than her when my father gave it to me."

"Yes, but you were a bold and hearty child. Syn is..."

"What?"

"Broken."

"She made the sacrifice today."

"Yes, at nineteen! The *shame*, Predon. Most children make their first sacrifice at fourteen. And even at her age I wasn't sure she'd be able to do it."

"But she did."

"And then ran crying into the woods." Vertah sighed. "I'm just happy she kept it together long enough to speak the

Divine Creedence. Can you imagine her having an episode in front of the Chief?"

"Our daughter is... different."

"Our daughter is insane."

"She's haunted."

"Oh, enough with your 'haunted' theories, Predon. You know that old crone was a bag of loose fortunes."

"But Syn proved herself. We can stop worrying. She is strong when it counts. We wouldn't have had the chance to save the Nighterrian if it weren't for her running into the woods."

"Are you saying you trust her?"

"She's my daughter, of course I trust her. She can't help it when she has an episode."

"You just don't want to admit it do you?"

"Admit what?"

"That we've failed as parents. You can make excuses all you want, but Syn is weak, and you know it."

Syn felt an army of tears march from her chest up to her tear ducts. Hurt and shame formed an egg in her throat. She backed away from the side of the house and ran toward the front door.

She forgot Rem waited for her there. His eyes widened at the sight of her distraught expression. "What is it? Is the Nighterrian well?"

"Enough about the Nighterrian!" A mixture of rage and embarrassment swirled through her like a tempest.

"What's wrong?" Rem asked.

"Just leave me alone."

A pair of teenagers—whom Syn recognized as the brother-sister duo, Varmah and Vedder—strolled by just as a tear escaped Syn's eye. Syn hurried to brush it away, but the twins turned to whisper to each other, and she knew they had seen.

Anger reared up inside her and latched onto Rem. Grown Legionites were not allowed to cry, yet here she was proving her mother right. Rem stood in her way, making her spill tears in public all because he insisted on talking. She moved to shove past him.

"Wait! We're friends, you can talk to me."

Syn turned on her heel and relinquished her fury. "Get lost!" Then quietly, with vehement spite, she said, "You're not my friend."

She immediately felt a prickle of guilt at the hurt that crossed his face. Too late to take the words back, she turned and ducked through the door to her home.

Inside the shadowed warmth, she curled into the darkest corner she could find and collapsed into a ball of shame. She would have stayed crying out her feelings until the hurt dissipated, but a voice in the dark cut short her self-pity.

"I heard Legionites never cry, that they're of a stronger brood."

Syn looked up through her tear-streaked vision to see a pair of red eyes in the dark.

7
A CURE

Syn sputtered as if she'd been thrown into icy water. She brushed at her face in a desperate attempt to wipe away evidence of her tears, but she knew the Nighterrian had already seen them. She stared, wholly mortified. Again, she had brought shame to her family.

Xedford stepped forward into the light of the small fire burning in the hearth. Color had returned to his face and his crimson eyes stared alert and calculating just below a dark bandana tied around his head. Syn guessed him to be in his early thirties. He stood handsome and powerful in the low light.

When he approached, his head nearly touched the ceiling crossbeams. He pulled up a stool and sat down in front of where Syn huddled on the floor. She noticed he wore a borrowed yak-hide cloak. Despite the warmth of the room, he had the dark fur gathered around him.

"I don't reckon Legionites are much different than any other folk." His voice rang with a deep baritone and the cadence of his Terraborn accent lent a finality to his words.

It took Syn a moment to register what he said. She stared up at the man who nearly died on her mother's table a few hours ago. "Please don't judge my village based on what you've seen here."

"Nah, you misunderstand." He shook his head. "You see, I've got much respect for the Legionites, especially after what you and your family have done for me. But I think, cry-wise, the guardians of the portals ought to be allowed a few tears every now and again."

Syn thought she must have heard him wrong. Surely, he didn't mean it. "I-I'm sorry you had to see me like this."

"It's Syndrah, right?"

"Syn, yes."

"Syn, believe it or not, I used to be very much like you as a child," he said. Syn found the slow drawl of his accent comforting in a strange way.

"How do you mean?"

"I was... sensitive." He ran a hand through his dark beard. "I cried at the smallest matter and I didn't ever feel like I quite fit in with everybody else." He leaned forward on the short stool. "Until I was cured, that is."

Syn perked up. "Cured?"

"That's right. When I joined up and earned my place as a Nighterrian."

Syn wiped her nose and scoured the face of the brave warrior professing to past weakness. "It *cured* you?"

She knew the imbuing granted the Nighterrians their powers. She heard stories of scars and wounds healing, but she never imagined it could fix afflictions such as a heart riddled with cowardice.

"The imbuing is a long and painful process, but afterward you emerge a different man—well, woman, in your case. The imbuing makes you stronger not only physically but mentally too." Xedford tapped the side of his head. "Everything I fought through in the trials was well worth it in the end."

Trials? "You mean you didn't inherit your Hallowed Point from your ancestors? You had to complete the trials?"

The edges of Xedford's mouth curled up into a smile that flickered in the light of the hearth. "Like I said, I used to be a lot like you."

"You were Legionite?"

"No, no, not quite. I was born in a village far from here, but not all too different. When I was fourteen, I met a Nighterrian who recruited me to join up and enter the trials. From there, I earned my Hallowed Point—or Hal'point as we tend to call it down below."

A Surfacer? Syn couldn't believe it. His eyes were Terraborn red, and they weren't the teardrop shape prevalent among the people populating the Surface realm. She looked into his eyes as doubt hardened in her chest.

It must have shown on her face for Xedford's next words were, "You don't believe me, do you?"

"No, I just... your eyes. I just thought, um, only those born in Interterra have red eyes."

"Yeah, that's true." He paused for a moment, perhaps considering something. "But the imbuing changes that too."

Syn said nothing as she processed the new information. "Thank you," was the only thing she could think to say.

"What're you thanking me for?"

"For being so kind."

"It's me who ought to be thanking you." Xedford stood from his stool and stepped toward Syn. He was a whole head and shoulders taller than her. He offered a hand to help her stand. "I might've fought my last fight out there in those woods if it hadn't been for you and your family."

Syn accepted his hand. His fingers wrapped around hers

with gentle warmth as she found her feet. "It was an honor to assist a Nighterrian," she said and bowed.

She was about to inquire about the events that brought him to the woods when she looked up to find him staring her up and down. Her heart stuttered as his intimidating eyes burned with hunger.

"I'd like to offer a token of thanks. Tell me, how old are you?"

Her skin smoldered with nervous fear while her hand remained in the possession of his grasp. "Nine-nineteen." She resisted the urge to take a step back.

Nighterrian men often took many wives. The honor of becoming a bride of the black was something Legionite women did not refuse, even if they were promised to another. Her mind raced with thoughts of Drekton. As sons of the black, both Drekton and Rem grew up never knowing their father. Syn did not want that fate for her future children, nor did she want to dispel her engagement—even if it meant gaining the respect of a bride of the black.

Xedford smiled at the sight of her discomfort. "You don't trust nobody, do you?" He didn't wait for an answer. "Good." He smiled and pulled an object from his pocket and placed it into Syn's palm.

Syn felt the cold touch of something small and metal. Breaking Xedford's stare, she looked down at her palm to find a tiny golden coin the size of her thumb nail. She knew coins were used in place of barter in Interterra, but they held no use in the village of Garon where everything was either traded or shared without cost.

"If you like, you can take this here token to the portal. On the other side, it'll grant you entrance into the Nighterrian trials."

Syn immediately felt embarrassed for thinking he intended

to thank her in other ways. "I-I..." She struggled to find the words as she held the priceless wealth in her hands.

Her mother's words echoed inside her head. *We've failed as parents... Syn is weak.*

The golden coin looked up at her from her cupped hands. Three crossed swords sat stutter-stamped into the metal, as if the coin hadn't been minted correctly. The edge of coin had a chip on one side. She imagined how lovely it would look among her collection of broken things, but the expectation of the precious metal burned in her grasp.

"I can't accept this," she said.

"I know it ain't much. It's only an invitation into the trials. It won't guarantee you'll become a Nighterrian, but I reckon you could make it."

Syn looked up at Xedford, his head bowed forward to escape the low hanging beam of the house. "Thank you, Xedford. Your faith in me is appreciated, but I know myself. I have a certain... affliction that would make it impossible for me to enter the trials."

"Whatever affliction you've got, physical or mental, the imbuing will cure."

The idea of being free of her haunting made her pause. Could there really be a life without the weight of ghosts dragging her down? No. She crushed the rising hope and tossed the idea away. Syn knew in her heart she would fail. Someone who could not even perform a ritual sacrifice would never be worthy of becoming a holy warrior. Even if she were brave enough to enter, her haunting would keep her from succeeding.

"Thank you for your kindness, but I don't think I'm fit to compete in the trials." Once steadfast in her resolve, her thoughts turned to Rem. Guilt seared her conscience at the unfair words she hurled at him a few minutes earlier. She looked toward the door where he was probably still waiting on the other side. "But I know someone who would make a wonderful Nighterrian."

———

Syn watched from the doorway as Xedford explained the coin and offered it to Rem. She stood too far way to hear the words exchanged, but the bright expression on Rem's face shined like a torch in the night.

Syn crossed the front yard and walked up to them in time to hear Xedford say, "Go on now and tell your family."

"Thank you! Thank you! Thank you!" Rem bowed with every thank you. "You will not regret it!" He clenched his fist around the coin and punched it to the sky. He then raced toward home, waving his fist through the air as he ran.

"I know he's young," Syn said, "but he has a warrior's heart. In a few years, he'll do the village proud in ways that I never could."

People poked their heads out of their homes as Rem's shouts of "I'm going to be a Nighterrian!" rang through the village.

Xedford chuckled, watching Rem retreat. "He'll do well." He turned to Syn. "Still, I wish we didn't have to wait so long for a worthy recruit."

Syn offered a bashful smile.

The curious onlookers turned their attention away from Rem and noticed Xedford. They stepped out of their doorways to ogle at the recovered Nighterrian.

"I best take my leave." Xedford squinted against the brightness of the snow-filled land.

"So soon?" She expected him to at least stay for dinner. She heard the Chief had ordered a special feast in honor of his presence.

"Yeah. I ought to return to my raid, let them know I ain't dead."

Syn's breath caught in a moment of panic. If he left through the portal of bones atop the Ancestral Hill, he might see the evidence of her failed sacrifice. "Are you certain your wounds are healed?"

"Completely. Thank your mother for me, I'm fit to rejoin the fight thanks to her."

"You didn't arrive through our portal, did you?" she asked over the sound of her heart pounding a rhythm of anxiety.

"No, I came through one a stretch north of here."

"Is that where you'll return to then?"

He glanced up at the Ancestral Hill. "I suppose so. Though I'd sooner be out of the cold, it'll be easier to catch up with my crew if I go back the way I came."

Syn gulped in relief. Her secret would remain undiscovered. She managed a single nod. The Legionites whispered their excitement and crept in for a closer look at the fabled brand of warrior.

Xedford stepped over the burned-out firepit in Syn's yard and crouched down to rub his fingers into the ashes. "I won't be short in remembering the devotion this village has shown me." He stood and swiped the black charcoal beneath his left eye, over the bridge of his nose, and beneath his other eye to aid in blocking out the glare of the snow.

Syn gave a deep bow. "Thank you for protecting the portals. We'd all be laid to waste if it weren't for Nighterrians like you fighting against the beasts on the other side."

"And if it weren't for Legionites like yourself guarding against the beasts that slip through our grasp, many more creatures would breed their slaughter here on Surface."

With these final words, Xedford turned and marched his way through the growing crowd. Villagers stepped back and bowed as he made his way toward the forest.

Syn felt a deep sadness envelop her. As the only one to ever truly understand her plight, she wished he would stay just a little longer. A snowflake landed on her cheek as she watched him walk away. Caught up in the panic of maintaining her secret, it was only then that she realized he never explained where exactly he came from or what caused his nearly fatal injuries.

Vertah ran up to Syn. "Where is he going?"

"He has to return to his raid," Syn said.

"But we were planning a feast!"

Syn swallowed back a scoff. Leave it to her mother to feel indignant over the inconvenient need to return to the fight. "His protection makes it so that we can live to *have* feasts."

Vertah turned a furious stare at Syn. "Don't you dare lecture me."

"I was just—"

"Perhaps you can put that smart tongue of yours to good use," Vertah said with a storm of controlled anger. "Chief Groth has invited us as guests for his feast. You can explain to him why the guest of honor will not be in attendance." She turned and stormed off.

Syn sighed, looking back at the crowd following Xedford's march through the opaque air as snow began to drift down and settle over the village.

<h1 style="text-align:center">8</h1>

<h2 style="text-align:center">FEAST</h2>

Syn watched the flames blaze from the center of the Chief's longhouse. Despite the rhythm of the drums and humming from singers at the far end of the house, the room felt dense with the rigidity of a stale ceremony.

Syn sat beside the stoic Chief with beads of dread rolling down her back. Antlers hung from the ceiling, decorating the walls. Their spiked shadows fell on the dinner party, making it seem as though they sat a in a thicket of thorns. The Chief's table took up most of the long, rectangular room. A brazier embedded in the table ran the length of the tabletop, lighting the room with blazing coals.

Syn leaned back from the heat and looked to her left where Drekton sat. He had also been invited to the feast for his part in helping Xedford. He seemed more serious than usual. Did he hate being amongst the Chief and the Elders as much as she did? Syn realized she was staring and looked away before he could take notice.

On the other side of fire, she caught her father's eye. She held onto the steadiness of his presence. Her mother sat beside him. She drank from the deep bowl of bone marrow soup and passed it to her husband. Vertah's sterile expression pierced Syn through the flames. *Don't embarrass me,* her face seemed to read.

Syn waited for the bowl of broth to make its way to her across the twelve Nameless Elders who took up the rest of the table. She knew she should feel thankful. It was a great honor to be invited to share the Chief's table. Indulgence in feasts was rare, even for the Chief and the Elders.

Mounds of raw meat sat piled on plates to her right. She recognized the goat she butchered earlier alongside stacks of yak meat, boar, and fish. The meat was cut into small chunks ready to be skewered and roasted in the fire before them. While the rest of Garon ate their rations, everyone at the table would gorge on the Chief's fare. Syn's stomach lurched.

"I don't deserve to be here," she whispered to the frayed, woven rug on the floor beneath the bench. She shifted in her wooden seat and tried not to itch at the cut on her forearm.

Drekton nudged her and Syn turned to accept the bowl of broth. Her hand brushed his as she took it from him, and she felt her face burn a bright red.

Growing up, her friendship with Drekton had been simple. They played together and shared each other's secrets, but when their parents arranged their marriage, it opened a chasm in their friendship. Gone were the days when she could run up and wrestle Drekton to the ground or annoy him by poking him in the ribs where he was ticklish. She handed the bowl of broth off as she wondered what it would be like to elicit a smile from him with a jab to his side. He looked so serious these days.

"I heard you played a part in getting Rem that coin," Drekton said without looking at her. A thread of resentment colored his tone, catching her off guard.

Syn watched his grim face harden further. Perhaps he was jealous? "I'm sorry I didn't put in a word for you. I didn't think you held any interest in becoming Nighterrian."

Drekton jerked his head to look at Syn. His brown eyes glowed with indignation in the light of the dancing flames. "I don't have any interest in becoming Nighterrian," he whispered over the sound of the drums and hollow throat singing.

Syn stared at him, confusion bunching in her brow.

"You don't get it, do you? Have you any idea how dangerous the trials are? Rem doesn't stand a chance at completing the trials or even surviving them."

"Rem has years before he's old enough to even qualify."

"A few years won't make a difference. Have you *seen* him? He's much too small and scrawny even for his age."

"You don't know what he will be like when he grows—"

"I do know." Drekton shook his head. "My mother and I have gone along with his ridiculous ideals, expecting him to grow out of it, but we lost that hope the second he received that gold coin. He'll persist now that he has an invitation."

Syn couldn't believe Drekton would be so cynical. "Do you really have so little faith in him?"

"There is no room for uncertainties at the edge of the world, Syn. Legionites are either strong or dead. And in attempting to become a Nighterrian, Rem will be dead." He turned away from her and stared into the fire. "You made sure of that."

Syn believed in Rem's ability to survive the trials—given enough time to grow up, that is. The room seemed to grow unbearably hot. She never imagined granting Rem his heart's desire would bring strife among his family.

Syn's family had always been close with Rem and Drekton's mother, Faylyn. Syn was both nervous and thrilled when her parents announced her engagement to Drekton. It was an agreement far in Syn's favor, one that Syn could never hope to outmatch. As a Du-Garon, Drekton would elevate her status from a third-ring citizen up to a second-ring citizen. Once she became Syndrah Du-Garon, maybe the condemnation of her peers would dwindle away.

She had reveled in her one opportunity to do her family proud. But more so, she fancied a simple, quiet life with her childhood friend. Even if he didn't share the same feelings for her as she did for him, perhaps he would grow to love her.

However, if Drekton's mother now held Syn in disapproval, they would never follow through with the marriage arrangement. The thought of being sent off to another village to marry a stranger filled Syn with terror and humiliation. She stared at the frayed rug while her heart receded into a dark corner of her chest. She racked her brain for the right words of an apology when the Chief stood from his pillowed seat.

"Legionites," Chief Groth announced. "Tonight, we have much cause to celebrate!"

"Hoy! Hoy! Hoy! Hoy!" the room chanted in agreement, and the singers rattled beads against their drums.

"Today, Garon has played host to a Nighterrian warrior. Although our honored guest had to return to his post in Interterra, we shall honor him from afar." Chief Groth picked up a bowl of fresh, spiced blood and presented it before the guests. "Please stand, Drekton Du-Garon, Predon Tri-Garon, Vertah Tri-Garon, and Syndrah Tri-Garon."

Syn stood, guilt flip-flopping in her gut like a fish out of water.

"The four of you have brought honor to Garon through your aid to warrior Xedford. Let us share a drink and may the Legon smile down upon you!" Chief Groth raised the bowl to his lips and drank a series of deep gulps. A red drop of blood dripped down his chin as he handed the bowl off to Syn.

Syn took a shallow sip and passed the bowl to Drekton. He accepted it without looking at her. The boar's blood tasted sweet with a savory finish, but Syn nearly choked. It flowed like sludge down her throat.

The singers hummed and played their drums while the spiced blood made a full circle past the Nameless Elders and back to the Chief. Groth set the bowl down and regarded the circle of Legionites. "It has proved to be an auspicious day as we also celebrate the final night of the Season of Slaughter. And we must honor Syndrah on her first sacrifice," he added with stale conviction and turned face her. "The life you took today will protect Garon. As Legionites, we must make sacrifices for the good of—"

A scream sounded from outside the lodge.

The singers halted and silence tore through the room as everyone held their breath to listen. The weight of the day's lies, misfortune, fear, and shame knocked Syn's breath from her chest. Her knees buckled, and she plunked down hard in her seat.

The sound of Scaler shrieks was common in Garon, but on this night their screeches resonated not from the trap atop the altar, but from just outside the door.

9
TURNLINGS

Syn found herself in a waking nightmare. Still frozen in her seat, a flurry of action swirled around her in a scene she could barely comprehend. She watched the guests grab their swords, axes, bows and arrows—all in a disassociated blur.

The clatter of weapons and shouts of orders did little to drown out the screams of the Scalers coming from outside.

"Syn!" someone shouted. "Syndrah!"

Syn surfaced from the swirling pit of dread long enough to focus her sight on her mother. "Stay here!" Vertah grabbed Syn by the shoulders and shook her. "Do you hear me? Stay here!"

Syn nodded. Her mother and father disappeared out the door along with the rest of the guests of the ruined feast. Even the singers and Elders raised their swords and spears with a war cry and ran to battle without hesitation.

Syn found herself alone. She stared at the fire still crackling on the table. *Coward,* the flames seemed to whisper.

Her mind woke up and went to work tracing the blame back to her morning on the altar. If the Scalers had made it into the village, that meant she hadn't spilled enough blood on the altar to draw their attention to the sacrifice. The trap wouldn't have sprung, as they would have ignored it and gone straight down the hill in search of fresh kills.

"This is my fault," she said to the vacant room.

A wave of hot rage and self-hatred crashed over her. A sudden all-consuming desire to smash the world to pieces pulled her completely from her dumfounded stupor. She stood, clenching her hands into fists as she screamed, "This is my fault!" A sob threatened to choke her, but she refused to let it take hold. "I have to do something."

She looked around the empty room before remembering the family sword she had hung at the door when she entered. Running to the pegs on the wall, she pulled the sword from its sheath. She repressed the fear climbing up her body and raced out the door into the snow.

Without the presence of the moon, the night air painted the sky a dark black. Snow fell in fat clumps. Syn peered past the falling flakes into the night. She couldn't see much, but she heard screams coming from the West.

After leaving the Chief's lodge behind, she crept past similar longhouses within the first ring of the village, half expecting the snapping jaws of Scalers around every corner. She followed the terrible shrieks into the night. The sounds of battle cries and shouts of fighting grew louder as she willed herself forward.

When she rounded a corner, the scene before her nearly sent her reeling back to the cover of safety. Three younger Scalers—Turnlings—prowled through the snow engaging easy targets. An adult Scaler stood towering over the slew of attacking Legionites. Arrows bounced off the full-grown Scaler without breaking its reptilian skin. Spears shattered to pieces as the men and women thrust their attack against the beast.

The Scaler shook off its assailants by swinging a clawed hand through the air. The soldiers dove out of the way of its sharpened talons.

Syn turned her attention to the Turnlings. They stood on two digitigrade hind legs and prowled forward in search of prey. Green and gray scales glittered in the torch light. Their mouths dripped hungry slobber from snouts filled with rows of thin, venomous teeth.

One took a lumbering step toward Syn. With only slits for nostrils and holes for ears, it whipped its head around with serpentine swiftness. The sight of claws and fangs retained a terror all their own, but the most horrifying aspect of the monsters sat embedded within its eye sockets.

The Scaler leveled its eyes on her—human eyes. Blue and intelligent as any man, the beast glared with the rage of a twisted and tortured human soul. It let out a piercing screech and barreled toward Syn.

She raised her sword to block the attack. The blade connected with its shoulder and sent a reverberation up through her hands as if she had struck a rock. The Turnling, surprised by the glancing bite of the metal sword, took a step back. It licked a forked tongue into the air and made another lunge at her.

Syn stepped back as she defended against the onslaught of snapping jaws and swiping claws. She swung her blade at the Turnling but accomplished little damage, its skin left unscathed. She dodged away from its claws, but it pressed its attack, forcing her to take retreating steps backward. She stabbed at the beast again but missed. After taking another step back, her back hit the wall of a house.

Though only a Turnling, the Scaler towered over her. Backed against the wall with the beast in front of her, she decided to make a run for it and darted to her right. But the beast was quick, it blocked her path to escape and snapped its jaws at her neck. She ducked and rolled away, missing its venomous bite by the space of a breath.

Syn tried to stand from her roll, but the beast was already upon her. From her awkward position in the snow, she made an upward stab and managed to draw a tiny droplet of blood from the Turnling's chest.

Syn scrambled against the wall trying to find her feet, but she slipped in the snow and fell back down. The beast loomed over her. The cloud of its breath steamed the air with the stench of gore. She slashed at it from the ground with violent desperation, but her tactless attempt only seemed to anger it. It slammed down onto all fours, trapping her sword arm beneath its clawed hand.

The humanoid blue eyes burrowed into her. It opened its jaws filled with rows of needle-like teeth. She tried to yank her arm free but to no avail. Trapped with nowhere to run, she could only await the inevitable crunch of teeth and slash of claws through her flesh. She prayed it would finish her off quick. Death would be a mercy compared to the transformation of its venomous bite.

The fangs closed in.

A cudgel bashed into the side of its reptilian face, cutting Syn's death prayer short. The beast reared up on its hindlegs and screamed. An axe bit into its side, sending out a spray of scales and blood.

Syn recognized the determined face of her mother as Vertah attacked the Scaler with another smash of her cudgel. With her arm now free of the Turnling's grasp, Syn jumped to her feet in time to see her father's axe come in for another attack to the beast's back.

"Run!" Vertah ordered over her shoulder before turning back toward the Scaler.

Syn dashed away, but a Scaler let out a deafening screech that stopped her in her tracks. She turned to survey the battle and found most of the villagers running in to fight the massive adult Scaler while a few smaller groups battled more Turnlings. How many were there? The dark night and the swirling snow made it difficult to see, but blood already sprayed the ground around her.

"No. I will not run." She redoubled her grip on the carved hilt of her sword and raced back to where her parents continued to fight the Turnling.

Predon hacked at the Scaler's shoulder blade, then leapt back to dodge the swipe of its claws. Vertah jumped in with her cudgel and swung at its head. The beast caught the weighted head of her club in its clawed fist and threw it to the side. Vertah's grip on the weapon sent her sprawling into the snow.

Syn jumped in to take her mother's place and delivered a shallow slash to the side of the beast's jaw. She received an approving nod from her father before he ducked and rolled to attack the Scaler's side. Syn went in for another strike when a hand grabbed a fist full of her cloak and yanked her backward.

"Stay back!" Vertah said as Syn fell on her back and dropped her sword.

Syn ignored her mother and scrambled for her blade. Determined to help bring down the Scaler, she climbed to her feet to rejoin the fight.

Vertah shoved her out of the way, this time with a painful elbow to Syn's gut. "I said, stay back!"

Bent over, reeling from the blow, Syn gathered her breath. "No, I need to fix this." But as she looked up at the battle around her, something caught her attention off near a cluster of sheds in the distance.

Through the windswept snow, she watched a small boy approach the battle scene with a spear held in his tiny grip. He wore two otter pelts over his slim shoulders to imitate broader shoulders.

"Rem." Syn's heart turned to liquid and slank from her chest.

She watched a Turnling knock two men off their feet and crouch down on all fours. It shrieked in bloodthirsty delight as it caught sight of Rem. The beast locked its stare on the easy target and flicked its tongue into the air.

It took off, tearing through the night like a rabid bear, racing straight for Rem.

10
BLOOD

Syn ran.

No, no, no, no! She knew she would never make it to Rem in time. Still, she sprinted as fast as her legs could carry her.

The beast closed in.

Syn was almost there, only a body's length away. She watched Rem raise his spear as the Scaler flew toward him in a powerful leap. The beast's jaws clamped around the spear and splintered it into shards. Unperturbed by his broken weapon, Rem jabbed at the Scaler's head with the broken shaft of his spear.

The Turnling pounced, knocking Rem down. It dug its claws into his tiny body just as Syn reached them. She attacked the beast's back with her sword, but the tough armor-like skin protected it from the worst of her blows.

The taste of blood drove the beast mad, and it took no notice of Syn as it tore into Rem. Syn screamed and hacked at the monster again and again. She cut a large gash into its side and finally pulled its attention away from Rem. It turned its head to look at her while blood dripped from its fangs.

"Rem!" screamed a voice of to her right.

Syn jumped out of the away of the beast's swipe. An arrow shot through the air and lodged itself into the soft flesh of the beast's armpit.

Syn glanced over to see Drekton toss his bow to the ground. He pulled out his sword and squared up to fight with vindictive rage sprawled across his face. The Scaler shrieked and broke off the arrow shaft. It bound after Drekton on all fours.

With the Scaler distracted, Syn knelt beside Rem. "Please don't be bitten, please don't be bitten," she pleaded as she looked over his wounds.

He lay unconscious and soaked with blood, but his chest still rose and fell with breath. Syn pulled the tattered fur pelts off him to examine his wounds. Deep slash marks covered his chest, but she didn't see any bite marks. She held pressure against his wounds to halt the flow of blood, but he bled from too many places for her to hold.

"Help..." The plea died on her lips as she looked around.

To her right, Drekton continued to fight the Turnling with a fury unlike she had ever seen. To her left, the full-sized Scaler bled from multiple wounds and its movement had become lethargic, but it continued to fight on. Behind her, Syn's parents danced around the body of a dead Scaler as they engaged in another fight against one of the other Turnlings.

Rem woke with a sudden gasp.

Syn snapped her attention back to him and redoubled the pressure on his wounds. "Rem, you're going to be fine. Don't move."

"Syn?"

"Yes, I'm here, Rem. I'm here."

"It hurts."

"I know, I know. Hold still. We'll stitch you up and you'll be fine, you'll be..."

Blood gurgled out from Rem's mouth as he tried to speak.

"Don't talk. You're going to be fine. You haven't been bitten."

Rem sputtered. His mouth bobbed open and close with silent words. With his last reservoir of strength, he raised his right arm.

Blood dripped out of his sleeve from an injury that went unnoticed in Syn's first examination. She grabbed his hand and removed the ties of his sleeve. Broken bones made his wrist droop in an unnatural way. His flesh glistened with blood and, when she looked closer, she could see distinct puncture wounds where the Scaler bit down and broke his arm.

A sob of torment broke free from Syn's chest. The world seemed to go silent. She stared into Rem's terrified brown eyes while tears streamed their way down her face. She held Rem in her arms, no longer bothering to put pressure on his wounds.

As she cried, her hand snaked through the snow to find the carved handle of her sword. "I'm sorry, Rem...I'm so sorry..." she said in between sobs. She gripped the hilt of her blade and looked down into his eyes. She read the same look of fear she saw in the sacrifice earlier that very morning.

Rem stopped spitting up blood. His body began to convulse.

Tears turned Syn's vision into a blur, but the tears didn't keep her from spotting the scales sprouting up through Rem's skin. She pulled the sword forward and held it up to his neck. She needed to do it soon, before he fully transformed. His teeth had already begun to lengthen, and more scales poked up through his skin to cover his exposed flesh.

Do it! She shouted at herself. *His soul will be destroyed if you don't do it now!*

Still, her hand hesitated at his neck. Rem opened his fanged mouth in a silent scream. His body ceased its convulsions. A crunch sounded as his bones elongated. Armored scales grew along his face, but his brown eyes remained the same.

"Rem?"

Syn looked up to find Drekton panting and covered in blood, though it didn't look like his own. "Don't let him turn!" Drekton ran and fell to his knees beside his changing brother. He waited for Syn to bring the mercy of death for a single breath. When she did nothing, he ripped the blade out of her hands and looked down at Rem.

"I'm sorry, little brother." Hesitation stalled his hand for the length of a heartbeat. Then, with a soul crushing wail—a simultaneous scream and sob—he drew the sword across Rem's throat in one swift motion.

A single gargling breath, and Rem laid still. Life left his eyes as his soul returned to the Abyss to await the mercy of the Legion.

Drekton tossed Syn's blade into the snow and clenched his trembling hands into fists. He said something then, but Syn didn't hear it. She could not find her ears or voice, only more tears.

She stayed locked in perpetual turmoil—a moment stretched into a thousand years as she stared down at the dead body of the brave little eight-year-old. Scales covered a portion of his face and his body lay half broken and disfigured but still recognizably Rem.

Drekton got up, perhaps to rejoin the fight or aid the injured. She didn't know, she didn't see him—only Rem. With all sense of self-preservation forgotten, Syn sat in the snow beside the body of her only friend.

She moved to place Rem's hands reverently over his chest when she noticed the glimmer of an object wedged in the snow beside him. She rescued the item from the snow. It was a gold coin with the chip on its side.

If guilt were lethal in doses, she would have died there on the spot. Instead, she tucked the Nighterrian coin into Rem's hand and curled his fingers around it before placing his hand on his chest.

Syn didn't hear the village fall silent. She didn't notice when the shrieks and screams died down and the world lay still in the aftermath of the massacre. How much time had passed? In her bubble of sorrow, she could only perceive the way Rem's blood colored the snow and the way she wished it all would end.

They found her there—her parents, the Chief, and the survivors of the attack. They gathered around her as she rocked back and forth whispering over and over, "What have I done?"

11
BLIZZARD

Syn sat in the dark, cramped retreat of the wood stockroom shivering and still wearing Rem's blood on her clothes. Melted snow dripped from her braids onto the pile of logs where she perched, hugging her knees.

She stared into nothingness. The tears had stopped an hour ago by her estimation. Now she felt something akin to the empty hour only deeper and without an end in sight. She blocked out the heartbreaking pain with numbness and focused on the dark. Perhaps it would swallow her up into a void where she would never have to face what she'd done. She longed for the Abyss where time and guilt didn't exist. The dark space among the stars where souls awaited reincarnation seemed like a peaceful place to float for eternity.

Perhaps that's where Rem is now. Syn gripped her head in her hands and pushed thoughts of him away.

Somewhere at the edge of her awareness she heard a knock come at the door.

The Chief's deep baritone pulled her attention toward the present. "We must speak," he said.

The door creaked. "Come in," Predon said.

Syn peeked behind the curtain hide that served as the doorway to the wood cubby. She watched Chief Groth enter with two of the Nameless Elders.

Predon ushered Vertah, Groth, and the Elders toward the workroom. "We can speak in here." He looked over his shoulder just as Syn ducked back behind the curtain.

Syn waited for the sound of footsteps to fade behind the door before she slipped from her perch. She padded to the door of the workroom and crouched beside it. Between the gap in the wooden door and the floor, she spied the group. Her mother stood wringing her hands while her father lit a torch.

"None of the injured have been brought to us," Vertah said.

"In light of the accusations, all of the injured have sought treatment from other families." The torchlight lit Groth's impassive face.

"Are there any more fatalities?" Predon asked.

"Some may still succumb to their wounds, but as it stands, Remmel remains the only death."

Predon shook his head. "I wish they would let us help. Surely the healers will have their hands full. It's not practical to let people go without treatment."

"Predon, the charges against your daughter are very serious."

"But they're only accusations." Predon ran a hand through his hair in frustration. "Soon they will see it was not Syn's fault. She performed the sacrifice, but the trap doesn't always work. I know the Du-Garon family is grieving, but the attack cannot be blamed on Syn."

The Elders exchanged looks.

"We found evidence on the contrary," Groth said.

Syn pulled away from the door, unable to listen to the rest. She buried her face in her hands as the muffled voices continued in the workroom. What would come of her? No doubt they had found the sacrifice frozen to death without a single cut to her body. By morning, all of Garon would know of the blood on her hands.

The image of Rem's mother, Faylyn, chased Syn like a predator through the weeds of her mind. Her face when she discovered Rem's body in the snow plagued Syn's memory. Faylyn's soul-tearing scream as she sank to her knees echoed in Syn's head.

Faylyn had proved a true Legionite woman. She didn't cry as she clung to Drekton, her last remaining son. She had turned her sorrow into rage and focused her sight on the gathering crowd. "Whose fault is this?" she had demanded. Her eyes, bloodshot and filled with hatred, found Syn crying over Rem's body.

"Whose fault is this?" The words echoed on repeat inside Syn's skull.

It's mine.

Syn crawled forward and peeked back through the crack in the door in time to see her mother put her face in her hands.

Predon leaned on the butchering table and shook his head. "What sort of punishment awaits our daughter?"

"We will hold a tribunal in the morning. Her fate will be decided then," Groth said.

Syn crawled onto her shaking feet and backed away. The tribunal could seek the death penalty, and why shouldn't they? Her haunting had brought pain and death to her village. The village would likely ask for her own pain and death to balance the scales.

Despite her desire to float along in the nothingness of the Abyss, she wasn't ready to die. Not as a coward. An overwhelming burst of self-loathing gushed through her. Her curse made her weak. Her curse had brought Rem's death.

"I will not let this continue," she decided in a sudden moment of desperate clarity.

Panic carried her to the front door, but shame stalled her hand. The family sword caught her attention as it bounced on her back when she ran for the door. She touched the leather strap across her chest.

"I need to make this right."

She pulled the sword off her shoulder and carried it over to the mantle where a small fire blazed at the hearth. She set the sword carefully on the hook where her father always hung it. The ivory handle still contained Rem's blood trapped in the divots of the intricate carving. She stepped back and allowed herself a silent goodbye. Then, she jumped into action.

She opened the weapons cabinet near the front door. A bow, a pair of cudgels, or a spear? No, none of them would do. She fumbled through the weapons in a hurry, fearing the party discussing her fate would exit the workroom at any moment. At the bottom of the cabinet, her frantic search turned up the only blade suitable for her disgraceful hands. Snapped in half, the sword resembled more of a dagger than a sword, but the angle in which it had broken left a jagged point perfect for stabbing.

"Hello, friend," she said to her new weapon. She shoved the discarded piece of scrap metal into a leather sheath and attached it around her waist as voices continued to sound from the workroom.

"Legion, help me," she prayed. She looked over her shoulder in a dark farewell, then reached for the door and slipped out into the blizzard.

12

HONOR

Wind whipped about in a torrent of snow as Syn made her way through the dark, freezing night. She ran as fast as she could despite the resistance of the wind and the attack of snowfall. She feared if she took her time, she would lose her nerve to do what needed to be done. With her heart pounding and her breath resonating in her ears, she almost didn't hear the howling.

She paused to listen. The howls, nearly lost to the wind, persisted near the western edge of the village. Could there be more beasts? It didn't sound like the shrieks of a Scaler, or the call of a wolf, but perhaps someone was hurt. Her weakness brought the attack to her people. If someone was injured or in danger, it would still be result of her failure to perform the sacrifice. She couldn't carry more blood on her hands.

Syn turned around and ran toward the source of the howls. She chased the call past the Outskirts and into the edge of the forest where she stopped and peered into the dark.

Through the icy blizzard she saw, not a beast, but a person. Syn ducked behind trees as she drew nearer to investigate. The enraged man screamed and beat a spear into a tree. With every distraught slam of the spear, he unleashed a wild roar into the wind. Syn got closer until she recognized him.

Drekton bashed his spear against the tree again and this time it snapped in half. He shouted and hurled the halves of the spear into the woods and fell to his knees. Self-hatred mounted an attack inside Syn's heart as she watched his despair. She felt like an intruder at the scene of his grief.

She glanced behind her toward the Ancestral Hill and gripped the handle of her broken sword. "I'm sorry I failed you," she whispered and backed away.

"Who's there?" Drekton looked up. He must have sensed her movement in the shadows.

Syn turned on her heel and ran. She heard Drekton's feet crunch in the snow as he gave chase. In the obscuring blizzard he probably mistook her for another Scaler. She could stop and prove she held no threat, but she feared the confrontation would keep her from her goal. And she couldn't bring herself to face him.

No turning back now.

Syn ran through the rings of the village while Drekton shouted and raised the alarm. She began to panic when Legionites raced from their homes at the sound of his call and joined him in the chase. What would happen if they caught her? Could Drekton be distraught enough take matters into his own hands and enact the Law of Retribution?

Skirmishes between families and individuals were often settled by the Law of Retribution. If your neighbor stole from you, you would take an item of equal value and the dispute would be settled. Syn imagined being forced to fight a Scaler with nothing but a spear, just like Rem.

No, the Chief said there would be a tribunal. This was

bigger than an individual grudge, it was far worse. She glanced over her shoulder; she couldn't let them catch her.

With her sight trained on the Ancestral Hill, she focused on her breath to carry her through the snow. Two breaths in, two breaths out. The Hill grew larger as she closed the distance. She passed the Scaler heads mounted on stakes and slipped through the gaps of the palisade.

She reached the base of the Hill and began to climb. With the mob closing in, she didn't have time to make for the stairs on the opposite side of the Hill. She scrambled up the icy bones as the tone of the mob behind her changed. They must have realized she was only a person and not a beast. They continued to call out to her, but their words fell victim to the wind.

A clatter of shifting bones below her indicated someone ascended the Hill in pursuit. Syn refused to look back as she slipped and scrambled her way up. The snow whipped at her face, making it hard to see. The frozen skeletons numbed her fingers, but she forced herself to carry on.

A skull dislodged and her stomach plunged to her toes as she began to slide down the icy slope. At the last moment, she caught another foot hold and clambered for purchase. After gaining her balance, she moved higher. Hand over hand, she climbed on with the knowledge of followers close behind.

The whiteout storm rained down with such cruelty, she almost didn't realize when she reached the top. Part of her was glad for the obscuring blizzard. Now she wouldn't have to set eyes upon the frozen body of the sacrifice.

Syn climbed to her feet atop the summit and spotted the portal shimmering with a dark, oily gloss. Roughly the width of her body, it sat like a gossamer lid on the ground. She felt the power of it calling out to her with a mixture of both dread and glory.

Shouts sounded from a short distance away. Syn knew she

had mere moments before her pursuers caught up to her and dragged her back down.

She looked up to the dark, swirling sky. "This is for you, Rem," she said.

Although she didn't have his golden coin, she would just have to find another way to gain entrance into the trials. If she returned a Nighterrian, perhaps she could regain a sliver of dignity and prove the Legion had forgiven her.

If she died in the trials, then at least she would meet her end with far more honor than the death penalty.

Syn stepped toward the pit where the pull of the portal's hypnotic presence beckoned her forward. With a deep breath, she stepped through the portal to another realm fraught with darkness and monsters, on a path toward redemption.

Or death.

PART TWO
INTERTERRA

13
LEKTRA

The aching grind of the wagon rattled Lektra along through the endless night. Comfort eluded her as she tried to find a better position that wasn't buried beneath sacks of potatoes and barrels of ale.

Behind her, the teamster sang off tune to the chorus of grunts from the beasts pulling the wagon past the lava pits that dotted the barren desert. Lektra grimaced at the sound of the grunts. She distrusted the dangerous beasts that everyone in Interterra seemed to revere. They resembled a hairless yak with tusks and four eyes that glared at you like you were a meal.

She sighed and shifted again in her cramped hiding spot. The hot night held her in a suffocating embrace. After wiping her brow, she pulled her knife from her belt and set to work carving another notch in her cudgel.

Day thirty-five. Back home in Veldt she knew the Season of Slaughter would soon be at an end, and her father would need her help in preparing for the winter ahead. But she couldn't bring herself to return. Not yet. Not until she found him.

She returned the knife to her belt and made sure it stayed positioned for easy retrieval. She patted the cudgel at her side. One didn't last long in Interterra without a handy weapon. Especially not Surfacers like herself.

Lektra had promised her father and her village Elders she would only search for thirty days, yet here she was stowed away and scanning the empty landscape. Through the open back of the canvas wagon, she stared up at the foreign stars hanging above her. They burned with an orange glow like an inflamed wound.

The stars were not like the shy pinpricks that scattered the sky back in the Surface realm. No, the stars in Interterra lit up the landscape. The ugly face of red dirt extended for miles in every direction. Natural rock structures punctured the wasteland and a few mountains rose in the distance but, for the most part, the land remained a flat, scorching nightmare. Travel through Interterra required the wagon to dodge around pools of lava that bubbled up from the ground like oozing pustules over the cracked completion of the land.

Barren. Treacherous. Lektra despised the heat and the incessant dust kicking up beneath the wheels. "This worthless place," she said.

"Hello?" came a voice from the other side of a barrel just behind her.

Lektra jumped and grabbed for her cudgel. A dirty face emerged from a hidden compartment among crates stamped with the word "fragile." The shadow crawled over sacks of potatoes and into the dim starlight.

Lektra breathed a half sigh of relief. The intruder proved to be merely a young girl, but Lektra still held tight to her weapon. In Interterra, even children could pose a threat. Over the past month, she learned to never let her guard down.

"What are you doing in here?" Lektra asked.

"Hiding." The girl plunked down on a sack of potatoes and took note of Lektra's crumpled position among the barrels of ale. "Same as you, looks like."

Could the girl have been there since Lektra snuck onboard back at the last town? Lektra glanced over her shoulder toward the teamster, but she doubted he would hear her talk over the oink of the grunts, the creak of the wagon, and his incorrigible singing.

She turned back to the young girl with the stringy blonde hair and a dirty face. "How old are you?"

"Ten and a half. How old are you?"

"Seventeen."

The girl's curious red eyes roamed over Lektra. "You're a Surfacer?"

"Yes, a Legionite."

"You talk funny," the girl said with a thick Terraborn accent.

"So do you. What are you doing hiding in the back of a wagon?"

The girl jabbed her thumb in the direction of the teamster on the other side of the canvas. "That's my papa. He said I couldn't come on the road with him. But I ain't no pants wettin' nilly. I'll show him I ain't afraid."

"You should be afraid. It's dangerous out here."

"I ain't never been afraid. No, not for one hot minute. Nobody goes around saying 'Caravinna's scared of this or scared of that.' No, they say, 'that Caravinna, she's a tough one,' which I am."

"Well, Caravinna, is it?"

The girl nodded.

"Caravinna, you might not be afraid, but I'm sure your mother is worried sick. She must be looking for you."

"Nah." Caravinna pulled at the lose seam on the sack

beneath her. "Mama died last year giving birth to my baby brother... but, well, he didn't make it neither."

"Oh. I'm sorry to hear that."

"Yeah, I miss her sometimes. My brother too, even though I didn't ever know him."

Lektra kept her weapon in hand but leaned back against a barrel. A bead of sweat dripped down her temple. She longed for the familiar comfort of her cold, snowy home. "I miss my brother too."

"Did he go off to meet the Fates?"

"No, he's still alive."

"Then why ain't you seen him?"

"He entered the Nighterrian trials last season, but he didn't come back."

"I don't mean to be rude or nothing but, well, how do you know he ain't dead? Papa always says those Nighterrians be nothin' to run with. He always says, 'Caravinna, don't you ever be getting wrapped up with one of those blue bloods, they live fast and dangerous.'"

Lektra leaned her head back and stared at the giant, orange stars. Nearly a year had passed since Tanok disappeared through the portal. Nearly a year since Lektra had felt safe. Still, she held tight to hope like gripping the ledge of a cliff.

"I just know. I can feel it, he's alive. I just need to find him."

Caravinna considered this for a moment, then shrugged. "Did you look at Ricksaw's near Outpost 55? I hear the failed competitors like hanging out around there."

"He wasn't there." Ricksaw was the first place Lektra had heard phrases like, "Surfacer scum" and "light-dwelling bitch." She had endured the shoves and the name calling in exchange for flimsy scraps of information. But all her leads amounted to nothing.

"What about Shepp's Valley? That's a famous place, yeah, it attracts all sorts of fellas. Did you check there?"

"I looked there too. I've gone from town to town all over this abysmal underworld. I've been thrown out and spat on just for asking questions about the Nighterrians."

"Yeah, folks around these parts are the secretive type. Papa says things've been tense ever since that Redd and his gang rolled through and took over this here land."

"So I've gathered." Lektra wanted to point out that the reason for her failure went deeper than the tight-lipped locals, but Caravinna seemed liked she was trying to be helpful. Lektra didn't want to offend her with complaints about the Terraborn people despite the racist glares she received when their red eyes fell on her Legionite features.

"What's your brother's name?" Caravinna asked. "So's I can ask around about him."

"I'd appreciate that. His name is Tanok."

"Tanok," Caravinna said, trying out the foreign name. She giggled. "That's a funny name."

Lektra smiled. "I used to call him 'Tan-Rock' as a kid."

That made Caravinna giggle even more. "And what's your name?"

"Lektra." She stuck out her hand in the customary Terraborn greeting. If she gained nothing else in her thirty-five days in Interterra, at least she knew how to properly shake hands. She at first found the gesture unpleasant, but she had grown used to it.

Caravinna took her hand in a tight squeeze and shook. "Lektra, that's not as funny as Tanok, but still strange."

It had been a while since Lektra had enjoyed the company of another person. She opened her mouth to offer thanks when the wagon began to slow.

"We're here!" Caravinna clambered over sacks to poke her head out of the back of the wagon.

"And where exactly is 'here?'"

"Shhh!" Caravinna held a finger to her lips and turned over her shoulder to listen to her papa shout at the grunts.

The grunts moaned and oinked as they slowed to a lazy walk. Lektra crawled over the stacks of goods to where Caravinna leaned out the back of the wagon. Together they watched a dusty town approach in their sights. It wasn't much of a town. A few sad rows of buildings sat in the dry dirt. A paltry attempt at civilization, like trying to grow seeds in the snow.

Lektra knew her stowaway presence would soon be discovered, and even if she were on good terms with the teamster's daughter, she couldn't count on the man's mercy. She'd have to make her escape soon. Too many times she had been forced to outrun the illegal weapons hidden beneath the sleaves of the Terraborn locals.

"I should be going," she said to Caravinna as she eyed a posse of riders galloping on leathery grunts headed toward the town.

Caravinna nodded. "I'll keep an eye out for your brother. What's he look like anyhow?"

"A lot like me. People always say we look like twins." Lektra rolled her eyes at the memory of family members cooing over their similar features. Tanok always teased her by saying it meant they thought she looked like a boy. "I always hated it when they said that. But Tanok is older, taller, and stronger... kind of like..."

The group of riders rode up past the slowing wagon and Lektra's heart tapped a hopeful rhythm as she scanned the faces of the men. It was silly. She knew better than to think she might stumble upon Tanok's face in a crowd. Surely that wasn't his wide shoulders, tanned skin, and Legionite-shaped eyes. A trick of the shadows, it couldn't be...

"That's him!"

"Where?"

"There!" Lektra motioned to the posse of six riders who halted their grunts as they reached the first building of the town. Caravinna huddled in closer. They watched the posse tie the ugly, gray beasts beside a trough of water outside an alehouse.

Lektra waited, sweating with anticipation, as the wagon drew past the riders at an unbearably slow pace. The youngest of the six men unstrapped the saddles from the grunts and hurried about his work. The saddle boy's face was dirty. Dust in the creases around his forehead and mouth gave him a solemn expression. He appeared aged and his hair hung wild at his shoulders, but Lektra would have known him in a whiteout storm.

"*Tanok.*" She didn't know if she said his name aloud. In her shock, she might have only voiced his name inside her head. She sat frozen in place as the wagon drew past. *Look over here!* She willed toward him.

The saddle boy looked up.

A single moment stretched out into a thousand instants that disobeyed the laws of time. Recognition raced across his expression as he stared at her with familiar storm-cloud eyes.

It's him, it's really him! Lektra stared back unable to find words amidst the astonishment of her fortune.

But then a dark shadow cast itself over Tanok's features and the reverie evoked by her sudden appearance turned grim. He set his jaw and his eyes flashed with warning. He gave a near imperceptible shake of his head. *No,* he seemed to communicate. Then he turned away and bent back to work unstrapping the saddles, as if he hadn't seen her at all.

14
OUTPOST 84

yn expected to fall through a great chasm when she stepped through the portal. Instead, she felt as if she entered a tunnel into the Abyss. Vertigo. Fear. Confusion. Time contracted and expanded. A force tugged on her soul and carried her forward.

Yet, it only lasted an instant. With a single step, she left behind the snow and emerged into a land of darkness. Syn found herself at the bottom of an empty pit. With nothing else to do but climb, she crawled her way up out of the hole while her fingers thawed in the warmth of the new climate. After glancing over her shoulder at the portal for the third time, she felt convinced her pursuers wouldn't follow her through.

Syn pulled her dagger from her belt as soon she stood on flat ground. Ready for an attack of monsters, she planted her feet and held her broken blade out in a defensive stance.

Her first glimpse of Interterra was nothing like she expected. She dropped her fighting posture and surveyed the barren land. No Nighterrians stood guard around the portal.

No beasts prowled within sight. The dry landscape stretched out into the perpetual night, quiet and vacant.

"This is strange," she said to her broken blade.

Syn traveled her gaze up and she gawked at the foreign night sky. The stars glowed in shades of red and orange in a series of unfamiliar constellations. They shinned brighter than the stars in Garon, as if they hovered closer to the earth. The stars provided more light than she expected. In the distance, she could see red craggy rocks rose from the dirt.

She turned around and discovered a series of buildings across the flat plain. If she listened carefully, she could hear sounds of life coming from the small village. She didn't know where to go to get to the trials, but she figured the village would be a good place to start. With her dagger in hand, she made her way toward the long buildings.

After only a few steps, she began to sweat beneath her fox-pelt cloak. Despite the non-existent sun, heat permeated the air. The warmth seemed to rise from the ground, and she eventually stooped down to feel the rust-colored dirt. Heat radiated from the earth as if a well of boiling water lay hidden just beneath the soil. The baking ground turned the world around her into a giant oven.

Syn wiped her brow with the back of her sleeve and continued toward the murmurs of civilization coming from the village. As she wandered closer, she could discern the noise of voices and laughter. An unseen instrument made bizarre sounding music that thrummed a melody across the wasteland.

She reached the village made up of just two parallel lines of buildings. The structures rose above her with an imposing presence. They weren't the cozy longhouses or circular huts she was used to. The buildings were twice as tall and had windows on the second story. Although many doors with various names painted across them indicated separate establishments, the houses stood connected to each other in two rows with long shared porches.

A towering contraption stood at the entrance to the village. Wooden scaffolding held up a series of blades at the top like a metal sunflower. The blades turned lazily in the light breeze. Syn wandered around its base. She couldn't imagine what the structure was for. A sign nailed to the wood read, "Outpost 84." She squinted to read a poster stapled beside it.

Attention:
Outpost 84 is under the jurisdiction of Redd the Collector.
Possession of illegal weapons will result in prosecution.

Redd the Collector? What a strange name. And what exactly classified as an "illegal" weapon? She doubted her broken blade would be cause for alarm, but she lowered it into the shadows of her cloak, just in case, as she moved on.

Sweat dripped down her back as she approached the row of buildings on her right. An old man sat on the steps in front of a door bursting with voices and laughter. In his hands he held a glass bottle from which he took clumsy sips. He looked at Syn with the red eyes of a Terraborn, but he lacked the wrist mounted three-barrel that would mark him as a Nighterrian. He appeared old enough to be a village elder, so Syn sheathed her blade and stepped up to him.

She swallowed to loosen her dry throat. "Hello, I'm here to enter the Nighterrian Trials." The old man swayed and looked at her with blissful confusion. "Can you tell me where to go?" Her throat itched as she waited for him to respond.

"Shhh-abernnnaan... ish..." he garbled and smiled a gaptoothed grin.

She backed away, realizing the man would be of no help,

and moved to climb the two steps of the porch. Voices and music sounded from behind a set of double doors labeled "Tibset's Alehouse."

She pushed her way through and paused as the pungent smell of sweat smacked her in the face. She wrinkled her nose and marveled at the scene inside. Tiny lights trapped inside mini glass lanterns illuminated the room buzzing with activity. People gathered around tables and drank from large metal mugs in a rambunctious celebration.

Women walked about scantily clad and adorned in jewelry. Some wore colorful dresses hitched up to show off their legs. The tight bust of the dresses exposed the tops of their breasts. Many sported ruffled skirts with layers of decorative scarves and jewelry hanging around their waists or necks. Syn had never seen so much color or opulence in her life.

The bearded men were, thankfully, more clad than the women. Despite the heat, they wore long, fitted jackets over vests and loose shirts. However, Syn glimpsed a showcase of dark chest hair from plenty of unbuttoned shirts.

Syn stepped out of the way of a fat man that nearly stumbled into her, then jumped as a woman sitting on a man's lap let out a cackle of laughter. The Terraborn woman wore a jingling set of golden medallions around her forehead that tinkled with every turn of her head.

"What do we got here? A fur-child?" The adorned woman laughed and grabbed Syn to pull her in.

Syn wiggled out of her grasp and pushed on though the crowded room. In the corner, a man played an odd musical instrument. He held the wooden instrument under his chin and rubbed a thin stick over the strings. The music rang with frenzied trills that only added to the ruckus of the alehouse.

A shout of anger caught her attention on the other side of the room where it appeared some sort of game was taking place. A pile of trinkets and coins glittered from the middle of the table where men sat staring at cards in their hands. Distracted, Syn nearly collided with a woman carrying a tray of cups filled with a mysterious bubbling liquid.

"I'm so sorry."

The woman ignored Syn's apology and stepped around her. She wore a cascade of beaded jewelry around her hips and bustled by to deliver the drinks to a group of men. The men cheered when she arrived and clinked the cups together before gulping the amber-colored liquid. A series of loud belches erupted from each of the men. One burped so hard he nearly fell out of his chair.

Syn tried to stop the woman who delivered the drinks on her way back, but the noise of the room drowned out her voice and the woman hurried on past.

Growing irritated, Syn made her way through the crowd of cleavage and hairy chests to find someone in charge. There had to be a Chief or an Elder around there somewhere. She wanted to ask, but each set of red Terraborn eyes slid past her with distaste.

She made it to the far end of the alehouse to a counter that stretched the length of the back wall. A man with bushy eyebrows and a white shirt drenched in sweat seemed to effuse an air of authority as he stood behind the tall counter.

"What'll it be?" he asked without looking up from loading cups onto a tray. White froth spilled over the edges of the mugs as a woman swept the tray away to distribute to various patrons.

Syn cleared her dry throat. "I'm wondering if you could tell me where—"

"Hey." He cut her off as soon as his red eyes looked down at her beneath his thick eyebrows. "You wrong in the head or something? I thought I done told you already."

"Excuse me?"

"Didn't I kick you out of here the other night?"

"No, this is my first time in this uh... alehouse." *This is my first time in Interterra*, she wanted to say, but thought it unwise to divulge her inexperience.

"Is that right?" He looked her up and down. "Humph." He shrugged and went back to pouring drinks. "You Surfacers all look the same."

"Right, so I'm looking for information on how to—"

"I don't give information to nobody who ain't drinking."

"Oh." Her throat did feel parched after her walk from the portal. "I suppose I'll take a drink then."

The man slammed a cup in front of her and a portion of the contents sloshed over the edge. He then dropped in a small, while tablet that made the drink bubble and fizz. Syn stared down at it with a quizzical eye. She wanted to wait for it to stop fizzing, but it didn't seem like that would occur any time soon. It looked like poison. She glanced over her shoulder and watched the other occupants continue to gulp away without falling over dead.

Syn picked up the cup and took a tiny sip. The drink tasted like the bitter juniper berry medicine her mother made her drink when she was sick. The bubbles burned as they popped on her tongue and traveled down her throat.

A shout from a table in the corner made her reach for her dagger. But when she looked over, she found it was simply the card game growing rowdy. Grown men slammed their cards down and hurled curses toward a girl at the end of the table. Syn hadn't noticed earlier, but something about the girl seemed strange. Messy blonde curls sprung from the girl's head like a wild mane. Unlike the other women in the alehouse, she didn't wear any frilly skirts. Her outfit included trousers and a vest made of a strange material that flashed in the lamplight.

That couldn't be... Scaler skin? Repulsed, Syn watched the girl gather a pile of wealth onto her side of the table. She looked up suddenly and locked eyes with Syn. The teenage girl stared with the red eyes of a Terraborn and smiled. Syn looked away, not wanting to catch the attention of someone who wore the skin of a Scaler.

Syn took another sip from her cup and tried not to grimace at the bitter flavor and offensive bubbles. She admired the potato-sized glass lanterns all around her and the mysterious way the light inside burned without oil to feed them.

Focus, Syn! She forced her attention back to the task at hand and stood on her toes to lean over the counter. "I am here to seek entrance into the Nighterrian Trials," she shouted over the noise of the room to get the attention of the rude man behind the counter.

"You're here to seek death then?" he said over his shoulder as he busied about his work.

Syn shrugged off the quip. "Please, can you tell me where to go or who to speak to?" The man ignored her and went about wiping out cups and pouring more drinks from a set of large wooden barrels. "Is there a Nighterrian around that I could ask?"

He glanced up from wiping a cup to glare at her. His thick eyebrows pinched together and resembled an eagle taking flight. "The blue-bloods ain't hard to find. The pissing scoundrels roll in here few every weeks and take what they want, the treacherous thieves!"

Aghast, Syn stepped back. She had never heard the great warriors spoken of with anything other than respect. Syn narrowed her eyes at the man. How dare he curse them.

"I tell you what, you clearly ain't from around here, so I'll do you a favor by offering some advice." He threw a rag over his shoulder and leaned over the counter. "Go home, little lady. Save yourself a bloody death and turn right around and go back the way you came."

Another bout of curses and shouts of discontent burst from the table in the corner where the card game took place. Syn flinched but refused to let it distract her. "You don't understand, I have to enter the trials. Please, will you tell me where to go?"

"Stubborn brat. Fine, if you want to go and get yourself killed now, you go right on ahead." He grunted and shook his head. "Give me your token and I'll tell you where you ought to go to get slaughtered."

"My what?"

He tapped his impatient hand out on the counter. "Your token, your Fates-damned invitation!"

"Oh, well, you see I don't have the coin anymore but—"

"Ignorant light-dwellers," he cursed. "All you pissing little sun-kissers come in here thinking you can pull one over on me, but it ain't gonna work, I'll tell you that."

"You don't understand, I had an invitation. I saved a Nighterrian named—"

"Enough out of you!" He slammed his fist down on the counter to truncate Syn's explanation. After a moment, his rage cooled and he relaxed to return to business. He glanced down at Syn's mostly full drink. "That'll be two clinks."

It took a moment for Syn to realize he meant payment for the drink. In Garon, unless a bargain was struck, if someone offered you something that meant it was a gift or a shared commodity.

"I-I don't have any money," she admitted.

The man's stare transitioned from annoyance back into

rage. "You tryin' to steal from me, girl?" He lunged over the bar and grabbed Syn by a handful of her fur cloak.

"No, I-I—" Syn reached for her blade, but the man shoved her back and released his grip. Syn hit the wooden floor with a thud.

"Get out!"

Strong hands closed around Syn's ankles and wrists. She struggled against the two burly men who carried her to the door. "Let me go!" she screamed and squirmed.

Once out the door, they swung her by her limbs and tossed her from the porch onto the hard dirt. Luckily, her thick fox-pelt cloak helped cushion the worst of the impact.

Without a word, the two men turned back inside, leaving Syn sprawled in the radiating heat of the packed earth. She groaned and sat up, rubbing the spot on her back where she hit the ground. Off to her right, she spotted a crushed metal cup lying in the dirt.

"I know how you feel," she said to the cup. She felt almost as battered as the poor thing.

Syn decided she could use a friend on the journey and crawled over to pick it up. A dent concaved half the metal mug. After wiping off the dust, she admired the beauty of its uselessness. She decided she would call him Gregory.

"What am I supposed to do now, Gregory?" She climbed to her feet and looped the handle of the cup through her belt.

Just then, the door to the alehouse burst open with a shout. The girl wearing the Scaler skin vest raced out holding a sack over her shoulder. She glanced at Syn, pausing to give her a wolfish grin, then sprinted away as angry hollers followed her out the door.

Men barreled out the alehouse and gave chase while hurling the foulest curses Syn had ever heard. Syn watched the blonde-headed girl disappear behind the row of buildings and escape into the night.

"This place is not at all what I expected," Syn said to Gregory.

After watching the furious men give up their chase and return to the alehouse, Syn wandered through the Outpost. She walked along the porch connected to the building opposite of Tibset's Alehouse. She hesitated to push through any more doors. Without the Nighterrian coin to prove her invitation, she'd need to come up with a new tactic.

Syn reached the end of the long porch and stopped to gaze at the dusty wasteland spread out around her. The flat landscape remained uninterrupted except for strange rock formations protruding up in the distance. Although she hadn't set eyes on a single beast, she found the dark land seemed to contain danger of a more insidious nature.

"What am I doing here?" she sighed.

"That's right, what *are* you doing here?" said a voice with a high-pitched drawl.

Syn whipped around as three dark outlines stalked up to her. A woman at the center stood twirling a dagger in her hands. Two men—one with a tattooed face and another with a gold earring—stepped at her flank.

"You lost, girl?" the woman asked.

Syn could sense an attack coiled in the woman's stance. "I'm just leaving." She turned to walk away.

A third man stepped from the shadows of the porch to cut her off. A mean set of scars stretched across his jaw and reminded Syn of the Severed one. She backed away and nearly tripped off the two steps of the porch. She managed to keep her feet under her, but she stood surrounded. Only the woman held a weapon in her hands, but each of the men wore swords at their belts.

Syn pulled her broken blade from her scabbard. "What do you want?" She addressed the woman.

The woman wore a purple scarf tied around her forehead and weaved through her hair. The purple scrap of fabric served as her only colorful adornment. She wore an outfit like the men in the alehouse with dark trousers and a long, brown jacket down to her knees.

"You're new here." The leader sheathed her dagger and stepped in closer. "And nobody new arrives in 84 without paying their dues to Magoila." She pointed to herself.

"I don't have anything to give you." Syn gripped the handle of her blade and glanced between the three men as she tried to guess which one would pounce first.

"Well, that's a rotten shame, ain't it? In that case, we ought to trade you to the slavers," the woman named Magoila said.

"Slavers?" spoke the man with the gold earring. "Way I see it, we'd be best off trading her to Morton. That bastard will pay a real hefty price for those organs she's got."

"Hmm, you make a good point," Magoila said. "In that case, don't slice her up too bad, boys. The doc will want all the goods intact."

The men drew their swords and stepped toward Syn.

15
GRUNT

The men brandished lethal swords and leered with vicious smiles. Syn switched the grip of her dagger for better use in a close-contact fight. She begged her years of battle drills and Legionite training to flow though her body, but paralyzing fear stood in her way.

The one with the earring lunged and she ducked out of the way. Another blade came slicing through the air. Syn knocked it aside with a swipe of her broken blade.

"Well, well, looky here, this one thinks she can fight!" the scar-faced one said with a devious smile.

Together the three men circled her while the woman watched from the porch. The attackers delivered tiny knicks and slices while they laughed like a huddle of oinking pigs. Syn did her best to defend against the sting of their bloody teasing, but her attempts made the cuts worse. Her heart pounded in her throat. The pump of blood and adrenaline made a rushing sound in her ears. A painful poke to her back made her whip around and lash out with her blade. She managed a slash to the cheek of the man with the earring.

"Light-loving whore!"

The laughter and cruel play faded in place of cold brutality. The three brigands converged in unison. Syn forgot her training as all sense of calm abandoned her. She swung in a tactless frenzy and managed to bloody arms and chests before they wrenched her blade from her grasp.

The tattooed man knocked her to the ground with a powerful punch. Facedown on the ground, Syn kicked and fought as she felt rope tie her wrists behind her back. Rough hands pushed her harder into the dirt.

She sensed movement out the corner of her eye. A couple walked hand-in-hand along the connected porch of the Outpost buildings.

"Help!" she screamed. "Help me!"

The couple glanced at her, then turned and scurried back the way they came.

"Keep her quiet," Magoila ordered.

"Hel—" A hand clapped over her mouth and nose, cutting off her airway.

"What say you, boys? Should we go and have a little fun with this one?" the tattooed man asked.

"Yeah, what's she got under all those furs?" The one with the earring lifted the edge of her cloak with the flat side of his sword.

The scarred man loomed in beside Syn's face, close enough that she could see the brown grime on his yellow teeth. "Morton won't mind if we bruise up her up just a little."

"Fine, but be quick about it," Magoila said.

Sheer terror ripped its way through Syn. She couldn't breathe against the hand holding back her air. She struggled with all her might as the men tugged at her clothes. Her defensive kicking lost power as her chest began to tighten and her head grew dizzy. The men laughed.

"Hold her still, will you?"

"This one's got fight!"

Beyond her sight, rumbling thunder vibrated the ground. Magoila shouted something that was lost to the night. And when the man with the tattoos looked up, his savage desire melted into terror. A boom cracked the air, and he fell back with a hole punctured through his forehead.

The hand over Syn's mouth face fell away, and she gasped a breath. She looked up to see the Legion incarnate. No—she blinked through the delirium of fear—a Nighterrian riding on a gray beast. He pointed his wrist mounted three-barrel at the retreating brigands and gave chase.

The two remaining men and their female leader fled into the night. Once they retreated out of sight, the Nighterrian dropped the aim of his three-barreled fist. He yanked on the reins of his beast and rode back toward Syn.

Syn struggled to her feet with her hands still tied behind her back. The Nighterrian neared and Syn froze at the sight of his familiar face. Long, dark hair, a towering frame, and a bandana tied around his head.

"Xedford?"

"Syn?" He hopped off his steed and produced a blade to cut her free. "Are you hurt?"

"N-no. I'm fine." Her freed hands continued to shake. She looked over her shoulder to where the gang retreated but saw no sign of them. "They were going to..." She looked down at the tattooed man with the bullet hole in his head.

"Don't worry, he's dead," Xedford offered her his hand.

"Good." Syn let him lead her away from the body and did her best to shake off thoughts of the unspeakable crime that nearly took place.

She followed Xedford who led his snorting beast to a

trough of water beside an empty stable. Taking his lead, Syn splashed water on her face and willed her heart to calm.

"Thank you for saving me," she said, then remembering herself, she bowed. "Warrior Xedford."

Xedford wiped a handful of water to the back of his neck and smiled. "We ain't in Garon anymore. You can call me Xedford, and you don't need to bow."

Syn sank down and sat at the edge of the water trough. She felt beneath her fur pelts to take stock of her wounds. "How did you know I'd be here?"

"I didn't. Believe it or not, I was just passing through on my way to the trials."

She found the shallow cuts were superficial. The tough hide of her furs protected her from the worst of the slices. In her current state she hardly felt them, and she figured they would heal on their own.

She looked up at Xedford and noticed he still had remnants of the charcoal he rubbed beneath his eyes from before he left Garon, but he no longer wore the borrowed yak-pelt cloak. She wondered what he did with it before her attention strayed to the way his tattered shirt exposed the muscles of his chest and stomach. The black garment hung open from a slice down the middle where her mother cut it to get to his Hallowed Point.

Did everyone in Interterra walk around half-clothed? She couldn't say she blamed them. The heat remained intense. Sweat poured from her brow and stung her eyes as her heart continued to pound in alarm from the struggle with the brigands.

A snort distracted her from her trail of thought, and she turned to regard the gray beast lumbering over to the trough. It slobbered and oinked like a pig as it sniffed at the water before plunging is face in. The beast had four eyes and spiked horns that poked out of the rough, gray skin along its face and chest.

With hooved feet and wide tusks that protruded from its mouth, it reminded her of a boar, but it stood much taller. The height of its leathery back ended just below her chin.

"What is that thing?"

"Ah, this here's my grunt." Xedford patted the beast on the back. He pulled a metal canister from the saddle bag and began rubbing what looked like a dark colored grease into the dry cracks of the creature's skin. "I reckon you don't see many grunts on the Surface. They don't do well crossing the portals."

"A grunt?" The creature raised its head from the trough and looked at her with four dark eyes. Its lips curled back from its tusks as it groaned an oink. Syn shied back.

Xedford chuckled. "Now, you can probably guess how it is they got their name. They're just about the only native creatures tame enough to keep around. If you keep them fed, that is."

"Aren't they dangerous?" The grunt ducked its head back to the water and slurped as it drank.

"Everything is dangerous around these parts. But"—he capped the canister of grease and returned it to his saddle bag —"if given the right purpose, they're mighty useful."

"Does it have a name?"

"No, why?"

Syn shrugged and looked abashedly down at her cup named Gregory. "It just seems you have a special affinity for the creature."

Xedford trained his crimson stare on Syn. She tried not to squirm against his evaluating gaze. "You're a perceptive one, Syn. Most folks don't notice my appreciation for beasts until they see my training sessions."

"Training sessions?"

Xedford leaned against the stable post. "Yeah, I train beasts. Scalers mostly."

"You *what?*"

"Well, I *try* to train them…" he ran a hand through his hair and looked away. "It ain't been going as well as I'd hoped."

"Of course it hasn't. The Scalers can't be trained or tamed, they're monsters!" Syn exclaimed, momentarily overtaken with incredulity before remembering she spoke to a holy warrior. "I mean, I'm sorry I didn't mean to criticize."

"No need to apologize. I don't expect you to understand."

Syn wiped her sweating hands on her fur-trimmed trousers. "I just don't see why you would risk such a thing."

"Sometimes even monsters have their uses." He clicked a series of levers at the elbow-end of his three-barrel. Syn watched, mesmerized, as he reloaded the barrel with a silvery bullet. He then clicked open a small round container attached to the weapon and used a funnel to pour a tiny amount of what looked like black sand from a leather pouch.

"How do you mean?"

He finished reloading his three-barrel and tucked his supplies away as he looked off into the night. "Just imagine an army of trained Scalers. Why, any threat would just about shrivel in comparison." His eyes twinkled with a faraway look, and Syn got the impression of him as boy with outlandish dreams.

It reminded Syn of the way Rem spoke about Nighterrians —no, she couldn't let herself think of Rem. "I can't imagine anything that would require such an army."

"Then you ain't been here long enough, darlin'." He winked before flicking his gaze over to the dead man lying in the dirt a few paces away.

Syn's gut churned. "I suppose you're right." The conversation had helped to distract her from the terrifying capture mere moments ago but now the world smacked back into sharp focus.

"So, you've changed your mind about the trials?" Xedford asked.

"I, umm..." She hesitated and glanced down at her hands. Rem's blood remained stuck under her nails. "I mean, yes, I'd like to enter the trials. If you'll still have me." She held her breath.

"Of course," he smiled.

A mixture of relief and fear flooded her at his acceptance. She tried to find the right words of thanks but came up empty.

"If you don't mind me asking, what made you decide to come?"

"I... just had a change of heart." She cleared her throat to choke back the threatening guilt.

"Well, we best get going then. We don't have long, and we'll need to pass through those crags." He nodded toward the rocks in the distance and grabbed his grunt by the reins. It snorted as it lumbered along beside him.

Syn jumped to follow, still in shock at the fortune of his valiant arrival and generous benediction. "I don't need that coin, do I? I'm sorry I—"

"No need to fret. The invitations are really only for non-Terraborn competitors who require a map to get to the trial grounds. But, seeing as I'm heading there myself, you can just follow me." He smiled down at her with an enigmatic grin "And I'm better than a map anyway."

Syn returned his smile as she followed beside him, but it fell from her face as they passed her dead attacker lying on the ground.

Xedford stooped to collect Syn's broken dagger. He regarded it with distaste. "This yours?"

"Yes, thank you." Syn took it hastily and returned it to her belt.

"You know, I reckon I could get you a better blade."

"No. Thank you, but I like this one." Syn blushed. She had decided to name it Elaine. Xedford shrugged. "What about him?" Syn nodded to the tattooed man.

Xedford gave the body a casual glance. "The Outpost will take care of him."

Syn looked back at the row of buildings. She noticed faces poking out of doorways and eyes peeking from behind curtains. She recalled the way the couple had run away in her time of need and how no one came to answer her cries for help.

"Where is your honor?" she said to the closed doors and curtained windows.

The Outpost seemed quieter than when she first arrived, as if it held its breath at Xedford's presence. The hush provided a sense of foreboding that tugged at Syn's back as she turned toward the crags in the distance and ran to catch up with her guide.

16
CRAGS

Syn kept expecting the sun to rise as she hiked. In the Surface world, she could judge the passage of time by the movement of the sun or the moon. Here, however, the dark filled the night with a timeless perpetuality.

The terrifying possibility that her haunting might strike at any moment lurked at the back of her mind while she walked. Exposed in the unfamiliar land, she would have no safe place to hide and recover. Her thoughts flashed with memories of the brigands' hands tearing at her clothes. She felt safe with Xedford by her side, but she couldn't help but imagine one of the brigands finding her passed out and vulnerable after an episode of her haunting. She forced her attention toward placing one foot in front of the other and prayed an episode wouldn't strike any time soon.

With the Crags permanently under the cover of darkness, the trail proved dangerous. Xedford had warned her of snakes that hid between rock crevices and venomous bats called "sky sharks" that swooped down from the sky. Syn asked if she could have a torch to search out threats, but Xedford explained it would only attract more predators.

Xedford stopped to consult the device he called a "pocket watch." Apparently, it was a way to measure time in a land without the sun. He clicked the lid of the circular item closed and returned it to his pocket. He walked on, leading his grunt by the reins.

The grunt snorted and glared at Syn. She was secretly glad when Xedford explained the beast wouldn't carry their combined weight up the steep rocks. Though he offered to let her ride it while he walked, she declined. She distrusted the creature and held no desire to climb atop its saddle.

"Where are the rest of your crew?" Syn hoped question wasn't too invasive. She needed something to take her mind off the oppressive heat and the annoyance of bruises and shallow cuts covering her body.

"Hmm?"

"When you left Garon, you said you were on your way to rejoin your men."

"Ah yes, my crew. I didn't find them at the crossing." Annoyance colored his tone. He paused and shook his head as if to cast away the bitterness. "With the trials only a day away, I suppose I can't blame them."

Syn trekked along in silence until another question occurred to her. "What brought you to Garon, anyway?"

Xedford cleared his throat and spoke over the sound of the grunt's snorts and slurps. "We chased a Scaler on through a portal to the north of you. We got separated in the woods as we were tracking it. Wretched fool I am, I tried to corner it to save it for capture and training but, well, you saw how that turned out."

Syn wiped the sweat from her brow as she picked her steps through the dark. She didn't expect his injuries to have come from a Scaler. They appeared more like stab wounds than claw marks. "You killed it though, right?"

"Yeah. Bastard cut me up pretty good, but I got him in the end."

"Good. I wouldn't be able to sleep at night knowing there might be a Scaler loose in the woods. Even if it were miles from Garon."

"Nah. We'd never let that happen," he smiled a heroic grin.

An unasked question prodded at Syn. She thought it might be inappropriate to voice, but Xedford's demeanor seemed welcoming. "Is it true Nighterrians are immune to the venom of a Scaler's bite?"

"That's right. Plenty of things change after the imbuing. Most venom and poisons become ineffective, your body heals right nice, and your strength increases. Even your bones harden, allowing you to shoot one of these." He raised his three-barreled arm in the air.

Syn imagined what it would be like to fire a three-barrel. She knew without the reinforced strength of a Nighterrian, the power of the weapon would break her fragile bones if she tried.

"Is there anything a Nighterrian can't do?"

"We ain't immortal if that's what you mean. If you part our heads from our shoulders, we'll die just as quick as anybody else. And we can't regrow any limbs if they get cut off."

Sweat continued to drip from her every pore as she tried to keep pace with Xedford's long strides. She felt her body completely drenched beneath her clothing and each dust-filled breath made her lungs burn.

"I assume being Nighterrian makes..." she panted for breath, "climbing mountains much easier?"

Xedford turned around. "Ah! My apologies, I up and forget myself. You must be needing a break." He stopped, detached a canteen from the saddle of the grunt, and handed it over to Syn.

Ashamed, she accepted the canteen. If she couldn't even make it through the crags without needing to rest, how could she possibly make it through the trials? She was thankful for the water, however. Her throat felt as dry as the landscape they walked through. She drank deep gulps but forced herself not to drain the whole thing. She handed it back to indicate her readiness to continue, but Xedford waved it away.

"Drink and rest awhile. We're nearly there." He nodded into the night.

With silent thanks, Syn guzzled the last of the water. She didn't know how he could discern their whereabouts. The jutting rocks rose in all directions, blocking out the landscape below. She tossed her braids out of her face and decided to take the opportunity to remove some of her sweltering layers. She unfastened her fox-pelt cloak and moved to toss it over a nearby boulder. As she threw her coat, she stepped on a rock and heard an odd mechanical clicking noise.

In the space of a single blink, the boulder with her cloak slid backward, revealing a pit dug beneath where a nest of snakes hissed and writhed. At the same time, the rock under her foot sprang upward, pitching her forward and into the uncovered pit.

On her way down, she locked eyes with a feathered serpent.

17
SERPENTS

A spike of fear appeared to stop time as Syn seemed to hover over the pit of writhing scales. She dangled in the air and realized she *was* in fact hovering. Xedford held a fist full of her clothing at her back which kept her from falling all the way into the pit of serpents.

A blue snake rose its head into the air and ruffled the mane of feathers on its neck. It opened its jaws and needle-sharp fangs glittered in the starlight. It reared its head back to strike just as Xedford yanked her out of the snake's reach.

Syn fell backwards into his embrace and watched the boulder click itself closed and side back over the pit of snakes. Xedford held her in his arms as she caught her breath.

"That was mighty close," he said.

Syn turned to face her rescuer. "What *was* that?" she asked, both astounded and fearful.

"A trap." Xedford let go of her and moved around to examine the boulder with careful steps.

A trap? Syn knew the movement of the boulder was no

magic, but the mechanics felt just as mystical. "How did the rock move?"

Xedford stepped around the backside of the bolder and touched something in the air. A quiet thrum rang out. Syn crept forward to investigate. When she squinted, she could just make out thin ropes nearly invisible in the dark.

"We call it, 'strangle wire.' Strong enough to hold the weight of three men but thin enough to go unnoticed."

Now that she knew what to look for, Syn could see a network of crisscrossing wires attached to a series of pullies and metal cogs hidden in the shadows behind the boulder. "Who put it here?"

Xedford sighed. "I regret to admit the posse you encountered earlier were only one of the many outlaw gangs among these parts."

"I was afraid to ask if that was a typical occurrence."

"Unfortunately, it is. Us Nighterrians try and keep the land safe, but we can't defend attacks on multiple fronts. When we ain't fighting monsters, we're fighting men. Oftentimes, I don't know which is worse."

"This place isn't at all what I thought it would be. I haven't seen a single beast, yet it's far more dangerous out here than I imagined." Syn glanced at the trap and felt at her shallow wounds.

"You got no idea." Xedford moved away from the wires and returned to his grunt. "And don't worry, you'll get your fill of beasts during the trials." He smiled and beckoned Syn over.

Syn said a silent farewell to her fox pelt still draped over the boulder and scurried over to Xedford. She hoped her face didn't give away the fear caged inside her chest.

"Stick close. I can't have you falling into a lava pit before we even get there," he said in good humor and placed a gentle hand on her back to lead her forward.

"A few hours here and you've already needed to save my life twice."

"Nah. The feathered serpent bite ain't lethal. The blue venom only paralyzes its victim for a few hours."

"What do these outlaws want with a paralyzed captive?" Images of Magoila's gang and her promise to sell Syn's organs flashed through her mind.

"Wealth mostly. Sometimes power."

"Power? How could a pit of snakes bring someone power?"

"The Hallowed Points—or as we call them around here, Hal'points—are exceedingly rare and powerful. The imbuing has the power to transform a man into a being with authority at his disposal."

"But you have to pass the trials to get one, and only teenagers can enter."

"That's the rule, but not everybody abides by the rules out here. Some gangs of outlaws use this pass to trap potential competitors. They intimidate them, and hold others hostage, to try and get one of them to win a Hal'point and return it to the gang."

"But wouldn't the imbuing of a Hallowed Point kill anyone unworthy of its power? I thought the whole point of the trials is to select only those found worthy enough to survive the imbuing."

"Adults and those untested by the trials can try it, and every now and again some lucky bastard might survive. But these outlaws, they live off risk. They'd rather die at the end of a Hal'point than a blade in the dark. Still, others trade the Hal'points for position or favor inside larger crime organizations."

"I had no idea things were so... ruthless."

"And that's why the path to becoming a Nighterrian is ruthless just the same. We gotta make sure the Hal'points fall, not only into hands tough enough to survive the imbuing, but into the hands of those who abide by our moral code."

"What would happen if the Hal'points fell into the wrong hands?" she asked, trying out the Terraborn vernacular.

Xedford lifted an eyebrow. "They already have. Who do you think runs the big crime operations?"

Syn stopped in her tracks. She didn't want to admit her ignorance in stating she didn't know large crime operations existed in the first place, but she could hardly believe the blasphemy. The Nighterrians were supposed to be protectors. How could the sacred blessing of the Legion be stolen by corrupt leaders? It was a scandal her people would never stand for.

After her brief shock, she hurried to catch up with Xedford's pace. "Have you ever caught anyone trying to win a Hal'point for an outlaw?"

"Yeah, we call them Converts."

Syn ruminated on this as she walked, and the conversation fell into silence. She did not typically fear the dark—perhaps it was all the near-death experiences of the past day—but she felt an eerie unease as she treaded on through the night. She had the itch of someone watching her, as if the rocks had eyes and might come to life at any moment.

Syn tried to focus on watching every step for signs of traps, but she found Xedford's proximity distracting. The sleeve of his shirt brushed her arm with every step, and he radiated the scent of leather and oil. His bare, muscular chest glistened with sweat, and she wondered why he didn't smell of body odor.

They reached a short wall of boulders blocking their path. Xedford scaled over the steep rocks effortlessly and offered his hand to help her over. Syn tried not to gawk at his strength as he pulled her up with ease, but she knew she left her mouth open for a bit too long when she watched him lean down and haul the grunt up and over by the tusks.

Once on the other side of the rocks, Syn fell into stride beside Xedford. She continued to feel as if she were roasting over a fire despite ridding herself of her fox cloak. Her tunic and trousers were still made of fur, and she couldn't very well remove them, or she'd be running around in nothing but her shift. She supposed she'd just have to get used to the heat.

Soon the terrain began to slope downward, much to Syn's relief. The further they descended the crags, the more she began to spot strange, bubbling holes filled with orange liquid. The holes sent steam into the night air and added to the climbing temperature. Fist-sized bugs flitted around the air above the holes.

"What are those?" she asked.

"Ghost moths. They're harmless but they make a racket if you disturb them."

"No, not the bugs. The holes."

"Ah, right. That's just a little lava," Xedford said. When Syn looked at him in confusion he added, "Molten rock."

Syn stared into the burning brightness of a nearby lava hole. "I thought you were joking about the lava pits!"

Xedford chuckled as Syn tried to wrap her mind around how hot rocks needed to get to melt into liquid. She blinked and saw the ghost of the bright light in her vision. The lava holes burned even to look at.

"I suppose everything here wants to kill you." She eyed the grunt with its dangerous tusks and sharp teeth, wondering what it would do if it didn't get fed.

"It's a fact of life that things want to kill you everywhere you go, even on the Surface. Nature has a way of testing the survival of a species." He nodded to a ghost moth hovering over a nearby lava hole. Faster than a blink, it whipped out a tiny pink tongue and swallowed an unsuspecting bug. "Only those strong enough to fight against the order of the universe will make it in the end."

Syn watched another unsuspecting bug get drawn into by the light of the lava. "You sound like my mother," she said without thought. She clapped a hand over her mouth. *Way to sound like a brat, Syn.* "I'm sorry, I didn't mean to be rude. I..." *What's wrong with me?* Perhaps the heat was getting to her.

Xedford looked down at her and offered a teasing smirk. "Sounds like you got a wise mother."

Syn nodded; glad she hadn't offended him with her petulant attitude. To be sure to keep her tongue in check, she said nothing more. Her mother's voice circled her thoughts like a vulture.

Weak.

Broken.

Perhaps her mother was right. Syn asked herself again what she was doing in the cruel, dark underworld. Could she really go on to enter the trials? She looked to the crushed cup bouncing along on her belt. She resisted the urge to talk out loud to it.

What do you think, Gregory? Am I running headlong toward certain death? Or worse, what if I survive but fail? In that case, perhaps I'd stay here in this dark, treacherous world for the rest of my days.

Gregory didn't respond of course, and soon Syn was distracted by the leveling of the terrain. She looked up to find a towering gray wall just ahead. She paused when she noticed the surface of the wall moved.

"We're here," Xedford said.

Syn walked past him, drawn in by the curious wall. When she stepped closer, she could see it wasn't a wall at all, but a chasm filled with lava. Over the orange river hovered thousands upon thousands of giant gray moths. They fluttered in their habitat, stacked on top one another over, creating a dense veil of wings that blocked out whatever laid beyond.

The head-sized moths hovering above the steamy crevice were much larger than the ones she spotted over the lava holes they passed. The ghost moths whipped out long, pink tongues and snatched smaller bugs out of the air quicker than lightning. She marveled at the moth wall that extended far above her head and curved around the landscape in a wide semicircle. She couldn't see where it ended.

"How do we get around?" she asked.

"You don't."

"You mean we go through? But how? There is lava below."

"The chasm is narrow. With a running start you'll make it through to the other side, easy."

Syn noticed the way he said "you" and not "we." She turned her attention away from the veil of bugs. "You're not coming?"

"No. My grunt here won't attempt the leap." As if in response, the grunt turned his head toward him and let out a deep moan. "Nilly beast," Xedford said, and patted the creature on the top of its spiked head.

He turned back to Syn. Orange light from the chasm danced off the side of his features. "Nighterrians enter from the sea to the East. This entrance here is for competitors only. Once you cross the veil, you'll officially be in the running for the trials."

Syn tried to look through the field of moths, but the buzzing of their wings kept her from catching a glimpse beyond.

"I understand your hesitation." Xedford mounted his slobbering grunt. "I won't hold nothing against you if you decide not to enter. The trials are brutal and unforgiving.

Plenty have died attempting them. But, well, I think you're here for more than power. You seek something else." He leaned forward in the saddle and whispered into her ear, "Your cure awaits."

A blush crept up Syn's cheeks. She felt the weight of her ghosts at the mention of her curse. "Thank you... for saving me and for guiding me."

"It was a real pleasure." Xedford winked, then turned his grunt toward what Syn supposed was East. "I'll see you on the other side." With a yank of the reins, he set off galloping along the edge of the burning river.

Syn watched him leave before turning back to the curtain of ghost moths. "I don't know if I can do this, Elaine," she said to her dagger. She looked over her shoulder toward the way back. She could probably find her way back to the portal, but traversing the crags proved dangerous, even with Xedford's protection.

She sensed movement in the dark. Her hand flew to Elaine's hilt. She paused, waiting for assailants to come bursting from the rocks.

No one showed. Perhaps it was merely a shadow given off by the light of the lava. She waited a few more breaths, then turned back to the wall. Danger lurked in all directions. At least the one ahead of her held a chance for redemption—and a cure.

She took a few steps back and sized up the jump. "We'll go on the count of three," she said to both Gregory and Elaine. "One"—she crouched— "two"—she took a deep breath— "three." Syn ran toward the veil at a gathering speed. She pushed off her last step at the edge of the chasm and leapt.

As she did, she heard a distant scream from behind her cry, *"No!"*

18

NEIGHBOR

The ghost moths screeched and fluttered in a mad frenzy as Syn parted through them in a blind, mid-air leap. A field of gray covered her vision, and the frantic flap of wings battered her body from every angle. For a split second, she thought she had made a grave mistake. The chasm had no end, and she would soon meet the molten rock in a blistering death.

Then her foot touched down on solid ground. She stumbled forward from the momentum of her jump and fell to her knees. She turned around, attempting to catch a glimpse of the person who screamed the warning right before she jumped.

The flurried blizzard of moths wailed shrill cries, but their fluttering wings revealed nothing of the other side.

She watched the curving wall of bugs for a few moments longer, waiting for someone to come through the veil after her. When the moths began to quiet and eventually fall back into their languid pace, she decided the voice must have been the screech of moths.

Or her own subconscious screaming at her to go back.

Turning her back on the veil, Syn beheld the trial grounds for the first time. Hundreds of canvas tents and makeshift shelters sprawled out around her in a disorganized mess. Competitors lounged by their camps, poking at their cookfires.

What stole her attention, however, was the massive structure at the center of the grounds. Nearly the size of a small mountain, the colossal rock formation took up most of the area inside the ring of moths. The rock towered above her in a tiered shape with three progressively smaller levels rising into the night sky.

A wide, circular base formed the bottom tier of the structure. On the ground level, an open archway at the center appeared to be the mouth of a cave. The cavern entrance swallowed the shadows of the night and obscured whatever hid within.

The second level housed a smaller rock structure with a flat ledge surrounding it. Based on the curving shape of the middle level, she figured a person could walk all the way around its perimeter without fear of falling off the edge.

A circular building composed of stone pillars perched on top of the second tier. Unlike the rest of the natural-looking rock formation, the top tier appeared manmade with perfectly even columns that held up a domed roof.

"The Imbuing Hall," she said to Gregory.

The sight of the fabled Hall drew her in. Following the pull of her curiosity, she walked toward the base of the rock to catch a better angle to glimpse the pinnacle on top. The memory of Rem's awed voice whenever he talked about the Imbuing Hall echoed in her mind. With her head tilted skyward, she didn't pay attention to other competitors littering the grounds.

"Hey!" shouted a boy with green hair as Syn bumped into him.

"Oh, I'm sorry I—"

The boy gave Syn a rough shove that knocked her to the ground. In one swift movement, he yanked a pair of swords from his belt with each hand. He pointed the blades at her throat.

"Fucking light-dweller." He spat on the ground. His red eyes glared with disgust.

Syn crawled backward and got to her feet. She backed way with her hands up.

"Don't you dare come near me again, you hear?" He sheathed his swords and flicked his green hair out of his face.

Syn retreated and surveyed the area around the rock monument. Hundreds of teenage competitors with their respective campfires and cloth shelters budded up against the side of the huge rock. The smell of roasting meat beckoned from various cookfires. Syn clutched the aching desire of her stomach and did her best to ignore her hunger.

The other competitors looked to be between the ages of sixteen to nineteen and wore the red eyes of the those who didn't need an invitation to enter the trials. Every one of the Terraborn competitors had swords, axes, or bows in their possession. Syn watched the campers exchange shifty glances at their neighbors and throw paranoid looks over their shoulders.

Hardly any open space remained to camp aside from a small buffer at the edge of the lava chasm. Not that she could pitch a camp anyway, she had no supplies. She tried to formulate a plan as she picked her way through the campgrounds. She explored around the perimeter of the rock, watching fights breakout over camp space. Hopping over a small fire, she was met with the hostile glances of territorial campers.

"What're you? A she-wolf?" spat a boy roasting a mysterious kill over a fire.

"Looky here, it's one of those Legion-worshiping Surfacers," teased a younger boy with a malicious grin.

"You know she ain't gonna last long," said the one at the fire.

To avoid a pointless scuffle, Syn absorbed the insults and slipped away to the sound of their laughter.

She picked her way around the wall of the rock formation. Once closer to the rock, she could see it contained colored layers of reddish hues. The waves of colors increased and the rough surface of rock smoothed out the farther she circled.

She came to an abrupt stop as the ground gave way to the rolling tide of a sea. Black waves lapped the side of the rock and halted her progress. Captivated, she gazed out into the vast sea. The sea churned like liquid obsidian, not just a trick of the shadows, the water itself retained an ominous black color.

None of the competitors made their camp near the beach. "It must be infested with monsters," she said to Elaine.

Syn looked around. To her right, the water lapped at the rock. She couldn't continue her circle around the rock formation without diving into the water. To her left, the wall of moths curled around until the lava river flowed into the ocean. Near where the land met the sea, a cluster of white trees grew up through the brackish water.

She crossed the rocky beach, making her way to the bone-like trees. Chunks of driftwood knocked against the trunks with every rolling wave as she sized up a route to the upper canopy.

She hoped the twisting limbs would hold her weight as she leaped, grabbing hold of the first branch. Getting to the next tree proved easy, but from there things got more difficult as the distance between weight-bearing branches increased and she was forced to push off one foothold to get to the next. She made it to the trunk of a larger tree, her years of scaling trees in

Garon and seeking solitude in the forest proved worthwhile. Soon she would have her own version of her hideout all to her—

A face swung down from a branch and nearly caused Syn to fall out of the tree. She made a desperate grab at a branch and clung into it, catching herself and steadying her feet on a branch below her.

"What in the surprise shit are you doing in my tree?" said the upside-down face attached to a wild tumble of blonde hair.

"*Your* tree?" Syn said, too stunned to utter anything else. She stared up at the girl hanging from a branch by the curl of her knees.

"I was here first, that makes it mine by claimer's rights." The girl bit into some sort of fruit and climbed right side up. As she did, Syn recognized the trousers and vest adorned with Scaler skin.

"Hey, I saw you at the Outpost," Syn said.

The girl squatted on a branch and peered down at Syn. She pulled the fruit from her mouth and chewed as she stared with narrowed eyes. "Yeah, I remember you. You're that one that got thrown out."

"And you're the one who got chased out."

Juice dripped down the girl's lips as she smiled. "Those grunt-fuckers were sore losers. I won my loot fair and square."

Syn disliked the girl's foul curses and distrusted her wayward attitude. "I'll find another tree." She moved to climb down.

"Wait up a second." The girl tilted her head as she looked down at Syn. "What's your name?"

"Syn."

"Syn, I like that, real fierce. I'm Relia."

"Nice to meet you," Syn said hollowly and moved to return to climbing down the tree.

"Where you off to?" Relia protested.

"To find another cluster of trees to camp in."

"You ain't gonna find any other trees than these. Why don't you take that one?" she nodded to the tree beside her.

"I prefer to be alone."

"I think you oughta stay. Afterall, there's more safety in numbers."

"Then why are you up here by yourself?" Syn challenged.

"Simple, it's the best spot. No way am I camping down there with those dick-swinging boys."

Syn looked down at the campgrounds. It was true, most of the competitors were boys. She saw a single female face for every hoard of males. She turned her attention back to Relia. After seeing her running away with a sack of wealth over her shoulder, Syn decided she didn't trust her in the slightest.

"No thanks." Syn figured she'd fare better in the dirt.

"Didn't you come with any supplies?"

"That's none of your business."

Relia shrugged. "Alright, maybe it ain't. But if you camp near me, I'll share mine with you."

Syn paused her descent. "Why would you do that?"

"Call it an investment. We can watch each other's back while we sleep. I don't trust those shifty Terraborn down there."

Syn lifted an eyebrow as she regarded Relia's red eyes. "Aren't you Terraborn?"

Relia laughed. "Maybe in origin. But not in spirit, and that's what counts."

Syn glanced down at another brawl taking place near the rock formation as she mulled over her chances on the ground.

A green fruit interrupted her sight as Relia thrusted it down in front of her face.

"You want a pear?"

Syn wasn't sure what a "pear" was, but she knew she wanted it. Her mouth began to water. When was the time she ate? Syn reached for the fruit with her one free hand, but Relia pulled it back.

"Only if you agree to watch my back. Just for tonight."

Syn's muscles cramped with her awkward, tiptoe stance on the narrow branch. "Fine. Just for tonight."

Relia grinned with a smile that showed too many teeth and handed over the fruit.

Syn bit into the pear and in moments she devoured the whole thing, core and all. She licked the sweet juice from her lips and climbed up to jump to the tree beside her strange new acquaintance.

"Here," Relia said.

Syn looked up and caught a bundle out of the air. She unrolled it to find enough rope and cloth to make a hammock. "Thank-thank you," Syn said, not sure what to make of her generosity.

She glanced at Relia lounging in her own hammock. Supplies littered the branches around her. A sword belt with multiple daggers laid draped over a branch to her right. Relia pulled out another fruit from a heavy sack on her lap and ripped into it. In a land that appeared barren, the fruit must be an expensive delicacy. Syn assumed most of Relia's supplies were probably funded from the loot stolen from the men at the Outpost.

"No wonder she needs someone to watch her back," Syn whispered to Gregory as she set to work tying together her hammock. "She has a treasure trove up here."

"Where ya from?" asked Relia.

"The Surface."

"Obviously. I can tell you're one of those portal protectors too based on all the fur and such."

"Legionite," Syn corrected.

"Right, Legionite. What village?"

"Garon."

"Never heard of it... But then again, I ain't never been this far west."

A shriek shuddered through the air. Syn flinched and looked to the veil as another competitor entered the trials grounds. The competitor's arrival sent out a ripple of alarm through the curtain of moths.

After the racket died down, Relia continued, "I'm from a town called, Averdale."

"Town?" Syn tied the last of her knots, securing her treetop bed. She gripped onto a branch and laid down to test its strength.

"Yeah, you know, a city."

Syn had heard of Terraborn cities. In the stories told by the Elders, the cities were where the privileged occupants lived in ignorance of the dangers of the outside world. Syn's resentment grew. People who lived in places far from portals didn't know the hardship and sacrifice her people made to keep the Surface world safe.

Relia continued despite Syn's silence. "It ain't everything it's cracked up to be. If you ask me, you Legion-whatevers got the fortunate face of the coin."

Syn scoffed. "Sure. If you like living at the edge of the world in constant fear that at any moment beasts could rip apart everyone you've ever cared about, then sure, it's a wonderful time."

"Hmm, you don't say..." Relia let the conversation drop and

took up humming an odd tune. She dug out another pear and bit into it with an obnoxious wet crunch.

Syn decided she would not trust someone with such haughty ignorance. The fruit-munching city dweller wouldn't make it through the first trial, anyway. Once satisfied with her hammock, she tied Gregory to a scrap of rope and hung him from an above branch. She tried to tune out Relia's humming as she went about making the tree feel more like home. The breeze off the sea helped cool the temperature, but Syn still found the heat nearly unbearable.

A barrel blast echoed over the water.

Syn and Relia sat straight up in unison. A shot fired again as the largest boat Syn had ever seen floated into sight from behind the rock formation. It didn't have any sails. Instead, the stern held an enormous wheel that churned through the water, propelling the ship through the water. Steam rose from a pair of cylindrical stacks at the center of the deck.

"What is that?" Syn asked.

"Shit on my grave." Relia marveled at the ship. "It's the Nighterrians." Her face split into a huge smile. She looked over at Syn—her expression ripe with eagerness. "It's time to meet our abusers."

19
RULES

Syn stood on the tip of her toes, looking over competitors' heads toward the Nighterrians lined up in front of the rock formation at the cave's entrance. She spotted Xedford standing beside a man wearing a golden three-barrel.

The Nighterrian with the gilded weapon stepped forward. "Welcome, competitors, to the Nighterrian trials." He was the oldest Nighterrian Syn had ever seen, though he only appeared to be around fifty years old. Gray streaks infused his dark hair and long beard. "My name's Revvor. I am the captain of this here raid of Nighterrians." Revvor motioned to the crew of burly men.

All fifteen Nighterrians wore similar black trousers, loose black shirts, vests with silvery three-barrels attached to their wrists, and long swords at their belts. The captain stood out from the rest with his golden three-barrel and a red sash tied around his waist.

Revvor turned to his right and beckoned Xedford forward. "This here is Xedford, my second-in-command."

Syn gasped. Second-in-command? She recalled her inappropriate questions and the casual way she conversed with him through the crags. *Idiot*, she cursed herself.

Captain Revvor continued, "Together we put together a unique set of trials for y'all this season. Some of you are meeting your future comrades, for whomever is successful in passing the trials over the next few weeks will be inducted into our raid."

Muttered whispers of excitement went up through the gathered competitors. Relia stood at Syn's shoulder and picked at her nails as she listened. Many of the teenagers decided to stay beside their camp and listen from afar. Still, Syn stood shoulder-to-shoulder packed in front of the tiered rock.

Revvor raised his three-barreled hand into the air to hush the crowd. "Be warned, these trials ain't for the weak. The next few weeks will reveal what you're really made of. Some of y'all will find you're but made of blood, bone, and muscle. A few of you'll be made of something more. That something more is what we're looking for. As you know, the trials are intended to weed out anybody who wouldn't survive the imbuing."

The green haired boy who pushed Syn down earlier shoved his way into the front of the crowd. Relia gave him a dirty look as he pushed past her.

"Moldy asshole," Relia cursed under her breath. Thankfully, he didn't hear her.

"Now that y'all been properly warned, I'll explain the rules—"

"Thank you, captain." Xedford stepped froward. "I'll take it from here." Revvor hesitated, as if deciding whether to let him speak. Xedford didn't wait for his permission. "Listen careful, we've got but a few rules here."

Syn's heart raced as Xedford paced in front of the cave. "Entry into the trials for this season is officially closed. Nobody else is allowed entrance into the trial grounds at this time. If you wish to leave the trials, you must do so before noon tomorrow. After that, you won't be permitted to leave unless you fail a trial."

Xedford paused to stare around at the faces of the competitors. "Now let me make this real clear: the only way out of here is by way of ship. Nobody is to cross the veil once the first trial begins. We'll take the injured and the defaulted back to the east bank after each trial."

Revvor stepped up beside Xedford. He wasn't quite as tall, but the weight of his gaze felt infinitely more intimidating. "I know what y'all are wondering, how many are we taking in this go-around?" Revvor scanned the crowd of hopeful candidates like a wolf in a chicken coop. "This season we'll be taking fifteen new inductees."

A cheer went up. Syn didn't know if that was a higher amount than usual, but it seemed like a very small number compared to the hundreds of teenagers hoping to obtain one of only fifteen Hallowed Points.

"I wouldn't be so quick to cheer," Revvor said, "the more spots we got available in our crew means that means many Nighterrians were slain without heirs. They died in the line of duty allowing their Hal'points to be picked up by new inductees."

The crowd hushed and Revvor continued, "The life of a Nighterrian is one filled with danger and death. Even if you succeed in the trials, don't be thinking life as a Nighterrian will be a stroll through the valley."

Despite the heat, Syn felt a shiver slither down her spine. Again, for the hundredth time, she wondered what she was doing there.

"Due to the limited size of our crew, we'll be doing things a little different this season." The captain smiled. His red eyes glittered in the light of the campfires. "Our usual operation would go something like this: After winning the trials, our new recruits would spend about a year as an apprentice before getting imbued. However, I'm happy to announce, this season each apprentice will be imbued *immediately.*"

A wave of excitement roared over the gathered competitors. Revvor raised his hand to silence them as he continued. "Also, we'll be recruiting apprentices from the first trial. Be one of the first six finishers to complete trial one, and you will go directly to the Imbuing Hall to receive your Hal'point. If you obey orders as an apprentice and survive the missions assigned to you, you'll earn yourself a spot in our raid at the conclusion of the trials."

Another murmur of excited whispers trickled through the crowd. From the shocked sound of their collective voices, Syn could tell this had never been done before.

Relia appeared the only one to voice disquiet at the news. "Fucking rigged odds. This is gonna to be a slaughter."

The competitors hushed as Xedford stepped in front of the captain once again. Captain Revvor bared his teeth in a smile that did not hide his displeasure as Xedford picked up with more rules.

"There will be three trials total. The first trial will take place here within the cave of the Rock of Reckoning." He nodded to the cave behind him. "We're only taking a hundred finishers to the next trial, so only the competitors able to claim one of these"—he motioned to a Nighterrian with long dreadlocks who pulled a red bandana from his pocket and waved it into the air—"will move on to trial two. The rest of y'all be shipped back to the other side of the crags."

"With your tails between your legs!" yelled a boisterous Nighterrian on the far right.

The crew laughed. Some of the competitors tried to join in the laughter but it rang stale.

"That's right." Revvor clapped Xedford on the shoulder. Xedford grimaced with a tight smile and Syn wondered if the captain was digging his grip into Xedford's shoulder. "If you're *lucky*, you'll return home a failure. Many never live to see home again."

The tension in the air strangled the attempted laughter of the crowd. Syn wiped at the sweat dripping from her hairline.

"Tomorrow, the trial begins at noon. So tonight, eat well and enjoy some sleep. For some of you, it'll the last thing you do in this life." Revvor scanned the crowd one last time, then retreated into the shadows of the cave.

The Nighterrians followed their captain into the dark. The crowd around the Rock of Reckoning began to dissipate, the competitors eager to return to their belongings to ensure no one had stolen anything.

Syn watched the crew depart and spotted Xedford's black bandana. He caught her eye from afar and winked. She felt a jolt of nervous excitement race through her before he joined his comrades into the shadows.

"This is a disaster," Relia said into Syn's ear.

Syn flinched. She hadn't realized Relia still stood beside her. "What do you mean?"

"They're taking apprentices after the first trial. It's grunt shit!"

Syn turned to make her way back to her temporary hideout. Relia bobbed along beside her and drew the attention of some of the boys. They watched Relia in her Scaler garb with hungry fascination while throwing looks of distaste at Syn's foreign features.

"Don't you know what this means?" Relia asked, either not noticing or not caring about the looks they drew.

"Yes, it means I'll have to try to be one of the first six."

"There ain't no way in the Fates' dark depths either of us is gonna claim one of those spots. You know who it'll go to?" She didn't wait for an answer. "It'll be stolen by those willing to suck face with treachery! That means sabotage of the worst kind."

Syn said nothing and tried to outpace her chattering companion.

Relia persisted. "You think these orphans and runaways with nothing left to lose will draw the line at bloodshed? Not a chance, no, they're desperate. They'll be killing each other next, just you watch and see."

Syn wished Relia would lower her voice. She looked over her shoulder and whispered, "As savage as they seem, I don't think our fellow competitors would resort to murder."

"You clearly ain't been in Interterra long, sister. Take it from me, I've been on this dusty side of the world my whole life, you can't trust nobody."

If that were that case, why did she seem to trust Syn? "What are you saying?" Syn asked. "You don't want to be one of the first six?"

"Exactly. Anybody cheating their way into an apprentice-ship will have a target on their backs."

"How so?"

"Don't you see? The more competitors that get taken out, the better your odds are for making it to the end. There's only fifteen spots available. Take away six after trial one and that's only nine! But if you knock off one of the apprentices, well, that adds another Hal'point to the mix, therefore increasing your odds."

"But the apprentices get imbued. They'll be Nighterrian in all but name. Do you really think anyone would be dumb enough to go toe-to-toe with someone that strong?" Syn reached the cluster of trees and swung out over the water to begin the climb.

Relia caught up and scaled the tree beside her. "The Nighterrians are hunted for their Hal'points all the time. This ain't no different." This was news to Syn, but it seemed to fall in line with that Xedford had said about the Converts. "Just you wait and see. We'll all be bloodier than a moon-time bleeding by the end."

Syn wasn't sure she followed Relia's line of reason. Perhaps too much was lost in translation between her strange sayings and her thick drawl. "The crew would never allow murder to take place," Syn said as she scaled her tree.

"You heard the rules. There's only one, and that's no crossing the veil."

Syn shook her head as she climbed. "The Nighterrians are honor bound, there's no way they would accept a recruit who —" Syn stopped her ascent and gasped.

"What?"

With her breath stolen by shock, Syn could only point. There, carved into the bark of her tree beside her hammock were the words:

LEAVE THE TRIALS OR MEET YOUR END.

20

TRIAL ONE

Syn stood among the jostling crowd outside the cavern entrance. Her fingers twitched with anxiety as she waited for the smoke blast to initiate the first trial. The crowd bucked and swirled like the waves of the black sea. The musky stench of sweating bodies clouded the air.

She pushed back against competitors attempting to shove their way to the front as the threatening note nagged at the back of her mind. The culprit hadn't touched any of Relia's items. Who would take the time to carve a message into Syn's tree but leave Relia's treasures undisturbed?

The message was a threat meant to intimidate her—that much was obvious—but who left it? And why her? These questions had pestered Syn long into the slumber hours. Whomever it was, they must have been watching her. Perhaps it was the same phantom she heard scream when she crossed the veil.

Relia shoved someone back who tried to force their position. "Pissing fart breathers!" she yelled in their general direction. She wore a blindfold over her eyes and pushed anyone who knocked into her.

"Would you please take that thing off?"

"No way, it's the instrument of my success!" Relia delivered an elbow to someone's gut. "You should really be putting yours on about now."

Syn shook her head. She would have suspected Relia of leaving the carved threat except the strange girl stayed beside Syn throughout the entirety of the meeting. She supposed Relia could still be in league with others and playing into a farce alliance just to backstab her later, but that seemed like a lot of work to take out one competitor.

"You're insane if you think I'm going into the trial blindfolded," Syn said. Relia had tried to offer her a blindfold earlier, to which Syn sternly refused.

"Don't worry, I'll take it off once we get in there," Relia explained. "The Terraborn and their creepy eyes got far better sight in the dark. For Surfacers like you, and others like me, it'll take our eyes way too long to adjust to the darkness."

"It's already dark." Syn had already tried to point out that Relia also had "creepy Terraborn eyes," but Relia refused to accept this, spouting something about her spirit and the cosmos.

"But it ain't pitch black, not like in there."

"Why don't you take a torch with you if you're so worried?"

"I got a feeling I'll be needing both hands for this trial. I can't be bothered with holding a torch." Relia shoved at the bodies wrestling against her. "Though it would be good for beating this Fates-forsaken crowd back!"

Syn looked around. Despite the total blackness of the cave entrance, no one in the crowd carried flames. "If you aren't going to take it off until you get into the cave, how do you expect to find your way in while blindfolded?"

"Simple. I just hold on to somebody who's headed in." Relia smiled her toothy grin toward Syn. With her blindfold on, she smiled a little too far to the left. "That's where you come in."

Syn said nothing, returning shoves to the jostling the crowd. For all she knew, it could be a trick to get her to fall behind. Relia had said herself the competitors would resort to sabotage. To help her would be to trust the thin ice of a frozen lake.

"You wouldn't leave a blind woman here to fend for herself, now, would you?" Relia asked.

"You're not blind, you—"

A shot fired into the cave and erupted a cloud of red smoke.

Syn didn't have time to debate. She grabbed Relia by the wrist and raced into the darkness. To her surprise, Relia didn't stumble or slow her down. Relia ran beside Syn and, with her free hand, threw wild punches in all directions. Instead, it was Syn who stumbled the farther they got into the cave as the darkness spread like a blanket of blackness over her vision. Caught off guard, she nearly tripped.

Relia caught her and took the lead, Syn's wrist in her grasp. With her eyes already adjusted to the dark, she must have pulled off her blindfold. They blazed ahead, careful not to waste a single precious second. Syn obeyed the yank of Relia's lead as they dodged right and left, racing through the tunnel of the cave.

Syn's awareness of her surroundings drifted into focus as her eyes adjusted. Once she could see shapes in the dark, she detached herself from Relia's grip to cut around a tangle of people wrestling on the ground. Syn caught a fist to the side of her head and had to shove her way forward. She lost Relia in the dark and the chaos.

Syn fought her way to the end of the pitch-black tunnel

and found herself in a massive cavern. The hollowed inside of the rock formed a domelike interior. The starlight shining in from the exit offered enough light for Syn to see that flooded water formed a lake that took up almost the entirety of the cavern floor. The wreckage of an old ship rose up from the murky depths.

The minimal light from outside illuminated rickety scaffolds zigzagging along the cavern walls. Ropes and swaying bridges connected the scaffolding to portions of the ship wreckage. The bridges intwined over and under each other in a crisscrossing maze of madness.

The competitors ahead of Syn sloshed into the water to swim through the cave to the other side. *Fools, it can't be that easy.* Syn set her sights on the finish line: the jagged hole at the far end of the cave where the ocean flooded in.

She tussled her way to the curving wall on her right and followed a set of boys who climbed up a knotted rope to get to the top of a scaffold. She began to climb but someone grabbed onto her foot as she tried to pull herself up. She sent out wild kicks to dislodge the grip of the person below her.

"Ruthless jerks!" she cursed once free and climbed to the sound of shouts and fighting echoing off the cavern walls.

Adrenaline pounded through her veins and aided in her strength. She climbed on, noticing the scaffold structure was made almost entirely of massive bones from some unknown species of monster. She didn't have time to marvel at how the joints connected before she reached the top of the rope.

A snarling face appeared before her. She glimpsed a whisp of green hair and saw the flash of a blade just before it cut the rope. She fell backwards through the air, screaming and wheeling her arms in panic.

The group of people gathered beneath the rope cushioned her fall, but she still landed hard on her shoulder. Syn detangled her limbs from the other competitors and tried to crawl free of the pile of humans, but a foot kicked her in the chest and sent her rolling into the shallow water.

The sound of screams stole her attention. Syn sat up in the water and looked toward the center of the cave near the ship-wreck where the hopeful swimmers thrashed. A beast rose from the black sea. In the dark she couldn't see anything more than the monster's sharp white teeth before it collapsed over the struggling swimmers and crashed down beneath the surface.

Syn scrambled out of the watery grave and back onto dry land just as limbs and various body parts floated to the top. She hurdled over wrestling bodies and dodged passed fistfights as she picked her way to the far-left side of the cavern.

Something caught her foot, and she found a face full of mud. Rolling to her side, she detangled her foot from the rope that tripped her. The rope disappeared into the water. Syn tested it with a tug and discovered it was attached to a scaffold near the shipwreck.

An idea blossomed.

Syn jumped to her feet and wrapped the rope around her arm. She took as many steps back as she could. Once up against the wall, she ran forward and leapt. With her feet tucked up under her body, she managed to only skim the surface of the water as she swung. She reached out her free hand and just barely grasped the edge of a broken plank protruding from the shipwreck.

She dug her nails in and pulled herself over until she could stand on the plank and reach the base of a bone scaffold. The unstable structure swayed and creaked as she climbed, but it held her weight and she made it onto the brittle bone platform.

What now? Three bridges branched off from the platform.

In the low light, it was impossible to track the route of one bridge to the next.

A chittering noise echoed off the walls and filled Syn with terror. The cavern walls multiplied the sound and informed of something lurking out of sight. Head-sized holes along the rocky dome rang with the source of the sound. On panicked feet she ran, choosing a swaying bridge to her right.

Syn reached the platform at the end of the bridge only to find the connection to the next bridge ended in frayed ropes, likely a sabotage from whomever passed through ahead of her.

She cursed her hasty choice and turned to go back the way she came. Halfway across the bridge, an infant-sized creature jumped out at her from a nearby hole in the cavern wall. She only caught sight of its huge eyes and ram-like horns before it latched onto her head and clawed at her face.

Syn fell to her knees to keep from falling off the rail-less bridge. The creature bashed its horns into the top of her skull. She grabbed hold of its hairy body and ripped it free. With the beast held at bay with one hand, she extracted Elaine with the other. Screaming, she stabbed the creature in the face. The hairy monster—roughly the size and shape of a human baby—stared up at her with yellow owl eyes as it died. No time to examine it, she yanked her blade free and ran to another bridge.

The giggling chatter of the tiny beasts increased as the walls came alive with them. They came pouring out from the holes along the domed cavern and crawled over the walls like spiders.

Syn ran as fast as she could while keeping her balance on the swaying bridges. The hairy creatures chased after her with their human-like faces and curling horns. She heard the shouts and cries of the other competitors around her as the creatures attacked. In the middle of a rickety bridge, someone called out her name.

"Syn!" a voice in the dark repeated.

Syn kicked a little demon off the bridge and turned over her shoulder. Relia sat stuck on a platform one bridge back. It looked like her foot had gone through the crumbing bone planks and wedged her in an awkward position as she fought off five horned creatures.

"Syn!" Relia called again.

Syn looked back toward her way out. Now in the middle of the cavern and closer to the light of the exit, she could see a route from the crisscrossing bridges up to a scaffold and from the scaffold to a rope that would let her swing to the finish line. Most of the other competitors were busy fighting the slew of attackers.

I can still make it into the top six.

Blood pounded in her ears and urged her to decide. She glanced back at Relia who hurled foul curses at the creatures as she defended against their attacks. Syn couldn't just leave her... could she?

A flood of chattering monsters poured out from a hole and raced on all fours along the bridge where Syn stood suspended in indecision. The army of little beasts threatened to collapse the bridge with their collective weight as they barreled over one another.

With her mind now made up, Syn threw a final look over her shoulder at Relia. "Sorry," she said, then she took off toward her escape.

She crossed another bridge and jumped to a nearby platform to avoid the hoard of creatures. One jumped down at her from a suspension bridge above her. She used Elaine to stab it in the face. Another grabbed her around the ankle and tried to bite her through her thick, fur trousers. She flung it off the scaffold and listened to it splash into the water below.

Syn stopped to catch her breath as she reached a perilous rope bridge. Every other foothold dangled uselessly from the suspension bridge. The missing planks made for wide gaps between each foothold.

Below her, she could see the opening of the exit. It loomed only another bridge and a rope swing away. She could even spy the red of the finisher bandanas tied to a wall of pegs on a floating dock just on the other side of the cave's mouth. One boy already looked to be crossing through to the dock. She squinted into the dark and saw a tail of others right behind him.

Hopes of making the apprenticeship urged her forward. "I can make it if I hurry!" she said to Elaine, stepping onto the precarious bridge. It swayed wildly beneath her weight, and she was forced to jump immediately to the next footing. She wobbled, her arms extended wide to help her find her balance. She readied herself for the leap to the next plank when an object whooshed past her head.

Syn froze and glanced around as she held her balance. *What was that?* She looked left just in time to get her answer. An arrow sliced past her face.

She crouched down, holding onto the single plank. The bridge swayed and creaked as she searched the dark for the source of the attack. Beyond the ropes and bones, she spied the silhouette of the culprit release another arrow.

Syn leapt from her crouch to the next plank just as the arrow flew past her. She missed the arrow but overshot her jump, catching the next foot hold under her arm. Her body dangled in the air. Vulnerable and exposed, she expected the piercing bite of an arrow to end her right then, but it didn't come. Desperation pulsed through her veins. She struggled and managed to haul herself up to make for the next jump.

Perched on the wavering bridge, she watched the shadowed outline nock another arrow. Before she could gain her balance, she jumped. Despite the chaos around her, she could hear the arrow whiz harmlessly behind her. *You're a terrible shot, whoever you are!* But her gloating cut short as her foot struck the next plank. The bone foothold broke in half.

She let out a squeal of panic and fell.

21

WATER DEMON

Syn expected to hit the water but instead her back smacked something solid. Rolling from the momentum of her fall, she scrambled to grab onto the edge of a platform. Her breath came in gasps as she hung by her fingertips and dangled above the water.

Syn looked up in search of the archer but the rope bridge above her hung vacant. A small mercy. She tried to pull herself up, but the scaffold shifted and groaned as she moved. She held fast and looked down to find the structure only stood on three legs where it rose from the ship wreckage.

Unable to move for fear of toppling the platform, she hung in the air and watched a slew of competitors race through to the exit. *No, I'm close!* Only a bridge away, she could see the red of the bandanas as one competitor after another swung onto the dock to claim their victory.

A wild cackle of triumph echoed off the walls. The starlight from outside lit a figure wearing shimmering scales. Regret felt its way through Syn's panic as she watched Relia swing through to the finish.

The platform let out a groan and shifted, dropping Syn down another foot. Between ragged gasps of breath, she noticed the structures all around her creak and shift as more battered teenagers trampled through the interconnected scaffolding. The hairy little creatures chewed at the supporting joints and bit through ropes.

The whole thing is going to crumble!

She redoubled her grip and readied herself to risk swinging a leg up when one of the horned creatures looked down at her. It paused for a moment to tilt its head and stare at her with huge owl-like eyes. Then it attacked her grip with its humanoid fingers. Its chittering rang like cruel laughter. She tried to hold on, but her fatigued grip fell victim to the demon's bite.

She fell again. This time, she dropped into the watery grave with a splash.

Syn clawed her way to the surface and bobbed up, sputtering in panic. With no choice left, she swam for the exit. The black water burned her eyes as she tore her way through the flooded cavern. Out the corner of her eye, she saw a barbed fin part the darkness.

Choking back the paralyzing fear, she forced herself to push forward. The splashing of black water filled her vision. She kicked and paddled as hard as she could, but the wet weight of her fur pants dragged her down.

Something soft brushed against her leg. She kicked out and connected with something solid. The sound of spilling water suggested a massive presence crested the surface behind her. She could feel the way it parted the water and knew jaws were coming. Syn fought through the black sea, knowing it would be futile. She wouldn't escape the beast's watery lair. Any moment now it would crunch her bones with its rows of sharp teeth.

Her knee struck something solid. A hand extended in front of her and pulled her out of the water.

Before she could process what was happening, she scrambled onto a dry dock in time to turn and see the jagged teeth of the beast's jaws snap close over thin air. It splashed down into the water and retreated, sending a wave of black liquid crashing onto the dock.

Shaking, Syn looked up to find Relia helping her to her feet —a red finisher bandana tied around Relia's wrist. Syn's mouth bobbed with wordless appreciation. The girl she left behind at the mercy of the attacking creatures had now saved her life.

A crash echoed from the cave and distracted Syn from her self-reproach. She turned to see the structure inside collapse. Scaffolds ripped free of their joins and fell, pulling all the connected bone bridges and people down with it. Screams and splashes resonated from within the cavern.

Now no longer under threat of certain death, a sudden recollection struck Syn's memory. She turned to the wall on the dock where a hundred red bandanas had sat tied on pegs only minutes before. Her heart liquified and dripped down to her toes. The wall of pegs stood empty. All one hundred spots in trial two were already tied around the proud wrists of the other finishers crowded on the dock.

Syn stood dripping wet and empty handed for a long moment. She turned away from the smiling faces of the finishers and watched the black waves from the ocean lap at the entrance to the cavern. From the floating dock she could see the back side of the towering rock formation for the first time. Carved steps only accessible by water led up to the second tier of the rock called Reckoning. Syn mused over the name as her joy of survival turned to gloom.

"I'm glad you made it." Relia pulled Syn in for a nonconsenting hug.

Syn suffered the embrace. Now was hardly the time for a hug, but Relia gripped her tight like they were old friends. Before letting go, Relia glanced over her shoulder and surreptitiously pulled something red from her pocket.

"For leading me into the cave," Relia said into Syn's ear.

Syn's eyes bulged with the swell of disbelief as Relia tucked a red bandana into her hand. Relia let go of the hug, and Syn looked down to behold the prize clutched in her grasp. She searched for words of gratitude, but her mind came up blank as she found herself the final finisher of trial one.

PART THREE
CONSPIRATOR

22

THE EXPERIMENT

Lektra replayed her reunion with Tanok over and over in her mind. The slight shake of his head and the whisper of fear that touched his eyes—what could it mean?

Despite Tanok's puzzling behavior, she pressed on. No way she was giving up now. Not when she was this close. Lektra could almost hear Tanok's voice in her mind. *Little sister, why are you always getting into trouble?* Or her father's constant complaint—*why can't you be more like your brother?*

She ground her teeth as she padded on silent feet around the back alley of the town. Once she had snapped out of her initial shock, she said a quick farewell to Caravinna and hopped off the wagon. She snuck back to where she spied Tanok and the group of riders enter a place with the words "Barbershop" over the door.

Lektra thanked her years of sneaking lessons from her third-ring friends back in Veldt. She found literacy an essential skill in navigating the dark underworld over the past month. Fourth-ring citizens weren't supposed to learn to read, but antiquated rules never stopped her from doing what she wanted.

She reached the back window of the barbershop and peered through the dirty glass into a storage room. The door leading from the storage room to the rest of the shop stood open, but a stack of boxes and crates blocked half the doorway and cut off her line of sight.

Lektra checked over her shoulder, then shimmied her knife beneath the edge of the window. It took a moment of wiggling, but she finally unlocked the latch. With painful slowness and prayers of silence, she slid the window up as far as she dared and hauled herself through. She pressed her back against the wall and willed her breath to slow so she could hear what was taking place.

"... how much longer?"

"You cannot rush the experiments," said a voice from somewhere Lektra couldn't see. Something about the eerie sing-song cadence of the man's voice rang a familiar tune in Lektra's mind. "Disaster arises from impatience."

She crept through the storage room and crouched on her hands and knees behind the stack of crates near the doorway. The bottom crate was empty, and she peeked between the gaps in the boards.

The shades were drawn over the front windows and five men stood around a figure seated in one of the barber chairs. The stances of the men appeared threatening, yet Lektra could see unease in the way they glanced at one another. A handsome rider with long, dark hair and a short beard with a deep scar across his forehead stood at the front of the posse, staring down at the person in the chair.

The barber chair faced away from Lektra, and she couldn't see who occupied it. Searching the room for Tanok, she spotted a mirror taking up the wall behind the counter near the door.

Her breath caught at the reflection of a teenage kid in the barber chair. His hands and feet were strapped down and a gag tied his mouth. For a split second she thought it was her brother, but his skin was too light, and his eyes were Terraborn red.

She searched further and breathed a sigh of relief when she found Tanok standing in the corner of the room with his hand on the hilt of a short blade at his hip. After ascertaining it really was her brother and not a heatstroke mirage invented by her subconscious, Lektra peeked back at the mirror.

A red-cloaked figure knelt at the captive's feet. He adjusted a set of bowls on the floor beneath where the boy's limp arms lay strapped to the chair. Violet blood seeped from the kid's arms and dripped into the bowls.

A shorter man with long dreadlocks jerked his head to the man with the scar on his forehead. "When is the Skully supposed to get here?"

Lektra tried to make sense of the scene. She had heard rumors of Redd the Collector's men being called "Skullies," but she knew very little about them. *Oh Tanok, please don't tell me you've gotten yourself wrapped up with the biggest crime lord on Interterra.*

"Any time now I reckon," answered the man with the long hair and scar on his forehead. Lektra guessed he might be the leader of the group based on the way rest of the posse stood at his flank.

"Those assholes are always late. High-nosed bastards. They're no more than personal henchman for wiping the boss' ass if you ask me," Dreadlocks said.

"He ain't a Skully anymore. He's with us now," the leader said.

"That's the problem with those brain-damaged freaks. You never know how slippery they're gonna be. If he can betray the boss for us, what makes you think he ain't gonna betray us the second he finds a better deal?"

"I think we're offering him the best deal he's likely to get," the leader said.

"That's supposing this here experiment goes as planned."

One of the other men spoke up. "If it don't go well, maybe it's for the best. Having the reputation of a Skully without the protection of the boss, shit, that's a death sentence if you ask me. He'll be getting murdered for his Hal'point, it's just a matter of time."

Hal'point? Lektra studied the men. Could this Skully they were talking about be one of Redd's outlaws *and* a Nighterrian? What had her foolish brother fallen into? She watched Tanok's face in the mirror. All she read was determination and impatience.

"We have it in good faith that this experiment will be a success." That eerie voice again. "We have already had one successful trial."

Lektra searched the refection of the mirror and realized the voice came from the figure in the red-hooded robe kneeling in front of the barber chair. She watched him draw a thin blade across the captive's wrists. The spooky voice, the red robe, it couldn't be... a Graver? What was a Surfacer body collector doing in Interterra?

"I'll believe it when I see it with my own eyes." The leader walked to the window and shifted the shade to the side.

"If he ever shows," complained Dreadlocks. "I say if he don't show up here soon, we take our leave. The captain will want us back before the trials."

"Patience now, we've got a mission to do here." The leader wandered away from the window to loom over the Graver once more.

Lektra kept her sights trained on the reflection in the

mirror with fearful fascination. Every few moments the Graver would drag his knife over the boy's wrists. After a minute or so the flow of purple blood would slow to a trickle as the wound healed. The Graver would then open his veins again, keeping blood flowing into the bowls.

Lektra only knew of one way to achieve the healing powers she witnessed. But the boy couldn't be a Nighterrian. His blood was purple, not blue. She wondered what sort of hybrid he might be as his eyes fluttered and rolled back in his head. He slumped further in the chair with a sallow, waxy face.

Three light taps came at the door followed by three heavy raps.

Lektra slank back behind the crates as another man entered the shop. He wore the black clothing of a Nighterrian, but unlike the other long haired, bearded men of the region, he sported a bald head and a shaved face. *The Skully.*

"Black?" the leader questioned, looking the man's clothing up and down. "I thought we agreed to go incognito."

"You don't see me wearing a three-barrel, do you?" the newcomer retorted. He shrugged a pack off his back and shoved it at Tanok.

"I would have thought a man in your position would appreciate some added discretion. That full-moon head of yours will get you killed soon as your wanted flyers make their rounds."

"How's about you let me worry about my own skin." The Skully looked around the room and his vision narrowed on the kid in the chair and the Graver collecting the blood. "Should we get on with it then?"

The Graver grunted in acknowledgement. He stood with a bowl of blood in each hand. The multitude of beaded jewelry around his neck clattered as moved. He offered the bowls to the man they referred to as, the Skully. "Drink these."

The Skully sniffed the bowl. "All of it?"

The Graver leveled his unsettling kohl-rimmed stare on the man. "All of it."

The bald man took the bowl to his lips and drank. The purple gore dripped down his chin as he guzzled it in a series of sickening gulps. He let out a loud belch after he finished the second bowl.

"Sit." The Graver gestured to the empty barber chair beside the kid. He turned to the posse and motioned to the captive teenager. "If you don't mind, I'll need you to hold this one down."

The men shrugged and moved in around the boy. Even Tanok grabbed him by the right arm, holding him to the chair. The Graver acquired a tray of glittering barber instruments and set it beside the unconscious prisoner. Selecting a straight razor, he tore away the right sleeve of the kid's shirt. Without a word, the Graver delivered a deep incision to his shoulder.

The boy's red eyes snapped open. He thrashed in the chair. The gag in his mouth muffled his screams, but it merely muted the sound of his agony. The posse held him down as the Graver took his time carving into his flesh like a sculptor etching into a fresh plank of wood. The Graver sliced away a chunk of flesh, exposing muscle and bone covered in indigo blood. From his tray of instruments, he plucked up a pair of pliers meant for pulling teeth and inserted them into the bleeding wound.

"Hurry up, will you? Somebody will hear," one of the men complained.

With a yank and a twist, the pliers came away with a blue glowing bullet clutched at the end of the pinchers. The boy immediately ceased thrashing and slumped lifeless against the chair. The Graver dropped the arrow shaped bullet into the Skully's awaiting hands. It was only then that Lektra hurdled over her own astonishment in time to realize she glimpsed a Hallowed Point.

"Get me my three-barrel," the Skully said to the leader.

"I can—"

"If I'm gonna die, it'll be at my own hands. Now go fetch it for me."

Lektra watched the leader nod to Tanok. Tanok hurriedly rummaged through the Skully's pack. With the obedience of a trained pet, he extracted a three-barrel and passed it to the bald man in the chair.

Once he had the weapon strapped to his wrist, the Skully loaded the Hal'point into the first barrel and adjusted some of the mechanisms at the back of the weapon. He then clicked the trigger into his hand and pressed the three-barrel to his right thigh.

What is happening? Lektra did her best to stifle the sound of her breathing. If the man was already a Nighterrian, another Hal'point would kill him.

"If it don't work,"—the Skully looked up at the men gathered around him—"then I suppose this is goodnight."

He fired.

Lektra clapped her hand over her mouth in time to silence her gasp. In her quick movement, however, her elbow clipped the edge of a precariously stacked box. It crashed to the floor.

Every eye in the room darted to the doorway of the stock room where she crouched behind the toppled crates.

23
CRAZY

"I can't figure why somebody would take the time to stop in the middle of the trial and shoot at you." Relia stabbed a dead moth with the tip of her blade. She brought the giant bug up to her face and sniffed it before depositing it in her bag.

Syn walked beside Relia as they scavenged for dead ghost moths along the burning edge of the veil. "It doesn't make sense. I don't even know anyone here."

Syn had mostly recovered from the trial of the previous day —or the equivalent of a day in the land of eternal night. The Nighterrians had rushed into the cave soon after the collapse of the scaffolds and rescued all they could. The dead were given no ceremony as their bodies were consumed by the water demon within the cave.

Syn rubbed at her sore shoulder. The muscle ached where she landed on it during the trial. Her forehead was badly bruised from the horns of the hairy little beasts she learned were called "pigmys." She needed time to recuperate and was glad to hear when Revvor announced the next trial would take place in six days to allow the crew time to set up the next set of brutal obstacles.

"And you're certain you saw a real person?" Relia asked. No semblance of accusation in her voice.

Could it all have been in her head? Syn knew her haunting didn't strike during the trial. And even if it had, an episode would have only warped everything around her into visions of nightmares. It wouldn't have caused her to hallucinate a rational threat, such as an archer with deadly arrows. "I'm sure."

"All I'm saying is, the mind does strange things under pressure of fear." Relia tapped the flat side of her blade against her curly head.

"If you don't believe me, go look at the carving in my tree." Syn kept the condemnation from her voice, knowing that she only remained in the trials because of Relia's magnanimous gesture.

"I believe you… just seems unlikely."

Syn couldn't fathom why Relia gave her the bandana Syn now wore around her neck. When asked, Relia's only explanation was that she did it because Syn led her through the passage when she had the blindfold on. Shame kept Syn from asking about the part where she left Relia behind to fend for herself against the pigmys.

"She made it through just fine without my help," Syn whispered to Elaine. She stooped down beside a fluttering moth hopping on the ground with a broken wing. With a stab, she used Elaine to put it out of its misery. She added the dead moth to Relia's sack as they continued their burning walk along the chasm toward where it flowed into the ocean.

Syn looked over her shoulder for the fifth time in an hour. Ever since she arrived at the trials, she felt watched. The campground spread out in disarray, almost resembling the aftermath of a battle. Broken tents stood half erect and personal items laid strewn about.

Immediately following the trial, the eliminated competitors were taken straight from the cave onto the huge ship. They were carted back to the other side of the veil, leaving their campsites available for plunder—an event to which the one hundred finishers took full advantage of.

Syn wore a freshly acquired set of Terraborn-style clothes. She found the loose flowing shirt and thin trousers to be a vast improvement, yet she continued to sweat in the heat of the night. She touched the handle of her new, unbroken sword bouncing at her hip. She didn't like it as much as Elaine, but she supposed it served as a practical addition. Sighing, she returned her attention to searching for dead moths.

"Maybe the somebody who's after you just hates Legionites." Relia wore a new set of leather bracers with tiny daggers tucked into the sides.

"Why would anyone hate Legionites? We protect the portals from letting monsters into the outside world."

Relia shrugged. "Maybe one got free, and that person blames you for it."

"A Scaler hasn't made it through our circle of fortitude in two generations."

"For *your* village," Relia said. "What about the rest of those Legionite villages? There's gotta be about a hundred or so portals that lead to the Surface."

"But it's not my fault what happens in villages on the other side of the world."

"I ain't saying it's logical. I'm just pointing out some folk's prejudice goes beyond reason."

"Hmm." Syn's brow creased as she explored the explanation Relia offered. She crouched down to pick up a square, wooden container. The tiny, discarded box had been trampled and left in the dirt. Its twisted hinges made the lid fit sideways.

"What are you gonna do about it?" Relia asked.

Syn toyed with the broken box. "There's nothing I can do."

"There's always something you can do."

Not if I deserve it. The memory of Rem's fearful, pleading eyes jumped into her mind.

"Howdy, ladies."

Syn looked up from the box to see a group of six boys. They approached with their hands on the hilts of their swords.

"What do you got there?" A boy with a broken nose nodded to Relia's bag of moths.

"None of your damn business," Relia said.

The boys fanned out, backing the girls up against the veil of ghost moths. "I been missing a few things from my camp. It wouldn't happen to be in that there bag of yours, would it?"

"It's just moths," Syn said.

"Let's have a look-see," said another boy wearing a heavy sword across his back.

"No." Relia glared in defiance.

"Relia, just give it to them." Syn wasn't about to get into a fight over a bag of worthless moths.

The one with the busted nose stepped forward to stand toe to toe with Relia. "You heard your sun-sick friend. Hand it over, or we'll take it." The rest of the group took a threatening step forward.

"I like that sword you got." Another boy on the far left pointed to Syn's newly acquired weapon.

Syn dropped the little box and clutched at her blade. She realized then that it wasn't about the bag or even the sword. The boys were lobbying for control. It's what wolves did when an alpha found a lone wolf in his pack's territory. She recognized the hunger for power in boys' red eyes.

She backed up and felt the flutter of wings near her head and the heat of the chasm roasting at her back. She drew her sword but, outnumbered and backed up against a river of lava, she knew her and Relia didn't stand a chance at fighting their way out of this one.

"We ain't giving you anything. Now piss off." Relia stared back at the leader of the ring of boys.

A tense silence passed as they locked eyes in a stalemate of glowering hatred. Relia broke the stare to look the boy up and down as if she were sizing up the threat. Then, she threw her head back and erupted in a shrieking fit of laughter.

Syn started. She watched the boys look to each other in confusion. One by one, each of them took a careful step backward. Relia continued to laugh, her body shaking as her cackle pierced the air. Tears leaking from her eyes, she clutched her stomach through the howling waves.

"What is this?" Broken-nose asked.

This evoked a fresh avalanche of laughter from Relia. Her cackle turned maniacal as she stepped up to the leader. He took a step back in response as Relia pulled a tiny knife from her leather bracer and sliced the palm of her own hand. Without breaking from laughter, she smeared her bleeding hand across her face and took another step toward the group.

The boys exchanged fearful glances, unsure how to react.

Relia lunged forward and dragged her tongue across her bleeding palm licking up the blood in a fit of giggles that was somehow more unsettling than her insane laughter.

"Freak!" Broken-nose stumbled back. "Let's go." He turned and raced away.

The rest of the group complied in the retreat. They ran, throwing weary looks over their shoulders. As soon as the boys were far enough away to no longer pose a threat, Relia cut her laughter short. She stood up straight and calmly wiped the blood from her palm on her trousers.

"What in the depths of the Abyss was *that*?" Syn watched Relia shed her adopted insanity and return to her normal composure as easily as sliding on a new coat.

Relia wiped at the tears and blood on her face and shrugged as if nothing happened. "Sometimes crazy is the best defense." She smiled at Syn's bewildered expression. "It's mighty useful for getting out of a losing fight."

Syn stared at her, dumbfounded, with her sword still in hand.

Relia plucked up her bag of moths and moseyed on. "When I bet in for cards, nobody ever expects me to win, and old men don't take kindly to losing to a girl. I can't tell you how many times I've gotten out of what would have been a brutal brawl simply through power of reputation."

"A reputation for being crazy?" Syn sheathed her sword but continued to look over her shoulder as she picked up the broken box she had dropped during the confrontation and hurried to catch up with Relia.

"For being unexpected," Relia corrected. She threw the bag of moths over her shoulder as she strode on with casual indifference. "People fear what they can't understand and what they can't predict. And since fear is adjacent to respect, I like to think I earned their respect tonight." She nodded in the direction where the boys retreated.

Syn could have laughed at the complete absurdity of her rationale, but she didn't want to press Relia's generosity. Afterall, she did owe her for saving her life and she had to admit, the crazy act had worked.

"I've been called crazy enough times in my life. But it never brought me any good." Syn said.

"Maybe you just ought to embrace it. Afterall, there's worse things you could be called. And most geniuses are said to be insane before folks discover their brilliance."

Syn said nothing. She had decided to tolerate Relia's imposing friendship, but she still didn't know if she could trust her. Everything about her aroused suspicion.

Relia began talking about food, but Syn hardly listened. She instead contemplated Relia's motivation. No one was this nice without an ulterior motive, especially not to Syn. She always had the sense that others could smell the weakness on her like a rotting stench. Even her father, as kind and understanding as he was, sometimes got the look in his eye like he felt ashamed to have her as a daughter.

By the time Syn and Relia neared their tree-camp, Syn still couldn't shake the feeling of someone watching her. She looked back toward where they had encountered the gang of boys and thought she saw a silhouette dip behind a tent. But when she stared harder, she decided it was probably just the tent entrance flapping in the breeze.

"...and once they've gone and dried out, I think they'll be fit to eat, though I've never eaten ghost moths before. I can't imagine they're worse than any other bug..."

Syn tuned out Relia's blabber about the moths as she turned the broken box around in her hands. She ran through a list of possible names: *Madison, Riley, Anna... Anna!* Anna fit the box perfectly. Her thoughts were fully focused on stringing Anna up in her treetop fort when Relia stopped in her tracks and Syn ran into her.

"Ugh," Syn shoved past her.

"Syn, I think you ought to see this."

Syn followed Relia's stare to the closest tree rising from the water a few steps away. There, in the center of the trunk, hung a makeshift doll with braided tassels for hair and a scrap of fur wrapped around its shoulders and waist. A knife stabbed through its eye held it to the tree.

Syn sloshed through the shallow water toward the tree.

"Careful!" Relia followed her into the shallows.

Reaching the trunk, Syn found a piece of parchment tucked behind the doll. She ripped it free from the knife and unfolded it.

The letter dropped from her grasp as she read it. It fell into the water and floated along the undulating waves.

"What'd it say?"

Relia's question went unanswered as Syn clenched her fist to keep her hand from shaking.

"Who left it?" Relia asked.

Syn shook her head, tears brimming her eyes. "I don't know... but whoever did wants me dead." Dread hardened into stone at the pit of her stomach. Inside her head, the words from the letter reverberated like a death sentence:

You don't belong here.

24
ALE

Alone, Syn walked the trial grounds while trying her best not to let the waves of guilt consume her. She had successfully kept thoughts of Rem at bay over the past two nights, but after the latest note, she could no longer stave off the wretchedness that flooded in like a broken dam.

"Whoever is leaving me these notes knows what I did to my village... what I did... to Rem," Syn said to Anna, the broken box. "But how?"

Anna's silent company offered no advice.

Syn fought back the onslaught of tears. Out in the open, walking through ransacked campsites, she couldn't let her weakness show. But stifling her tears was worth the price of being alone.

After a sleepless night and a hundred unrelenting questions about the note, Relia had caught wind of a card came taking place on the eastern side of the campground and finally took off to seek fortune. Syn felt relieved at her absence, and she didn't desire to be around whenever Relia returned. Her prying questions about the note only heightened Syn's shame.

To multiply the dread, Syn feared another attack from her haunting. She couldn't tell if her aching head resulted from the heat, her injuries from the pigmys, or if it signaled a coming episode. Showing weakness in front of the other competitors would be her undoing. The one hundred remaining teenagers were nothing but ruthless scavengers waiting to pick off the easy meals—proven by the run in with the six boys the previous night.

Cheers of excitement echoed off the Rock of Reckoning, distracting Syn from her dark reverie. She let her curiosity lead her toward the beach where a group of competitors gathered around the posse of new apprentices. The six finishers had been taken to the Imbuing Hall after the trial two nights prior. This was their first return to the trial grounds as imbued apprentices, and it seemed everyone wanted to get a glimpse of their changed forms.

Syn edged closer to satiate her curiosity. The apprentices were dressed all in black and they smiled as they rolled wooden barrels off their beached skiff. Physically, they appeared unchanged, but the clothing made them look just like young Nighterrians sans the three-barrel weapons.

Syn gritted her teeth. Among them she noticed the green haired boy who pushed her down on the first day and who cut her rope during the trial. Four other boys rolled barrels behind him and... was that a girl at the back?

"We've got ale to share!" announced the red-haired girl.

Whooping cheers went up around the crowd of competitors. "Are you really imbued?" someone asked. "Give us a demonstration!" demanded another.

The leading apprentice swiped a handful of mossy hair out of his face. He exchanged a look with the girl and shrugged.

Together, they picked up their barrels and easily raised them over their heads in a display of their newly-granted strength. The rest of the apprentices followed suit to the shouts of approval from the growing crowd.

Syn examined each of the apprentices and wondered where in their body they decided to keep their Hallowed Point. Her sight fell over a broad-shouldered boy at the center of the pack. She paused as she noticed something strange. The rest of the apprentices had red Terraborn eyes, but the one at the center looked around the crowd with brown eyes. Syn stepped closer to gain a better look. She didn't recognize the boy. He was a Surfacer, but not a Legionite as his skin was too light and his eyes weren't the right shape.

"I thought Xedford said the Imbuing changes your eyes," Syn said to Anna as she thought back on her conversation with him inside her home back in Garon.

The apprentices stacked the barrels into a triangle and began filling cups with the amber-colored drink Syn recognized from the Outpost. She joined the crowd to get a closer look at boy with the brown eyes.

The mass of competitors grew as more people pushed their way in to get their cups filled. Syn tried to make her way up to the apprentice but after catching a painful elbow to the rib, she decided to step back and wait in the queue. When she reached the front of the line, however, she ended up in front of the green-haired boy.

He looked her up and down. "No ale for light-dwellers."

Before Syn could respond, the red-headed girl knocked him in the shoulder. "Be civil, Torrance," she said.

Torrance ignored her. "No more furs, huh?" He blocked Syn's path from getting around him. "You finally gone and figured out the weather here?"

Syn ignored the remark and pressed on with her mission.

"I'm here to talk to..." Where did the brown-eyed apprentice go? She couldn't spot him through the crowd.

The redhead rolled her eyes and pushed a large cup into Syn's hands then stepped out of the way to usher her out of Torrance's presence. Teens, thirsty for the taste of ale, pushed Syn forward and through the jostling crowd. She soon found herself at the end of the line, still clutching the full mug of ale.

She weaved her way through the crowd and eventually spotted the brown-eyed apprentice drinking and chatting with a group of competitors. "They don't begrudge *him* for not being Terraborn," Syn said to Anna as she watched from afar.

Without much else to do but wait her turn to talk to him, she took a gulp of her ale. The drink still tasted bitter, but it lacked the foaming tablet that added bubbles and she found she could tolerate it. It tasted better than the dried ghost moths Relia had prepared. The rich drink filled her stomach as she sipped on. It quelled her appetite and soon the hunger pangs weren't the only thing that lifted. The burden of her guilt seemed to lighten and the fear of a coming attack from her haunting evaporated.

"This is wonderful," she said to Anna. "I've never felt... light before." She felt as if she could run for miles and not tire. The looming dread of the next trial withered away as she drank.

By the time Syn finished her cup, she was smiling. She stumbled toward the barrels for a refill. The back of her mind whispered about something she had planned to do, but it seemed less important now. She refilled her mug and gulped down the bitterness. While musing over the possibility of retaining this weightless feeling forever, she spotted the green-haired boy named Torrance out the corner of her eye.

"Perhaps he's the one who has it out for me." Syn narrowed

her eyes and took another sip. "He could have killed me when he cut the rope during the trial."

Syn stood drinking and stoking the fires of her anger as she pierced Torrance with her stare. By the time she finished her second cup, she felt fit to confront him.

She set off toward him and nearly tripped. Were her feet always this uncoordinated? Once she found her balance, she resumed her quest toward her target. Someone's back interrupted her view of Torrance. Broad shoulders. Black clothing. An apprentice stood in her way. The sight of him triggered a memory that struggled to the surface. What was it?

"Eyes!" she yelled, triumphant in her ability to remember.

The brown-eyed apprentice turned toward her with confusion across his face.

"Why... haves... those eyes?" Words were hard. She felt like a wall of inebriation stood in the way of her ability to articulate.

Torrance hopped off his barrel and stepped in front Syn. "I thought I told you, no ale for light-dwellers."

"Stop... trying... kill me..." She brought her fists up. His green hair floated in circles in her vision.

Torrance laughed and crouched down to get eye level with Syn. "Get lost, weakling."

Syn swung at him with the empty cup in her hand. He dodged out of the way and the momentum of her miss carried her off balance. She staggered and fell to the ground. The sound of laughter from the crowd bubbled around her.

Syn climbed to her feet and tried to charge toward Torrance, but the hoard of competitors swept her up and pushed her back. She tried to fight against the crowd of people, but her attempts amounted to nil. A final shove sent her sprawling to the packed red dirt.

Defeated, she sat up holding her head. The world churned

in dizzying swirls, and she started feeling nauseous. She found her way to her feet and began the uncertain trek back to her camp. Curses and laughter crept behind her as she made her retreat.

In the clutches of nausea, the weight of her fears began to crash back down. She picked her way through destroyed camps while muttering to herself and crying. She drew curious looks from competitors gathered around cookfires as she passed. She paid them no attention and stumbled on through the night. The brown eyes of the apprentice made slow revolutions around her thoughts. They reminded her of Rem's brown eyes.

She rounded the bend, leaving the party at the beach and the judging stares behind. Finally, she stood alone in the dark. Sweet solitude. If Rem could see her now, what would he think? He would probably—

The world went black. Confusion registered before the realization of a fabric bag over her head. Someone swept her feet out from under her and she hit the ground.

25
ENOUGH

Syn screamed as her attacker knelt on her back, holding her to the ground. The bag came away, only to be replaced with a gag that quieted her screams. She choked on the gag and yelled out stifled cries. A hand shoved her head to the earth. Struggling and helpless, she couldn't see—couldn't make out the shape in the dark as her sight remained blurred from drink and tears. She flailed her limbs, but she couldn't recall the maneuvers of her training. Her attacker gained control of her arms and she felt the rough scratch of rope binding her wrists behind her back. Her perception tumbled in darkness filled with bright stabs of terror as the unseen assailant tightened the ropes around her wrists.

I'm going to die.

Panic and drunken vulnerability opened the door to thoughts of Rem. Was this what he felt before he died? She struggled to free herself as memories assaulted her. The utter terror in Rem's face as scales sprang from his skin—the moment his soul vacated his eyes—the voice that haunted her memory. *It hurts.*

Visions of memories colored the blackness of her blurred sight and bludgeoned her soul. Helpless. Hopeless. The door to the cage of her pathetic rage burst open. She embraced surrender. Suddenly, and miraculously, strange shadows burst into her vision in an apparition of clawed hands. The pressure on her back lifted, and she heard a grunt a few paces away.

What just happened? The hands of shadows receded from her vision and slunk back into her skin as if they never existed. Confused, she lifted her head from the dirt and rolled to her side. It is over? She looked around. There! A figure in the night. Who was it? Shouts. A female voice? Confusion eclipsed her awareness as she blinked into the darkness that swirled with her intoxicated vision.

She tried to get to her feet, but with her hands still tied behind her back, she felt too clumsy. The sound of retreating footsteps skittered through the dirt. She rolled over again and looked around the dark. No one leered within sight.

Syn flopped on the ground and managed to get to her knees. When she looked up again, a figure ran toward her. She tried to grab around her back for her blade and missed. The figure closed in. Her bound hands touched the hilt of Elaine's handle, and this time she ripped her free. She held Elaine awkwardly with her arms behind her back and the broken edge pointed near her hip.

"Put it away, it's me," Relia said and untied the gag from Syn's mouth.

The removal of the gag seemed to uncork a wave of nausea. Bile burned its way up Syn's throat. She dropped Elaine, doubled over, and threw up. Relia held her back from falling into the pile of her own vomit. When the heaving ceased, Relia went to work cutting the ropes binding her wrists.

"Relia? What are... what are you doing here?" With her

hands now free, Syn picked up Elaine and tried to sheath her, but after missing twice Relia did it for her.

"Saving your drunk ass." Relia pulled Syn's arm over her shoulder and helped her walk.

"Who... was it?"

"I didn't get a good look at him, but I think I saw where he ran off to."

"Where? We need to..." Syn fought back the urge to vomit again. "... go after him."

Relia jingled a laugh as they reached the trees at the edge of the water. "Not right now. Right now, you gotta get some sleep."

Syn let Relia help her into the first tree branch. She then began a tenuous climb up to her hammock. Twice she almost fell to the waters below, but Relia caught her and shoved her back on balance. After what seemed like an eternity of climbing, they finally made it to the top. Syn flopped into her hammock and immediately threw up over the side. The acrid bitterness of the ale tasted even worse on the way out.

Relia handed her a canteen of water which Syn accepted with gratitude. Syn sipped as she waited for her vision to stop spinning.

"I've been poisoned," Syn said after a while.

Relia chuckled. "You poisoned yourself, Legion-woman. Interterran ale is sinfully strong, especially for a Surfacer such as yourself."

"You've had it?"

"Sure I have. It's one of my all-time favorites. Thanks for inviting me to the party by the way." She flashed her toothy smile. "I remember getting sick the first time too. The liking for it is an acquired thing, but I'm betting you develop a taste for it."

"I'm never drinking that shit again," Syn vowed.

"I said that too. Give it time, sister."

Syn let the conversation lapse. She was tempted to bring up the strange thing that happened with the shadows, but she decided it must have been a delusional remnant of the drink.

She stared down at her hands and the raw rope burn around her wrists. Rage gently twisted its fingers around her chest. *Threatening notes, arrows in the dark, and now this.* Perhaps it was the fading numbness of the alcohol, or maybe she had finally reached her boiling point. But, like the final snowflake that caved the roof of a hut, something shifted in her as she sat thinking about what the assailant might have done if he had succeeded. Would he have drowned her in the ocean? Thrown her into the chasm of lava? Violated her like brigands from the Outpost had planned?

"I've had enough." Syn clenched her jaw against the threat of bile crawling up her throat.

"What are we gonna to do about it?"

"I don't know, but it's time I put an end to this."

Relia grinned a dangerous smile. "I reckon it's time we go on the offensive."

Syn couldn't agree more. She laid back in her hammock and let thoughts of vengeance soothe her while Relia's use of the word "we" circled around in her mind. Eventually, the fog of ale drifted her off to sleep.

26

MIRAGE

Syn followed Relia on sneaking feet as they picked their way through the campsites with torches in hand. Snickers and crude laughter followed them as they crossed the trial grounds. After the previous night's drunken display of humiliation, Syn expected it. Yet, the stares and whispers continued to sting.

"Want a drink?" teased a tall boy. He then threw a full mug of ale at her.

Syn stepped out of the way of the worst of the splash but half of it splattered her face. The smell nearly made her gag. Her stomach still ached from heaving up ale and stomach acid the night before.

Relia pointed the flaming end of her torch at the boy and jumped up to fight but Syn yanked her away. "Leave it, we have a mission to accomplish."

Relia backed away, glaring and snarling like an animal.

Syn pushed on with the depressing idea that perhaps she should feel at home. She endured similar treatment in Garon, if only less blatantly cruel. Memories of home coiled around her mind as she followed Relia. She recalled a snow-filled day in the woods as a child.

Syn had managed to keep evidence of her condition a secret from the other children until the age of ten. Her haunting struck one winter day while tracking an elk on a hunting expedition.

All she remembered was screaming and sprinting through the trees as the branches tried to grab at her. All sense of direction abandoned her as she tried to outrun the terrors that jumped into her path. She found the hollow of a tree just as the horror reached its pinnacle and she fainted.

By the time the empty hour came to dull the fear, she was alone and completely lost. The day had grown dark, and the snow fell in a torrent of white. She shivered inside the tree for hours on end, whispering to herself and trying to remember the songs her mother sang to soothe her.

In a forest of saplings, you are an ancient oak. The words of the senile old woman circled her mind while she sat trembling in the freezing cold. Syn hadn't felt like an ancient oak that day or any day since. *You must embrace the shadows cast by your branches.* How could she embrace what would certainly be her end?

Syn knew she would die when the merciless cold reached out and numbed the feeling in her legs and arms. Frozen in the fetal position, she couldn't move or even cry out by the time night fell and she heard the call of the search party.

"Syndrah!"

"Syn! Where are you?"

I'm here! She had tried to scream, but words froze in her throat. She cowered there, helpless, and unable to force her voice to answer their call. Panic had stolen through her as she heard them move away in the wrong direction. *No! Don't leave me!* She pressed every drop of strength she had into reaching out to them, but only a dry croak escaped her. She heard their footsteps crunch away and the voices begin to fade.

It was Drekton who found her that night. The sight of his face peeking through the hollow of the tree was a vision of salvation she'd never forget.

"I found her!" he yelled, calling back the search party.

Syn had shivered with silent gratitude. Hands extracted her from the tree. She felt the painful creak of her joints, heard the relieved voice of her father as he carried her away. But behind the icicles of her eyelashes, she kept her sights trained on Drekton and vowed to repay him one day.

The following day she learned the consequences of her episode. The rest of the children shunned her for her weakness. A Legionite never runs away, the Divine Creedence declared it. *I will defend. I will never abandon a fight.*

"Coward." The whispers followed her everywhere she went. Shortly accompanied by "insane," "unstable," "weak."

It seemed the trial grounds were a repeat of her childhood disgrace. Sneers and curses followed Syn and Relia as they traversed the campgrounds. She did her best to ignore the other competitors as she trained her focus back on the task at hand.

Syn grew nervous as she followed Relia toward the supposed campsite of her attacker. Although she desired to find the person who seemed intent on terrorizing her, she no longer felt the vindictive confidence of the previous night. After the emboldening effects of intoxication wore off, she feared the confrontation. Whoever it was knew about the Scaler attack in Garon. And they knew it was her fault.

"Are you sure about this?" Syn asked.

Relia looked over her shoulder. "I seen him come this way."

"No, I mean are you sure we should do this? What if he attacks and kills us?"

"Well, then we'll just have to kill the bastard first," Relia spoke with cool confidence, as if it were that simple. "Hush up now, we're almost there."

Despite Relia's continued show of loyalty, Syn tensed at the thought that Relia could be leading her into a trap. Before Syn could backout of the mission, they reached a campsite attached to the wall of the Rock of Reckoning. A cloth tarp used the side of the rock as a lean-to. The entrance flaps flittered in the breeze, inviting them in.

Relia nodded toward it to indicate it as the one. Torch light flickered shadows over her calm expression. With weapons drawn, they exchanged a silent look. Syn crept in closer and Relia ripped back the cloth doorway as Syn prepared for an ambush.

No one emerged. Relia shined the light of her torch inside to reveal the vacant space within. She looked to Syn and shrugged. Relieved, Syn led the way into the tent.

Inside it opened to a much larger space than it appeared on the outside. Whoever built it had dug out the floor to create an area large enough to stand up in. Relia's firelight illuminated simple supplies. Bowls, cookware, dried jerky, and extra firewood lined the ground beside the rock wall. Two shallow holes appeared to be beds, but only one contained a sleeping roll. A shiver rippled down Syn's body. Could there be more than one person after her?

"Look." Relia pointed her sword toward a pack in the corner.

Syn sheathed her weapon and shoved the butt of her torch into the dirt to kneel beside the pack. She flung it open and dug through it while Relia explored the rest of the supplies. Syn pulled out three sets of sharp knives and set them aside along with a ration of dried jerky.

"What do you make of these?" Relia held up a hand full of small vials filled with dark blue liquid.

"No idea." Syn continued digging through the pack. She froze as her hand touched something soft and hairy. She yanked it free and held it up to the torchlight. *An otter-pelt cloak?*

"Whoa." Relia looked up from the vials. "Is that yours?"

For a moment Syn thought it might be, but she remembered she arrived wearing a fox cloak. "No." She looked to the stitching and exchanged a warning look with Relia.

"Legionite?"

"Unmistakable Legionite craftsmanship." Syn dug again through the nearly empty pack. Her hand closed over one last item. She brought it up to the firelight and opened her fingers.

A gold coin sat in her palm. The three crossing blades were stutter stamped into the metal like a mistake in the minting. The top edge had a flattened chip on it.

Memories of Rem's corpse struck her in a sudden breathtaking punch—the golden glimmer she plucked from the blood-stained snow, the cold white of his tiny hands as she closed them around the Nighterrian coin.

"I know who it is." Syn jumped to her feet without looking away from the coin. The headache she'd been nursing in the ale's aftermath suddenly flared into an inferno inside her skull.

"Who?"

"My fiancé."

The entrance to the tent flew open. Syn looked up as Drekton burst through. The memory of his face emerging from the tree in the woods flicked into her mind, but this was not the Drekton from her childhood. Reality ruined the mirage as Drekton's wild expression greeted her with undeniable hatred.

27
CONFESSIONS

Relia dropped the vials she held and whipped around. "Stay back!" She pointed the torch at Drekton with one hand and pulled out her sword with the other.

Drekton ignored Relia as he stared icicles at Syn. "Syndrah," he greeted with coldness Syn had never heard in his voice before.

"Drekton." Syn couldn't meet his eye. She looked at the floor where the shattered vials sat in a mess of blue liquid.

"Why're you doing this?" Relia shoved both blade and torch closer to Drekton. "What're you after her for?"

Drekton looked to Relia as if seeing her for the first time. "Why don't you tell her, Syn? Tell her what you did."

"I-I..." Her head throbbed, warning her of the arrival of darkness.

"You killed my brother!" His words felt like a knife burrowed in her gut, all the way to the hilt.

"I didn't-I didn't mean to."

Relia jumped closer to Drekton. "Give me one good reason

not to slice you from sack"—she motioned her sword to his crotch and drew a line in the air up to his head— "to skull."

"Relia." Syn raised her hand in peace. "This isn't your fight." She turned to Drekton and fought back the alarm ringing in her head. "You followed me here?"

"No. I came to fulfill Rem's dream. But then I saw you here and I wouldn't stand for it. Rem's killer living out his dream?" He shook his head in disgust.

She couldn't get the image of Drekton as an innocent ten-year-old out of her mind. The man before her now was but a vindictive corruption of her childhood savior. "So you tried to kill me?"

"Kill you? Don't be ridiculous, I'm no murderer," Drekton said.

"But during the trial you—"

"Do you really think I couldn't have shot you between the eyes if I wanted to? I was just trying to keep you from the finish line."

The promise of a coming attack from her ghosts made it hard to think, but Syn found his words rang true. Drekton's dead aim was known throughout Garon. Syn had once witnessed him shoot a rabbit through the eye in the dark— during a snowstorm.

Relia interjected, "What about the other night? You looked pretty criminal to me, what were you trying to accomplish?"

"Criminal?" Drekton hissed the word like it tasted bad on his tongue. "The only criminal here is Syn. Removing her from the trials is the least I could do as I'm well within my right to enact the Law of Retribution."

Syn nearly sank to her knees. Of course, Drekton remained the ever-perfect Legionite. If the law said to bash your head against a wall three times a day, Drekton would have his maiming done before sunrise.

Drekton continued, "I don't know what you were thinking in coming here, Syn. You don't deserve to become a Nighterrian, not after what you've done."

"I thought it—"

"You thought wrong!" Drekton's fists clenched like he wanted to swing at her.

Syn decided she would let him if he did. Her ghosts were coming and the pressure of panic in her chest made it feel like her heart would explode. She needed to get away before her curse took hold.

"You want to enact the Law of Retribution? Do it. We both know I deserve it."

"Syn," Relia objected, but Syn silenced her with a look. Relia relaxed slightly but maintained her power stance, ready to strike at Drekton if need be.

"To follow the law exactly I'd need to call down a Scaler attack on you, but that's not going to happen." He clenched his jaw and shook his head. "Consider the Law fulfilled. I want nothing more to do with you."

Defeated by her own guilt, Syn stared at the coin in her hand. She could feel him glaring down at her. Without looking Drekton in the eye, Syn held the coin up in her trembling palm as an offering of her surrender.

Drekton only glowered at her, making no move to take the coin. "Look at me."

Syn could hardly make out his words over the ringing in her ears. She didn't want to look at him. She could feel the haunting staking its horrible claim as darkness crept at the corners of her vision.

"Look at me!"

Syn looked up at Drekton's face contorted in rage. His deep brown eyes—eyes just like Rem's—held sorrow that fueled his anger. In the moment before her vision transformed his expression into horror, she saw his soul laid bare. She saw the pain, the loss, the guilt, and the misery that lashed his heart.

Then his skin melted from his face as the haunting took hold. Syn let out a whimpering cry.

Drekton pushed her hand away. "Keep the coin. Let it remind you of Rem and what you've done. I hope you carry it with you the rest of your days." He spoke with a face of exposed sinew and muscle. The illusion turned Syn's stomach, but no more than her own shame. He stepped aside. "Do the honorable thing and go back to Garon."

Syn closed her fist around the coin and felt tears burning her eyes.

"Go!" Drekton ordered. "Before I change my mind." His exposed eye sockets glared at the scales of Relia's clothes. "And take your savage friend with you."

In a jolt of self-preservation, Syn bolted out the exit of the tent. She ran headlong into the night air in search of sanctuary. Curious competitors peeked out of their tents. Their faces morphed into hairy beasts and undead corpses.

"Wait!" Relia called after her.

"Leave me alone!" Syn ran faster, hurdling over tents in desperation.

Tears streamed down her face as the night appeared to grow darker. She reached the beach and saw multi-eyeballed creatures unfurl their tentacles from the waves and reach toward her. Fear pounded through her veins like poison as she sought refuge.

Syn scrambled up her tree to retreat like she always did during an episode, but this time she wouldn't find solitude. Relia kept pace in the tree alongside her. Syn reached her hammock at the same time as Relia arrived at hers. The branches made of skeletal hands provoked her with frightening daggers. Syn ducked for cover as they came toward her, though she knew they wouldn't cause her bodily harm. Relia climbed over to Syn's tree.

"Get away from me!"

Relia's hair transformed into golden snakes. The scales of her vest took on a life of their own and turned her flesh into the green and gray skin of a Scaler. Syn screamed and tried to scramble away from Relia. The hammock swung beneath both their weight.

Hands fused together in a stream of shadowed mist and grabbed onto the edge of the hammock. Syn clambered backward, but her back hit the trunk of the tree. The Relia-Scaler and the black hands were coming for her. With nowhere else to run, she huddled in terror as the fear crawled up inside her and latched onto her senses. The shadows yanked on the edge of the hammock. The sudden swing dumped Relia off the side.

Relia yelped as she grabbed onto a branch to arrest her fall. Syn tried to process what just happened. Did her haunting just *move* the hammock? Relia clung to the limb of the tree and stared at Syn in fright. Her face popped back into reality. For a moment she was no longer a beast but a frightened girl clinging to a limb.

"Relia..." Syn reached for her, but the visions returned, and she retracted her hand. Shadows swirled around Relia as she pulled herself up. Scales reigned over her body once again. Her face lengthened and took on the shape of snout with the sharpened fangs of a Scaler.

Syn screamed.

"Calm down, calm down dammit!" Relia reached for her.

Syn cowered and shut her eyes. She could feel fear stealing its way up her body. Soon it would dominate her with a dizziness that would make her black out.

"Look at me, Syn, look at me. I ain't gonna hurt you."

Hands grabbed hold of Syn's shoulders. Syn flinched, but

the hands felt like human hands, not the claws of a monster. "It's not real," Syn muttered to herself. "It's-not-real-it's-not-real-it's-not-real."

"Yeah, it ain't real. You're safe here."

Syn cracked an eye and stared down at Relia's hand on her arm. Pink flesh with dirt under her nails. It looked normal. Still breathing in gasps, she slowly dragged her vision upward.

"It's alright now. Everything is alright, just breathe," Relia said.

Syn focused on the sound of her voice as she peeked up at her face. She recovered a split second of relief as Relia's blonde curls and red eyes looked back at her, but it faded in a heartbeat. The beast emerged again, replacing her features.

"Just breathe," Relia urged. The vision of her as a Scaler flickered in and out from human to monster.

"It's... not... real." Syn stared hard into Relia's eyes and could almost see past the illusion. But the hands of the tree branches crawled toward her out of the corner of her eye, stealing her focus. When Syn glanced back at Relia, a forked reptilian tongue licked the air. She clamped her eyes tight and cried, longing for escape. Why hadn't she fainted yet?

Syn remained conscious as an eternity passed—or perhaps just a matter of minutes. Part of her retained awareness of Relia's presence as crashing waves of terror squeezed her in rhythmic contractions. When the seizing power of the haunting loosened its grip, Syn emerged from her fetal position. Finally, the comforting nothingness of the empty hour drove away the demons.

Relia sat beside her on her hammock. She looked over at Syn with... curiosity? Surely, Syn read her expression wrong. Hadn't she just seen her crumble into a weeping pile of cowardice? Where was the condemnation, the disgust, the pity? Syn sat up and offered Relia a tentative look of apology.

"What in the flaming fuck just happened?" Relia threw her hands in the air in exasperation.

"I... have an affliction."

Relia tilted her curly head and lifted an eyebrow. "Well, I'll say."

"You must think I'm insane."

Relia shrugged. "We're all a little insane. Nobody escapes life without some bang ups."

"And I've lived hundreds of lives." Syn looked up at the orange stars.

"What do you mean?"

Syn sighed. "Legionite souls are reincarnated. After death, life begins again... and again, and again."

"You mean you can remember all these past lives of yours?"

"No, but I can feel them sometimes. My father calls it my 'haunting.' Ever since I can remember there's been times when the ghosts turn everything around me into monsters." Syn paused. She realized she had never explained her haunting to anyone before. What inspired to her talk about it now?

"Well shit me a brick and call me a mason, that sounds terrifying."

Syn gave a hollow chuckle.

After a moment Relia asked, "What sort of monster did I look like?"

"A Scaler."

Relia pulled an appalled expression.

"Are you surprised?" Syn asked. "You're wearing their skin."

Relia picked at the scales of her pants. "I loathe the wretched beasts."

"Then why do you wear all that?"

"I like to keep my enemies close." Relia sprouted a mischievous grin. "So that any other Scaler who sees it will know I murdered their cousin."

"Seriously?"

Relia chuckled before growing pensive. "It's also to remind me of my purpose."

"And that is?"

"To kill as many of those scaley abominations as I can." She clenched her fists. "To bring the Fates-damned beasts into extinction."

Syn appreciated her gumption. "I hate the Scalers too. Is that why you want to become a Nighterrian?"

Relia nodded. "Those soul snatching bastards killed my parents." She joined Syn in staring up at the bright stars. Her chin quivered as she spoke. "It was a long while back, but I remember it clear as yesternight. It was two of them. They slaughtered my ma and pa while I hid in the closet and did nothing." A tear dripped down her cheek. She didn't wipe it away. She didn't even seem embarrassed about it.

"Your parents, did... did they turn?"

"No, thank the Fates."

"I'm sorry." Syn didn't feel like it was the most adequate response to Relia's story but what else could she say? "I brought a Scaler attack to my village." The admission breezed out of her without thought.

"How's that?"

Why did I say that? Too late to take it back, Syn wiped the salty remnants of tears from her face and began the story. She explained her failure to perform the sacrifice and the ensuing massacre that resulted in Rem's death.

"I never meant for any of it to happen. If I could go back, I'd do the sacrifice in a second." Syn felt more tears threaten. What happened to the empty hour? Where was the comfort of detachment? Her confession seemed to obliterate the safety of numbness.

Relia put a hand on Syn's shoulder. Syn looked over to see her crying. "It ain't your fault," Relia said.

Syn felt a stab of pain. The welling lump in her throat threatened to break her. But somehow, through the pain, she felt something lift. The heaviness of her soul, like the weight of boulder sitting on her chest, seemed to lessen just slightly.

"Thank you." Syn let go of her strangled emotions and allowed the tears fall as her and Relia swayed in her hammock consumed by their separate sorrows and regrets.

The empty hour hurt more than ever before but, for the first time, Syn found she was not alone in the enduring of it.

28

PYRE

"And that's why I'll never swim naked in the Lake of Misdeed again. I was pulling leeches off my ass for a week!" Relia laughed. "I swear, they kept multiplying!"

Syn chuckled at the story as she dangled her feet from her hammock, her baited hook plunked into the black sea below. "I don't know why you would go swimming nude in the first place."

Syn no longer felt embarrassed about Relia witnessing her episode. And in the two continuous nights that followed, a tentative form of trust began to develop. Mostly through the way Syn no longer slept with one eye open, expecting Relia to betray her at any moment.

"It was a dare. The Fates willed it and the other kids said I wouldn't do it, so I had to prove I wasn't nilly."

Syn learned "nilly" meant something akin to "coward." Many of Relia's odd phrases and Terraborn sayings were still lost on her, however. She watched Relia fish from her own hammock with an air of absolute certainty that she would catch something.

"Who are these Fates you keep talking about?"

"The Fates, you know, the gods in charge of destiny." Syn returned a questioning look. "The gods of luck and karma." When Syn offered no sign of recognition, Relia continued with exasperation. "Aw, come on! They hold up the bridges between realms."

"Your gods live in the portals?"

"No, dummy. They *are* the portals."

Syn stared at her for a moment, waiting to see if she would burst out laughing. But Relia sat with brows furrowed in serious conviction. Syn shook her head and chuckled. "Perhaps one of those leaches burrowed into your brain."

Relia stared toward the red, starry sky with a faraway look of wonder. "You know, the Fates *have* favored me since then. I reckon I carry the ichor of the gods by way of parasite."

Syn stared, bewildered, clutching at her fishing line. Relia turned to her, and laughter bubbled out of her like the fizzing ale tablets. Syn laughed as she marveled at Relia's strangeness. She couldn't remember the last time she laughed with anyone. It felt natural and comforting, if only for a moment.

When the hiccups of giggles died down, however, her mind turned back toward the future. A reminder of the second trial stood before her. She grew grim staring at the Rock of Reckoning, wondering what the next trial would bring.

"Why do you do that?" Relia asked.

"Do what?"

"Get all serious all of a sudden. Don't you ever let yourself be happy?"

"I'll be happy once we defeat the trials and I get cured."

"Cured?"

"Xedford said that the Imbuing would cure me of my

curse." Syn regarded her friends dangling from a branch to her left. Gregory swayed next to Anna and between them hung Rem's golden coin.

"You hate yourself that much?"

Syn flicked to gaze to Relia. "You don't know what it's like."

"What is it like?" Relia asked, and Syn could tell she honestly wanted to understand.

"It's like... like anchors attached to each of your limbs and trying to go about life dragging them everywhere you go. Day after day the chains get tangled, and you get stuck on the smallest bumps. And then, when the haunting strikes, it's like... like running from a killer in the dark, one you can't see but is all around you. Then you realize the killer is yourself, and you're helpless to fight her."

Relia stayed quiet for a moment, pondering Syn's words. "Shit on parade, no wonder you're here." She turned back to her fishing stick without an ounce of pity or judgement, just gentle acceptance.

Syn smiled. She had never openly talked about her weakness to anyone, but perhaps Relia could understand. She too had a tortured past and a pained soul. But Relia delt with it like the burden weighed nothing.

"I'm only here because of the good grace of a generous Nighterrian," Syn said.

"Aw, does somebody got a crush?"

"What?"

"Don't be playing all bashful-like. Xedford! I can tell by the way you talk about him that you like him."

"Don't be ridiculous." Syn had told Relia about her journey to the trials, but she didn't think she had included any swooning over Xedford.

"I am the mayor of Ridiculous, thank you very much. And I think he likes you too."

"He's only nice to me because I helped save his life."

"Sure, sure. You know, as far as older men go, he is on the rugged and handsome side of things. I just wonder why he wears that awful bandana all the damn time. You think he's covering up a bald spot?"

Syn shook her head, trying to banish the insufferable blush from her cheeks. "He's not *that* old." Plenty of women Syn's age had married far older men back in Garon.

"Just be careful now," Relia grew serious. "I never trust the handsome ones. Especially when they got power and position behind them."

Eager to change the subject, Syn nodded toward the Rock of Reckoning. "It looks like the crew is setting up the next trial."

"Yeah. I wonder what kind of torture maze they'll shove us through next."

Shouted voices rang off the water. Syn squinted through the dark to the massive, tiered rock. Although they had a higher vantage point from their place in the trees, she still couldn't see what they were doing in the darkness. All she could perceive were movements on the ledge surrounding the second tier.

"Maybe Drekton won't try to sabotage me this time." She hadn't seen Drekton since their confrontation two nights earlier, but his words remained with her. If she had any honor at all, she would do what he said and return to Garon to meet her punishment. But she had come too far to give up now.

"The other night you said he was your betrothed?" Relia asked.

"He used to be. Our parents arranged our marriage a few years back. We were supposed to marry after I gained my citizenship. But all of that was before... well, you know." She focused on the waters below, but she could feel Rem's coin glinting from the branch beside her.

"I guess he ain't bad to look at, neither—in a frozen-waste-land-next-door kind of way. If only he weren't such an asshole—"

"Relia!" Syn spotted something floating along the waves in the water.

"Sorry, I know you still got remnants of feelings for him, but I think he's an asshole."

"No, look! What is that?" Syn pointed down at the black sea.

Relia squinted toward the waves. "Is that... a person?"

"They're not moving." Syn exchanged a look with Relia.

They jumped into action simultaneously. With fishing poles abandoned, they climbed down their respective trees in a hurry. Relia splashed into the water first.

"Careful," Syn said as she joined her in the black water. They had no way of knowing what sort of deviant creatures lurked beneath the surface.

The human shape floated only a few yards away. Together they risked the waves and swam toward the immobile body. As they neared it, Syn could tell the person was dead. They swam the body back to the shore anyway.

Back on the rocky beach, Syn got her first good look at it. It was a boy, broad-shouldered with whisps of a patchy beard. Syn gasped. She recognized him. His dark brown eyes stared open and vacant into the night.

"He's one of the apprentices."

Relia cursed and sent Syn a worried look.

Syn stared down at the boy. His face was pale, as if all the blood had been drained from his body. His lips stood out against his skin in a sickly shade of blue. Flashes of the girl on the altar jumped into Syn's memory: gray eyes and blueberry lips. Syn shook her head, focusing her attention back on the dead apprentice. Something seemed odd about the shape of his chest. Syn pulled up his black shirt to reveal a gaping hole in his chest.

"Aw, what in the depths of damnation?" Relia complained.

His skin furled up at the edges of the wound in tattered scraps as if something had dug its way into his chest. Syn stuck her hand into the remnants of his chest cavity.

"What are you doing?"

Syn didn't respond. She focused on feeling around inside the dead boy. If being a butcher's daughter had taught her anything, it was a familiarity with the insides of animals. All mammals were similar in design. As she explored his chest, she found a notched hole in one of his ribs. The gap in the bone felt like the appropriate size for the home of a small, pointed object.

"His Hallowed Point is gone." She pulled her hands free. They came away slick with purple gore.

Relia looked to her in silent alarm. Syn could read the thought on the edge of her lips; sabotage had reached a new height. It appeared some competitors were desperate enough to win that they would murder an imbued apprentice.

***

NIGHTERRIANS LITTERED THE BEACH, THEIR GRIM EXPRESSION illuminated by the flames of the pyre. They spoke in hushed voices amongst each other as the mutilated body of the apprentice burned behind them.

The boy's name was Gordon, Syn learned after a crowd of competitors whispered it over the flames of the pyre. The air weighed heavy with smoke and paranoia as the teenagers eyed one another.

The remaining apprentices stood together beside the fire. Their faces were stowed tight, as if they wore blank masks. Syn ran her eyes over them and counted only four. Where was the girl with the red hair?

"Who do you think did it?" Relia asked. She stood glaring at the competitors, as if she could discern the culprit by piercing them with her gaze.

"I don't know."

Syn had explained to Relia how Gordon's blue lips reminded her of the lips of the sacrifice. Could they have shared the same disease? Relia thought it was unlikely as the imbuing was supposed to make one immune to disease, but Syn couldn't shake the thought.

Captain Revvor emerged from behind the pyre. He looked exhausted. Deep circles lined his eyes and he walked with a near stagger as if it were difficult for him to stay on his feet.

The crowd hushed as he raised his golden three-barrel. When he spoke, his voice came out slow and filled with gravel. "I think we've all experienced a mighty sobering night here tonight. As you know, the apprentices are tasked with aiding the crew on some of our more dangerous missions. And, unfortunately, we've lost one of our own." He bowed his head as he spoke the next words. "May his soul go bravely into the night."

The crowd echoed the prayer. "May his soul go bravely into the night."

Syn did not repeat the phrase. It was all wrong. The Legionite prayer for the dead was, "Into the Abyss and born again." She knew the Terraborn did not swear fealty to the Legion, but what about the Nighterrians? Weren't they supposed to be loyal to the Legion? Afterall, it was the Legion whose power infused their Hallowed Points.

"While we're gathered here, I might as well go on and let

Xedford explain the next trial." Revvor stepped back. His eyes glittered with malice as he ushered Xedford forward.

Excitement trickled through the crowd, as if the smell of burning flesh wasn't still present in the air. Only the four apprentices continued to look solemn.

Xedford cleared his throat and pointed up at the second tier of the Rock of Reckoning. "Tomorrow, a gauntlet will be erected leading up to the second tier. From there, you'll go on to collect a prize from one of the boxes stationed around the outside of the tier. The key to each box will have been swallowed by a beast guarding each of the prizes. Your task is to find a way to get the key, unlock the box, and return to the campgrounds with your prize.

"Also, there's something else unique to this trial." Xedford paused, staring around the faces of the competitors. Syn had the ridiculous thought that maybe he was searching for her. "When you step back onto the campgrounds, whoever is touching the prize will continue to the next trial."

Murmurs of tentative allegiances traveled around the competitors as they began to plot. Xedford continued, "Yeah, that's right. This trial will allow you to team up with as many people as can touch the prize at the same time. And it will be real difficult to make it through the gauntlet without a teammate. But be warned, should you make it to trial three, it's every competitor for themselves. And, as it stands, we are down an apprentice. So, the first person to complete this trial *solo* will win an apprenticeship."

The transitory friendships spoken a minute before died in the silence following Xedford's speech. Syn could almost hear the crowd's thoughts of backstabbing over the sound of crashing waves and the crackling of the pyre.

Revvor spoke up to dismiss the meeting. "Rest up, trial two

will begin tomorrow at noon." He grunted and swaggered away.

"Shit on a stick." Relia pulled her hands through her hair.

"This isn't right," Syn agreed. "And they didn't explain what happened to Gordon. His Hallowed Point was retrieved, so how did he end up in the water after failing the mission?"

"It don't make a lick of sense."

"And did you notice? There's another apprentice missing. Where is the red-haired girl?"

"Yeah, I noticed."

Syn watched the crowd disperse. She scanned the retreating Nighterrians and spotted Xedford turning toward a group of skiffs littered along the beach. "Wait here," she said to Relia and took off, pushing through the crowd.

"Where you going?" Relia called.

"To get answers!" Syn zigzagged her way through the competitors. She caught up with Xedford just as he swung a leg into the small boat. "Xedford, wait!"

He turned to her and smiled. "Syn, what is it?"

"I just had a few questions, and I was wondering if, well, if you're willing to answer them?"

Xedford's smile faltered with brief hesitation. Then he nodded. "Climb in. I'll answer what I can."

29
CONVERT

Syn fidgeted on the wooden bench of the skiff. Xedford sat opposite her, rowing them across the waves. The other Nighterrians winked and snickered at them as they drifted past in their own skiffs.

"Sorry about them." Xedford chuckled and shook his head at a rude gesture made by a massive Nighterrian rowing by. "They're a crude bunch."

"It's fine." Syn felt too distracted by the dangerous waters to care. The tiny boat would offer no contest against the colossal beasts lurking in the black depths. She looked away from the water, attempting to stow her anxiety. She needed to focus on getting the answers she sought. She opened her mouth to begin the conversation when Xedford spoke up first.

"What brought you here?" He held both ores and rowed backwards at an easy pace.

"I wanted to know what happened to Gordon, I—"

"No," Xedford interrupted. "I mean, what brought you to the trials? You never explained what inspired you to go and change your mind."

"Oh, I umm…" Why was he asking? She wasn't here to talk about herself, she needed answers. "I just figured taking my chances for a cure would be better than living with it the rest of my life."

"Ah, that's right. Your 'affliction,' as you called it. What exactly is it you're suffering from?"

Syn didn't like the way his tone implied some sort of culpability. She began to feel more like this was an interrogation of her rather than of him. "It's just something I inherited," she answered.

"A plague of the mind?"

Syn narrowed her eyes. "I'm happy to talk about myself all you like, but first I'd like some answers." When her words sounded too harsh, she added, "Please." He was a Nighterrian after all, what was she doing demanding answers from him?

She began to regret her words as Xedford stopped rowing. He folded his arms in his lap with his left wrist containing the silvery three-barrel on top. He examined her in the orange starlight as if he were trying to determine the honesty of her character. Syn's indignation faltered. She was about to apologize when he spoke up.

"I understand your fear." A soft smile creased his bearded face, restoring the likeness of a kind mentor. "An apprentice is dead. That proves that sometimes even the strongest competitors don't make it to become Nighterrian in the end."

Syn let the pressure of the air held in her chest whoosh out. It appeared she passed whatever test she was under. "I just don't understand how we found Gordon's body in the water if he died during a mission. His Hal'point had been removed when we found him. Is that how the dead are treated around here? Thrown to the waves?"

Xedford seemed to consider something. He looked over his shoulder to take stock of his surroundings. They were alone on the black water. The rest of the Nighterrians had already made it back to the huge ship anchored near the backside of the Rock of Reckoning.

"I shouldn't be talking about this with you," he began, "but you and I've been through quite a bit together. I reckon you've earned some answers." He cleared his throat and settled into the wooden seat that appeared far too small for a man his size.

Syn leaned in. Sweat slicked her palms as she listened.

"Captain Revvor took the apprentices and a handful of the crew on a mission through a nearby portal."

"To the Surface?"

"No, no. Some of the portals around here don't just take you to the Surface, they can take you to other parts of Interterra. We were looking for a nest. You see, the goal of the mission was for the apprentices to get their swords wet by defeating as many beasts as they could while the rest of the crew captured the ones needed for the next trial.

"Now Gordon didn't look right from the start. We figured it was just a side effect of the imbuing. But he insisted he was fine and so we didn't think much of it at the time. It wasn't until we made it to the nest of monsters that we realized something was wrong.

"We fought hard, and under normal circumstances we would have gone without casualties. But Gordon began to slow, and it became obvious he'd taken ill. His lips turned blue, and he collapsed. There wasn't enough of us to defend him when the worms closed in." Xedford paused and sighed. "We got him back through the portal, but it was too late. You see, the newly imbued are real fragile. If their Hal'point gets knocked around before its fully infused, it's a death sentence. Gordon was a goner."

Syn's skin crawled. "What happened next?"

"We had our hands full after that. We had to get control of

the beasts for the trial and keep them apart, so they wouldn't kill each other. We set the apprentices in charge of retrieving Gordon's Hal'point and respectfully burning or burying his body. But, when the crew and I got back to the ship, we arrived during the aftermath of a mutiny. It seems one of the apprentices tried to take the Hal'point for herself. She fought like a demon and Gordon's body got thrown overboard during the struggle. The rest of the apprentices had just gotten her under control when we got there."

"Her? That red-headed apprentice?"

"That's right. Ortha was her name."

"But why would she want to steal a Hal'point if she's already imbued with one?"

"Now that's the question, ain't it?" He leaned in. "You remember those Converts I talked about when we crossed the crags?"

Syn recalled her encounter with the serpent trap. She sighed as she put the pieces together. "Ortha must be trying to steal a Hal'point for the outlaws."

Xedford's face bobbed against the night sky as they floated along. His piercing red eyes burrowed into her. She felt exposed, like he was about to ask more invasive questions about her past. "Shortly before Ortha died, she revealed she had an accomplice, another competitor still in the trials."

Syn leaned back. "You don't... You suspect *me*?"

He explored her with his stare for a moment, then straightened. "Nah."

Syn felt a drop of relief, but her heart still sprinted in her chest.

"Ortha's co-conspirator is out there," he said. "She admitted her and the accomplice poisoned Gordon to try and take his Hal'point."

"I thought the imbuing made one immune to poison."

"Not for the freshly imbued. The power of the Hal'point infuses over several days. The newly imbued—plumb-bloods we call them—won't be full-fledged Nighterrians until about thirty nights after the initial imbuing."

Syn had always imagined the transformation was instant. At least that explained Gordon's brown eyes. "What kind of poison turns a person's lips blue?"

"You recall those blue feathered serpent from the crags?"

Syn nodded.

"Well, their venom mimics a disease called, Captive-Para-lytica. The venom makes the body unable to move or speak. But it would require a real heavy dose of that blue poison to take down a plumb-blood."

Syn's mind flashed with the memory of the blue-lipped sacrifice, then jumped to the multitude of blue vials she discovered in Drekton's campsite. She nearly sprang out of the skiff. Could the second Convert be Drekton? No, that was nonsense. Drekton would never do such a thing.

"Relia was right," she said instead. "The apprentices do have targets on their backs, but not from who I thought."

Xedford gave a grim nod. "Nighterrians are always hunted for their Hal'points, but the plumb-bloods are targeted more often. We were able to keep the Hal'point from the outlaws this time, but I think there's still more to come."

"The girl, Ortha, she's dead?"

"Yeah. I wish we could've gotten more information out of her. But by the time we got there, the other apprentices had had their revenge for Gordon's murder."

"What would make someone turn convert? I would rather die than betray honor and join a band of outlaws."

"It's not as uncommon as you might think. The outlaws got a real insidious approach to their manipulation, one which they've refined over the years. They got a way of sniffing out those in turmoil, especially those who've suffered a loss. Lots of teens who've got nothing else to lose come to the trials looking for a purpose. The converts lure them in with the idea of living a life doing as they please. With the power of a gang of outlaws at your back to defend you, it can be tempting. Those in the right headspace fall victim to their persuasion quite easy."

Relieved that Xedford's gaze no longer held the scrutiny of suspicion, Syn's mind flitted back to Drekton and how deeply he grieved over Rem's death—almost to the point of madness. Amid his anguish, could he have fallen into the clutches of an outlaw and emerged a convert?

"Do you know anybody like I just described?" Xedford asked. "Somebody in enough pain to crumble into treachery?"

Syn kept her expression solid. She remembered the two beds dug into the dirt of Drekton's camp. The evidence of the blue vials was enough to raise her suspicion, but she needed to be sure before she voiced her concern. She owed the memory of her childhood friend that much.

"No," she lied. "But I'd like to help you find whoever it is."

"I thought you'd say that." He smiled his roguish grin.

Another question occurred to her as they floated on the waves. "What about Ortha's Hal'point? Will another spot open up in the running?" She hoped the question didn't sound too insensitive; the girl had just died after all.

"Actually, I was hoping to keep that particular Hal'point for whoever catches the conspirator." Xedford placed his hand on hers.

Shocked, Syn sat staring wordlessly into his crimson eyes. His large hands encircled hers. They felt strong and warm. Nervous bats took to the air inside her stomach.

"You'd make an excellent Nighterrian, Syn," he said with his hypnotizing drawl. He reached a hand to her cheek. She could smell his scent of oil and leather over the sea breeze as he leaned in close.

"I-I'll do my best," she said.

"I know you will. There's something about you, you know…" He leaned forward until their faces were only inches apart. "Something powerful… but smothered by your affliction."

Syn lost the ability to form words. She thought she might float out of the boat at his touch. She felt drawn to him like the powerful pull of a portal.

Xedford leaned in and kissed her.

Syn tumbled on waves of confusion and desire as she kissed him back. The pounding of her heart drummed so loud she was sure he could hear it. He pulled her into his arms until she was nearly sitting on his lap. She embraced the rough scratch of his beard and met the caress of his lips in time with her own. His tongue tasted of a hunger she wanted to satiate. She reached her hands up and tangled her fingers in his hair and the tie of his bandana.

Xedford pulled away to break off the kiss. Syn stared at him in breathless surrender. He smiled and traced his fingers around her face. "I apologize if that was a bit… unexpected."

Syn smiled back at him, still trying to catch her breath. She returned to her seat on the bench in an awkward retreat. Her body felt flushed with desire, but her practical senses screamed questions at her.

"I suppose I should take you back to your camp before we get too, uh, carried away." He winked.

Syn gave him a bashful smile, but inside she felt at odds with herself. What would have happened if they continued? Her mouth still tingled from where his lips met hers. The tingling bespoke her temptation, but how could that be? It wasn't like her to let impulse dictate her actions. Her mind teetered back and forth from desire to self-reproach. Would she have let him continue? No, no, she wouldn't. But a secret part of her whispered, *maybe.*

Xedford plucked up the ores and began rowing. Syn tried to focus on the revelation of everything he uncovered before the kiss.

She cleared her throat. "How do I discreetly get in touch with you if I uncover something about the convert?"

"Don't worry, I'll find you after tomorrow's trial," he said as he rowed.

Syn's stomach lurched. She had nearly forgotten the trial loomed so near.

"I know it's only a short slice of time, but the smallest lead could help," Xedford said. "The next trial might even weed out whomever this conspirator is, but we can't count on that."

"I'll find out what I can between now and then," she promised.

Xedford smiled and rowed the skiff in easy silence, a contrast to the storm roaring inside Syn. Could he really grant her a Hal'point if she uncovered the conspirator? And what of Drekton? Were her suspicions genuine or a product of paranoid conjecture?

And what about that kiss?

Too many questions swirled around in her head while the replayed memory of Xedford's kiss invaded her every thought. She hardly even noticed when they made it back to the beach. The skiff bumped up against the rocky shore, knocking Syn from her distant thoughts. She turned her attention to Xedford and smiled, trying not to stare at his lips. He certainly was ruggedly handsome, but she couldn't let herself get caught ogling at him.

"Thank you for answering my questions." She moved to climb from the boat.

Xedford grabbed her by the wrist. Syn's breath quickened at his touch. "You still owe me an answer you know, about your affliction. One day I hope you feel comfortable enough to tell me all about it."

"Maybe one day."

Xedford seemed to accept her flimsy promise. "Tread real careful now, both during the trial and while trying to sniff out the conspirator. I'd hate to put you in more danger than you already are."

"I'll be careful," she said.

Xedford pulled her in. She shivered with pleasure as he whispered into her ear, his voice dripping with promises, "I can't wait to fix you."

30
KISS

"**A**nd you think this conspirator is Drekton?" Relia asked.

Syn had considered keeping the information she learned from Xedford a secret, but Relia pestered her until she spilled all the details. Afterall, an added pair of eyes might help find the convert faster. However, Syn pointedly left out the part with the kiss and Xedford's promise of handing Syn a Hal'point if she uncovered the conspirator.

"You saw the blue vials at his camp," Syn said. "What else could they be but feathered serpent venom?"

"I figure it could be a number of things." Relia leaned in from her position in Syn's tree. She sat straddling a branch and toying with Syn's hanging trinkets. "There are plenty of elixirs and such peddled all over Interterra. They're always promising overnight cures to this and that. Most of them are grunt piss in a bottle, but they ain't poisonous. What makes you so sure it's him?"

"I just have a feeling."

Relia turned Gregory in her hands, trying to observe her

reflection in his dented surface. "You got a feeling of hatred, that's for sure."

Syn threw Relia a sour look. She expected her to be excited over the prospect of espionage.

"Hey, I ain't saying you shouldn't hate him. In fact, if I were you, I might have killed him already." Relia lost interest in Gregory. She grabbed Anna, opening and closing her crooked lid. "I hear you talking to these things, do they talk back to you in that haunted head of yours?"

"No, they don't talk back, that's the point." She rolled her eyes and returned to the problem at hand. "I promised Xedford I'd try and get him some answers by tomorrow night."

"Tomorrow night? I think you're forgetting this little thing, what's it called? Oh, that's right, the second trial!" Relia let go of Anna and moved to reach for the golden coin.

Syn caught her by the wrist before she could grab it. "Are you saying you don't want to help me?" She released Relia's hand.

Relia frowned. "Now don't go getting all dramatic on me. Of course I want to help. I just don't think now is the best time to go snooping around, stirring up trouble. This next trial is gonna be full to the brim with backstabbing. If they think you're some kind of snitch, it will be incentive enough for them to go after you."

Syn said nothing as she pondered her resolve. "Fine," she seceded, at least for the time being. "In that case, we should get some sleep."

"Right." Relia swung from the branch to her own tree.

Syn settled in her hammock and stared up at her friends twisting from their cords.

"Hey," Relia whispered. "We're teaming up for the trial tomorrow, right?"

"Sure." Syn knew it would be suicide to go it alone, but for as many times as Relia proved herself trustworthy, Syn still had her doubts.

Relia told Syn goodnight. Syn closed her eyes and let thoughts of Xedford's promise echo back to her as she drifted in and out of a troubled sleep.

SYN WOKE WITH A START WHEN SOMETHING HIT HER HEAD. IN HER LAP she found the small rock that had pegged her forehead.

She looked over the edge of her hammock, but no one lurked in the water at the base of her tree. She continued to scan up the beach, past the rocks and driftwood, to the red dirt. She blinked once, then twice. Written in the damp dirt were the words, *TRUST NO ONE*.

A figure stood in the shadows. Terrifying familiarity paralyzed her at the uncanny impression. Syn saw *herself* standing on the beach.

It couldn't be. Syn rubbed her eyes. The apparition was gone.

She looked to Relia snoring in the tree next to her. When she turned back to the beach, the words had disappeared as well. Either the waves had swept them away, or they were never there at all.

"Just a half-waking dream, Syn," she told herself as she settled back in her hammock.

Dream or not, the vision rattled her. She lay awake and alert, unable to return to sleep. Without a watch, it was unclear what hour it was, but the rest of the trial grounds seemed quiet, indicating it was still the slumber hours.

She tossed and turned in her hammock, trying to find sleep —or at least a peaceful state of mind. Her thoughts wore over and over the possibilities of what lay ahead but, like the inevitable change of the seasons, her thoughts transitioned to Xedford. She touched a finger to her lips as she recalled his kiss.

I can't wait to fix you.

Syn longed for her cure, but she found thoughts of Xedford troubling. He stirred something inside her that she couldn't face. What if she failed him in the search for the convert? *What if he hadn't stopped that kiss?* As if in response, her mind landed on a memory of another kiss. Her first kiss.

It wasn't long after Syn's brush with near death in the frozen woods at the age of ten. For months afterward she had shouldered the blows of the other children's teasing and name-calling. Instead of fading from their thoughts, their revulsion for her cowardice only grew more intense as time wore on. It probably didn't help that, around this time, Syn had taken up collecting broken treasures and talking to them as her friends.

She remembered the weight of the dull, wooden sword in her grasp as she practiced the battle drills alongside the twelve other kids her age. Block, duck, lunge, strike. Block, duck, lunge, strike. Her muscles ached, and she was glad when the instructor was called off to attend to a matter at home.

"Keep practicing your drills. I'll be back shortly," he said before racing off.

As soon as he was out of sight, Syn dropped her fighting stance and rested on her wooden sword. The other children did the same. All but Drekton who continued with the drill, slicing and ducking with speed and skill beyond his years. Drekton the Dutiful. Syn watched him practice, doing her best to ignore the cruel whispers taking place behind her back when an icy snowball smacked her in the face. Laughter burned her ears as she wiped the snow away only to catch another to the back of her head.

"Oh no, *snow!*" A bug-eyed girl named Varmah clapped her hands to her cheeks in mock fear. "Are you going to go screaming into the woods now?"

Syn tried to ignore her, but another snowball pelted her in the mouth. Syn turned to find Varmah's twin brother, Vedder, packing another snowball.

"Our dad nearly lost a toe to the cold while he was searching for you!" Vedder launched another chunk of snow at Syn, but this time she was ready for it. She sliced it with her wooden sword before it hit.

"Coward!"

"Freak!"

Snow came flying at her from all directions. She did her best to block them with her sword, but they soon over-whelmed her dull blade and her juvenile skill. Another snow-ball smashed her in the face and this one had rocks in it that cut her lip.

"Stop!" Syn yelled, but this only egged them on. More rock-filled snowballs came flying. "Stop or I'll tell on you!"

"Who are you going to tell, Syn? Those sticks you talk to?" Varmah said, giving up on the snowballs and striking Syn in the side with her wooden sword.

Vedder began the chant, "Syn-the-Insane! Syn-the-Insane!"

Vedder and Varmah took turns swinging their practice blades at her. Syn did her best to defend against the twins with the iron tang of blood in her mouth. Soon, however, they over-whelmed her. More kids took up the chant, "Syn-the-Insane!" and drew their weapons on her.

Vedder swept Syn's legs out from under her with one powerful swipe. The practice blade fell from Syn's grasp as she hit the ground. The wind knocked out of her lungs with the force of her fall. She struggled to gasp a breath. Varmah stood over Syn and raised her sword. Syn panicked. She grappled for air that would not come. Curses chanted around her, and rocks showered down on her.

Varmah fell face first into the snow.

The chanting of "Syn-the-Insane" ceased as the collective stares of the children turned to where Drekton stood behind Varmah. He held his practice sword poised incriminatingly above his head.

Finally, Syn gasped a lung full of air. She saw Vedder run in to avenge his sister. Syn kicked out her foot just in time to trip him, sending him sprawling into the snow.

The world erupted into a frenzy of flying wooden swords and punches. She found a hand in the chaos that helped her to her feet. Drekton defended against the blows of the rest of children as he pulled Syn along.

Hand in hand, they raced through the snow out of the practice grounds. They weaved in between the huts of the Outskirts to outrun the mob of children. Into the fifth ring of the village, Syn took the lead. She knew every good hiding spot in the village. She pulled Drekton into a wood barn where they shimmed in between piles of logs. They reached the dark corner she had last used to recover from her haunting and leaned against the stacks of wood to catch their breath.

By the time their breathing slowed, they were still hand in hand.

Together they waited in the dark. Syn wiped the blood from her lip and searched for the proper words of thanks. She came up empty. How could she possibly put into words the full weight of her gratitude? First, he saved her life by finding her in the woods, then he saved her from what would have been a devastating beating. He probably also caught some painful blows in the process. Worse, his show of gallantry would now have earned him the scorn of his peers.

"I think they're gone," Drekton said.

"Oh... we should probably go then," Syn said, though she didn't want to leave.

"My mother will be looking for me." He moved to slide out from the stacks of wood.

"Wait." Syn stayed rooted in place and tightened her grip on his hand.

He turned back to her. In the dark, all she could see were the whites of his eyes. Without the proper words to thank him, she had only one idea left. Before allowing herself to reconsider, she leaned forward and kissed him. Due to the dark, her aim was slightly off. She ended up kissing him more on the side of the mouth but that seemed okay.

When she pulled away, they stood in awkward in silence. Syn's pulse pounded like ceremonial drums. She counted her heartbeats as she waited for him to react. *One, two, three—idiot, why did I do that?—four, five, six.*

Her fear ended as a sliver of darkness parted with the white of Drekton's smile. He squeezed her hand and they stared at each other as time wandered away. They shared no other words or kisses; they simply stood there in the dark, happy to be in each other's presence.

The reminiscence of her first kiss, as clumsy and awkward as it was, remained a coveted memory. Syn let it fade away from her mind's eye as she lay swaying in her tree, searching for sleep in the scorching night.

A heavy cloud of sorrow rained through her chest at the thought of her childhood friend. The Drekton she knew now was but a ghost of the boy she once held dear. But could he really have fallen so far as to ally himself with the outlaws?

Unable to sleep, she watched the black waves crash and pondered her options. She decided there stood no guarantee that she would succeed in the coming trial. A part of her knew she would fail. But if she survived, perhaps the information she gleaned would be enough to earn her an exception to the rules—at least in Xedford's eyes.

Her resolve hardened as the hours dragged on. "I need to know," she said to her friends hanging above her.

Without Relia's support, she would have to face her mission alone. There remained a heavy chance that she could die during the trial tomorrow. If she did, she at least wanted to uncover Drekton's secrets. She owed it to her childhood self to know the truth about the boy she once kissed in the dark.

31
CONFRONTATION

Syn kept to the shadows as she sidled along the side of the Rock of Reckoning. She kept her sights trained on the back of Drekton's head, her hand hovering over Elaine. He had his long, dark hair tied back and he sat sharpening his sword beside a small fire.

A growl thundered through the night from the second level of the Rock of Reckoning. Drekton looked up from his sword and Syn jumped back to hide herself behind a nearby tent. He glanced up at the Rock where the crew worked on stationing the beasts for the trial. After a moment, he returned to running the whetstone over his blade. Syn watched the dancing flames of the campfire light his dark features.

"And to think," she said to Elaine, "I was once dazzled by his square jaw and sharp eyes." Now she could only see him as a criminal.

Behind her, the screeches of monsters echoing off the wall of the Rock reminded her she needed to get on with it. Soon the second trial would start, and Syn would be out of time. She cursed herself for getting such a late start. After her fitful night of sleep, interrupted by the vision on the beach, she fell into a deep sleep for a few hours into the morning. When she woke, Relia was already absent from her tree. She left a stolen watch and note inviting Syn to come gamble with her on the beach along with a warning not to be late for the trial.

Syn clicked the pocket watch open. She thought it read 10:45, but she second guessed herself. Could it be 11:45? Relia had taught Syn how to read the time, but the many dials confused her. It was much simpler to discern the time by the position of the sun back in Garon. She missed the light of day and the predictable nature of its path across the sky.

When she looked up from her watch, she gave a start. The stump where Drekton had previously been sitting now stood vacant. "Shit storms." Syn found herself adopting Relia's curses. "Where did he go?" She stepped out from the cover of the tent to look around.

Hands grabbed her from behind. Before she could extract her blade, her attacker arrested her arms. A familiar voice sneered in her ear. "Why are you following me?"

"I know what you're plotting, and I want in," Syn said, just the way she had rehearsed.

Drekton didn't respond. He pulled Syn backward, dragging her past the campfire, and shoved her through the entrance to a tent. Syn stumbled in and realized it wasn't the same camp as the one she entered before with Relia. This one was smaller, but still big enough to stand up in.

"I thought I made it clear that I never wanted to see your face here again," Drekton said.

"I've come to join you and the Converts." She crossed her arms and glared at him in the hope of exuding confidence.

"Converts? What are you talking about?"

"I know you're with them. I saw the vials, Drekton, I know it's you."

"What vials?" His brow creased and Syn could read confusion behind his anger.

"The blue vials of feathered serpent venom I found at your camp."

"I've been hopping camps. I'm not responsible for what others leave behind in their tents."

"Come on, Drekton. I know you probably have a huge stash of them around here somewhere." She looked around the tent, but at a cursory glance found nothing incriminating.

"I have no idea what you're talking about."

"Oh, give up the act. I know it's what you gave to Ortha to poison Gordon with. You did good work, but Ortha's been compromised."

"You think I had a part in Gordon's death?" Drekton gave a bitter laugh. "This is insane, even for you."

Syn ignored the sting of the insult and pressed on with her act. "Now that Ortha is out of the picture, you'll need another hand to help you deliver the Hal'point to the outlaws, and I'm your only option."

Drekton stepped forward. "I don't know what it is you think that I've done, but don't you dare accuse me of working for outlaws." He spoke with a quiet voice teetering just on the edge of violence. "You think I have no honor? That I've abandoned the Legion?"

Syn took a step forward. "I think you're like me, and you realized the outlaws offer protection and more if we succeed."

They stared at each other in stalemate. This was not going the way Syn rehearsed it in her head, but she stood her ground. She waited for him to make the first move as the sound of monsters roared through the campground. She thought she could feel the ground tremble, but maybe that was just her nerves.

The cacophony of the coming trial stole the fury from

Drekton's eyes. He stared at her for a long moment and Syn watched the flame behind his eyes dwindle. Was that sorrow in his expression?

"I shouldn't have tried to sabotage you the way I did," he said. "I'm sorry. But this doesn't excuse what you're doing now."

Syn had no response. The last thing she expected from him was an apology. Perhaps the fear of death for the coming the trial softened him. Or, more likely, it was a ploy to distract her from her purpose. It was working. She let her anger flare in response.

"You're not sorry. Don't try to manipulate me, it's not going to work!"

Drekton shook his head and stepped back. "You don't understand, I shouldn't have shot at you or tied you up without showing my face, that was cowardly. I should have just confronted you when I first saw you here."

"You won't get rid of me with empty apologies." Syn felt her resolve crack. She had never seen him like this. He looked almost defeated by self-hated. She knew exactly what that felt like.

"Accept my apology or don't, but I'm sorry, Syn. I was angry, I still am. And I still hate you for what you did, but..." He looked away. "It's not what Rem would have wanted."

He's lying, it's all an act. Syn seized hold of her willpower and pressed on. If she could convince him that Ortha had tried to recruit her, maybe he would let her in.

"Don't play the innocent, good guy. I know you and Ortha have been stalking me from the beginning trying to recruit me. Well, job well done. I'm here now to prove myself."

"Recruit you?"

"Yes. When you tried to keep me from crossing the veil, and

all the threatening notes you left me. I'm here to prove myself worthy of the cause."

"All the threatening notes? What are you talking about? I left you one note. And I didn't even know you were here until I saw you at the first trial, so how could I have tried to keep you from crossing the veil?"

"Quit playing games, Drekton. Was it you or Ortha's idea to carve threats into my tree? Is that your way of trying to test me?"

"Have your senses frozen over? I've never carved anything into your tree. And who in the empty Abyss is this Ortha you keep talking about?"

Why would he confess to one note but not the other? Syn looked into his dark eyes and found honest confusion, but also fear. Something wasn't right.

The screech of beasts increased outside the tent.

"The trial is starting soon. I don't have time for this." Drekton turned as if to leave, but Syn caught him by the wrist.

"No. I won't let you go to the trial until you let me in on your plan."

"You think you can stop me?"

Shuddering shrieks rippled through the campground. Both Syn and Drekton stiffened as they listened. It wasn't the roars of the beasts from the Rock, but the screams of the ghost moths.

Someone had crossed the veil.

Distracted by the sound, Syn dropped her guard. Drekton took the opportunity to sweep her legs out from under her. Before she could recover, he knelt on her back.

"Let go of me!" She struggled as she felt him tie her wrists behind her back. No! Not again.

"I can't risk you going after me during the trial." He grabbed hold of her ankles and tied them to her wrists. "I'm sorry, but this is for the best. Honor won't allow me to let you go through with the trials. You wouldn't survive the next trial anyway. At least this way you'll live."

Drekton proved his skill as a practiced hunter. Within seconds Syn laid on her stomach with her face in the dirt, hogtied and unable to move. Drekton shouldered his bow and quiver of arrows and made for the door of the tent.

"You can't do this!" she yelled.

He turned over his shoulder and, for a moment, he was the boy she kissed in the dark, her savior in the woods. His heavy brown eyes bespoke earnest sincerity as he said, "The crew will find you after the trial. Go home, your family needs you."

The unmistakable blast of a three-barrel boomed its starting call. Drekton raced from the tent. The trial had officially begun.

"No!" she screamed after Drekton. "Come back!"

She heard footfalls and shouts of other competitors as the trial began. She struggled in her restraints, but her effort only tightened the ropes binding her hands and feet. Shouts of competitors sounded outside the tent. The clash of metal and screams of pain joined the roars of the beasts as the trial commenced without her.

"Help!" Syn yelled, though she knew it was useless. As if her voice could be heard over the battle of the trial, as if anyone would come rescue her. "Help!" It was hopeless.

Syn laid her head down in the dirt. "Help..."

No one was coming. She had failed. And without uncovering any proof of Drekton's subversion, any prospect of amnesty remained crushed alongside her chance of finishing the trial. She laid there, helpless, listening to the battle just out of reach.

"Blazing shit sticks!"

Syn turned her head to see the most magnificent sight in all the world. "Relia!"

Relia sported a swollen eye and a bloody lip along with an expression screwed up in concern as she entered the tent. She slipped in and cut Syn free.

"A mountain of capable allies and I, of course, team up with the one who goes gets herself tied up before the trial begins!"

Syn burst free from her bindings and leapt to her feet. "Thank you."

"Yeah, yeah, it's Relia to the rescue again. I expect a basket of fruit delivered to my tree later. But right now, we gotta catch up to the trial!" She grabbed Syn by the arm and ran out of the tent.

Syn ran beside her. They skirted around tents along the perimeter of the Rock and skidded to a stop at the front face of the Rock of Reckoning. Syn's heart withered in despair.

A huge, newly erected ramp sloped from the campground up to the wide ledge on second tier of the rock. On the underside of the ramp, crisscrossing scaffolding held the wooden structure together and wheels at the bottom showed how the crew installed it so quick. All they had to do was roll it into place just before the trial.

It was a truly horrifying marvel. The gangway contained chained beasts of differing sizes. They shrieked and hissed at the competitors gathered near the bottom of the ramp. Syn could see the hairy textures and leathery wings of the beasts clawing at the wooden ramp near the bottom, but the monstrosities near the top remained lost to the shadows. She could only make out their outlines. Over the sound of roars, Syn could hear the clatter of thick iron chains that anchored them to a spot where they couldn't eat each other.

"We're never going to make it," Syn said.

The ramp's impenetrability stared back at her. Hungry creatures snapped their rabid jaws toward competitors trying to make their way up the ramp to the second tier of the Rock. The farther up the ramp, the longer the chains holding the vicious creatures at bay. *No wonder the captain called it a gauntlet.*

"But we got something nobody else has." Relia pulled a glass jar from her pocket and shook it toward Syn. Small, white tablets filled the inside.

"What is that?"

"It's what I just spent the past hour gambling to win." Relia slipped a pack off her shoulder that Syn hadn't noticed she carried. She opened the flap to a rotting stench. Inside sat a huge chunk of raw meat too many days past its expiration. Relia tucked the jar beside it, then slung the pack back over her shoulder.

"How is that supposed to help us?" Syn asked.

"Simple, you'll see."

She didn't waste time questioning further. Syn motioned to the gauntlet. "How are we ever going to get up there?"

Their late start would make crossing nearly impossible. Almost half the competitors already stood at the top of the gangway defending the entrance to the second tier. Shouts and clanks of metal echoed in the night as the competitors fought, not just monsters, but other competitors.

"That alliance there is big enough to fill a small raid." Syn pointed to the group at the top of the gangway. "And it looks like they teamed up to keep anyone else from making it up to the tier."

"They'll likely be killing anybody who comes up the plank so they can split each of the prizes amongst themselves."

"But what are those others doing just standing there?" The other half of the competitors appeared to have an alternate strategy. A mass of teenagers stood at the bottom of the plank. They looked almost bored staring up at the top of the ramp as they waited with steel in hand.

"That's obvious," Relia said. "Their plan is to murder whoever returns down the gauntlet and steal their prize before they make it to the campground, the motherless barbarians. I knew this would be a bloodbath."

"This is hopeless. Even if we fight our way past the gang defending the entrance to the tier and kill a beast, we'll never make it past the group waiting at the bottom to rob us of our prize."

Relia pulled her sword from her belt. "That's true and all, but we've got no other choice but to fight." She stepped forward with determination.

"Wait." Syn scanned the Rock. "What if we don't enter through the gauntlet?"

"My apologies, I didn't reckon you could fly."

"No, the crew has been stationing the beasts up on the second tier for hours, but they didn't install the gauntlet until a few minutes ago. There must be another way up." She recalled what she noticed about the Rock when she stood on the dock at the end of the first trial. "There are stairs carved into the back of the Rock from the sea!"

Relia looked to Syn smiled with mischievous delight. "You wily genius. But how do we get over there? We'll be nothing but supper for the water demons if we try and swim."

Syn surveyed the rough texture of the rock wall and the surrounding beach. It was her turn to smile. "Simple, you'll see."

They took off running toward the beach.

32
MONSTERS

Black water licked over the top of Syn's boots as she stood balancing on a log barely large enough to keep her and Relia afloat. The pair drifted along with the log, mostly submerged in the brackish sea. It was the biggest piece of driftwood they could find in a frenzied search of the beach. They figured it would do, but one wrong move would send them both into the perilous water. Progress came slowly as they clung to the rock wall and used it to pull themselves around the perimeter of the Rock. Any time they wobbled on the undulating waves they would have to stop and hold onto the wall to catch their balance.

Something splashed beside Syn. She looked over her shoulder to make sure it wasn't Relia falling into the water.

"Piss-drinking water demons," Relia cursed at the water.

"They must be drawn to the smell of that rotting chunk of meat in your pack."

Syn wiped her hand on her trousers to dry the sweat before reaching for another handhold on the wall. She tried her best to grip the wall, but the surface of the rock had grown smoother the farther they went. Their advancement stalled as the water-beaten rock provided little to grip onto.

The clamor of battle bounced off the water and amplified the sound of the trials above them. It cut at Syn's patience. She felt as if they had been at it for hours. Syn's fingers were raw and cut from holding onto the wall. Their tedious progress around the Rock made her fear they might be too late once they reached the tier. The growls and shrieks of beasts still rumbled above them, proving that some of them were still alive, but it sounded like less than before. The curvature of the rock formation made it impossible to see how much further they had to go.

"Do you think anyone has stolen a prize yet?" Syn asked.

"Don't worry yourself about that, just keep going." Relia continued to scan the water for threats while she helped pull their raft along.

Syn continued to worry, however, as they made careful progress. One misplaced grab and it would all be over. She caught the glint of white teeth. A wolf-sized mass leapt from the water. She retracted her foot just in time for its piranha jaws to snap shut in a narrow miss. Its slick body bounced off the side of the wall and splashed back into the water. The shock sent Syn teetering to the side. She nearly fell into the sea, but Relia caught her and shoved her back on balance.

"Hurry!" Relia yelled.

Syn clawed at the wall. The beast was almost bigger than the log they perched on. She didn't look over, but she could feel the current of the water change with the demon circling back around. Snapping jaws and splashing sounded all around them.

"There's more!" Cornered against the wall and floating on a tiny log, they didn't stand a chance.

"Go! Go! Go!"

Syn scrabbled. She pulled them along, hand over hand as ribbed fins of varying sizes rose from the water. How many? Syn didn't look over her shoulder to check. She scraped her hands as she tried to keep balance and hasten their escape. She could feel Relia slash at them and wobble their piece of driftwood.

"There's too many!" Relia said.

On the verge of giving up and suggesting they climb up and cling onto the wall, Syn spotted the stairs. "We made it!"

She grabbed the wall, and with one last desperate shove she pushed them over to the stairs carved into the Rock. Syn grabbed hold of the ledge and hauled herself up to the third stair. Relia followed behind and pushed off the log, but it shot backwards in the water. Syn grabbed her wrist and helped swing her momentum forward to catch the edge of the second stair. With Syn's help, she clambered up. They perched on the huge stairs and watched the log drift away.

"There goes our way back." Syn looked to Relia who let out a colorful curse.

They stood and sized up the crooked set of stairs. The steps disappeared up into the night, hiding whatever beast lie in wait at the top. After catching her breath, Syn used all four limbs to climb up the gigantic steps. The rattle of chains and the hungry calls of the monsters grew louder the farther they traveled.

Relia grabbed Syn by the back of her shirt and yanked her backward. A burst of fire exploded just past Syn's face, singeing the small hairs of her eyebrows. When the flames burned away, she turned to her left to find the source of the eruption. A grotesque porcupine reared up on its back legs. The thing was the size and shape of a bear but without fur. Its naked, pink skin contained sharp needle-like spikes extending over its body.

Syn scrambled up to the flat ground of the tier with Relia in tow. The spiked beast roared and lunged after them. The iron collar around its neck stopped it short and its guttural cry choked off in a hacking cough. They ran as the beast belched another burst of flames. Syn could feel the heat of it explode behind her as they ducked against the side of the Rock for cover.

Relia looked to Syn with wide eyes. Together they exchanged a silent agreement: *Not that one.* They moved on to find a different beast—hopefully one that didn't breathe fire. Once they reached a safe distance away from the fire-spitting porcupine, they spared a moment to catch their breath.

Relia crouched and took the pack off her shoulder to prepare the poisoned meat while Syn took stock of their surroundings. She could hear the growls and shrieks of other beasts just around the bend but couldn't see them.

Every few paces along the rock wall, wooden doors of varying sizes stood out against the rough red stone of the second tier. No handles extended from the wooden doors blocking up the circular holes. The one beside them came up to Syn's waist. Perhaps it could provide an escape route. Syn kicked at it, but it didn't budge.

Relia looked over her shoulder at Syn while she shoved the white tablets into the wet chunk of meat. "What are you doing?"

"What do you think are these for?" Syn leaned her ear against the door but heard nothing on the other side.

"No idea." Relia handed Syn the empty pack. She stood from her crouch with bait in one hand and a sword in the other. "Let's go."

Syn drew her own sword and stepped beside Relia. They inched their way forward while keeping to the side of the Rock for cover. When they rounded the bend, they found a reddish lizard-like beast huddled against the wall about ten paces away. It was a smaller monster, roughly six feet long from head to tail. The drooping jowls of its face formed a mane of pendulous skin around its neck. The texture of its body resembled rough rock and if it weren't for the sixteen clawed arms protruding from the sides of its belly, it could have blended in with the stone. It made no movement and the set of eyes on either side of its head remained closed as they shuffled forward.

"Is it dead?" Syn whispered.

"I don't think—"

The beast's head suddenly appeared right in front of them. Its teeth snapped within inches of Relia's face. She hit the ground to avoid its jaws.

How was that possible? The beast was ten paces away. Syn dragged Relia backward as she watched the head of the monster retreat. It pulled its face back and Syn realized how it covered the distance in an instant. The body stayed where it was, but its head moved on an extendable neck that stretched out the loose folds of skin around its face.

"Loaded dice!" Relia climbed to her feet. "Where are they getting these things from?"

The beast's head swayed from its deceptively small body and stared them down with a look that promised slaughter.

"What *is* it?" Syn asked.

Relia didn't get to answer as the beast thrust its head out at them again. Syn slashed at its neck with her blade, but the tough skin rejected the blow like a suit of armor. She brought her sword up to chop at it again, but she knew she was too late. It opened its mouth and lunged in for Relia. Syn's blade harmlessly glanced off its neck just as rows of sharp teeth closed around something with a wet crunch.

No! Syn was sure it ripped Relia's throat wide open but

when the beast darted back, Relia stood with her neck intact. Syn looked her up and down to ensure she was whole. Syn found no blood or gaping wounds, only Relia standing empty-handed.

Syn whipped her attention back to the beast in time to see it swallow the poisoned chunk of meat in one revolting bite. The piece of flesh traveled in a bulbous lump down the creature's long throat as it retracted its head. Thankfully, the monster didn't seem to care that the meat was weeks past its expiration.

"Now what?" Syn asked without removing her eyes from the monster.

"Now we wait." Relia plucked up her sword she had dropped in the scuffle.

They retreated out of the beast's reach and stood on edge of the second tier waiting for the thing to strike or fall over dead. The sound of other monsters' screams filled the night and made Syn's pulse roar like a rushing river as she waited and stared. The beast stared back, its hunger paused but not satiated.

"How long is it supposed to take?" Syn asked.

"Damned if I know. Believe it or not, this is my first time poisoning some freakish rock fiend with a bunch of ale tablets."

"Ale tablets? I thought you said it was poison?"

"Yeah, if you eat them without—"

Movement in the dark. Two figures approached out of the shadows with weapons held high.

"Clear on out!" Relia called. "This one here's ours." She nodded to the sixteen-legged creature. The beast turned its vicious gaze toward the newcomers.

"It don't look dead," said a boy with a broken nose. Syn

recognized him as the gang leader Relia had scared off with her act of insanity.

"Well, look who it is," said the second kid. Blood dripped from his busted lip when he smiled. "It's the insane-o twins!"

"This here beast is fair game if you ask me." The broken-nosed leader nodded to the rock fiend.

A third and fourth shape appeared from around the bend. The new arrivals stepped up next to their teammates. They looked like a pair of brothers. Both wore blood splatters and bled from various wounds while their eyes bore the same sanguine ferocity of their bloody clothing. Syn tried to guess at the amount of bloodshed the gang must have committed to get to the back of the tier. Was the blood on their clothes more human or beast?

"We don't want to fight you," Syn said. "There's another beast back that way." She nodded behind her where they passed the flame-spitting monster.

One of the brothers smirked and prowled forward. "Look, Charmen. A couple of girls think they're gonna tell us what to do."

"We don't take orders from nobody, especially not the likes of you," said the brother named Charmen. "Let me show you how it works." He charged at Syn.

Syn met his attack with a parried slice. They crossed swords, but the power of his strike pushed her back. She stumbled and caught the ground with one hand, just barely blocking the next blow that sliced down at her. She could sense two of the boys attacking the monster while Relia engaged the fourth. She pushed off from the ground and jumped back from for another strike.

Charmen's next jab nicked her in the shoulder. Syn gasped, not from the pain, but from the salivating lizard jaws that entered the fight. Charmen jumped over the extended neck of the beast to avoid its attack. The distraction gave Syn time to catch him off guard. She thrust toward him as the beast's neck retracted, but he was too quick. He knocked the blow away with a powerful block that nearly sent the sword from her grip.

Syn felt the edge of the tier beneath the back of her foot where the ground ended in a sheer cliff drop. She shuffled around to avoid being pushed over the edge, but each retreating step traveled her closer within range of the beast. Charmen dove in with a powerful slash. Syn blocked it poorly and his blade glanced off hers. A shallow cut sliced her cheek and one of her braids dropped to the ground. He lunged in again and she blocked, meeting his fiendish red eyes. She found no mercy in them.

A shadow sprung out of the corner of her vision. Syn dropped to the ground to dodge another head thrust from the beast. She rolled out of the way as the rocky face retreated. *Did it dump Charmen off the edge?*

A blade stabbed the ground within a breath of her face. *Nope.* She rolled again as Charmen's sword came down once more. Her training taught her the ground was the worst place to be. She needed to get up, but stabs rained down in quick succession and all she could do was roll out of the way.

She rolled again and her right foot felt the ground end. Panic jolted through her. With nowhere else to go, she looked up at her attacker and tried to raise her sword, though she knew it would be useless. He smiled then—an evil, hate-filled smile—as he raised his blade above his head.

The world exploded.

33
GUTS

Blood ripped through the air along with rotten guts and sharp chunks of bone. White foam, turned pink by blood, burst into the night and scattered pieces of rock-colored flesh.

Distracted by the gory eruption, Charmen stalled his swing. The split second was all Syn needed to recover and strike. She kicked out at his feet just as he returned to deliver the killing strike. He tripped and fell, the swing of his sword carrying him forward. Syn tucked into a ball and rolled out of the way as he tumbled off the edge of the cliff.

A scream and a splash. Silence.

I've killed someone. She peeked over the edge. She didn't have time to feel the weight of it. "Relia!" Syn crawled her feet and left the edge of the cliff.

The scene she found was a putrid disaster. The beast's insides lay open in a frothing mess of blood and guts. Its limbs and organs—many of them now disassembled—lie strewn across the ground.

"Relia!" Syn picked through the scattered carcass that

continued to fizz from the ingested ale tablets. She heard a grunt off to her left and ran toward it. The severed head and neck of the beast sat beside a body face-down in the dirt. A sword stood skewered through the person's back with the bloody tip pointed toward the sky.

"No!" Syn jumped over the beast's head and rolled the body over.

It was the ringleader with the broken nose. Syn gasped in relief. She rolled the body to the side to reveal Relia trapped beneath the weight of the dead boy.

"I told you it would work." Relia smiled her toothy grin.

"I'm sorry I ever doubted you." Syn helped her to her feet.

Relia wiped a trickle of blood from her brow and yanked her sword from the dead body. She returned it to its sheath and put her hands on her hips. "Well, I reckon we ought to start the search."

Search? Syn had nearly forgotten the trial's task. "Right, the key."

The pair held their breath and began rooting around in the bloody sinew and gurgling foam. Syn dragged her hands through the sloppy gore in a hurry. She found the bodies of the two other boys but otherwise came up empty-handed.

"What if the key was flung over the edge when the thing exploded?" Syn asked.

"Shh, the Fates will hear you! Don't tempt 'em." Relia tossed a clawed limb over her shoulder.

Syn braved the stench of the putrid innards and dug her hands further into the foaming mush. She touched something cold and hard and hurried to wrestle a large metal chest from beneath the wrecked carcass.

"I found the box."

"Good, now we just gotta find the..." Relia stopped to listen.

Over the distant sounds of fighting and beastly rumbling, voices sounded from around the corner. Syn exchanged a nervous look with Relia and together they dug in a frantic attempt to locate the key before more trouble arrived.

"I got it!" Relia held a slimy key into the air.

Syn pushed the box toward her. Relia's hands shook as she struggled to undo the lock; her hands kept slipping in the goo. She unlocked it on her third attempt. Relia ripped open the lid and seized the prize just as company rounded the corner.

Quick as a lightning strike, Relia shoved the silvery object into the empty pack on Syn's back. Too occupied with the coming trouble, Syn didn't get to see what it was, but it weighed heavy on her back.

"What in damnation done happened to this thing?" A kid with a high-pitched twang and a bloody bandage tied over his left eye surveyed the mess until his one good eye landed on Syn and Relia.

A bloodied group followed behind him carrying weapons and looking feral. Syn lost count after the seventh one appeared. Desperation drowned her heart to the soupy pit of her stomach. They were too many. In the dark, they may not have seen Relia slip the prize in Syn's pack, but they would soon figure it out.

"Oy, how did you two scrawny bitches get up here?" said one boy. Syn watched his eyes fall on the open box at Relia's feet.

"Run," Relia said.

Syn didn't need a second nudge. She took off toward the way leading to the stairs. Shouts and footfalls followed them as the ruthless alliance hunted them down. Syn willed her legs to carry her faster as Relia kept up pace beside her. She could hear the murder party closing in. Any moment she'd feel the icy stab of metal penetrate her back. Lost in fear, she nearly ran headlong into the spiked beast that jumped into their path. Syn skidded to a stop. The monster let loose a billow of flames.

Syn ducked, instinctively grabbing Relia by the arm to make sure she missed the scorching fire. They huddled on the ground as the beast reared up in its hind legs and staggered forward. A broken chain dangled from its neck.

"It's off its leash!" Relia yelled.

The monster roared at the mob of pursuers and the gang jumped a step back at the sight of the formidable beast. Syn estimated their distance from the stairs and realized they weren't nearly close enough to make a run for it past the porcupine beast. Trapped between the fire breathing monster and a mob of killers, Syn wasn't sure which was worse.

The beast growled and closed in. Syn looked to edge of the cliff. "Climb down!"

She ducked out of the way of the beast's swipe and rolled toward the edge. Relia followed suit and dodged away from the flames that burst into the air. They scrambled over the edge, breathing in ragged gasps, and struggling for purchase. Shrieks of pain and death met Syn's ears as she climbed down the sheer rock cliff. She told herself to focus only on finding the next hand hold and reaching her foot to the next tiny ledge.

They made a diagonal descent from the cliff edge down toward the front face of the Rock. Syn tried not to think about how much farther they would have to climb as sounds of battle increased up on the second level. She could only assume the clans of competitors had gone to war with each other over the prizes. Were these really the type of people needed to become Nighterrian? The more ruthless, the better?

It felt like they had been climbing for hours though she knew it must have been only a matter of minutes. Her fingers felt weak and her grip had begun to lose strength as they reached a small jutting section of rock halfway down the face. Together they clung to it and paused for a brief rest.

Syn looked down toward the water, dread wringing out her guts. Without a form of raft, they would still have to rock climb their way around the entire rock formation to reach the ground.

"I don't know if my grip will hold the whole way back to the beach," Relia said.

"It will have to." Syn was thankful her years of tree climbing back home in Garon. "Besides, we're almost there."

Relia shined an exasperated, yet hopeful look toward Syn, but then it was gone.

Relia shot her gaze up at the sound of fluttering from above. Syn followed her glance. A body fell from the cliff edge and tumbled toward them through the air. They didn't have time to move, it was right above them. All Syn could do was hold tight to the rock as body hit the protrusion they clung onto. The kick of its foot nearly ripped Syn free of her hold, but she managed to cling on. However, the weight of the body hit Relia square in the chest, knocking her off the rock.

A shrill cry lanced the air as Relia fell.

"No!" Syn screamed and looked down.

A splash announced Relia's arrival into demon infested waters below.

34
WOLF PELT

"Relia!" Syn clung to the wall and listened.

Splashing. *She's alive!* But she wouldn't survive long. Misery seized Syn's heart with an icy grip.

The weight of the prize in her back encouraged the selfish impulse that told her to keep going and not look back. She knew she could finish the trial. All she had to do was make the climb back to the beach and she'd be granted entrance into the final trial. She looked around the bend of rock and could just barely see the trees of their camp.

So close.

"There's nothing I can do," Syn said to Elaine. "I have to keep going."

Guilt ricocheted through her conscience as she considered leaving Relia to die. How many times had Relia come to save her? She had already left Relia behind once. The memory battered her into submission, and she glanced below. The water churned with evidence of a fight.

"I can't leave her again," she said at last. She drew in a deep breath to gather her courage. If the trials were a test of ruthlessness, Syn had failed.

She pushed off the rock and let herself fall.

Her stomach dropped as the blackness of the water came rushing up toward her. She fought against the panic and ripped Elaine from her belt as she plunged into the water.

The cold bite of the sea hit her first. Then a fin smacked her in the side. A gasp of air. Splashing water. Where is Relia? Something slithered against Syn's leg. She kicked in blind panic. A slick, powerful body ripped at her clothing, pulling her underwater. Darkness. She couldn't see anything, but she felt a ribbed fin. With her free hand, she dug her nails in and pierce her fingers through the slimy webbing of the fin and held on. The water demon bucked as she stabbed—once, twice, three times. She let go when it stopped moving.

Syn came up for air and found Relia using the dead body of the boy who knocked her into the water as a shield against a pair of jaws.

"Fates divine!" Relia exclaimed when Syn crested the surface beside her.

Syn coughed up a mouthful of salty water. She stabbed the beast attacking Relia and her corpse-shield.

"You didn't think I'd leave you to die, did you?" Syn asked, as if she hadn't considered doing that very thing. The water demon she killed floated up to the surface next to her.

"Yeah, actually. I thought for sure I was a goner."

"We might still be."

A mountain of splashes announced a hoard of water creatures a few yards away. Syn shoved the carcass of the dead water demon toward the rising fins hoping they would take the easy meal. Relia did the same with her human shield.

Together they swam in a desperate dash for escape. Syn prayed to the Legion while she fought against the dark sea. The water stung her eyes, making it difficult to navigate. The weight of her pack dragged her down and slowed her pace.

Hope breathed its dangerous relief as she spotted the beach looming up ahead. But fins, and now tentacles, rose out the corner of her eye. They were closing in. Syn swam with Elaine in hand. She slashed out at anything that moved and sensed Relia do the same. Syn's vision filled with thick water and even thicker fear. Her foot touched something hard. A spike of terror peaked. She kicked at it only to connect with something else. Relia grabbed her arm as she flailed in the water. Syn nearly stabbed her by mistake.

"We're here, come on!" Relia pulled Syn up by the elbow.

Syn realized they had nearly made it to the beach. The thing she kicked was a rock, and she found she could stand up in the water. They sloshed through the rocks toward the shore.

"Wait!" Syn sheathed her dagger and stopped as she shrugged the pack off her back.

"There ain't time!" Relia kicked at snapping jaws and sliced a slithering tentacle.

Smaller creatures jumped at them from the shallows. Syn extracted the prize from her pack and recognized it as a three-barrel. She stomped on the fin of an attacking demon and dragged Relia toward land, making sure Relia grabbed hold of the three-barrel as they stepped onto dry ground.

They didn't stop once they reached the beach. They ran headlong through the campground, sharing hold of the prize. Fear retreated in place of triumph. Relia smiled her carnivore grin as they made it to the front side of the Rock of Reckoning where members of the crew stood with a handful of bloodied competitors. The two Nighterrians watching the ramp for finishes waved them over. They regarded Syn and Relia with confusion as the sopping wet girls pulled to a halt and presented their prize.

"Well, I'll be a virgin in a whorehouse... where in damnation did you two come from?" A Nighterrian with a gold tooth surveyed the girls' dripping clothing and their out of breath gasps as he accepted the three-barrel.

The Nighterrian beside him sipped a mug of ale and smirked with a lopsided grin. "Look at them, they swam!" He pounded Syn on the back in congratulations.

The two Nighterrians knocked their drinks together and broke into dumbfounded laughter. "Cheers," said the one with the gold tooth. "You scrappy gals just made it into the third trial." He pushed Syn and Relia toward the small crowd of bruised and bloodied finishers making their way toward a large tent near the underside of the gauntlet.

"We did it! Holy Fates in a pocket of fortune, we did it!" Relia linked arms with Syn. "Thanks for not leaving me behind."

"Of course." Syn smiled. "Just returning the favor."

Relia skipped along, leading Syn toward where the other finishers entered the inviting glow of the finisher's tent. Although she was covered in bruises and bleeding from the glancing bite of water demons, Syn felt like her feet hardly touched the ground as she floated on glory and fading adrenaline.

Syn scanned the line of finalists for Drekton. Her eyes fell instead on Xedford who stood beside a pack of fellow Nighterrians. Her heart pattered a fluttering rhythm. She smiled at him with pride, but when Xedford met her eyes, his expression remained grim. A pang of disquiet struck her. Was he not happy at her success? Syn extracted herself from Relia's linked arm before they reached the finisher's tent.

Xedford stepped forward from the gathered crew and opened his mouth to say something to Syn, but he was shoved aside.

"Is that her?" Captain Revvor pushed past Xedford and narrowed his feral gaze on Syn. He looked even worse than the previous night. Even in the dark, Syn could see tiny blue veins around his eyes. He appeared disheveled to the point of derangement.

"What's going..." Syn began, but the crowd of Nighterrians parted to make way for a man wearing a white wolf pelt. Her words disintegrated into ashes as she struggled to make sense of the apparition before her.

"Chief Groth?" It was all she could manage to utter through the veil of astonishment. The sight of him brought her back to Garon. Scalers screamed, or was that the beasts of the trial? Snow. Blood. Rem's dying stare.

"That's her," Groth said to the captain.

"Seize her," Revvor ordered. "She's under arrest."

PART FOUR
GHOSTS

35
PARALYZED

Every pair of eyes in the barbershop fell on Lektra's hiding spot. She ducked back behind the door for cover, but she knew it was too late. They had seen her.

"Who's there?" called the leader.

She heard the scrape of weapons pulled from scabbards. Footsteps approached. The window sat open at the back of the stockroom. She didn't think she could make it, but she had to try. She raced toward escape.

Her hands clasped the windowsill to the sound of shouts behind her. Half her body was out the window when she felt hands close around her ankles and yank her backward. She kicked and struggled, but strong arms overpowered her.

Lektra glanced up. The sight of her attacker made her stop fighting. Tanok caught her in a chokehold. Rage ran hot across his face.

"Tanok," she rasped as he tightened his arm around her throat.

"You shouldn't have come here," he said into her ear. He

used his teeth to rip the cork from a small vile. He shoved the vial into her mouth and tipped the contents down her throat as he released the chokehold.

Lektra coughed and tried to spit out the sour liquid, but it coated her throat as she gasped for breath. Tanok released her and she fell backward. Her limbs grew heavy. She tried to climb to her feet, but they felt numb, as if they didn't belong to her.

The paralyzing numbness staked its claim, and she collapsed into a heap on the floor. *Fight,* she told her body, but it refused to respond. Panic enveloped her. She stared—petrified and vulnerable—as Tanok and three of the men formed a circle around her.

"Good work, boy." The leader with the scar on his forehead nodded to Tanok.

Move. Move! Lektra pressed every ounce of concentration into willing her body to react. Still, she couldn't manage to even twitch her fingers. All she could do was blink her eyes as tears of betrayal formed.

One of the riders with a long, dusty beard leaned over Lektra. "Who is she? A spy?"

"She ain't one of Redd's spies. He'd never have hired a Surfacer," said another man.

"She's probably just a thief who happened upon the wrong place," Tanok said.

The leader ran a hand through his beard. "Either way, she's seen too much. Even if she's just a regular thief, we can't risk it."

"Why didn't you just kill her?" The long-bearded man looked to Tanok.

Lektra found her eyes were the only part of her still able to move. She swiveled them around in their sockets and flicked her gaze back and forth between her brother and the man suggesting her death.

"I thought she'd be useful." Tanok shrugged.

"We ought to kill her and be done with it."

"She'll be dead soon enough," Tanok said. "Why don't we make her a down payment for our arrangement?" He nodded to the Graver who stood beside the door to the stockroom.

The leader clapped Tanok on the shoulder. "A wise foresight." He looked to the Graver. "How's about this one as one of your test subjects?"

The red-robed body trader glared down at Lektra. The beads of his jewelry jingled as he leaned over her with a rotten-toothed smile. "We have enough test subjects. However, since we are spending much of our time on this experiment. It has not allowed us to procure our regular duties. What we require is revenue to continue work on the experiment."

"It's money you want then?"

"No, we don't need your coin. What we need is more like this one here." He nodded to Lektra. "Surfacers to carry on our work with the Legionites. They will grow suspicious if we suddenly cease our vocation."

Legionites? Lektra's mind raced with the mention of her people. What was going on? And why couldn't she bring her voice to scream? It was as if she were trapped in a nightmare where every attempt to run, fight, or shout become impossible.

"Consider her yours."

A gasp and moan from the other room cut the conversation short. Lektra had nearly forgotten about the man who shot himself with the Hal'point. The last two riders dragged the Skully under the arms and entered the crowded stockroom.

"He's alive," said the one with the dreadlocks.

"Barely," said the other man.

"How long will it take him to recover?" The leader looked to the Graver.

"It's unclear." The Graver tilted the bald man's face up to

examine him. "Our only other tester took several days to regain his strength."

"Several days? And you couldn't have mentioned that before?" Long-beard complained.

"It was not asked before."

"You rotten-tooth bast—"

The leader pressed a hand against Long-beard's chest. "That's enough, Duster." He turned to the Graver. "Is there anything else we ought to know about the Second Imbuing?"

A *second* imbuing! Lektra's bewilderment trumped her fear. *It's not possible.* Out the corner of her eyes she stared at the Skully. He looked like he would easily crumble to the floor if the two men didn't hold him up. Yet, his eyes fluttered open and close, and he moaned in pain, proof that he was still very much alive after a second Hallowed Point.

"We will let you know how our other experiment progresses," the Graver said.

The leader narrowed his eyes. "We'd also appreciate a measure of discretion on your part."

"Certainly. Discretion is all we know."

Dreadlocks spoke up. "How do we know you ain't gonna sell us out to the next highest bidder?"

"If you mean the Collector, you have no reason to worry. My intelligence tells me he has no knowledge of what you and Revvor have been up to. However, should he catch wind of our more..." The Graver traveled his gaze to the moaning Skully. "Clandestine experiments, I can assure you he could not whittle answers out of us. That is, if you continue to keep up your end of the bargain." He turned his unsettling stare down at Lektra.

She would have kicked him in the face, or at least squirmed under his gaze, but instead she just laid there defenseless as a lame calf.

"A deal is a deal," the leader agreed.

The Graver nodded. "I will require one of you to accompany me back to the Surface to meet with my colleagues and assure the agreement is kept."

"Fine. I'll go with you to the Surface." The leader turned to the rest of the posse. "Tanok, come load the girl up in the Graver's cart. The rest of you lie low, keep an eye on the experiment, and wait for my return."

"What about the captain? He'll be sore if we ain't back in time for commencement," said the one named Duster.

"Revvor can wait. First priority is to make sure our test subject here don't drop dead." He eyed the Skully with uncertainty. He then turned to the rest of the posse. "Barrels on, boys!"

Lektra watched the men leave the cramped stockroom and seek out their packs. Through the open door, she watched them switch out their light-colored shirts for black. Once changed, they removed silvery three-barrels from their packs and strapped them to their left wrists. *Nighterrians.* Lektra wanted to scream at the sacrilege. Was Tanok one too?

No. He retrieved no further weapons before he crouched down to scoop Lektra's limp body off the floor. He stared straight ahead without glancing down at her, as if she were a sack of potatoes. *Look at me!* She tried in vain to scream.

The leader attached his sacred weapon to his arm and tied a bandana over his scarred forehead. He strode out the door and held it open for Tanok. Lektra bounced along in Tanok's arms as they exited the barbershop.

Outside, the Graver led the way around the backside of the row of shops. Lektra searched for witnesses to help. A tall man hitching his grunt took notice of the Graver and paused to stare at him. *Help! Help me!* The plea could not escape Lektra's lips. It didn't matter. As soon as the man noticed the three-barrel strapped to the leader's wrist, he looked away and hurried about hitching his grunt.

Tanok looked to the Nighterrian. "Do you really think it can be done?"

"You having doubts? Even after what you just seen?"

"It's just…" Tanok flicked his eyes down at Lektra, then looked away. "A second Imbuing has never been accomplished. We know nothing of the lasting effects."

"Just because it's never been done before don't mean it's impossible. I reckon there simply never been the right person to go and do it," the leader reasoned.

"But the risks…"

"There is risk in everything we do out here, Tanok. It is our way of life. Yeah, we take risks, but we fix high rewards. It's all about weighing the risk verses the reward. The risk of doing a bad deal with the Gravers, well, that's worth the reward of finally prying ourselves free of Redd's stranglehold. With the second imbuing, we'll be free to build our own raid the way we want."

With her mind still whirling, Lektra struggled to fit the pieces into place. Redd the Collector's power extended far and wide along with his dreadful reputation. Many feared to speak his name without glancing over their shoulders. But the Nighterrians couldn't really be under his control… could they?

How did her brother, the honest and true Tanok Qu-Veldt, end up in a posse plotting to overthrow the most powerful outlaw in Interterra? The night shadowed him in a cloak of suspicion as he carried her through the town's back alley.

Do I even know you anymore, big brother?

The Nighterrian leader continued, "It's natural to be apprehensive. In fact, it's a good survival skill. But you needn't worry yourself. You've done well as an apprentice. After we learn to harness this new power here, you'll earn yourself a Hal'point and a place among us."

The Graver stopped in front of a small shack. Tanok stopped and Lektra watched the eerie man roll a pulling cart out into the night. The flaming starlight lit the cage filled with rotting body parts. The Graver opened the door to the cage and Tanok stepped forward.

No. You're not putting me in there!

Tanok bent through the door of the cage and maneuvered Lektra's body to fit inside. As he leaned over, he said, "I'm sorry, little sister."

The stench of rot rushed Lektra's senses. Her eyes filled with hot tears. *How dare you call me 'little sister' while you sell me off to the Gravers.*

"This was the only way to keep them from killing you on sight." Tanok tucked her legs in to fit through the door. "I just you need you to trust me." He closed the door to the cage and fussed with the latch long enough to whisper, "I won't let you die. I promise."

He turned and walked away.

The Nighterrian exchanged a few words with Tanok then said something to the Graver. Lektra couldn't hear past the screaming in her head. *Don't leave me! Tanok, don't leave me here!*

The Graver began to pull the cart. It drew her away from her brother. Lektra's vision blurred with tears, but she could still see Tanok stop and glance over his shoulder at her. Between the bars of the cage, Lektra thought she saw sorrow in his eyes. Could he be sincere about his promise? He gave her a single nod, as if in answer to her question. Then he turned and strode into the dark.

And away she rolled.

36
BRIG

Syn's captors shoved her into a prison cell on board the Nighterrian ship. One of the crew members locked her to the wall with her arms and feet spread wide like a star.

"Wait here," he said.

As if she could do anything else but wait. Anxiety thrummed a melody of distress and despair that rang through her tired body. Syn had given up on asking why she was under arrest. Her questions were met only with, "Ask the captain," by the two Nighterrians who dragged her onto a skiff and across the waves to the massive ship.

She watched the pair of men leave down the brig filled with empty cells. The lanterns lighting the narrow passage swayed with the nauseating churn of the water beneath them. The floorboards above her creaked and she could hear the mumble of voices above.

Her mind raced with the implication of Chief Groth's arrival. It seemed impossible that he would have ventured into Interterra. Why would he leave Garon? Had his hatred for her extended beyond her expectation? Had he been pursuing her all this time?

Shouted voices from the room above interrupted her march of questions.

"... and you think... trust you?" It sounded like the captain's voice.

"... matter of time... Collector... himself!" Was that Xedford? Syn pricked her ears but could still only make out every few words as Xedford's voice continued. "...break with... now! ... solidify our order."

A pause, then Revvor's voice again. "Xedford... remind you... last apprentice?"

Xedford said something unintelligible.

"It does! ... Surfacers... trouble ... girl you're grooming."

Whatever was said next was too quiet for Syn to hear. She strained against her chains and tried to listen but could only hear soft mumbles through the floorboards above. A door creaked open and slammed closed. Footsteps. Silence.

What was that all about? With the words "Surfacer" and "girl," the captain could only have meant Syn. Her gut clenched to think her arrest had brought Xedford strife. Everything she touched exploded into violent disaster she realized as she sat commiserating in the dark.

She had been unarmed during the arrest and felt the raw rub of loneliness without the comfort of her friend at her side. "How did I get here?" Syn asked her empty scabbard where Elaine normally sat.

Syn groaned and leaned her head back against the wall. If she stayed in the brig much longer, she thought she might be sick. The ship undulated on the waves while the thick air around her smelled of fish and mold. Her body ached from the nip of partial bites from the water demons during her and Relia's escape from the second trial. Could it really have been only a matter of hours ago? It felt like a year had passed since their fleeting moment of victory was squelched by Groth's arrival. How long would they keep her in the damp prison?

As if to punctuate her thought, a door squeaked on metal hinges at the end of the brig. Two figures emerged into the swaying light of the prison. Revvor produced the keys to the cell and unlocked the door.

When he stepped inside, Syn nearly gasped. The captain looked horrific. Blue veins clawed up the side of his neck in a network of pulsing spider limbs. His eyes were bloodshot and rimmed with redness that gave him the appearance of madness.

Chief Groth stepped into the cell behind the feral captain. They impaled Syn with their combined glares. Despite her hunger for answers, Syn thought it best not to speak first.

The captain kept his eyes on Syn as he spoke to Groth. "You ought to know, Chief Groth, that we don't just up and allow deserters to enter the trials. This was a real lousy screw up on our part."

"You are not at fault in any way, Captain Revvor," Groth said, stern and grim as always. Calm abhorrence laid within his eyes.

"Deserter? What are you talking about?" Syn asked.

Captain Revvor unfolded a piece of paper and read. "Syndrah Tri-Garon, you are guilty of fleeing punishment for your crimes, you—"

"I didn't flee. I came here to redeem myself, to win back my honor."

"You deserted!" Groth yelled. The level of vehemence in which he condemned her made Syn cringed in her chains. "You fled, like a coward in the night." His voice returned to calm displeasure as he stepped forward and stood before her as rigid as a carving. "What are we, Syn?"

Tears threatened to spring from Syn's eyes if she spoke. She remained silent to hold them back. She glanced at Captain Revvor, but his monstrous face offered no comfort. He must have already heard what Syn had done.

"What *are* we?" Chief Groth asked again.

"We... are Legionite." Syn nearly choked as nausea climbed up her throat. Tears welled in her eyes.

"And what is your oath as a Legionite?"

"I will defend," she tried to blink the tears back, but it was no use. "I will... I will..."

"Say it!"

"I will... *sacrifice*." Drops of incriminating evidence leaked down her face.

"That's right. But you did not perform the sacrifice, did you?"

Syn hung her head in shame.

"We held a tribunal for your failures and deception," Groth said. "When you weren't present, we were forced to find you guilty."

She had hoped she would never have to confront her greatest sin. She realized now how foolish she was in seeking to exonerate herself with the title of Nighterrian. Of course, she could never make it to the Imbuing Hall.

"Why have you come?" Syn could no longer contain her hysteria. She wept as she sought her answers. "Why not just leave me here to die in the trials?"

"I am Chief. I am responsible for my citizens, and I take upon my shoulders every mistake and every transgression that takes place in my village." Groth looked upon Syn's tears with disgust. "When we received notice of your location, the Elders and I agreed to carry out justice."

Notice of her location? Syn opened her mouth to ask who turned her in when Groth cut her off.

"You should know that when you were absent for your punishment. Remmel's family demanded restitution along with the others who were injured. Therefore, your family has been excommunicated."

Syn felt her insides melt into liquid. Excommunication meant her parents would not be allowed to partake in the community resources. They would receive no rations and would be forced to hunt and forage on their own all winter in the frozen wilderness.

"No... you-you can't!"

Life in the hostile village continued only because of the community effort of the people. The punishment ensured her family would suffer a future filled with hunger and strife as they scraped for every meal.

"I can and I have," Groth said.

"For how long?"

"Until the village has forgiven your family."

That meant forever. The village held tight to grudges like prized possessions and passed them down for generations. Visions of her parents falling destitute brought forth more tears.

"You can't do this! It's not their fault, it's mine!"

"It is done," Groth said. Captain Revvor shifted his stance and his frightful features flickered beneath the light of the lanterns. Groth looked to him and nodded. "There is more. I've come, not only to collect you from the trials, but to deliver your punishment."

"My punishment?" What more could there be?

"Like you said, I could have let the trials finish you, but then your soul would return to bring weakness to another village. As a faithful Legionite, this I could not allow." Groth paused. Then, with slow indulgence, like each word was a savory delight, he said, "I've come to sever your soul."

It was as if he had thrown her beneath the ice of the frozen lake. Trapped and downing, she choked on the freezing flood of cruel justice. Fear shot memories of the Severed man through her mind like strikes of lightning.

"No..." Her voice came out in a whisper.

"It is decided."

"When?" She already knew the answer. They had bound her to the wall for a reason. She jerked against the iron shackles.

Groth pulled a knife from his belt and stepped forward.

"No!" Syn shrieked and yanked against the shackles.

A commotion sounded beyond the rows of cells. A metal creak, and the door to the brig banged open. A man ran up to Syn's cell. As he approached, the dim lamps cast light into handsome features beneath a dark beard. Xedford.

"What's going on here?" he asked, taking in Syn's disposition—tears and all.

Syn wanted to crawl into a dark corner and never emerge. Why, of all the important people in the room, did she feel like she let Xedford down the most? She didn't want him to witness her severing.

"Xed, you got some nerve, brother. Clear off, this ain't none of your concern," Revvor said.

"I think it's every concern of mine. I brought her here," Xedford said.

"Did you bring her here knowing she was a renegade?" Revvor challenged.

"Captain Revvor," Groth spoke up, "I feel it is my duty to assure you warrior Xedford knew nothing of Syn's crimes when he met her."

The captain acknowledged Groth with a perfunctory nod, then turned back to Xedford. "It don't matter. The chief here has come to collect his prisoner. There's nothing to be done."

"Captain, you wouldn't up and forget the decree for the enactment of the trials, now would you?" Xedford asked with a raised eyebrow. Revvor opened his mouth to speak, but Xedford cut him off. "Syn can't be removed from the trial grounds until she is eliminated from the competition or until the trials conclude." From under his arm, he pulled a slim, withered book open to a specific page and handed it to the captain. "Our own laws declare it."

Revvor looked down at the book and flipped through the waterlogged pages. He then shoved the book back at Xedford and glowered at him for a moment. A silent standoff seemed to pass between them as they stared at one another.

"I reckon you're right," Revvor said with measured words. He turned to Groth. "My apologies, Chief, but our laws supersede any existing warrants against an individual while still in the competition. The girl can't be hauled off to face judgement just yet."

Xedford gave Revvor a self-satisfied smile and put out his hand. Revvor smacked a ring of keys into his open palm. Xedford went to work unlocking the heavy shackles that bound Syn's wrists and ankles.

Captain Revvor continued, "We *will* hand her over to you, Chief. Just as soon as she has been eliminated from the next trial." He looked at Syn. The blue veins pulsed through his face. "Listen here, girl. We'll let you continue with the trials, but know that if you fail, you'll be severed right quick."

"But not if she wins." Xedford gave Syn an encouraging wink.

Beneath her shame, Syn nurtured the budding seeds of gratitude. She could hardly believe what was happening. She brushed away her tears and forced her mind to move toward plotting how she could retain the longevity of her soul by escaping the severing.

Groth gave a quick bow. "I am at the mercy of your laws, of course. But I must return to my village soon."

"You won't need to wait long," Revvor said. "We're fixing to have the final trial take place tomorrow."

Tomorrow? Did she hear him right? Syn reeled from the whiplash of discoveries.

Groth nodded his consent and Syn saw a glimpse of his agitation. She could tell he disliked the dark realm, it made him uncomfortable. Realization ignited as she finally understood why he came. If the Nameless Elders were holding Groth responsible for Syn's crime, his position as chief would be threatened. He must have been forced to seek absolution by delivering Syn's punishment or else risk losing his Chiefdom.

No wonder he hated her. But one question remained, how did he find her? *When we received notice of your location.* Who turned her in?

"Follow me." Revvor hobbled out the door of the cell and motioned Groth to follow. "You've had a real long trip. We'll clear a room for you to get some shut-eye."

"It would be an honor." Groth followed Revvor out of the cell.

Revvor ordered to Xedford, "You'll take her back to the grounds." He turned and led Groth past the prison cells.

Conflict lingered on Syn's mind. It might be her final chance to obtain the answers she sought. Someone was responsible for turning her in. She gritted her teeth and hurried past Xedford into the narrow passage outside her cell.

"Chief Groth!"

He turned to regard her with a fuming stare.

"How did you find me here?" she asked.

Groth stared at her for a long moment. Syn thought he wasn't going to answer, then he finally spoke. "A girl arrived at Garon claiming to know of an escaped criminal belonging to our village." He pierced her with eyes of accusation. "A criminal responsible for the failure to perform a sacrifice." Before Syn could prod further, he turned and walked out the brig door.

Syn was left standing in a pool of revelation and confusion. One thing was certain, however, Syn's saboteur was a girl.

37
REPRIEVE

Silence pressed between Syn and Xedford as they emerged onto the upper deck of the ship and lowered themselves down to the water on a skiff. Syn noticed the growl of beasts and the sounds of fighting had ceased. She didn't know how long she was imprisoned on the ship, but it appeared the trials had concluded.

Xedford rowed while Syn eyed the stairs leading up the back of the Rock of Reckoning to the second tier. If seemed like her and Relia had fought the monsters and gangs a lifetime ago, despite feeling the fresh pain of cuts and bruises covering her body.

Once they were out of earshot, Xedford spoke up. "I understand now why you joined up for the trials."

Her mind lurched and begged for escape. It was all too much: Rem, Groth's revelation about the messenger, her potential severing, the coming trial, her exiled parents.

"I..." Syn looked down at her scraped and torn hands as she stalled for words. "I'm sorry for deceiving you. I just... I didn't want you to know what I'd done."

"You don't need to apologize. I figure you're allowed to keep a thing or two private. I might have even done the same myself."

How could he remain so kind to her after learning the truth?

"Thank you for keeping me in the trials. I would have been severed and sent home in shame if it weren't for you." Just when she thought she couldn't be more indebted to him, he goes and saves her again.

"Much obliged." He smiled as he rowed along the rolling waves. "Now you just gotta win the next trial."

Syn nodded. *If I don't, my family will suffer for the rest of their lives.* She felt like an utter ignoramus. *Am I really so selfish that I didn't think what would happen to my parents in my absence?*

"I got faith that you'll come out a winner. Once you're imbued, you can return to your village and exonerate your family."

"Yes... I suppose I'll meet my fate soon." *As either a hero or a branded criminal.*

"It's a damn crime you won't get much time to prepare," Xedford said.

"It wasn't planned this way?"

"No," he sighed. "The usual way of things is to give the competitors six days between each trial. But considering recent... occurrences, the captain has decided to go on with the trial immediately."

"What occurrences?"

The skiff glided into the opening of the cave of Reckoning and plunged them into the dark. Syn tensed, unsure why he rowed them through the cavern.

"Isn't there a giant water demon in here?" Syn whipped her head around to search the waves for evidence of the beast.

"Nah, we cleared that one out after the trial." Xedford

paused his rowing to put a hand on her knee in reassurance. "I just figured we could use a private place to talk."

Syn relaxed at the warmth of his hand on her knee. But his comforting touch was distracting. "What was it we were talking about?" she asked.

Xedford chuckled and removed his hand to return to propelling them farther into the dark. Syn finally remembered her trail of thought. "You were saying something about certain occurrences?"

"There's been a breach in the veil."

Syn recalled the wave of moth shrieks she heard while confronting Drekton. "Someone left the trial grounds?"

"Or somebody trespassed in. We ain't been able to find the culprit, but I've got my suspicions."

Syn leaned in toward Xedford to whisper, "You think it was Ortha's accomplice?"

"I reckon so. Were you able to uncover any information?" he asked.

Syn thought back to Drekton's confusion when provoked with questions about Ortha. She found it unlikely that Drekton was the conspirator. Plus, Syn was with him when the alarm of ghost moths sounded, so it couldn't have been him.

"No," she said. "My lead turned into a dead end."

Chattering sounds of the pigmys echoed off the cavern walls and sent a shiver down Syn's spine. She realized most of the wreckage from the first trial had been cleaned up. The place still made her gut clench with memories, nonetheless.

"That's mighty unfortunate." Xedford said. "Tensions are high between members of the crew."

Syn remembered the argument she overheard while in the brig. Something about the phrase "girl" and "grooming" stood out in her mind like a mountain in a valley of snow.

"I heard you and Revvor arguing through the floorboards above my cell."

Xedford stopped rowing. Syn couldn't interpret his expression in the darkness, but she felt the alarm in his rigid posture. "What did you hear?"

"I'm sorry." Her palms went clammy. "I didn't mean to eavesdrop, and I didn't hear much, just something about, umm..." Too embarrassed to voice her theory that they were arguing about her, she grasped for another word from the argument and went with it. "An apprentice?"

He seemed to consider something as he ran his hand over his head and tightened the tie of his bandana. "I've made some mistakes in my life." Syn remained silent and waited for him to continue. "Last season I trusted an apprentice that turned on us. Since then, Revvor's had it out for me. He doesn't trust my opinions about what would be best for the raid."

At the sound of his pained words, Syn reached out and placed her hand on his. She knew exactly what it was like to make a grave mistake. Maybe this was why he continued to help her. Perhaps he felt broken too.

He returned the gesture by placing his other hand on hers as he continued. "I don't like the third trial coming so soon. I argued against it but the captain—he's changed you see. It's a long story, but what it comes down to is I can see him losing his grip over the crew."

"He does look a bit, uh, unraveled?"

"You got that right. I don't want a mutiny on my hands, but I can't help but recognize the warning signs. With a captain going mad and a Convert lurking around the dark, nobody knows who to trust."

"Why don't *you* lead the raid?"

The white of Xedford's smile hatched through the darkness. "Perhaps one day I will." He leaned in so their noses where nearly touching. "If I ever had my own raid, I'd make you my second-in-command."

Nerves shuddered Syn's breath as she inhaled in his familiar scent. Perhaps the intoxication of his presence inspired the brashness of her next words, for she wasn't sure why she said them. "Am I the Surfacer you're grooming?"

"You heard that part, did you?" He chuckled and offered her his signature smile. "That's Revvor's take on it. He says I harbor a special interest in Surfacers. But the way I see it is, I simply got a knack for glimpsing the potential in the underestimated. Take my Scalers for example, nobody ever thought it possible to train the beasts, but I'm on the cusp of a breakthrough."

Syn felt the breeze of his breath and leaned in to capture it. "Do you always see the good in things?"

He whispered into her ear, and she felt the tickle of his beard beside her cheek. "I always see things in the way they might serve me best. Everything is a weapon if given the right" —he brushed his lips up against her ear—"incentive."

The shiver that passed through Syn's body melted away the world around her. The trials no longer existed. Assailants no longer stalked the dark out to get her. She ached with a longing to keep the world at bay.

"You see me as a weapon, then?" she asked.

"I see you as a woman, and women are always dangerous in their own right."

"Dangerous even to you?"

He placed a finger beneath her chin and tilted her face up. "Especially to me."

He kissed her.

Syn fell into his arms as their lips met. She kissed him with the frantic need to retain her grip on the momentary reprieve from the fear and chaos of her world. Her skin came alive with desire as she felt his arms envelop her. He picked her up and maneuvered her onto the floor of the boat. His three-barrel knocked against the wood, and he unbuckled it in a hurry. Syn hardly had time to realize it was off before she heard the weapon clunk onto the bow.

His unarmed hands explored their way beneath her clothing, and she gasped with delight at the euphoria of his touch against the skin of her back, her stomach, her chest. His lips found hers once again and for the first time since she entered Interterra, she didn't feel afraid.

More! More! Her mind begged to never return to the state of horror and dread that raged in the land outside his touch. Their lips never parted as he unbuckled her belt and unlaced her trousers. With rushed movements, as if the cave might come crashing down if they slowed, they tore at each other's garments.

Clothed only in shadows, Syn felt the warm rush of his skin on hers. It didn't matter that the wooden seats of the boat jabbed into her back. It didn't matter that the boat could tip them into the dangerous waters with one careless movement. Her body begged for his and her breath came in gasps between his lips.

With too much to confront outside the cave, she declared she would not let herself pause to reconsider. She gave herself over to desire and whatever it took to stretch the moment into eternity.

38
TRAITOR

Syn tugged her clothes back on with a bashful glance toward Xedford. She felt herself slowly emerging from the temporary rapture that had overtaken her.

"That was unexpected." Xedford grinned as he sat on the boat's bench and strapped his three-barrel back on.

Syn chuckled while weaving in and out of conflicting thoughts. What had come over her? Her mind felt muddy and slow. Worse, reality seemed to draw into focus as the fear and uncertainty of the future returned with added burden.

A flash of steel severed the dark.

Xedford pulled a dagger from his belt. Syn panicked, nearly jumping out of the skiff. "I believe this is yours." He twirled the blade around and offered her the hilt.

Syn breathed a sigh of foolish relief. "Thank-thank you."

She accepted the broken blade and tucked Elaine back into her belt. With her friend at her side, she accomplished a smidgeon of reassurance.

"I suppose we ought to be getting back." Xedford smiled and plucked up the ores to begin rowing.

Syn felt the soreness of her body as the boat floated along. A twinge of regret began to sink in. For some reason her thoughts jumped to Drekton and their arranged marriage. She had no valid reason to feel guilty, but shame tumbled through her like a blizzard. *Don't be silly, Syn.* Her engagement to Drekton had effectively ended the moment Rem died. And her empty doorstep in the days following the announcement of their engagement proved he never wanted to marry her in the first place.

None of that mattered. She watched Xedford row with a satisfied smile gracing his features. She marveled at him; the man who saved her life countless times; the man who saw her secrets laid bare; and the man who, somehow, still wanted to be with her.

But the self-assurance of Xedford's acceptance only lasted a short while. Once the intoxicating cloud of his touch evaporated, the glaring reality of her uncertain fate loomed above her like an anvil on a pendulum. Her thoughts circled toward what she had been afraid to confront earlier.

"Chief Groth said someone turned me in," Syn said.

"I was going to ask about that. I don't reckon the breach in the veil on the same night as the arrival of your Chief was a coincidence. Now, Groth didn't cross the veil, but he did arrive by sea just a few hours later."

"You mean you think whoever crossed the veil was on their way to deliver the message to Chief Groth?" she asked.

"Or on their way back."

Syn tried to estimate if it were possible for someone to sneak out of the trial grounds and make the trip through the portal and back in a single night. "How long would it take to get to Garon and back?"

"For somebody familiar with the terrain, it'd have taken about four or five hours round trip."

"And Groth said he received the message from a girl." Syn didn't want to listen to voice the that prodded the back of her mind. She had already tried to deny it, stomp it to the ground, and toss it from her suspicion only to have it come back around.

"There ain't too many girls here in the trials," Xedford said. "Tell me, how much do you trust that gal you've gone and teamed up with?"

Syn remembered Relia's empty hammock when she woke that morning, and how the alarm of moths sounded mere minutes before Relia found Syn in Drekton's tent. *It can't be her! It can't be!* Syn wanted to scream, wanted to cry.

"She-she saved my life," Syn said, more to herself than Xedford. "She helped me through the first trial. I wouldn't still be here if it weren't for her."

"I'd be careful not to underestimate a gambler's bluff. What all does she know about your past?"

Syn recalled the night after the episode of the haunting. "Everything."

Thoughts of Relia's Scaler garb filled her mind, and the true meaning of her words sank in. *I like to keep my enemies close.*

"Listen, now I don't mean to try and tell you want to do, but I've been around these trials for a while. I've seen all kinds of tactics. Just because she saves your life one night, don't mean she won't end it the next. It's a risky gambit, but one I've seen work. She would have latched on to you in the beginning because she knew she'd need help through the second trial. But the third trial is where she's likely to hang you with that same friendship."

The boat bumped up against the shore as they reached the end of the lake. Syn jumped, gripping the wooden sides of the skiff. Dread weighed her down into her seat. If only she could stay in the comfort of the dark cave forever.

Xedford continued, "The trials are your own. I can't interfere in any way, but I'd be careful of that girl. If she is the sort I'm fixing her to be, she won't kill you outright, but she'll take care to rattle you up. The knife will come to your back when you're at your most vulnerable."

"But if I stay away from her, how will I find out if she's the Convert?"

"We'll let things play themselves out. Just don't let her sabotage you during the trial. If she makes it through to the end, we'll deal with her before the imbuing."

Syn mulled over every conversation she had with Relia, trying to uncover the truth hidden beneath her duplicity. She forced herself to climb out of the boat and prepare for what lay ahead.

"Thank you again for helping me."

"Of course. Good luck tomorrow, and Syn." He held her wrist before she could step away from the shore.

"Yes?"

"Watch your back for knives." He placed a kiss on the top of her hand. "I'll meet you at the top." He let go and nodded up toward the ceiling of the cavern where, through layers of rock, the third tier stood with the pillars of the Imbuing Hall.

She nodded and watched him sit back down and push the boat into the water. A promise whispered on the edge of his smile as he rowed away. Syn clutched at her body and bundled her clothes in around her as she made her retreat through the mouth of the cavern.

She ducked around the wooden structure on the underside of the gauntlet and skirted past its large wheels. The ramp sat silent and empty except for the bodies of dead monsters. Off to her left she could see the finisher's tent. Light blazed from within, throwing long silhouettes against the linen walls. She heard cheers of merriment and possible drunkenness—a true celebration. While to her right, a series of blazing fires made up the pyres for the dead. The stench of death permeated the air.

"They burn while you celebrate," she said to the finisher's tent.

She moved on, making her way through the camp. She needed to be alone to sort out her next move, and she desired the peaceful silence of her friends. Perhaps Gregory and Anna would help her figure out what to do about Relia. Should Syn pretend ignorance and try to subvert Relia's plots? Or would that be inviting undue danger?

Scenes from the boat invaded her deliberations. She bit her lip at the memory of Xedford's touch as she reached the crop of trees and began her climb. She never thought a man could make her feel so light. He lifted the weight of her heavy soul better than ale. But just like ale, there seemed to be a price. The hangover of her act with Xedford left part of her feeling conflicted by her decision. Did everyone feel this way after their first time?

Preoccupied by flashbacks that evoked both guilt and pleasure, she almost forgot Relia could have been waiting for her in the canopy of her own camp. Syn breathed a sigh of relief when she reached her hideout and found herself alone.

"She must be celebrating with the rest of those savage finishers," she said to Elaine.

Syn climbed into her hammock. Her body ached with fatigue, and she felt the soreness of muscles she didn't know she had. She found her mind a befuddled mess of thoughts that continued to stray toward Xedford to avoid contemplating Relia's duplicity.

Her friends dangled above, offering her stillness. She sighed and set her mind toward straightening her priorities.

The best thing to do would be to pretend like she suspected nothing while secretly keeping watch over Relia.

"I thought she was my friend," she said to Gregory. "Stupid. I should have known better than…"

No. Something was off. She accounted for Gregory and Anna, but the cord where she hung Rem's coin fluttered in the light breeze. The golden coin was absent, and in its place, hung a folded scrap of paper. Syn shot up and ripped it from the string. With breathless anxiety she unfolded it and read:

REMEMBER THE ALTAR.

A cold stab of shame. Then, the confusion and sorrow hardened into hatred. How dare she steal Rem's coin? After she knew what it meant to her. Syn's entire body trembled like a boiling pot. Unable to contain the overwhelming rage that bubbled and overflowed inside her, she tore the note to pieces and made up her mind.

"I saved your life," she spat at torn pieces of parchment she crushed in her fist. "I confided in you … and now you throw it in my face."

She threw the pieces of the note and sat simmering in her fury for a moment as she watched the scraps flutter down to the water. In a rush of decision, Syn ripped Anna and Gregory from her tree and gathered up her belongings. Xedford's words came rushing to her mind. *She won't kill you outright, but she'll take care to rattle you up. The knife will come to your back when you're at your most vulnerable.*

Syn would not stay in the camp beside a traitor. She hurried down the tree and splashed into the water. Relia obviously didn't fear Syn's retaliation. Perhaps she assumed Syn would run packing back to Garon with tears in her eyes.

"And maybe I would have done just that a week ago," she said to her true friends tucked inside her pack. But things had changed. The trials proved that only those willing to seize life would survive. "I'm no longer as meek as you think."

She stalked through the camp in search of solitude while she reveled in a brainstorm of ideas on how to show Relia just what her treachery had earned her.

39
SACRED RULE

"We had but one rule." Captain Revvor paced in front of the wooden gauntlet. He glowered at the small crowd of finishers with his blood-shot stare. The orange starlight lit his monstrous veins with tallow light.

Syn had arrived just as the meeting began and snuck into the back of the group of fifty or so competitors. No other Nighterrians stood present, only the apprentices lined the ramp leading up to the second tier. The ramp had been cleared of beasts and body parts, but it still wore a fresh coat of blood. Syn eyed the new apprentice at the end of the line. She didn't recognize him, but she could guess what sort of person lie beneath his bloodthirsty smile.

"One rule... and somebody here broke it." Revvor paused and stroked the back of his three-barrel. "Can any y'all tell me what that one rule was?"

A tense breath, and the crowd spoke in jumbling words. Their combined voiced equivocated to, "No crossing the veil."

Syn spied around the crowd to try and see if Drekton had

made it through to the final trial. She didn't spot him anywhere. Pressure on her shoulder made her spin around to find Relia's curly head and bruised face.

"Where in the bleeding dark have you been? I've been looking all over for you!" Relia didn't bother to hush her voice.

Syn jerked herself free from Relia's touch and turned back toward the captain.

"That's right," Revvor said with a slow, gravelly voice that sounded like it pained him to speak. "No crossing the veil. And yet, here we are." He continued prowling before the crowd. Was it possible he looked even worse than last night? The competitors at the front shied back from his mad stare.

"What happened to you?" Relia persisted.

"I found a new camp," Syn answered without looking at her. "One where I wouldn't have to worry about blades finding my throat in the night."

Relia scoffed. "How do you figure?"

Syn ignored her.

Captain Revvor continued, "Now that the cardinal rule of the trials was up and broken, we're forced to enact a punishment."

"What happened? Why did they arrest you?" Relia asked again.

Syn continued to ignore her as she listened to the captain explain that the next trial would take place in exactly four hours. This information distracted Relia from her interrogation. Sounds of dissent and grumbling exasperation rose through the crowd.

Captain Revvor raised his arms to silence them. "Trial three will begin on the second tier. Each of the doors stationed in the walls will open to a platform. From the platform, you will have a set of pullies to choose from. Some of the pullies will take you up to the next platform and the next door, and some will take you down. Your objective is to try and select the correct series of ropes to travel up to the Imbuing Hall on the third tier. But each platform will only hold your weight for a short time. If you go and take too long to decide, you'll fall to your death."

That didn't sound so bad. Syn could tell from the tense air edged with confusion that others had similar thoughts. After surviving man-eating beasts and murderous gangs of competitors, the third trial almost seemed anticlimactic.

The captain's face cracked with a deranged grin, as if he were holding back a joke. "The first nine competitors to make it to the Imbuing Hall will imbued. These nine will join our crew along with our apprentices to complete our raid and earn the title of Nighterrian."

The competitors waited for further explanation, but Captain Revvor concluded the meeting by leading the apprentices around the back of the ramp and through the mouth of the cave.

Syn stomped off.

Relia ran after her and jumped into her path as she tried to walk away. "Hey! My apologies, I've gone and thought we were friends here."

"Friends? Really?" Gripped by fury, Syn leaned in to shout in her face. "Friends don't slip out in the night to delivers messages to get the other arrested!"

Relia took a step back. "You mean me? You're joking, right? How in the depths of Damnation would I be responsible for your arrest?"

The crowd of competitors began to disperse, but their shifty gazes lingered on the quarrelling pair.

"I know it was you who broke the veil." Syn had worked through the timeline in the early hours of the wake cycle when she couldn't find sleep. The math fit. "You must have slipped through another way yesternight, but by the time you returned from delivering a message to my Chief, you were late for the trial, so you had to go through the veil."

"Hah! You've gone and lost your pissing mind! I was late for the trial because I was looking for your sorry ass!" She stepped forward with fists clenched. "Or should I have left you there tied up and helpless as a legless hare?"

Rage thrashed within Syn at the word helpless. "You can drop the act. I know it was all a part of your plan. You can't deny those bruises on your face! I'll bet you got those while traversing the crags."

"I already told you, I entered a fighting bet to win the tablets."

"Yes, it was very convenient how you showed up with the exact items needed for you to win the trial."

"For *us* to win the trial!"

"There is no more 'us.'" Syn glared with the full weight of the betrayal she felt. "Tell me, did you go into it knowing you would betray me from the beginning? Or did the decision arise out of convenience?" Syn didn't wait for an answer. She stepped to leave, but Relia caught her arm.

"Who's been feeding you these ideas?" Relia's eyes lost some of the anger, but her grip spoke to desperation.

"No one. I just finally woke up to the truth."

"Do you really got so little faith in your own judgement that you're willing to believe whatever somebody tells you?"

Syn yanked free of her grasp and shoved her backward. Relia stumbled back as Syn yelled, "What about Rem's coin then? I didn't need anyone to tell me what that means! How dare you take the one thing that matters to me out here? After I told you everything, you'd stoop so low as to use it against me?"

"I didn't take your precious coin, Syn. I came back to the

camp to find all your shit gone. You talk about betrayal, but you're the one accusing me of all kinds of gruntshit and *you're* the one who left *me*!"

"I know you're lying. I'll bet you've been deceiving me this whole time. Was your family really even killed by Scalers or as that a well-crafted lie as well?"

Wild fury rippled across Relia's expression. She shoved Syn hard with both hands. Syn tripped and landed in the dirt. Relia spit on her and watched with satisfaction as the saliva caught Syn on the cheek.

"Seeing as you're so bent on being alone, you can take your stupid fake friends with you to the next trial. See if a cup and a broken box will save your lousy life like I have." Relia turned on her heel and walked away to the gasps of nosy onlookers.

Rage and embarrassment colored Syn's face as she wiped the spit off her cheek. "You were never my friend!"

Relia parted the crowd of gathered spectators with a rough shoulder check.

"You were only using me to get through the trials anyway! I'll be glad not to get a knife in my back!" Syn called, but Relia was already gone.

Syn cursed. She found her feet and pushed past the small crowd. Egged on by the outrage of Relia's denial, she resolved to shove thoughts of her away and focus on winning a Hal'-Point. *I don't need you.*

In the familiar company of solitude, she left to ready herself for the coming trial—alone.

40
APPARITIONS

The doors on the second tier of the Rock of Reckoning were diminutive in size, yet they stood with an imposing presence. Most of the arched doorways came up to Syn's shoulder, while some appeared only big enough to crawl through.

Syn stood in front of one of the medium-sized holes with a wooden door that came up to her chest. A few paces away, a lanky boy stood in front of one of the bigger doors. His presence felt too close for comfort, but Syn refused to move and give up the opportunity to begin the trial at a somewhat larger door than most.

She looked over her shoulder in nervous anticipation. The second tier no longer held any growling beasts, but evidence of the previous trial lay splattered about. Blood darkened the rock wall and pieces of broken weapons scattered the ground.

On her tenth glance over her shoulder, she noticed the Nighterrian with dreadlocks named Quent approach from around the bend of the rock. He carried a wooden crate. The contents of the box tinkled as he walked up to Syn. He handed her a lidless jar filled with a mysterious green substance that glowed in the dark.

"Rub this on your body," he said, his face impassive.

"What?"

Quent rolled his eyes and shoved his hand into the open jar. He smacked a handful of the goo onto Syn's chest and rubbed the glowing substance down her arms.

"I can do it." She jerked away from his hand and began working the strange goo over her chest and arms.

He shrugged and offered the competitor next to her an equal handful.

"What is this stuff?" asked the boy as he slathered the glowing substance over himself.

"Night moss."

"I guess this means it's dark in there." Syn regarded the way the night moss pushed back the darkness where it glowed green on her arms and chest.

Quent grunted and dug in his crate again to extract an orange, finger-sized vial. He uncorked it with his teeth and thrust it at Syn's face. "Drink." He walked over and handed one to the boy next to her. "Drink."

Syn shared a distrustful look with the boy. "Is this a test?" She tried to gain a better look at the liquid by using the night moss to illuminate the vial, but it didn't resemble anything familiar.

"Drink, or you ain't allowed to compete." Quent waited.

The boy shrugged and tipped the contents into his mouth. He handed the empty vial back to the Nighterrian as Syn waited for him to take ill or fall over dead. When nothing happened—and Quent glared at her expectantly—she followed suit and swallowed the orange liquid. The drink burned her throat on the way down. She coughed and handed the empty vial back. Quent grunted again and left to continue to make his round through the tier.

The awful flavor lingered in Syn's mouth. She spat into the dirt, attempting get the taste out, but it didn't help. Her nerves pressed her to consult the pocket watch Relia had given her. Her gut twisted with thoughts of her ex-teammate, but she couldn't let herself dwell on past mistakes. The watch informed her the trial would begin any moment. Adrenaline brought sweat to her palms and a twitch to her fingers as anxiety thrummed inside her like a vibrating war cry.

She patted Elaine at her side and whispered, "This is it, one last trip through torment." She thought of her parents back home. "I'm going to make things right." She stared at the door in preparation. If she could make it, she'd soon have her cure and her family's absolution.

The door pulsed in her vision. She blinked. The surface of the door seemed to crawl with movement. *No, no, no.* What was this? She could always tell when the haunting was about to strike but this vision came upon her too suddenly.

"What..." said the boy off to her right.

Syn looked over and noticed him step back in fear. She let out a half breath of relief. *It must be the drink.* It was not an episode of her haunting but perhaps this was just as bad.

"This is how they get us. I knew the trial seemed too easy," she said.

"They poisoned us!" the lanky boy said.

Syn began to voice an explanation, but a crack of barrel fire sounded.

The trial had begun.

Syn ran toward the pulsing door and crouched down to give it a shove. The top of the wooden door fell forward. Hinged on the bottom, the door formed a platform into the darkness.

She ducked her head to step through and stand on the door-turned-platform. To her immediate distress, she could feel the trap door begin to tilt beneath her weight. It tipped a gradual slope downward and she knew she had only seconds before she would slip off.

Before her—and just out of reach—were two sets of pullies she could barely make out in the dark. The darkness was so complete, she could barely even see the boy who entered the tier beside her. The glow of the night moss covering her body provided the only source of light, allowing her to glimpse the ropes. One pulley contained thick ropes the size of her forearm, the other hung with thin ropes the width of two fingers.

The thicker ropes might be the safer bet, but the trials cared nothing about safety. Syn decided to risk the thin ropes, but which side? Each pulley had two sides to it. One would take you down and the other would, supposedly, pull you up. She looked up and down, but the ends of the ropes disappeared into darkness on both ends. Out of time, she slid forward on the falling platform and jumped to grab onto the left side of the thin pulley.

She shot upward through the dark.

Yes! But her joy snuffed out as the rope in her hands transformed into a snake. She yelped, nearly letting go of the rope as it hissed and slithered.

"It's not real," she told herself as she focused on the feeling of the coarse strands in her hands. The rope remained covered in scales in her vision, but she was able to see past the illusion just as the pulley yanked to a halt.

Screams sounded through the blackness below her—likely the other competitors battling their own minds. She thought she could already hear the distant scream of someone falling through the dark.

Syn forced herself to focus through the wave of nausea that

washed over her. The darkness pulsed in her vision as she clung to the rope. She spotted another platform just below her and off to the left. But was it real or imaginary? Only one way to find out.

She kicked her legs out to swing to the side. The spread of darkness obscured everything around her. Only the light glow of the night moss allowed her to see a few feet in front of her. The platform appeared to float in the air beneath her, yet she knew there must be structures and spires hidden in the blackout.

She swung out to gain momentum then dropped down onto the platform. In that same instant, the platform pitched forward at a rate far quicker than the last one. Forced to make a split decision, she leapt for the first rope she could touch as the ground fell away beneath her.

Her choice proved erroneous. She dropped down. She tried to reach for the rope of the opposite side of pulley to arrest her descent, but it was too far way, and she was falling too fast. The slack line of the pulley sank her farther and farther while tendrils of tentacles formed from the oppressive dark. The pulley yanked to a stop and the visions reached out to touch her.

Hands emerged from dark and wrapped themselves around her body. Her chaotic mind could feel the tingle of their touch. Fingers trickled down her body. Or was it only a cavern breeze? She climbed with wild intent up the rope, but the darkness was all around her and transforming into human outlines. Formless faces took on color and shape. Syn gripped with her feet and pulled hand-over-hand in a desperate attempt to get away. She tried to ignore the imagined apparitions, but she felt herself choking on the fear.

A figure jumped out in front of her, stopping her progress. Syn gasped as the round face of her father materialized from the shadows. "I'm embarrassed to have you as a daughter," he said.

Sickness and panic sprang to her gut. *What fresh realm of horror?* Never in all her haunted hallucinations had her visions spoken to her. She did her best to ignore it and forced herself to climb on.

"I hope you never come back. We're better off without you. We're all better off without you!" said the disembodied head of her father.

Syn scaled the rope as terror threatened to overwhelm her. A new face fused together from the dark. She tried not to look, but it followed her and bobbed into existence in front of her face. Long braids and a displeased face. *Mother.*

"You're not worthy," Vertah said. "It's Legionite custom to leave defected children out in the snow when they're born. I wish I had left you out there." Syn cried as she climbed on. Her mother's voice followed her. "You're weak! You're broken! You're pathetic!"

"You're-not-real-you're-not-real," Syn chanted to herself. She knew the illusions were fake; her parents weren't really there. But a dark corner of her mind insisted the hallucinations spoke the truth.

With tears falling down her face, she noticed a door in a wall to her left. The wall seemed to rise from the middle of the darkness. It wasn't the wall to the outside, nor was it same platform she fell from. She figured the craggy walls must rise into a mad clutter throughout the whole inside of the upper cavern. But she didn't have time to discern the labyrinthine inner workings of the second tier.

She managed a clumsy swing from her rope and kicked open the door. Before she could jump to the platform, more screams echoed in the cavern. Syn felt the whoosh of the air as someone fell right past her. In the split second in which she glimpsed the competitor's face, a terrifying hallucination made the falling kid appear to have Syn's face.

In a blink, the victim of the trial fell past her sight into the dark. Below, a faraway thud ended the screaming.

No more time to delay. Syn swung past the reach of imagined hands and leapt into the hole in the wall where the door she had kicked formed a platform. She landed in a clumsy crouch that bruised her knee. She stood up to gather her bearings, all the while the wooden door tipped beneath her weight.

Three pullies hung in front of her: one set made of bloody, human sinew; one set of writhing worms; and one set that transformed into blue feathered serpents. The serpents raised the feathers on their collar and hissed. One struck out at Syn. She jumped to the side and teetered on the edge of the platform. With an adrenaline spiked gasp, she regained her balance and attempted to reach for a rope—any rope—when the lined face of Chief Groth twisted into shape.

"It's time to sever your soul!" He lunged out with a knife that floated in the darkness.

Instinct made her duck away from the imagined knife. But the distraction ate up her time. Before she could regain her balance, the platform dumped her into the air.

Syn fell screaming through the dark as she plummeted her way toward a life-ending crunch.

41
DOWN

Syn hurtled through the air. She flailed her limbs, attempting to latch onto something, anything, but found no purchase.

Her back hit a metal pulley the size of a wagon wheel. The force of the impact turned her around, and she hooked her leg around a rope. Still falling, she tried to grab hold of another rope, but it slipped from her grasp.

The tension tightened around her ankle, yanking her to a stop. At the mercy of the rope around her foot, the trajectory of her momentum carried her face first into the side of a rough wall.

Syn dangled in the air and felt blood drip down her face. Her back seared in pain, and her head throbbed from the fresh bludgeoning. Blinking away the dizziness, she sat up to grab the rope around her foot, but she couldn't reach. Thoughts came slowly and her skull pounded with the weight of blood gathering toward her head.

Shapes shattered and reformed in her splintered vision. Whatever potion they had forced her to drink made the world swirl in a hundred broken images. But between the spaces of clawed hands and beastly talons, she could make out the rough wall beside her.

A hole sat in the wall next to where she smacked her head. The opening swelled and trembled in her vision. She fought back the fear as the hole roared at her like a beast. She wiggled her body to swing forward. Once she gained enough momentum, she swung toward the hole and grabbed ahold of the edge. She pulled half her body into the hole and untangled the rope binding her foot.

Once free, she realized the space in the wall led out into a tight tunnel. Where did it lead? She held her bleeding forehead as the obscurity of darkness filled her sights and pulsed in time with her throbbing head.

A voice sounded from farther within the tunnel. "Syn?"

Syn grabbed Elaine. "Hello?"

"Syn, help me," the youthful voice cried.

"Rem?" Syn went to crawl through the tunnel but the awkward angle of the sword on her hip wouldn't let her fit through. She hastily unbuckled the scabbard and blade, hardly caring when it slipped off the ledge of the wall and fell away.

Rem's voice called to her.

With Elaine in hand, she felt her way through the rough stone by slithering on her stomach and using her elbows to crawl forward. Deep down, she knew it couldn't be Rem. Rem was dead. Still, she couldn't keep herself from answering his call. The tunnel widened to where she could crawl on her hands and knees. Ahead, the path split into two forks.

"Rem? Where are you?"

A whimpering cry sounded off to her right, and she crept forward. Shadows solidified into the shape of a small boy holding his knees and crying into his arms.

"Why did you do it, Syn?" he asked without looking up.

"I'm so sorry, Rem... I never meant for any of it to happen."

"Why did you kill me?"

Syn bobbed for words as a sob escaped her chest.

"I said." He looked up from his hands to glare at Syn with the decaying flesh of the dead. "Why did you kill me?" Tattered, rotten skin hung from his cheeks and morbid slime dripped from his chin. His eyes burrowed into her like black holes filled with hatred.

"*Why did you kill me?!*" He lunged at her.

Syn screamed and ducked away. Crawling as fast as she could, she took the tunnel to her left. Rem's ghost followed behind her. She could feel his hateful presence. His ghastly stare burned into the back of her head.

"It's all your fault!" His voice rang near her ear.

Frantic in her desire to escape, she clawed her way through the winding tunnel on all fours. Rem rained condemnations, all the while she tried to tell herself he wasn't real, but she could almost smell his rotting flesh and feel his rank breath at her ear.

The tunnel split off into fractured routes, some of them too small for Syn to climb through. Fearing she might get stuck, she chose the largest options. Beyond her panicked flight she could feel the tunnel sloping downward.

"I'm dead because of you!" Rem screamed at her.

Swallowed by terror and overwhelming guilt, she didn't see the horned pigmy shoot out from an adjoining tunnel until it was already upon her. The creature chattered with delight and bashed its horns against the back of her head. Elaine fell out of her grasp as the pain of the beating horns proved the beast was real.

Syn bucked her head against the tunnel ceiling to get it off, but the pigmy clung on with its humanlike hands. It crawled around to the front of her face and sank its teeth into her neck. Syn screamed in pain.

With one hand, she wrestled with the flesh-hungry creature while she felt around the floor for Elaine. Where was she? She abandoned the blade and grabbed the creature with both hands. Screaming, she stabbed her thumbs through its owl-like eyes. The pigmy screeched and fought with all its feeble weight, but Syn pushed harder until she felt its eyeballs pop. Only once her thumbs disappeared into its skull with a revolting squish did it finally lay still.

Syn slumped against the tunnel and held her bleeding neck. She looked around to find Rem's ghost had finally abandoned her. She sighed with relief. With the vision gone, he would stay silently buried in the depths of her subconscious. For now, anyway. She knew she'd carry the weight of his death for the rest of her life.

Looking over at the desecrated pigmy, she realized she was a trespasser in their tunneled domain. With a grunt, she pushed herself off the wall to locate Elaine. She found her just beyond the dead pigmy.

"Some help you were." Syn gripped her tight and continued through the tunnel in search of an area large enough to turn around in.

After crawling a few paces forward, the ground fell out from under her. Syn pitched forward, tumbling head over feet as the tunnel widened and dropped at a steep angle. Unable to arrest her descent, she tucked in her extremities and pointed Elaine away from her body.

The steep incline ended with an abrupt halt. Syn groaned and uncurled herself from her protective ball. Cut, bruised, and dazed, she sat up. The power of the hallucinogenic potion still staked its claim over her senses, but it had abated slightly.

Perhaps it was all the hits to her head, or maybe she was just used to seeing ghosts.

She sat up and felt the top of her head touch the ceiling. *Where am I?* She squinted into the dark. The glowing night moss on her body cast a dim green light. She swept her arms around the wide area, feeling more tunnels splitting off in different directions.

Echoed voices sounded from far away. She froze and listened. The sounds traveled in from one of the splitting intersections. Syn pushed away the pain of her various injuries and followed the sounds. She crawled through the tunnel to her right and the voices grew louder. Still unable to make out what they were saying, she crawled on.

"Don't be using too much of that serpent venom. The good doctor won't pay the same for damaged organs," a woman's voice said with a drawling Terraborn accent.

Serpent venom? Syn scooted closer to where the voices rang.

"Would you rather have them waking up and causing a ruckus mid-way through the crags?" came another voice, rough and deep.

The tunnel ended as it opened into an enormous cavern where a small light blazed at the center. Syn gathered her bearings and realized she had traveled all the way down the Rock of Reckoning and arrived at the bottom tier where the first trial had taken place.

The light came from a lantern. A woman carried it by the handle and set it down on a dock in the middle of the black water. Two sets of boats floated on either side of the dock. Syn peered around the remnants of the ship wreckage and the sunken pieces of scaffolding. The one boat looked more like a small, flat barge containing a pile of dead bodies. Syn recognized the five apprentices standing on the dock along with an unfamiliar man dressed all in black.

Syn tried to puzzle out an explanation as she watched the mysterious woman with the lantern. Syn could only see the back of her head. The woman wore a purple scarf weaved through her long braid which swung side to side as she paced opposite the apprentices. Two muscled men arranged bodies into the barge behind her.

Syn's vision still pulsed, but she focused past the undulations of her inebriated sight and spied the green haired apprentice named Torrance dragging a body along the dock. Zeroing in on the body, she recognized the sharp jawline and straight, dark hair.

She restrained a gasp. "Drekton," she breathed in whisper.

"Hold it right there, boy. That one there's mine." The woman with the thick accent pointed at Torrance.

One of the muscular men grabbed hold of Drekton's feet and tried to tug him from Torrance's grasp. Torrance held fast to Drekton's arms and looked over to the man dressed in black for orders on how to proceed.

"Don't you be going and getting greedy in your old age, Magoila. You only paid for ten," said the man in black.

Magoila. The name pounded a familiar sound in Syn's memory. The woman turned her face toward the light to glare at the man. Recognition struck Syn like a blow to the gut. It was the same gang leader who attacked Syn at the Outpost. What was she doing here?

"I take what I'm owed after paying the egregious sum you charge, you filthy thief!" Magoila said. Her burly ally with the gold earring yanked on Drekton's feet, but Torrance stood his ground and held fast to Drekton's dead weight.

Syn reevaluated the scene through her pulsing vision. The bodies on the barge weren't dead bodies at all. They blinked their eyes and drew breath. She breathed a sigh of relief. Drekton wasn't dead, but his lips were blue. All the incapacitated victims wore evidence of feathered serpent venom on their lips.

Syn clapped her hands over her mouth. *I've found the conspirators!* Could it be that all the apprentices had turned Convert?

"You calling *me* a thief?" The man in black strode forward with menace. The lamplight cast an eerie glow over his features. A series of healed burn marks bubbled the surface of his cheek. Syn caught the glint of a three-barrel on his left wrist. A Nighterrian? Syn didn't recognize him as part of the crew, and she had never seen scars on a Nighterrian.

The scarred man glowered at Magoila. "Boss says to keep all the Surfacers for ourselves. You got what you need, go on and clear off now."

Magoila shoved the lantern close to the man's burn-marked face. "One of y'all killed one of my men. I think one more boy is the least I'm owed."

"As if you care about any of your men." The man pushed the lantern away and shook his head. "You pay us skim from the ale compared to what I know those slavers and black market surgeons will pay for healthy young boys."

"You're free to go straight to the source yourself. Oh, but that's right, you Nighterrians can't very well go about trading slaves and body parts out in the open. You have your honorable reputations to uphold." Magoila scoffed.

Syn's concern bristled at the way she called him a Nighterrian. Could the conspiracy really go as far as to include outlaw Nighterrians from other raids?

The Nighterrian shook his head. "Don't think you ain't expendable. There are thousands of other lousy bandits we can sell to."

"You know damn well the rest of those slippery gangs would report straight back to Redd." She poked the man in the chest with her finger. "You sell to me for a discount because of the discretion I provide."

The scar-faced man sneered. Another Nighterrian with graying hair, whom Syn didn't recognize, rowed up in a small boat. "What's taking so damn long?" He wore a three-barrel on his wrist and his eyes pierced the dark with their blueness.

Blue eyes? Were these real Nighterrians or imposters?

"Magoila is up to her usual tricks," the scarred Nighterrian explained.

The blue-eyed Nighterrian looked to the outlaw. She stared proudly over her loot of teenage boys. "Get on with it," he said to her. "We got our final batch coming after this trial." He nodded upward toward the ceiling of the cavern. "If you want to get in on that haul, be back here in ten hours."

"But she's tryin' to take more than she paid for," the burned man said.

Magoila scoffed. "I'm owed compensation for the man I lost after one of you put a slug through his damned head!"

"We ain't got time to argue," said the older man.

"But the captain—"

"Let her have him and let's be done with it."

The scarred Nighterrian stared Magoila down for a moment, then nodded to Torrance who still held Drekton's wrists. Torrance tossed him away with a sneer and let the brigand pull Drekton into Magoila's small barge stacked with other paralyzed teenagers.

No! In a sudden moment of clarity, Syn realized she still cared for Drekton. He was her childhood best friend, her first kiss, and her savior in the woods. She couldn't let him be sold into slavery.

Magoila snapped her fingers, and the two thieves began to

paddle. "Mighty fine of you boys." Magoila called over her shoulder in a saccharine voice. "See y'all in a few hours!"

"Bloodthirsty bitch," said the scarred Nighterrian.

Syn backed away from the opening of the cave and retreated into the tunnel. "This can't be happening..." she said to Elaine. The conspiracy went far deeper than she thought. They were operating right under the crew's noses!

"I need to tell Xedford before it's too late." She fought against the sickening swirl of the mind-altering potion. His words circled back to her in her drug-riddled memory. *I'll meet you at the top.*

She took off sprinting through the tunnel on all fours. There remained only one way to make it to the Imbuing Hall. With all six of the apprentices in on the exploitation of failed competitors, she decided Xedford was her best hope. She needed to get to him soon to catch the conspirators in the act.

With frantic desperation, she climbed and made her way through the maze of tunnels. She followed the passageways that contained flecks of her night moss and knew she was on the right path when the tunnels sloped upward.

Adrenaline, mixed with the power of the potion, raised her paranoia. Pushing herself forward kept her from full-fledged panic. "Calm down, Syn," she said to herself. "Make a plan."

By the time she reached the end of the tunnels, her palms and knees were bloody and torn. She breathed in a deep, shaking breath of relief for making it back to the second tier, yet she couldn't let herself revel in success. The whole trial still loomed above her and she needed to traverse the dangerous ropes before she could get to the Hall.

Pandemonium raged inside her. She realized alone she'd have no chance at making it through the trial in time to unveil the hatching plot. With an effort, she set aside the hurt and the resentment as she accepted what she needed to do next.

"I need help," she confessed to Elaine.

With a deep breath, she jumped from the ledge in the wall and grabbed hold of the rope that had previously caught her foot. Her body protested along with the torn skin of her hands, but she held on. She dangled there for a moment, just long enough to harden her resolve. She needed help, even if it meant recruiting an enemy.

"I need to find Relia," she decided, and began to climb.

42
HELP

The climb up the ropes continued at a slow and grueling pace. The effects of the potion had lessened to a bearable degree, but the shadows still slithered and writhed with the promise of attack.

Breathless and dripping in sweat, Syn made it to the third platform of her ascent and nearly collapsed in exhaustion. No time to rest; she forced herself to focus on which pulley to select as the platform began to tilt.

Through the glow of the night moss, she could see the rope on the far right contained what looked like a blood stain. Syn tried to decipher if the blood translated to an ominous or auspicious sign, but the floor beneath her continued to pitch forward. She decided to chance it and jumped to the blood-stained rope.

"Auspicious it is." Syn caught her breath as she rode the pulley up through the dark.

The rope stopped short in front of a curved wall with a thin ledge and a series of doors. Syn stepped onto the ledge and edged her way around the wall.

Some of the doors contained hasty slash marks carved into the wood while others were marked with symbols smeared with blood or night moss. A clever strategy. It appeared the other competitors had started marking their progress through the maze-like trial so if they dropped back down, they could determine where they had already been. But which marking was Relia's?

Syn selected a door with an X carved into the upper right corner. She pushed it open and stepped forward into the dark only to find nothing laid beyond. She swept her glowing arms right and left but found only complete darkness.

The door hinged forward forcing her to scramble backward. She gripped onto the ledge just as the door fell away. With a grunt, she pulled herself back up onto the ledge of the wall. Either some of the doors on the level were designed with the trick of no pullies, or the ropes had been cut. Mechanical clicking sounded as unseen mechanisms cranked the door back up into place.

Syn edged forward along the slim shelf of the wall. She was about to select a small door with a night moss handprint when something caught her attention out the corner of her eye. A tiny glimmer reflected off the glow of her night moss. She moved onto the next door in line and found a green scale wedged into the crease of the wood.

Hope surged through her. She pushed open the door and stepped onto it but faltered as it pitched forward at an alarming rate. Without any time to deliberate, she leapt for the first rope she could reach.

Mid leap, and without the ability to change her trajectory, she realized the rope was sliced halfway through. A shock of fear resonated through her grip as she grabbed hold and prayed it wouldn't snap beneath her weight.

"Thank the Legion." Syn shot upward. Perhaps the half-sliced rope made a clever trap for the boys, but it bore Syn's weight just fine.

"Relia, you abysmal genius!" Syn realized the only person close to her own weight and still in the competition was Relia. By slicing the rope to the point where it only carried her weight, Relia had made sure no one else could follow the path she blazed. No one except Syn.

On the next platform she selected the option with the frayed rope and traveled upward again. At the top of the pulley, a series of doors awaited her. She examined each of them until she spotted the one marked with a scale.

Syn made accelerated progress as she followed the trail of scales and half cut ropes. The other competitor's markings became less and less prevalent the higher she traveled as fewer competitors had made it up that far. Her course stayed true as she tracked Relia's expert route. She soon lost count of how many doors she had traveled through. All the half-severed ropes took her higher.

Syn couldn't celebrate yet though, her battered hands were losing their grip. The higher she traveled, the more she could feel exhaustion spreading over her limbs. Lightheaded and dizzy, she drew upon the fear and anxiety of the potion's waning influence and forced herself into the moving shadows.

She fixated on sorting out her strategy as she followed Relia's trail. Was it safe to ask for Relia's help? Relia had manipulated Syn to try and win the competition, but that didn't make her one of the Converts. Unless the apprentices had coerced her into it. *Maybe she's not guilty of sabotaging me.* No, that was the delirium talking. Syn couldn't let her desire for Relia's innocence get in the way of reality.

By the time Syn reached another set of doors along a short wall, her thoughts became sluggish. Her vision had gone fuzzy around the edges as she glanced paranoid looks over her shoulder. The green light of the night moss lit a flick of blonde hair beside a door just in front of her. The sight jolted Syn back to the chase. She lunged along the slim ledge and caught hold of Relia's arm just before she stepped onto the door.

Relia rounded on her and lashed out with her blade. "Get away from me!"

Syn dodged just in time, but Relia captured Syn by the throat and slammed her to the wall. She poised her sword at Syn's neck.

"Scaler scum!" screamed Relia.

Syn froze in place with her hands raised in surrender. She read the fear in Relia's eyes—the wild look of a cornered animal.

"Relia, it's Syn!"

Relia continued to point the blade at Syn's throat. Her expression gave no indication of recognition and Syn realized she must still be suffering from the hallucinatory potion. Still, Relia hesitated. Part of her must have known that what she was seeing wasn't real.

Syn knew how that felt. "It's me." Syn tried for a calming voice as she carefully brought her hand up to touch Relia on the wrist. "You can feel my hand, it doesn't have claws or scales."

"Syn?" Relia dropped her sword, her hands trembling in fear. A flash of relief passed over her eyes at the sight of Syn. Then it was gone. The fear abated only to be replaced with hatred. She returned to holding the blade at Syn's throat. "What're you doing here? Come to push me off the edge?"

"No, I came because I need your help."

"Help yourself," Relia hissed and sheathed her blade. She stepped out onto the open door.

Syn followed her onto the hinging door. "Please, I need you

to listen." The door pitched rapidly forward beneath their combined weight.

"I've heard enough out of you." Relia jumped for a rope.

Syn followed and leapt for the rope opposite her. She latched on and the balance of weight on either side of the pulley caused them to hang motionless.

"Please, Relia, you have to listen."

"Get off the shit-be-damned rope!"

"Not until you listen to what I have to say."

"No, I've heard—"

"I found them. I found the conspirators! It's so much worse than we thought. All the apprentices are in on it, along with some Nighterrians. I saw them in the cave trading the failed competitors to the outlaws."

"It's the drugs, Syn. None of it's real. I've seen all kinds of shit that ain't really there."

"No, I swear. This was real. They poisoned the competitors with serpent venom. The outlaws are going to trade them as slaves and cadavers!"

Relia scrutinized Syn's expression for a moment as they dangled from the ropes. She must have found Syn earnest because the coldness in her eyes melted just slightly.

"Please, you have to believe me," Syn begged. "If we fail this trial, we'll be captured and sold like the rest."

"How many Nighterrians did you reckon you saw?"

Syn's hope took flight. "Two, but I didn't recognize them as part of the crew. We need to get to the Imbuing Hall and find Xedford before the trial ends so we can catch them in the act."

Relia pursed her lips, her face drawn with suspicion.

"I know you don't trust me, but this is bigger than either of us. We need to put everything aside. I don't care what you did to sabotage me, it doesn't matter right—"

"What I done to sabotage you? You're still on that train, huh?" Relia barked a bitter laugh.

Syn's gut dropped knowing she had said the wrong thing. *Why did I have to bring up the betrayal?*

"If, after everything, you still think I betrayed you, you must be more messed up in that sick head of yours than I thought." With one hand, Relia swung and grabbed hold of another pulley rope off to her left. The look on her face nearly convinced Syn she was innocent.

Could I have been wrong? Could she be... innocent? "No, Relia, I—"

"Mighty fine try, Syn. You almost got me, but I won't be tricked that easy." The sting of betrayal settled deep within her red eyes. She swung onto the other pulley, leaving the one Syn clung onto to become unbalanced.

"No!" Syn's pulley carried her down as Relia's pulled her upward and out of reach.

Syn dropped, but she didn't miss the sight of a trapdoor springing open in the ceiling. Soft light flooded in. Before falling out of sight, she watched Relia's rope carry her all the way up and into what could only be the Imbuing Hall.

43
LIES

Despair converged in Syn's chest as she continued to descend through the dark. She watched the trial whoosh past her while she clung to the rope like a wingless bird. Surely the pulley would stop soon, but no, the slack continued to carry her farther and farther toward the bottom. Syn held on in hopeless anguish, completely unable to arrest her descent or reach any of the other platforms or pulleys that flew past her.

The rope finally yanked to an abrupt stop. The force of it ripped her grip free and she fell a few feet before hitting solid ground.

After coughing to recover breath to her lungs, she rolled from her back and climbed to her feet. The ground of the second tier looked like a maze of narrow rock spires that made up the labyrinth of walls and doors in the darkness above. The dead body of a boy laid a few feet away where he must have fallen from a lethal height. The glowing night moss wrapped the crumbled corpse in disturbing light.

"This is a sick joke." Syn stared around. She couldn't

believe the cruelty of reaching the top of the tier only to make one wrong choice that carried her all the way to the bottom.

All her work now undone, she stared up at the rope dangling above her. She wouldn't let despair take over. She gathered her strength and jumped as high as she could, but her attempt was still many feet away from catching the end of the rope. She backed up to go at it from a running start.

"Don't bother, it's useless," said a voice.

Syn looked over to see a group of despondent looking competitors emerge from the other side of a rock.

"We've all tried it," said the tall, lanky boy Syn remembered from the start of the trial. "It's pointless, the ropes are too high up."

"No, it can't be the end." Syn tried again to catch the end of a rope but to no avail.

"We've failed," said the boy.

"No!" Determined not to give up, Syn ran to one of the rock walls surrounding the space. She clawed at the wall, but its smooth surface provided too little purchase and her torn hands couldn't hold on. She turned to another rock and tried again. She hardly made it a foot off the ground before sliding down.

"It's useless," said the boy with a hollow voice.

Panicked rage vibrated through Syn's body as she slid down from another attempt at the rock. "No. There has to be a way..."

The tall boy gave up on trying to convince her. He turned and led the silent group of teens away without waiting for Syn to follow.

"Wait, where are you going?"

"To the way out," he said without looking over his shoulder.

Syn hesitated, then hurried to catch up. Maybe she could find a rougher rock to climb up. *This can't be it… I was so close.*

She followed the group of failed competitors through the maze of rocks. She tried to scale a few of the rock walls, but all of them proved too smooth and steep. She realized the ground she walked on must serve as the ceiling to the cavern with the shipwreck on the first tier. The converts were conspiring just beneath her feet!

She hurried after the solemn group with impatience and soon they escaped the maze, reaching what she assumed was the outer wall of the second tier. A large set of wide doors indicated an exit. When she asked the lanky boy why they hadn't left, he explained that the doors were locked. More failed competitors sat or leaned against the wall. Most nursed various injuries while some sat rocking and muttering to themselves as they stared into the dark.

The combined glow of the gathered teens helped to illuminate the vast room. Syn scanned the walls for holes that might lead to pigmy tunnels but found nothing. She was about to make a sweep of the perimeter to explore further when a creak sounded, and the wide doors flung open.

In walked captain Revvor with all five apprentices.

"Our nineth and final finisher has entered the Imbuing Hall," the Captain announced. Syn's thoughts flew to Relia. "Which concludes this trial. Unfortunately, none of you fellas made the cut. Follow the apprentices, they'll be taking you to the ship where we can treat your injuries and give you the antidote to the hallucinogen."

Lies. "No, don't follow them!" Syn screamed, her voice echoing off the walls. Could the captain be in on it too?

Some competitors gave her curious looks, but most ignored her as they accepted defeat and walked calmly to their unknowing demise.

"No, listen to me! They'll kill you!" She drew her dagger.

Revvor stepped toward her. His monstrous face rippled with worming veins while his eyes blazed with hunger. "This one's still tripping." He leveled his golden three-barrel at her face.

Syn refused to lower her blade but took a step back in retreat. Two apprentices grabbed her from behind and twisted Elaine from her grasp. "No—" She tasted a weathered rag shoved into her mouth. She struggled and kicked as she was rushed from all sides. A knee landed in her gut. Cruel, powerful hands detained her arms behind her back.

"Take her to that Legionite Chief," the captain ordered. The apprentices jerked Syn to her feet and Revvor grabbed a fist full of her shirt. "Don't be thinking you can escape your punishment that easy." He gave a mad, twisted smile then shoved her backward into the custody of the Convert-apprentices.

Syn screamed muffled cries as they dragged her toward her fate.

44
CUT

"Syndrah Tri-Garon, you have been found guilty of desertion from your post, deception to cover up your crimes, and failure to perform a sacrifice which led to the endangerment of the entire village of Garon." Chief Groth's stare punctuated the list of Syn's crimes with a sneer of disgust.

Syn dragged his vision up to meet his eye. Thick iron manacles around her wrists and ankles held her to the wall of the brig and detained her ability to thrash against the restraints. She tried to speak, but her words came out muffled by the gag of fabric in her mouth. Even if she could cry out, it wouldn't matter. No one would come to her aid. She found herself again hanging deep in the belly of the Nighterrian ship, shackled to the wall of the damp prison.

"As Chief of Garon and dutiful servant to the Legion of the Nameless, it is my responsibility to carry out sentencing. Your soul will now be severed to ensure you will no longer be reborn into another life."

He stepped forward and ripped Elaine from where she had

been returned to the scabbard at Syn's belt. The apprentices had chuckled at it as they locked her up. Elaine's edge flashed in the lamplight as he held her up. He took note her broken edge and scoffed.

Pure panic threatened to rupture Syn's pounding heart. *No! The Nighterrians are corrupt, you must stop them!* The unintelligible words came out as grunts from her gagged mouth. Syn yanked on her shackles and screamed—all to no avail. Stretched out tight by the iron manacles around her wrist and ankles, she couldn't even bend the joints of her arms or legs.

"You'll want to hold still for this." Groth leered in. "Or it will be much worse."

He grabbed Syn's chin with his left hand. She tried to turn her face away as she continued to shout stifled warnings, but Groth's grip tightened and crushed her head against the wooden wall of the ship.

No-No-No!

With his right hand, Groth brought Elaine up to her left eye. The broken, jagged edge came toward her face to bring the cut. Syn fought with all her strength, but it didn't stop the arrival of the blade. Searing pain traveled through her as the dagger opened her skin. Groth burrowed it into her flesh and traced a diagonal line from her brow, across her eye, and down onto her cheek. The thick scent of iron filled her nose as blood dripped down her face from the fresh wound.

Syn's lungs pumped in and out in shallow breaths that came out as a whine through her gag. She attempted to wriggle her head free, but Groth's grip held true as he made his second incision. It seemed to last a lifetime. The burn of the slice traveled across her eye, crossing the first cut to form an X. More blood spilled and soaked the cloth of her gag. The salty, metallic taste filled her with calamitous dread.

She knew he wasn't finished.

The scar across the face of a Severed indicated a criminal status at first sight. The severing of her eye would inform the Legion not to reincarnate her soul when she reached the Abyss after her death.

Syn gathered her wild strength. She employed every drop of energy to help her thrash. *Success!* Blood splattered Groth's face as she managed to rip her head from his grip. He stepped back with a growl of displeasure.

Please! Ungag me! Syn shouted through her blood-soaked muzzle. If only she could explain. Blood drenched her vision in her left eye, but she could see two Nighterrians from the crew enter the cell and nod to Groth. They took hold of either side of her and held her steady. Groth moved back in.

Syn watched through her blood-covered vision as Groth pulled on a pair of padded gloves. From a thick pouch insulated in multiple layers of animal hide, he extracted a tiny vial with a dropper attached to the cork. The worst kind of poison sat inside: An extract made from the oils of the inferno plant. Just brushing up against the leaves of the plant found in the shade of the woods would leave your skin covered in blisters. The concentrated oil could burn a hole through leather.

Groth brough the dropper out of the vial. A single drop of white liquid trembled at the end of the tube. The imbued strength of the Nighterrians cemented Syn's face to the wall while Groth pulled back her tattered eye lid. Unable to move or look away, she watched the poisoned droplet come closer and closer.

Drip.

It seared through her pupil. It burned—oh Legion how it *burned*. Panic erupted and transported her to a new realm of pain. She had never felt pain like this before. She screamed and thrashed against her captors.

When Groth stepped back, it was over. The poison forever ended the sight in her left eye.

Syn slumped against her restraints. Agony ripped through her face. Her eye felt as if Groth had lit it on fire. It burned deep into her skull. Her entire body trembled with the torture.

Groth returned Elaine to Syn's belt. *Severed by my own friend*, she thought through the tragic despair. Defeated, she could no longer fight or think straight. She felt dizzy with agony and blood loss, but she was distantly aware of someone new approaching. She could only barely make out the faceless voices at the edge of the cell.

"Patch her up and make sure she don't bleed out."

Syn knew that voice, but she couldn't focus, couldn't see. She wavered on the edge of unconsciousness. All she could perceive was her own blood and bolts of searing agony radiating from her left eye. Hanging from her shackles, the darkness converged; she surrendered to it.

Syn returned from the momentary blackout. How long had it been? Seconds? Minutes? A familiar voice echoed in through the outskirts of her awareness.

"...if you prefer to wait, you can take her with you in an hour's time once she's fit to travel."

"No, I've been away from my village long enough." *Groth's voice?* "I cannot delay my return."

"Alright. We'll deliver her to the portal in due time."

"No rush. My village no longer has a desire for her. Let her find her own way back... if she chooses to return at all."

"We'll take you back to the East bank."

"Thank you. It's been an honor."

"Is there anything else you need, Chief?"

"No. I am glad I was able to execute justice. I'll have to thank that Legionite girl for leading me to our renegade."

Footsteps. The clank of metal. Unseen hands unlocked her

chains. An inkling of something she needed to do, something she needed to tell someone, lurked at the edge of her memory but she couldn't remember. Brutal waves of pain stole her ability to makes sense of the world.

A face swam in her sight. A man. Long dark hair, a deep scar across his forehead. "So much wasted potential," he said.

Unable to extract thoughts from beneath the power of the excruciating torture, she fell unconscious.

45
ABYSS

Syn woke thinking she emerged from a terrifying nightmare. For a sliver of moment, she was back in her own bed in a world where she could run outside to see Rem and her parents.

Reality collapsed back into place as she felt desecrating pain on the left side of her face.

She bumped along in a rocking motion to the sound of snorts. She managed to crack open her single sight-filled eye and saw a mass of dry gray skin swaying in her vision. Peering beyond the veil of agony, she noticed her surroundings. She was flopped belly-side down over an oinking grunt. Her hands and feet were tied together around the beast as if she were a human saddle.

Syn looked up at the red-orange stars of the night sky, seeing dust and rugged red rocks jutting up in all directions. The Crags.

She tilted her pounding head to the side and saw a line of grunts tied together with blue lipped boys strapped to their backs in the same fashion as Syn. The beasts followed a burly man and a woman riding at the front. *Magoila.* How long had Syn been unconscious? Apparently long enough to be sold to the outlaws.

Down toward the end of the line of grunts she saw other injured competitors bobbing along, dripping blood with their eyes closed. Their lips weren't touched by the blue serpent venom and Syn wondered what kind of bargain Magoila had struck for them. Injured teens would make poor slaves. Unless they were going straight to the surgeon. With a start she realized she was one of the injured they hadn't bothered to paralyze with the venom.

A part of her felt relieved. She would die soon. That same part of her said to give in to the misery and fall into the pit of oblivion. Soon, she'd float along in the Abyss for eternity. Perhaps she would find no pain there. No guilt, no fear. She longed for nothingness, yet something kept her from enjoying the fantasy of a dark void.

The image of Relia's face surfaced in her mind's eye. The final look of betrayal in Relia's eyes before she disappeared through the dark pierced through Syn's pain. The severing of her soul brought with it a certain clarity. With an effort, she remembered Groth's voice just before she blacked out.

I'll have to thank that Legionite girl for leading me to our renegade.

Between the blinding throbs emanating from her eye, Syn realized Relia had never been the one to betray her. Relia was many things, but Legionite was not among them. Syn discovered a new low. Wretchedness, interrupted by curiosity, tore at her attempt to revel in her self-hatred. If Relia hadn't been the one to deliver the message to Chief Groth, then who?

She glanced back over at Magoila riding at the front of the pack of grunts. Could it have been her? No, she was no Legionite either.

No, no, go back to feeling nothing. She begged herself to return to the state of numbness—to accept her fate and meet death—but her mind kept returning to Relia.

At least she made it to the finish. Syn recalled the light of the trapped door at the end of the trial. So long as Relia didn't have to suffer the fate of the failed competitors, she could rest easy. Relia was cunning, perhaps she would uncover the corruption of the apprentices on her own.

Syn mulled over her mistakes and regrets as the grunts carried her through the crags. Maybe she would get to see Drekton one last time before she met the oblivion she sought. If he hadn't already been sold. Now, at the final verse of her life, she felt ashamed for accusing Drekton of conspiracy. Her thoughts rolled over to the boy she grew up with, the one she was supposed to marry. The image of his blue lips and para-lyzed body deepened the wound of regret.

She had failed him too.

She thought of her parents doomed to suffer in exile for the rest of their days. Waves of torment and the agony of her severed soul pulled her up and down through a sea of anguish. She watched the landscape pass by and decided she deserved every ounce of pain she received.

A squeal sounded from a grunt in the back of the line. Syn looked over but she couldn't see past the spiked rump of her grunt. She heard the scraping metallic sound of a sword being drawn. The grunts broke out in a cacophony of shrieks as they bucked in panic. Syn's grunt kicked in circles, but she caught a glimpse of slender figure in the dark.

"Kill her!" came Magoila's voice from beyond sight.

Her? Syn couldn't see much between the blurred frenzy of beasts and her own rearing grunt. She saw a flash of a muscular brigand as he jumped off his bucking grunt and ran after the shadowed figure.

The silhouette of the mysterious woman slashed the bridles connecting the beasts to each other at the back of the line. She smacked the flat of her blade against the grunts, ushering them onward in escape. They galloped away, carrying with them the immobilized captives strapped to their backs.

The brigand dodged his way toward the attacking woman and struck out with his blade. She ducked past a rock and slipped behind the cover of the aggravated grunts. The outlaw slashed his way toward her again, cutting down grunts and captives in the process.

"Stop, you idiot! We need them!" Magoila pulled up her sleeve and aimed something silvery, but her panicked grunt yanked her back and forth by the ropes connecting her to the pack of crazed animals.

Syn's grunt turned her away from the fight and she lost sight of what was happening. She heard the clash of blades and the squeals of grunts.

A crack of thunder split the air. Barrel fire? Where did that come from? Dust kicked up by the stomping hooves choked her airway. She tried to roll her weight around to spur the beast in a direction of escape, but it continued to kick in frenzied circles.

From the plumes of dust emerged the woman. She ran headlong toward Syn. The female attacker raised her blade as she closed in. Syn gaped in disbelief. The woman wasn't a woman, but a girl. Younger than Syn, perhaps sixteen or seventeen. She sliced through the rope attaching Syn's grunt to the rest of the pack and met Syn's stare. Her eyes blazed with irises the same shade of gray as Syn's single eye.

The girl jumped onto the grunt and landed on Syn's back. The air rushed out of Syn's chest as the girl kicked the steed into a run. They raced through the dusty crags leaving the chaos of the scene behind them.

In a state of utter shock, Syn played the image of her rescuer over and over inside her mind as they rode away. The girl looked different than when Syn had last seen her. She no longer had blue lips, but her eyes remained unmistakably familiar.

PART FIVE
RESCUE

46
SACRIFICE

Lektra felt no comfort upon her return to the Surface. The freezing air bit at her through her light clothes designed for Interterra. She watched through the bars of the cage as snow-covered trees passed by. Winter had come early. She tried to discern if she was anywhere near home, but she didn't recognize the forest.

Outside her sight, the Graver and the Nighterrian pulled the cart of bodies along. The pair stayed eerily silent as they traversed the frosty land. The rocking rhythm of the cart sent Lektra's mind spiraling toward Tanok. Part of her felt guilty for thinking he was in on the brutality she witnessed. Of course, Tanok had found himself up against a villainous plot to take down a conspiracy from the inside. A spy among the most dangerous of men, he was bravery personified.

If only they had more time together.

A pang of nostalgia burrowed into her heart. She recalled the day her brother left for the trials. Their entire village had arrived to offer their prayers and shove various gifts into Tanok's pack. Tanok had smiled, accepting the gifts and praise like a hero as he waved goodbye. Lektra, of course, insisted on following him all the way to the portal.

"Don't forget us simple Legionites once you're a big, powerful warrior," she had teased.

"Oh, I fully intend to make you grovel on your knees, little sister. Perhaps I'll make you my steward and you can shine my boots and feed me fruit as I lounge about," Tanok said.

"How about I shine your fruit and feed you your boots?"

He laughed. "I wouldn't put it past you."

"Don't get yourself killed in the first trial," she said in jest, though a tiny chill had entered through the thick layers of her fur cloak.

"Don't die of boredom while I'm gone." He grinned his champion smile. Then, with the certainty as if he were strolling through the doors of the Imbuing Hall, he stepped through the portal toward greatness.

Lektra was left standing in the snow, beaming with pride and a touch of envy. It never occurred to her that Tanok might not return. He was the strongest and bravest in all of Veldt. She was certain the next time she saw him he would be an imbued Nighterrian.

It was only after the days and months dragged on that Lektra slowly concluded that something had gone terribly wrong. But she never could have imagined things had gone *this* wrong.

I won't let you die... I promise. Tanok's words rang back to her as her thoughts turned toward the present. *I just need you to trust me.* Lektra wanted to trust him, but fear grew insidious roots through her heart. How could she trust him when her future looked so bleak?

Lektra tried to think of a way to escape. She had grown used to the stench of decaying offerings that surrounded her through the journey into the woods, but she couldn't get used to the way her body wouldn't respond. As the cart passed through the uneven terrain, the severed arms and legs shifted and fell upon her. The dangling skin of a severed thigh hung in her face, blocking half her vision. She remained helpless to move it away. She wished she could scream or move or do *anything*. Instead, she laid there as useful as a carcass.

The cart rolled to a stop. Trepidation spiked through Lektra. She could hear voices, but a large portion of her sight remained obscured.

"We expected Revvor to meet us." A Graver's haunting voice. Not the one they arrived with, but a second man.

"Yes, does he know you're here?" *A third Graver?*

"I'm second-in-command," the Nighterrian's voice responded. "He'd not risk himself, should the deal go sideways."

One man tsked. "You put so little faith in us."

"I put faith in myself. Now, you got the answers we seek?"

A short pause. "The original experiment has been a success," said one of the Gravers.

"How long's it been since his second imbuing?"

"First, I must remind you the deal we have struck. Your people will forever owe us a debt. A debt which can be cashed in at any time."

"Yeah, yeah. Tell me how long," the Nighterrian said.

"A year."

"And no adverse side effects?"

"If you're referring to his health, I can assure you he is far superior to any Nighterrian with only a single Hallowed Point."

"Is that so? What sort of abilities did the second imbuing get him?"

"He—"

Lektra couldn't be certain of what happened next. She heard a shot fired from a three-barrel. A cry of pain.

"You!" shouted the Nighterrian, betrayal in his voice.

Tanok! He's come to rescue me! The cart began to draw away as the Gravers shouted in panic. She couldn't see, unable to turn toward the fight with her body still paralyzed.

"This is what you get, Xedford!" returned the attacker.

Lektra's hope crumbled to ash. The voice of the attacker sounded rasping and unfamiliar—not Tanok's voice at all. *No, what's happening?*

"Why are you doing this?" demanded the man named Xedford.

"I've come to give you what you deserve," the unseen attacker returned.

Another shot rang through the woods. The cart rolled away to reveal drops of blood in the snow.

I'm here! Help! She couldn't get her voice to work. Tears of rage and frustration clouded her vision. The fling of limbs fell on top of her as the panicked trio of Gravers pulled the cart away in a hurry to retreat from the fight. She couldn't see. She begged her arms to move or her legs to kick; she willed her voice to scream, but she remained a prisoner in her own body.

Sounds of battle faded behind her. Fear ripped through Lektra's immobile body. She knew she had missed her opportunity to seize her freedom. She needed to let her people know of the treachery of the Nighterrians. She needed to escape.

She needed to save her brother.

Instead, the Gravers rolled her on through the snow. If they spoke to each other, they must have used the silent hand signals of the secret Graver language. She wished they'd speak aloud. Who was the attacker? Was he coming back?

Lost in her own storm of fear and regret, she hardly noticed when the silence of the woods broke, and they entered a village. Through the shift of body part offerings, she could see the faces of Legionites. A twinge of hope struck her for a fleeting moment. *I'm home*, she thought. But the faces remained unfamiliar. Despair overtook her as realization set in. A stranger in a new village, carted in by Gravers.

What's to become of me?

"I was beginning to think you wouldn't show." A deep voice drifted over from somewhere she couldn't see. "Need I remind you it's the final day of the Season. It is imperative we have bait for our trap."

"We know. We always deliver."

"You're injured. What happened?"

"Nothing of matter. Just a scrape in the woods."

"Go seek the butchers, they'll patch you up."

"Many thanks." The snow crunched with footsteps.

The deep voice of authority again, "Is there a sacrifice in there somewhere?"

"Yes, she's terminally ill. A genetic disease, no need to worry about contagion."

"Hurry and prep her. We'll need her ready in an hour."

The cart rolled forward a few paces and beneath the frozen limbs Lektra could see a snow-covered hill in the distance. It looked just like the one in her own village. Her eyes zeroed in on the altar erected at the top of the hill—the place where she would undoubtably draw her final breath until the Legion delivered her into another life.

47
INSANE

Syn couldn't hurdle over the shock of her savior. The girl whose life she spared upon the altar had returned to rescue her, but how? Syn bounced along on the grunt while buried in a pit of disbelief.

Once they had ridden a safe distance away from the bedlam, the girl pulled the beast to a stop amongst a crop of enshrouding rocks. The Legionite girl jumped off Syn's back and immediately cut Syn free.

Syn slumped off the grunt, wobbling on weak legs before catching herself against a boulder. Her hand instinctively went to her belt where, she was glad to find, Elaine still sat. She held onto Elaine's hilt as she watched the girl sheath her blade and secure the grunt so it wouldn't run off.

The girl carried a belt of weapons and supplies around her waist and a slim pack on her back as if she had been traveling. She wore Terraborn-style trousers, and a tunic made of thin material ideal for the hot climate, but her tanned skin, round face, and braided hair spoke of her Legionite heritage.

The girl turned to Syn. "I'm Lektra."

Syn reached for the first words she could find. "How are you not dead?"

Lektra gave a sad smile. "I suppose I have a lot to explain." She strode over to Syn. "But first, I have to know, why didn't you do it?" Her hand remained hovered over the hilt of her blade. "Why didn't you kill me?"

How many times had she asked herself this very question? "I don't know why. I saw the look in your eyes, and it was like... like I knew you didn't want me to do it and I just... I just couldn't."

Lektra relaxed her stance. Her hand moved from her hilt to her pocket. She produced a small object and offered it to Syn. Syn plucked up the golden coin with the chipped edge. Rem's coin? With her head fuzzy and scrambled from her injuries, it took her longer than it should have for her to realize her stalker stood before her.

Remember the altar, the note had said.

"*You!*" She shot her gaze up to level Lektra with accusation. "You're the one who's been after me. Leaving me notes and..." Her hand flew to her throbbing face. She felt at her left eye for the first time. It was painful to the slightest touch, swollen and tender. Someone had sewn the skin closed.

"Yes." Lektra's expression creased with sorrow as her sight traveled over Syn's severing wound.

"Why me?"

"I was looking for my brother, Tanok. I had been looking for him for over a month before I was captured and put on the altar. After your mercy, I resumed my search for him when I found you instead."

Lektra sighed and leaned against a rock as she explained her search for her missing brother and how she stumbled upon the discovery of the Nighterrian corruption.

Syn listened, doing her best to comprehend the story through her muddled brain. Could the girl be trusted? Or was she in on the plot as well? Hearing the desperate quiver of Lektra's voice at the mention of her brother proved at least that much of the story was true.

"I needed someone to help me unravel the exploitation, but other than my brother, I didn't know who else I could trust. Then, as I was looking for him and scouting out prisoners from Magoila's base camp, I saw you on your way to the trials. I thought if I couldn't find Tanok, maybe I could trust you because you and I somehow shared an understanding that day on the altar.

"I tried to keep you from entering the veil and I tried multiple times to warn you, but with Xedford and that girl watching you so close, I couldn't be certain where your loyalties lied. I couldn't risk approaching you or explaining further for fear you'd turn me in."

"So you turned *me* in instead?" Syn felt at the stitches crisscrossing an X over the left half of her face. The edges of the wound seeped dribbles of blood or perhaps drainage fluid.

"I'm sorry, I'm so sorry," Lektra pleaded. "I was running out of time, and I need a way to get you out of the competition. I thought if I informed your village that you were in danger, your Chief would pull you from the trials and I would get my chance to intercept you. I didn't learn about the attack on your village until after I had already told your Chief where you were, and by then it was too late." She shook her head in remorse.

Syn found Lektra earnest in her regret, but she couldn't trust or forgive her just yet. After a moment of searching her expression, Syn let the anger die. She slid down against the rock and sat down hard in the dirt.

"I suppose you couldn't have known," Syn said.

"I didn't, and you must believe me, I had no idea you would be severed."

Beneath the pain and exhaustion, Syn swam through the sea of questions. "Why didn't you go back to your own village and explain the truth?"

"And tell them that the holy warriors we've been worshiping are actually malicious criminals? I'd be whipped for blasphemy. No one would believe a Qu-Veldt anyway."

Syn understood. The word of a fourth ring citizen would never hold up against the reputation of the holy warriors. It was the same reason Syn couldn't simply return to Garon and expose the raid. Who would believe a severed girl?

Syn held her throbbing head. "I still can't believe you're alive."

Lektra unstrapped a canteen from her belt and handed it to Syn. Syn accepted it as Lektra sat down beside her. "You thought I froze to death on the altar?"

Syn nodded.

"I probably would have if I hadn't recovered from the effects of the serpent venom in time to roll myself through the portal."

Syn gripped hard onto the canteen in her hands as she tried to ground herself. "You said the Nighterrians traded you to the Gravers, but why?" A flash of the body collectors filled her mind and sent a shiver trickling down her back.

"Magoila and her gang are only half of the scheme. The Nighterrians themselves take care of the rest. They've been selling failed competitors to the Gravers in exchange for information."

"Information on what?"

Lektra looked to Syn, weariness filling her gray eyes. "You should drink." Lektra pushed at the canteen in Syn's hand. Syn sniffed at the water before guzzling it down with thankful appreciation. Lektra continued, "The Gravers found a way for a Nighterrian to survive a second imbuing."

Syn choked on the water she gulped. "*A second imbuing?*"— she coughed— "As in *two* Hal'points?"

Lektra nodded. "The Gravers have been tinkering with cadavers for centuries. Their more recent experiment into the second imbuing was funded by Revvor's raid."

Syn sputtered for words. Rumors of the Gravers' clandestine experiments were often whispered about in the village, but no one had cause to believe they posed a real threat. "That's not possible, everyone knows imbuing a second Hal'-point is a Nighterrian death sentence."

"Things have changed."

Syn thought back to her mother's vehement reaction that day in the workroom when Syn inquired about multiple Hallowed Points. She was beginning to grasp the depth of a sacrilege more than one Hal'point could prove. Still, she couldn't deny her curiosity.

"How is it done?"

Lektra studied Syn, as if deciding whether she could trust her. After a moment she leaned in. "The plumb-bloods are the key. I don't fully understand it, but what I do know is if a Nighterrian consumes the blood of a newly imbued, when the second Hallowed Point is harvested and given to the new host, his body will not reject it."

Syn's thoughts flashed to Gordon's lifeless body and his purple blood. A new terror struck her as she thought if Captain Revvor's transformation over the course of the trials. "The captain, is he...?"

"Yes. From what I can tell I think he's already achieved a second imbuing. It won't be long before the whole crew steals their second as well."

"You mean the entire raid is in on it too?"

"Yes."

"Even... Xedford?"

"Especially Xedford." Rage crossed Lektra's expression as she spoke his name.

But he saved my life. It occurred to Syn that Lektra could be lying. She regarded her with scrutiny. "How do you know all this?"

"I was there. I saw it happen."

Lektra dove into a gruesome story of a bald man and a plumb-blood in a barbershop. She followed it up with the explanation of a trip through the woods with Xedford and how the meeting with the Gravers was cut short by an attack.

Syn puzzled through the timeline fitting together the pieces of when she found Xedford stumbling through the woods on the brink of death. Exhaustion and loss of blood made it hard for Syn to think. She had to walk herself through each event, but the fragments began to fall into place. A spike of horror echoed through her with every revelation of Lektra's story. Syn studied Lektra's face as she spoke and found naked truth.

"... and then I met you shortly after when I was put on the altar in Garon," Lektra concluded.

All Syn could think of was Xedford touching her in the dark of the cave. Her skin crawled, and she feared she might be sick.

A sudden bolt of realization jumped through her veins. She sat up straight, dropping the empty canteen.

"There are fifteen Nighterrians in the raid... and-and they're taking fifteen inductees. That means they're using everyone who makes it through the trials as an incubator for a second Hal'point!" She clapped her hand over her mouth. "Relia!"

"That blonde-headed girl?"

Syn jumped to her feet. "She's just finished the final trial.

We have to get to her!" She felt like a fool for not thinking of her sooner. Syn's mind churned with calculations. "By now she might have already been imbued. But even if she hasn't, she's still in danger."

Lektra offered a grim nod. "I'm sorry, but there's nothing we can do."

"We need to save her!" Syn raced toward the grunt. All pain and exhaustion retreated from her awareness as plans for Relia's rescue thrust all else aside.

"Wait!" Lektra followed and grabbed the reins out of Syn's hands. "What are you doing? You can't just ride up to the Imbuing Hall. And even if you could get up there, the crew would shoot you on sight."

"I have to try. I can't just let them kill her."

"I'm sorry about your friend, but this is not the way to do this. We need to find proof to bring back to our people. We can't bring down the corruption if we're dead."

"There's no time for proof! We need to get to her before it's too late."

"We'd never make it."

"I can't leave her behind, not again. What if it was your brother? You can't tell me you wouldn't at least try to save him."

Something shifted in Lektra's eyes, and Syn knew she had said the right thing. "So, what do you want to do? You want the two of us to infiltrate the Hall alone?" Lektra asked. "We'd be running straight to our death at the end of a three-barrel."

"No, not alone." Syn mounted the grunt and looked down at Lektra "You said you've been to Magoila's base camp?"

"Yes, why?"

"Could you find it again?"

Lektra hesitated, then nodded.

Syn extended her hand. "Then let's go get our reinforcements."

Lektra shook her head, but a smile crept over her mouth. "You're insane," she said, but grabbed hold of Syn's outstretched hand and jumped onto the grunt's back.

"I get that a lot." Syn smiled and kicked the grunt into motion.

48
SINGLE-BARREL

Tucked away behind a plot of jutting rocks, Magoila's base consisted of three wooden buildings and a large, fenced pen for the grunts. A campfire blazed outside where four rugged men sat laughing and drinking from a glass jug they passed around.

Syn and Lektra left their grunt behind and out of earshot so it wouldn't alarm anyone of their presence, but it seemed the added oinks would have made little difference. The four men took up singing a lurid tune about women and drinking.

Syn followed Lektra around the back of a rock to get a better view of the camp. Syn narrowed her eyes at the brigand wearing a gold earring. She gripped her fist around Elaine as she identified him as one of the men who attacked her at the Outpost.

"What now?" Syn asked in a hushed tone.

"You tell me, this was your idea," Lektra said.

"Which one of these buildings holds the prisoners?"

Lektra pointed to a windowless shack on the far right.

One of the men let out a loud belch to the cheers of the

other three. They quicky picked back up with their crude song. *"With whores galore and ale on pour, what could a man want more?"*

"Do you think they'll even notice if we just sneak over there and break the lock?" Syn asked.

Lektra studied the singing men with a frown and shrugged. "It's worth a shot."

Syn valued her bravery. The determined look on Lektra's face reminded her of Relia. Syn took a deep breath to calm her nerves and stepped out from behind the boulder but stopped as she recognized the sound of hoof beats. Back into the shadows she slunk just as Magoila came riding up, a single grunt and captive in tow.

Through the dust covering her face, Magoila's expression radiated coldhearted rage. Her left sleeve hung unbuttoned, exposing a hidden weapon. The small barrel strapped to her wrist caught the firelight as she dismounted and stepped over to the men.

"Is that a *single*-barrel?" Syn asked. It must have been the source of the shot she heard earlier when Lektra rescued her.

Lektra nodded. "They're illegal, but a lot of the Terraborns around here carry them in secret."

Syn put the marvel of the sacrilegious weapon out of her head as she watched Magoila reach the campfire. Three men fell silent while one who had his back turned continued to sing despite the warning expressions of the others. Magoila announced her presence by kicking the jug out of the singing man's hands.

"What are you useless bags of shit doing?" Magoila demanded.

"We was just having us a drink," slurred the one with the earring.

"'*Just having a drink,*'" Magoila mocked. "Our posse has been set upon and you four sit here getting drunk?"

The men looked around as if noticing for the first time that she hadn't returned with a retinue of grunts and prisoners. They jumped to their feet and clumsily grabbed at their swords as if the threat lay imminent.

"Useless nincompoops!" Magoila threw her hands in the air and stomped over to the grunt carrying her single captive.

"Where's Bo?" asked one of the men.

Magoila extracted a short arrow from her quiver attached to the grunt and loaded it into her single barrel. "Dead," she said without looking up as she added powder to her weapon. "Two of you go and search for the rest of the grunts, they can't have gone far." Magoila handed the reigns of the grunt with the boy tied to the back to a potbellied man. "And the two of you go on and put this one with the rest. Stay here and keep watch."

The brigands mumbled agreements and moved to obey orders. Magoila jumped onto her steed and rode off leading the two men on foot.

The remaining two went about securing the prisoner. Syn nodded to Lektra. "Now is our chance." With her good eye, she glared at the familiar brigand. "I call the one with the earring."

Lektra drew her short sword. Together they crept from their hiding place.

"Nothing like Mags to go and ruin a good old time," complained the man with the earring as he fumbled with the lock on the shed.

"Bitch is always giving us orders... do this, kill that." The potbellied man worked on untying the ropes holding the paralyzed prisoner.

Syn padded with care through the dirt. She emerged from behind the shed and waited to hear the lock click open.

"You know, I been thinking we could start our own damn posse of—"

Syn bashed him over the head with the butt of her dagger. However, he didn't drop him to the ground like she hoped. He grabbed the top of his head and whirled around.

Syn ducked the heavy fist that flew at her face. She heard Lektra engage the other outlaw as she dodged another blow. Syn's drunken opponent drew a sword from his belt. She stepped backward and did her best to remember her training, but it felt like her limbs were too slow to obey and her severed eye made her unbalanced.

The man swayed with drunkenness but lunged, forcing her to take another step back toward the campfire. He reared back for another strike, but Syn got inside his swing and slashed at his stomach before stumbling out of the way of his falling sword. Distracted by the cut, he staggered and cursed. Syn shuffled around him. She delivered a powerful kick to his back, and he toppled forward into the campfire.

Flames devoured his face and clothes. Shrieks filled the night. He ejected himself from the pit and ran screaming into the dark. With half his body ablaze, panic carried him directly into a boulder where he smacked face first and fell to the ground.

Syn turned over her shoulder to find Lektra pulling her sword from her opponent's gut where he lay in a pool of blood.

"Someone will have heard that. We need to hurry." Lektra yanked her sword free and turned to the shed.

Syn ran to the door and pulled it open. Inside, fearful eyes looked up at her from huddled positions. With relief, she noticed they wiggled against their restrains, indicating the effects of the venom had worn off. *Thank the Legion.* It would have been nearly impossible to liberate them if they couldn't run.

Lektra joined her and they bent about cutting free the gags from their mouths and the ropes that bound their hands and feet. Among all the red Terraborn stares, Syn spotted Drekton's brown eyes as they widened in disbelief. She hurried to cut him free.

He coughed as she removed his gag. "Syn? What in the Abyss are you doing here?" His eyes fell on her severed face, and he drew back in revulsion.

It wasn't the warm welcome she wanted, but she supposed she couldn't hope for more. "Saving you," she said and helped him to his feet.

Syn looked around, only six captives occupied the shack. If she counted the boy tied to the grunt outside, all together they had a team of nine. Not the best army to storm the Imbuing Hall, but it would have to do, it was all they had.

The freed captives stood; their bodies seemed to need a moment to adjust to movement after being bound. They didn't have a moment, however. If Magoila heard the dying screams of her men, she could be headed back their way any minute.

"We have to go." Syn ushered the group forward.

"Follow us." Lektra helped the final boy to his feet and dashed out the door.

Confused and shaken, the freed captives stumbled out of the shed and followed Lektra. Syn took up the rear. With their original Grunt far off in the other direction, Syn left it in favor of the grunt with the blue-lipped boy bound to its back. She grabbed hold of the reigns and yanked it along as they made their escape.

After a hurried retreat up into up into the crags, Lektra came to a stop to allow the boys to catch their breaths. She looked to Syn with an eyebrow raised as if waiting for instructions.

Syn dropped the reins of the grunt and trembled inside. It

occurred to her the task ahead included convincing a troop of boys—who just barely escaped with their lives—to risk returning to the site of their demise. Most of them were bitter Terraborns already prejudiced against Surfacers. And Syn was but a Severed Legionite outcast. She didn't know where to begin, luckily Drekton started for her.

"What's going on, how did you find us?" he asked.

Syn cleared her throat. "As you all probably figured out, the apprentices—along with Revvor's entire raid—are corrupt. The past couple seasons they've been trading the eliminated competitors to outlaws and Gravers."

"Why?" asked a boy. His red eyes bounced between Syn and Lektra.

Syn wasn't sure how much to divulge. The secret of the second imbuing was dangerous information. In the wrong hands it already proved disastrous. "Revvor's desire for power has driven him mad." She paused to peer around the small group. They were hungry and tired. Behind their confused stares she read doubt but most of all, fear.

"What do you want from us? Why did you go and save us?" asked another boy.

Syn realized they wanted assurance that she didn't rescue them only to throw them back into captivity.

"Please," she began, groping for the right words while attempting to command an air of authority. "The competitors who passed the third trial are in danger." She looked over to Lektra who nodded for her to continue. "We have reason to believe they will all be murdered by the crew. Lektra and I plan to infiltrate the Imbuing Hall and rescue the newly Imbued before the Nighterrians murder them. I know you all have been through a lot, and all of you now have your freedom, but we need your help. I ask that you to join us."

A tense moment passed. Syn held her breath trying not to let her brave façade crumble as she waited.

A boy near the back of the group broke the silence. "You've up and lost your damned mind. I'm out of here." He turned to leave.

The rest of the crowd echoed similar sentiments and began to disperse.

"Wait," Syn pleaded, desperate now, "you can't leave, we need your help!"

"You said we're free, or are you fixing to hold us captive and force us to fight?"

"No, but... the raid's corruption will never be exposed unless we take a stand."

Heads shook. Two boys took the opportunity to ensure their freedom and scampered off. Another jumped onto the grunt and, despite Lektra's attempt to stop him, rode it away with the paralyzed boy still attached. Lektra gave up the chase as they raced away. There went their only grunt.

"No, please, you have to..." Syn abandoned her plea as more boys used the distraction of the stolen grunt to slink away into the shadows.

"Looks like this is the thanks we get." Lektra said.

Syn shook her head. She couldn't say she blamed them. Her plan was foolhardy. She looked up as someone stepped forward. Drekton, the only recruit remaining.

"Tell me why you're really doing this," he said.

Syn looked into his eyes and felt the familiar ache of shame she'd carried since Rem's death. The guilt was accompanied by a twitch of nervous energy. Drekton the dutiful. Perhaps she could rally the part of him who valued honor above all else.

"There's no time, I can explain on the way if you're going to join us," Syn said.

"I'm not about to throw myself into a hopeless rescue

mission. I'm here for answers."

Syn looked to Lektra for help. She sighed and began the explanation. Together they took turns expositing the crew's hunger for power and the instrument of their desire.

"What kind of power would a second Hallowed Point grant them?" he asked.

"We're not sure," Lektra said. "But we can only imagine it increases the Nighterrian's strength and abilities significantly."

"Haven't you seen the captain lately?" added Syn.

Drekton responded with a serious nod. His eyes roamed over the ugly side of Syn's face in a way that made her want to cover it. "Did the captain sever you?"

"No." Syn looked away in shame.

Drekton remained silent as Syn explained Groth's arrival after the second trial. He continued to scrutinize her as Lektra went on to explain the depth of the raid's exploitation. Syn watched his apprehension solidify into indignation.

By the end, he shook his head. "You're never going to make it to the Imbuing Hall. Even if you do, they'll shoot you dead before you can accomplish anything."

Syn's hopes fluttered to the floor like dead leaves. She tried to think of what else she could do to convince him, but she stuttered for words.

Lektra piped up, "The Nighterrians lied about a lot of things. We may not be as helpless as you think." She shrugged the pack she carried off her shoulder and began to undo the ties. "I have something that could give us an advan—"

Her words stopped on the way to her lips as a bang exploded her chest with a splatter of blood. Syn hardly had time to register the sight of the arrow tip jutting out from Lektra's sternum before she fell to her knees.

Behind her, obscured beneath the cover of night, Magoila smiled and lowered her single-barrel.

49
TRAP

Syn grabbed hold of Lektra and yanked her back behind a boulder before she fell to the dirt. Syn could hear Magoila laugh and load another steel arrow into her single-barrel.

Blood spewed from Lektra's mouth as Syn held her. "Please..." Lektra choked. More blood coughed from her lips. "... find... Tanok..." With a fleeting breath of strength, she half lifted the pack still in her grasp.

Syn took the bag. Her hands trembled over the arrow protruding from Lektra's chest. She had to do something! What could she do? Nothing, she realized in a moment of hope-shattering despair.

Lektra's lips mouthed a single word. *Please.*

Syn read her imploring stare and felt as if she were on the altar in Garon once more. "I'll find him, I promise."

Part of Syn registered the metal clicking of Magoila's fully loaded single-barrel, but she couldn't abandon Lektra.

"Syn, we need to go." Drekton tugged at her.

Syn stood in place holding the girl she barely knew as footsteps approached from the other side of the bolder. "I'll find your brother," Syn promised again.

It was all she could offer, and she thought she could read relief in Lektra's pained expression. Lektra stared up at Syn as her body jerked with the drowning of blood and her gray eyes went wide with acceptance.

Her stare unfocused and her body went limp.

Locked in a state of shock, Syn would have stayed there holding her as an arrow found its home in her own chest if it weren't for Drekton. He yanked her backward and forced her to duck as Magoila rounded the corner and fired at them. The arrow burrowed into the boulder behind them.

"We have to go!" Drekton yelled. Magoila reloaded.

"I can't just leave her!" Despite her words, she lowered Lektra to the ground.

"She's dead, there's nothing we can do." Drekton pulled her along in retreat.

Syn shouldered Lektra's pack and let Drekton lead her away. She looked over her shoulder for one last glimpse of Lektra's body. "I'm sorry," she said to the poor girl with gray eyes.

Then she ran.

She glimpsed Magoila gather her grunt to give chase as they ran through the dark. They dodged boulders and jumped over jutting rocks. Shouts and hoofbeats followed close behind.

They made their way up the steep incline of the crags with adrenaline pounding them forward. Syn scrambled over boulders in a route she hoped the grunt couldn't follow. She helped Drekton over a short wall of rocks and noticed the empty scabbard at his belt. Her terror mounted as she realized Elaine was their only weapon.

Just as this thought crossed her mind, the hulking shadow

of a brigand jumped from behind a boulder. The barrel-chested man slashed out with his sword.

Syn leapt back as Drekton ducked and delivered a punch to the man's side. Unperturbed by the blow, the outlaw stepped toward Syn with another swing of his blade. Her blind eye left her exposed to darkness on one side and her defense suffered. Syn threw up her dagger with a clumsy block that just barely kicked the sword off its trajectory.

Drekton dispensed a hard kick to the man's ribs which threw him off balance as he swung again. Syn dodged away but heard hoofbeats close behind.

Magoila was coming.

Syn stepped in for a killing strike. She brought Elaine down on the man's face, but he regained his balance just in time to knock her arm away with such force she fell backward. Someone caught her from behind, however, and she just had time to register it was Drekton as he wrapped his fingers over the hand she had clutched around Elaine. He carried both their grips forward and slammed the dagger into the man's chest.

They held the blade there, hand on top of hand, as shock registered across the man's face. Drekton let go and Syn pulled Elaine free. It uncorked a fountain of blood. The brigand dropped like a heap of rocks.

The ground trembled with hoofbeats. Syn whirled around just as Magoila rode past. Syn jumped out of the way as the air cracked with a boom and a steel arrow sailed past her face and burrowed into the dirt.

She turned around to watch Magoila gallop away when she noticed the final brigand emerge from the dark. Drekton had his back turned as he commandeered the dead man's sword.

"Drekton, look out!"

Drekton whipped around with his new weapon in hand and faced the massive outlaw. Any sign of the man's previous drunkenness evaporated in the place of hostile anger. The two squared up for a fight.

Syn whirled back to Magoila. She watched her pull her grunt to a halt and jump gracefully off its back. Magoila didn't bother to reload her barrel. Instead, she pulled a curved sword from her belt. Syn tightened her grip on her trusty friend and readied herself for the fight. She heard the clang of metal as Drekton engaged the outlaw behind her.

"You done cost me a year's worth of profit, girl." Magoila stalked forward. "No one messes with Magoila and lives to tell about it." A smile crackled at the edges of her mouth as she closed in.

Panic burned up through Syn's body as the cutthroat woman circled her. Syn knew she was vulnerable on her blind left side, so she shuffled to keep Magoila on her right.

Magoila's predatory eyes twinkled with mirth. "It's a real shame I gotta skin you alive. You'd make a fine little outlaw... or a pretty little *whore!*" —she jumped in with the speed of a serpent's strike.

Syn just had time to raise her dagger to deflect the blow. Magoila's sword bounced off Elaine and sliced Syn's shoulder. Magoila coiled up for another attack.

Syn spotted something upon a rock a few paces away.

Invigorated by her discovery, Syn pressed forward. She turned out of the way of Magoila's next strike and caught a shallow slice to her back. She hardly felt the pain as she danced backward, allowing the woman gain on her.

"You can't run from me, girl!" Magoila pushed Syn back with a swing that met only air.

"I don't have to run from you." The farther Syn retreated, the more familiar the landscape appeared.

"Then quit your running and fight me!"

"You know what I think?" Syn took one final step back.

Magoila smiled knowing she had Syn cornered against a boulder. "I don't give a damn what you think." She swung down with a killing strike.

Syn stepped out of the way of the blade and stuck out her foot. Magoila's swing carried her weight forward and Syn's intercepting foot caused her trip. Magoila caught herself with her other foot and remained standing on a flat rock. She smiled at Syn's pathetic attempt for a split second, then the clicking of gears sounded and a boulder slid backward. The rock under Magoila's foot popped forward and dumped her into a pit of hissing snakes.

"I think you'd look lovely with blue lips," Syn said.

The sound of Magoila's scream cut off as the boulder with Syn's fox pelt coat slid back into place and the serpents' bite went to work.

50
THREE-BARREL

Syn didn't dare revel in Magoila's defeat as the clang of metal echoed off the rocks behind her. She dashed away to Drekton.

The brigand had him pressed up against a rock with a massive axe locked against Drekton's sword. The man forced his enormous weight forward and the double edge of Drekton's blade cut into the soft flesh of his neck.

Syn arrived on padded feet to carry out a single slice. She snuck up behind the outlaw and, in one swift motion, she ripped Elaine across the man's throat. Blood spewed over Drekton and drenched him in a thick rain. He shoved the dying man backward and the brigand fell to the ground with a gurgle, then silence. Drekton looked to Syn, bleeding and covered in gore, yet his eyes shone with gratitude.

"Thanks." Drekton spat blood from his mouth and leaned against the rock to catch his breath.

Syn returned Elaine to her belt and rescued the sword from the dead man's hip to add to her own arsenal. "We should go.

Magoila's operation could extend past the few outlaws we saw, and they could be coming this way at any time."

After wiping the blood from his eyes, Drekton uttered the very words Syn feared. "We need to get back to Garon."

"The crew is about to Imbue Relia, then drink her blood and rip out her Hal'point for their own sick gain."

Drekton shook his head. "There's nothing we can do. There's only two of us against the whole crew plus the apprentices."

"I know it's hopeless, but I have to try." Syn touched the throbbing half of her face and felt at her stitches. "I can't return to Garon. Not anymore."

Drekton's expression softened. He opened his mouth, then closed it. Was that pity or disgust Syn read in his eyes? "Do you even have a plan?" he asked.

Syn nodded. "Get to the Imbuing Hall, steal Relia away from the crew, and make our escape."

"So, you don't have a plan."

"I—"

"What's in the pack?" He motioned toward Syn's back.

Lektra's pack hung nearly forgotten over Syn's shoulder. She felt nauseous thinking of Lektra, and the arrow tip plunged through her chest. Syn pushed the image if her dying stare away and pulled open the pack. She reached in and her hand closed around smooth metal. With her mouth agape, she extracted the single item.

A silvery three-barrel dangled from her grasp.

Drekton dug his hand into the pack and searched around. He came up with a small pouch and handed it to Syn.

"Blackpowder." Syn recognized the dark sand inside the pouch as what Xedford used to reload his three-barrel.

Drekton felt around the pack but didn't produce anything else. "No ammunition."

Syn sighed and joined Drekton in leaning against the rock. She glanced over at Magoila's grunt as it wandered around slobbering and oinking. An idea struck her. She handed Drekton the three-barrel. He held it by the leather straps as if, after everything, he still believed it too sacred to touch. Syn left him and his foolish piousness behind to tread over to Magoila's grunt.

She approached with care so she wouldn't spook it. It snorted and stepped back as its four eyes caught sight of her. "Don't worry... I'm not going to hurt you." She held her hands up in surrender before grabbing hold of the reigns. The grunt moaned and stamped his feet but didn't protest otherwise. "Good boy."

Syn searched Magoila's saddle bags. She found a supply of hard crackers and a half-full canteen, but the real prize she sought hung near the front of the saddle on the right side.

She unbuckled a small quiver of metal arrows. Two remained, but they weren't the wooden shaft and feather arrows Syn was used to. Drekton walked up, three-barrel still dangled in his grasp. Syn handed him one of the arrows. He held it up to examine it in the starlight. The arrows were short and made entirely of metal with tiny holes at the back of the shaft.

"I don't get it," he said. "What are you thinking? Without being imbued ourselves, we have no way to use a three-barrel."

Syn supposed she could pull Magoila's paralyzed body from the trap and take her single-barrel, but the serpents posed too high a risk. *No, this will have to work.* She knelt to the ground and told Drekton to set everything down on the dirt. She had watched Xedford load a three-barrel and she closed her eyes for a moment to revive the memory. She then went about clicking the various gears the way she remembered and filling the metal container at the elbow end of the weapon with blackpowder.

Lektra's final words came back to her with sudden clarity as she loaded the weapon with the two arrows. *The Nighterrians lied about a lot of things.*

"The Nighterrians lied about the trials, maybe they lied about other things too." She thought of the blue-eyed Nighterrian, and the scar-faced Nighterrian she glimpsed in the cave during the third trial.

"You think you can shoot it without breaking your arm?"

"Not me." The two arrows made satisfying clicks as she loaded them in. If only she had one more.

"You want *me* to shoot it?"

"No, us." Syn stood and started searching around in the dirt.

"Are you serious?"

"Deadly," Syn said, unable to keep from chuckling at her dark joke. Perhaps, after the events of the previous two days, she truly *had* begun to lose her mind.

"What are you looking for?"

"Ah-hah!" Syn spotted the last arrow Magoila shot buried in the dirt. She dug it free as Drekton continued to voice his protest.

"You can't really be thinking of going back there. It would be suicide."

"You don't have to come with me." She extracted the arrow from the ground and looked over her shoulder at Drekton. "You can take the grunt back to Garon and tell them what happened here. You're loved by the village. They might even believe you."

Drekton gave Magoila's grunt a look of contempt. "No. I told myself I would come back a Nighterrian or not at all."

Syn remembered promising herself something similar.

With her hand clenched tight around the arrow, she waited for him to make his decision.

Eventually he sighed and pulled his hand through his hair. "I suppose coming back as someone's hero would be close enough."

Drekton, you wonderful, honor-bound fool! If their situation weren't so grave, Syn would have leapt for joy. "Are you sure? Like you said, it's a suicide mission. Who will warn our people about the Nighterrians if we die?"

Drekton shrugged. "I suppose we'll just have to not die."

Warmth gathered in Syn's chest. "I'll do my best."

"You know that once we cross the veil they'll know were coming."

"I know," she said.

"And how are we supposed to get all the way up to the Imbuing Hall?"

That was a problem. If only they could sprout wings and fly to the top of the Rock of Reckoning. Syn toyed with the arrow in her grasp as she racked her brain. She felt at the hole at the back of the arrow shaft. A wild thought hatched into a creative solution.

She turned to regard the serpent trap. If she squinted into the dark, she could just make out the lines of the strangle wire holding the gears in place in a series of crossing webs.

Although it hurt her face to do so, Syn grinned. She resisted the urge to begin laughing in maniacal victory. She would leave that to Relia once they rescued her.

51
THE HALL

The scream of the ghost moths echoed their warning call as Syn and Drekton leaped through the veil. Their feet pounded the ground on the other side, and with thankful relief, Syn saw the ramp up to the second tier still stood in place. She raced alongside Drekton with a stolen sword bouncing at her side and the loaded three-barrel in her grasp.

The scream of agitated moths faded as they ran up the ramp. Syn wished Lektra could have explained how she moved in and out of the trial grounds without setting off the alarm. They made haste knowing the captain probably already dispatched a team to investigate the breach in the perimeter. They reached the second tier, panting in heavy breaths. Syn's eye throbbed with every beat of her heart, but she pushed the pain away to focus on their next steps.

Syn had considered working their way up the system of doors and pulleys or searching out a tunnel inside the rock walls, but it would take far too long. The risk of getting lost in the maze of tunnels or taking the wrong pulley remained too great. They needed to get to the top before it was too late. It if it wasn't already.

"Are you ready?" she asked.

"If we break both our arms, it's your fault." He held out his left wrist.

Syn placed the three-barrel over both his left arm and her right. She held the weapon in place while Drekton secured the leather straps on the underside of their arms and notched the three buckles as tight as they would go. Once secure, they stepped back to the edge of the tier and pointed the three-barrel up toward the lip of the Rock towering above them. Syn could just see the stone pillars of the Imbuing Hall that made up the third tier.

"Here goes nothing." Syn sent a silent prayer to the Legion.

With her free hand, she extracted the strangle wire they had collected from the trap. One end of the strangle wire was tied to the shaft of the arrow loaded into the middle barrel. The other end they had spooled up around a stick. She held the spooled wire out to the side to let it unwind in preparation for the yank of the arrow. With her right hand, she did her best to steady Drekton's aim.

With delicate hands, Drekton extended the little contraption at the underside of his wrist. The mechanism clicked into place, and he curled his fingers around the metal trigger. Neither of them knew exactly how to operate the weapon, but based on what they witnessed from the Nighterrians, all they needed to do was squeeze down on the trigger.

"Here we go."

Drekton fired.

The recoil of the blast sent a jolt though both their arms and they nearly fell backward off the edge of the cliff. But they regained their balance and marveled at their fully intact arms. The kick of the weapon proved strong but far from risking bone breakage. With their combined strength, they were able to keep the weapon controlled.

Syn looked up at the arrow. It found its mark wedged into the rock at the top of the second tier, but her hopes dropped as she noticed the spool of wire was not connected to the shaft of the arrow.

She glanced down at the three-barrel and realized her mistake: the first barrel on the right sat empty. They only had enough strangle-wire to connect it to one arrow and she assumed the first round to leave the barrel would come from the center.

She angled the good side of her face to Drekton with a look of innocence. "At least our arms aren't broken."

Drekton lifted an eyebrow without a word.

"Again." Syn raised their conjoined arms.

She couldn't be certain the next round to fire would be the center barrel, but there remained no other option but to test it out. They took aim. Syn caught the glint of steel out the corner of her right eye. Two apprentices slipped from behind the curve of the rock and sneaked toward them on silent feet.

"Shoot!" Syn shouted as she returned to holding their aim.

Drekton fired the weapon and the metal arrow burrowed itself into the rock at the top of the tier with the wire stringing off the end.

The apprentices hurdled toward them. Drekton flicked the trigger mechanism out of his grip. He drew his sword with his free hand and held it between his teeth. Syn looped the end of the spool of wire around her belt and together they started to climb up the wall, using the wire to haul themselves upward.

The first of the two boys reached them. Drekton held onto the wire with this three-barrel hand and took his sword from his mouth to slashed out with his free hand. Syn heard the metal clank of their blades as she turned to meet the second incoming apprentice. She held onto the strangle wire and tucked her legs out of the way of his slash. His sword bit into the rock. When he went to yank it free from the wall, Syn used the split second of opportunity to land a brutal kick to his face. She heard his nose crunch and he fell backward.

Syn tried to climb higher but with her arm still attached to Drekton through the three-barrel, she couldn't get far. Drekton defended the best he could but their position dangling from the wall put him in a vulnerable spot. The apprentice knocked the blade from Drekton's grip and smiled.

Guessing his next move, Syn fell in sync with Drekton's final line of defense. The apprentice reared back to lunge in with an overhead strike, just as Syn and Drekton pushed off the wall. Together they kicked the boy in the chest with the power of their combined weight. The apprentice flew back; the force of the kick carried him over the edge of the tier.

They returned to climbing as the second apprentice found his feet and wiped purple blood from his nose. Syn glanced over her shoulder to find Torrance arrive on the scene.

Drekton and Syn scrambled up the rock as best they could, but the attachment of their arms beneath the three-barrel made the climb clumsy and awkward. The apprentice's sword slashed at their feet. Syn felt the tip of the blade graze the bottom of her boot. At the rate they were going, they were never going to make it.

Drekton stopped climbing. With his free hand, he reached for the three-barrel and began unbuckling the straps.

"What are you doing?"

"Go save Relia. I'll take care of them." He nodded to the apprentices gathered below just as two more apprentices rounded the corner.

"What are you crazy? It's four on one and you don't even have a weapon."

"Sometimes crazy is all you need."

He loosened the last strap of the three-barrel and let himself slip free and drop to the ground. The apprentices surrounded him on all sides with weapons drawn. Drekton stood from his crouch—unarmed and outnumbered.

A breath of heart pounding silence. Then, the unexpected. To Syn's shock, as well as the rest of the apprentices, Drekton began to laugh. He let out a bubble of laughter which grew into a maniacal cackle that reeked of insanity. Syn stared in awe as the rest of the apprentices hesitated. A few even lowered their blades in confusion as he continued to laugh.

Syn stole the opportunity. Extracting her stolen sword from her belt she yelled, "Drekton!"

His laughter cut off as he looked up. Syn dropped her sword and Drekton caught it out of the air. Without a second of hesitation, he dove into battle seizing his opponents' momentary confusion.

"Go!" he yelled without looking up at her.

Syn climbed to the sound of clamor below her. *Legion bless you, Drekton Du-Garon.* She cut her hands on the sharp, unforgiving wire and forced herself not to look down. Drekton was the best fighter his age in Garon. He could hold his own against the apprentices. At least that's what she told herself as she focused on rescuing Relia.

It must have been Drekton trailing them on that day beside the veil. It seemed they both had learned from Relia's clever antics.

With bloodied hands, Syn reached the spot where the arrow sat burrowed into the rock. Voices carried out from the open columns of the Imbuing Hall. Syn quietly hauled herself up onto the ledge and scrambled for cover behind a pillar carved with scenes of battle. She untied the strangle wire from her belt and tightened the straps of the three-barrel on her wrist.

After waiting a moment to ascertain no one had seen her, she pulled Rem's coin from her pocket and kissed it for good luck. "Rem, grant me strength." She returned the coin to her pocket and yanked Elaine from her belt. "It's just you and me now."

She peeked out from behind the pillar. The Imbuing Hall laid out before her with the open walls holding a domed roof up by stone columns. She felt a strange tug at her soul and recognized the feeling before she set eyes on the portal. The glimmering gate hovered its presence on the ground like a small pond.

Her head pounded with the sound of her racing heartbeat as she flicked her gaze toward the ritual taking place. Captain Revvor stood in front of the portal holding his golden three-barrel up against a boy's chest. The tall teenager wore a black cloak and stood with his chest puffed up against the barrel.

"Welcome to the raid," Captain Revvor said, and fired the three-barrel into the boy's chest.

The boy gasped and stumbled backward. An older Nighter-rian with blue eyes caught him by the arm. Syn froze at the sight of the man she glimpsed in the cavern during the third trial. The boy moaned and doubled over as the blue-eyed Nighterrian escorted him through the portal. The pair disappeared through the other side toward whatever lay beyond.

Syn surveyed the rest of the Hall. A throng of Nighterrians lined the room. There were more than the fifteen crewmen she had come to recognize over the course of the trials. Who were these other men? She scanned the crowd looking for Xedford, but instead her sight landed on the other man she recognized from the cavern: the Nighterrian with the burn scars. He stood at attention watching the captain.

Revvor walked around a set of nine pedestals positioned in a semi-circle around the portal. Each pedestal contained an open empty box. Revvor waltzed up to the final box and plucked up the final object. He held it up between his fingers. The object was the size of a bullet but shaped like the tip of an arrowhead. A strange, ephemeral glow surrounded it with a soft blue aura.

A Hallowed Point.

Syn had never seen one before, but she knew nothing else that glowed with such an unnatural, awe-inspiring light—as if power emanated from the pointed bullet.

Syn tore her eye away from the Hal'point and risked a further glance around the Hall. The other finishers must have already left through the portal after being imbued. She searched for Relia, but the stone pillar blocked her sight of the far end of the Hall. She didn't see Xedford either.

Revvor loaded the Hal'point into his golden three-barrel. "And for our final finisher, and I ought to add, a mighty fine addition to our raid..." Revvor smiled, and Syn watched the spidering blue veins pulse from where they crept up his neck to his face. "I must say, darlin', you up and surprised every one of us. Women-folk don't often make it through the trials."

Syn watched a short, cloaked figure approach the captain. A lock of wild blonde hair bounced out from beneath the hood. Syn recognized the confident cadence of her walk. *She's alive and not yet imbued!* Syn nearly jumped out from behind the column but forced herself to remain tactful. She looked down at the three-barrel strapped to her own wrist. One arrow remained.

Revvor smiled a monstrous grin and pressed the Hal'point-loaded barrel against Relia's neck. "What's your name, darlin'?"

"Relia."

Syn extended the little lever at the bottom of her wrist and held the trigger of the three-barrel in her palm. She raised her arm to take aim, pointing the final arrow at the captain's face.

"Well, Relia, welcome to the rai—"

Syn pulled the trigger. The force of the recoil knocked her backward and she nearly fell off the ledge but caught the carved pillar by her fingertips. She recovered in time to watch the arrow pierce through the air and whoosh harmlessly past Revvor's face.

With his hand still holding the three-barrel poised over Relia's throat, the captain slowly turned his head to where the shot originated. His red eyes pulsed with vicious delight as they slid over Syn. Every head in the Hall jerked toward her. Tense silence froze the air for the length of a heartbeat.

Then the Hall erupted into chaos.

52
FRIENDS

Shots cracked the air. Syn scrambled to her feet on the edge of where the stone column met the sheer drop below. The tiny ledge allowed her enough room to hide but no space to fight. She moved to her right to escape her vulnerable position only to meet the end of a three-barrel. Syn knocked the Nighterrian's arm away with her own three-barreled fist just as he pulled the trigger. The shot went wild.

Bullets pounded the stone column. Through the cacophony, she heard the captain yell something that sounded like, "I want her alive." The shuddering crack of bullets ceased only to be replaced with the scrape of swords.

A blade swung out of the darkness from her blind left side. She barely ducked in time to miss the slice. The man reared back for another strike but Syn dove around the pillar into the Hall. She rolled out of the dive and jumped to her feet with Elaine in hand.

The glint of pointed steel flew out from every direction. Syn blocked and dodged, but her blind eye left her open to unseen attacks. She shuffled back in retreat as she felt the sting of slices and cuts nick her body. The onslaught of Nighterrian blades forced her further into the Imbuing Hall.

Outnumbered against an army of superhumans, desperation made her forget her years of training. She swung Elaine around in wild arcs like a cornered animal. The faces of the Nighterrian men creased into ragged, hungry smiles as they closed in like a pack of wolves. The imagery morphed into reality with a gut-sinking twist when one of the crewmen's sneers sprouted fangs.

Syn's defense faltered. A slice caught her in the side, and she stumbled. The faces of the men began to melt and transform into monstrosities. *No!* Terror dug in and clouded her senses. She realized she had been too distracted by her rescue attempt to recognize her pounding headache as a sentinel's cry for the onset of her haunting. Her broken mind seized her, and the hoard of creatures pressed in.

The captain yelled something, and the tips of blades halted at Syn's face. The brutal strength of Nighterrian hands ripped Elaine from her grasp and tossed the dagger away. She screamed as she fought the ghosts of her fractured soul. The crew arrested her struggling body and smashed her onto the hard stone floor.

Syn glanced up to find swords in every direction. She searched the crowd of terrorizing faces for Xedford, but she couldn't find him.

The swords parted to let the captain through. With him, he dragged Relia by a fist full of her hair. She struggled and flung curses, but Revvor didn't seem to notice. Syn realized he no longer looked sickly and frail, just monstrous. He pulled Relia along with the ease of a man dragging a mouse by its tail and threw her to the ground beside Syn.

Relia snapped her attention toward Syn and glared. "What have you done?" Her voice cracked with hurt and rage.

Syn crawled toward her. "Relia, I'm sorry. I—"

The captain yanked Syn up by the collar. "Come to try and steal a Hal'point, have you?" The pulsing veins crawled up his neck and came to life in Syn's vision. They swarmed over his features, turning him into a grotesque swirl of twisting spider legs.

Syn cringed back but forced herself to speak. "I know what you're doing with the newly imbued." She glanced down at Relia to make sure she heard what she said next. "I know you're only using them as incubators for your Hal'points before you slaughter them for a second imbuing."

Revvor's face contorted and Syn thought he might be smiling but she couldn't make it out over the mess of writhing veins. She had to look away as he chuckled.

He threw her back to the ground. "A real pity…" He held his golden wrist into the air and stroked the barrel loaded with the Hal'point. "I was fixing to give the crew some amusement by letting the two of you fight to the death over this here Hal'-point. But now I reckon your lousy spying has ruined all my fun."

The Nighterrians hissed and took a step forward with their blades. Syn squinted past the pounding headache that threatened to collapse her. She saw Relia's look of bewilderment as she glanced back and forth between the captain and Syn.

"Second imbuing…" Relia uttered under her breath.

A commotion at the far end of the Hall stole Syn's attention. The crowd of Nighterrians parted again to usher the apprentices forward. They dragged a struggling form in tow. His face was so swollen and bruised, Syn almost didn't recognize him. The apprentices tossed him forward.

"Drekton!" Syn jumped up to catch him, his weight carried them both to the ground in an awkward slump. Syn took a quick scan of his injuries. Blood and bruises covered him nearly from head to toe, but he was still cognizant and running on the adrenaline of the fight.

"Sorry I couldn't have been more of use," he said.

Syn could have kissed him then if it weren't for the haunting crawling up her spine and digging its way through her body to spread its reign of darkness.

The end had come.

The three of them knelt before a bloody death looming at the end of sharpened swords. Deep down Syn knew the mission was doomed to fail. What were a couple of teenagers against a raid of near immortal soldiers?

She thought she would feel regret at her failure, and fear for the end of her soul's final life. Instead, she felt proud. She would do it over again because she knew Relia would have done it for her. Drekton also proved magnanimous in his decision to battle at her side. Syn only wished she could have saved them both.

Is this what it's like to have friends?

Syn climbed to her feet and stepped in front of Relia and Drekton to stand tall in defiance before the captain. "Take me instead, let them go."

Revvor smirked. "Ain't none of you leaving here alive." He turned and walked away. "Kill them," he ordered over his shoulder.

Drekton leapt to his feet and roared like a demon. "You won't get away with this! We aren't the only ones who know about the second imbuing!" But the captain ignored him.

Relia stood and put a hand on Syn's shoulder. Syn wanted to tell her how sorry she was for getting lost in the paranoia of treachery. She wanted to tell her that she didn't deserve Relia's friendship but that she was grateful for it all the same. But when she turned to Relia, she realized the words weren't needed. Syn's heart nearly burst as she read forgiveness in Relia's eyes.

The circle of melted-faced Nighterrians smothered her happiness as they converged. Unarmed, yet standing to meet death, the three of them huddled together with brave faces. With no other weapons, they raised their fists and planted their feet. Syn would not go down without a fight, and neither would her friends.

An unhuman shriek pierced the air.

The sound vibrated the ground beneath them and echoed off the stone floor. Time froze as Syn turned toward the portal to see two green and gray beasts lumber forward on hindlegs. One of them tilted its head to the domed roof and let out another shrill cry. Their human eyes scanned the room.

"Scalers." Syn wasn't sure if she said the word aloud or if it died on her lips. Her first thought was that her haunting had reached a new height, but then she noticed the expressions of her friends and the way the Nighterrians took up defensive stances against the beasts. Only then did she accept the reality of the threat before her.

One of the Scalers lashed out with a clawed hand. The crowd of Nighterrians jumped back and Syn got her first good look at the beasts. They were no Turnlings. The full-sized beasts towered above the Nighterrians and wore strange muzzles over their snouts which attached to long leather leashes that disappeared past the portal.

A pair of hands grasping the ends of the leashes emerged from the shimmering blackness. Syn's mouth fell open as the man attached to the hands took one tilting step forward and rose from the portal like a phantom from the shadows.

Xedford strode into the Hall with his charismatic smile spread across his face and a red sash tied around his waist. The

Scalers roared and thrust forward, but he held them back with the power of his grasp on their leashes.

"Xedford!" Revvor stomped toward him, seemingly unafraid of the bloodthirsty Scalers. "What in damnation is the meaning of this?"

"This is a coup," Xedford said with a dark chuckle. His eyes fell on Syn and sparkled with malice. "I've come to rescue my conspirators."

Syn thought she saw him wink, but then again it could have been the haunting.

53
FINAL TRIAL

Syn stood beside Relia and Drekton, unsure of whether to run or stay where they were and let Xedford rescue them. Could he be trusted? Syn's head hammered with dizzying throbs that made her thoughts lurch and crawl. She remembered Lektra's incriminating story of Xedford's allegiance, but perhaps he had planned to double cross Revvor the whole time.

"This is the end of your reign, Revvor. I'm takin' over the raid," Xedford said, a leashed Scaler in each hand.

Revvor leveled his golden three-barrel at Xedford. "Over my dead body."

"Now, I was hoping it wouldn't have to come to that. But I'm happy to oblige." Xedford let out a length of slack and the Scaler on the right jumped forward. It snapped at the captain beneath its muzzle.

Revvor recoiled with a hiss. "The crew will never follow you." He gestured at the Nighterrians poised with barrels aimed and swords raised. "Get rid of him."

Xedford responded by marching forward with measured steps. The Scalers screamed their shrill cry. Syn felt Relia tense at her side.

"You do that, and I set these two free."

The crew paused to exchanged shifty glances.

"You limp-dick cowards! Kill him!" Without waiting to see if his crew would follow, Revvor charged forward with madness in his eyes.

Xedford transferred one of the leashes to the other hand and ripped his sword from its scabbard. The captain hurdled forward in a mad charge, but Xedford calmly stepped to the side and delivered an expert slice to Revvor's left arm.

Caught up in inhuman rage, Revvor didn't appear to notice how Xedford's cut severed his left arm from his body. Revvor lifted his sword hand, as if to continue the fight, but a loud plunk alerted him as his three-barrel hit the stone floor. Agony curled across his face in a moment of realization. Dropping his sword, he grabbed at the stump where his elbow used to be and sank to the floor. A chorus of gasps filled the room as the crew stared at their captain.

Revvor's arm began to regrow.

"It's not possible!" someone said.

"Behold the power of the second imbuing!" hailed another.

The crowd watched Revvor's skin regenerate at a rate faster than a normal Nighterrian had ever healed. Revvor shrieked in pain and writhed on the floor beside the portal.

Stalled by indecision, Syn watched the scene unfold while attempting to puzzle out Xedford's motives. Maybe Lektra had been wrong about him. He certainly looked like he was there to save them, but should she risk it?

"I'll be taking this." Xedford plucked up Revvor's severed arm. As he bent over, he whispered to the captain, but loud enough for the whole Hall to hear. "I'd head on through the portal now if I was you." He nodded to the shimmering gateway at his feet.

"I'll... kill you!" Revvor's face continued to worm with living veins in Syn's eyes, but she could tell his expression contorted in pain as he remained paralyzed by the torturous regrowth of his limb.

"Not if you're still fixing to have a crew. These are my two best Scalers." He gave a small yank at the pair of leashes in his hand. "The rest, I'm afraid, proved too difficult to control once they caught the scent of blood. All your precious incubators are down there getting torn to pieces before they're ripe."

With one hand, Xedford clicked a mechanism on the captain's golden three-barrel and the Hal'point dropped into his grasp. He tossed the empty weapon away.

"It's a mighty hard dilemma you've got here, Revvor. To extract vengeance or save your crew? But I'm feeling real generous today, so I'll help you decide." In a blur of movement, Xedford delivered a powerful kick to Revvor's chest that sent him sliding through the portal.

Syn decided it was time to make their escape. Taking advantage of the crew's shock, she grabbed Relia and Drekton by the hands and pulled them away from the army of undead Nighterrians.

Xedford spread his arms wide and addressed the remaining crewmen. "Welcome to my new raid. Who here wants to join up?"

At the sight of the brutal treatment of their captain, the loyal Nighterrians yelled and charged forward.

"Very well," Xedford said.

Syn led Drekton and Relia toward the back of the Hall. Which pillar had she come up from? She needed to find the arrow and the strangle wire, but dark shadows began pressing into her vision. She finally located the correct pillar when they heard what sounded like the crack of a whip.

Syn looked over her shoulder to find the Scalers free of their leashes. The beasts hunched over and ran on all fours. They raced toward the crew, their human eyes alight and hungry with the promise of flesh.

"Shit-shit-shit! We gotta get out of here!" Relia screamed.

Syn yanked her friends toward cover behind a column. "Drekton, how did the apprentices get you up here?"

Drekton looked away from the Scalers and shook his head. "That way requires the strength of an imbued to travel through."

"That leaves us with only one option." Syn led them farther around the pillar. They balanced on the edge of the cliff and shuffled forward. She continued to peak out from behind the column and monitor the chaos within. From amidst the frenzy of claws, teeth, swords, and barrelfire, Xedford strode forward with cold calculation and made straight for Syn and her friends.

"Hurry!" Syn's hands shook as her vision pulsed with bright flashes.

Relia located where Syn had left the spool of wire and handed it to her. Syn looped the end around Relia's belt. "Relia, you go first. Drekton and I will—" Syn looked up to find Drekton missing. She turned just as Xedford grabbed her and Relia and hauled them back into the Hall where Drekton laid sprawled on the floor. Drekton scrambled to his feet and reached for a discarded sword. He stood tall with weapon in hand. Xedford released Syn and Relia and they ran to flank him.

The three of them flashed cautious looks over their shoulders. The screech of Scalers and the smell of blackpowder clouded the air while shadows coalesced and invaded Syn's vision. She watched the crew begin to dive through the portal toward escape despite Xedford's promise of further Scalers on the other side.

"What do you want with us, lizard-lover?" Relia's eyes stared, vacant of fear. Her red irises smoldered with pure hatred as she watched the Scalers attack the Nighterrians.

"Don't worry about them. They only kill when ordered." Xedford's face remained normal in Syn's vision, yet haunted shadows snaked around him.

Syn pressed her hands to her head. "Quit playing games, Xedford. What do you want?" Beneath the weight of her curse, part of her still hoped for a believable explanation.

Xedford flashed a smile. "Like I said, I've come to take over the raid. I was hoping more of the men would join up, but I figure it don't matter much." He looked around the fading chaos of the Imbuing Hall. "Soon I'll be able to harvest enough Hal'points to create my own raid."

The battle cries and clamor of metal and barrel shots dissipated as most of the crew joined their captain on the other side of the portal.

Syn ventured a test of his bluff. "How? It looks like the crew has escaped."

"Not once they arrive at the nest of Scalers I assembled on the other side."

He wasn't bluffing. She watched him load the Hal'point he stole from Revvor into his own three-barrel.

"It was a real surprised finding you here, Syn. I suppose you and I were just meant to be. You've proven yourself worthy of a Hal'point. I got no doubt you're strong enough to survive the imbuing. But there remains the need to prove yourself worthy of joining my crew."

"What makes you think I *want* to join your crew?"

"Ain't that everything you ever wanted? To restore honor to your family, and to earn yourself a cure?" Xedford asked.

Syn glanced around at the carnage. Although the Nighterrians healed from the wounds caused by the Scalers, she could hear their screams of pain as the last few dove for the portal. Clearly, they didn't believe Xedford's promise of the ambush that awaited them on the other side.

"Not if it means joining you," she said.

"You certain? I've been rooting for you this whole time. I'll Imbue you right here, right now. You can join me as my second-in-command like we talked about that night in the cave." He gave her a lustful smile.

It sickened her. How could she have been so blind to his treachery? "And what about my friends?"

The room fell to near silence as the last trickle of men jumped through the portal to join the rest of the raid. The two beasts stalked around the Hall on all fours, snarling and licking their forked tongues into the air.

"You friends can join us..." Xedford stepped forward to loom over Syn. "*If* they prove themselves worthy of my crew. With a new raid comes new traditions, you see, and I got a little trial of my own." He whistled, and the Scalers snapped their attention to him. He grabbed Syn around the waist and yanked her into him as he pointed at Relia and Drekton.

The Scalers flicked their soulless human stares toward Drekton and Relia and stalked forward.

"No!" Syn made to run toward her friends, but Xedford pulled a sword from his belt and held the weapon in front of her face. Syn looked past the blade to watch Relia collect a discarded sword and take up a fighting stance beside Drekton.

Relia beckoned the Scalers forward. "I killed your cousin, you know. I ate his eyes for breakfast! Come get me, fuckers!"

The beasts shrieked and barreled toward them.

"You can't do this!" Syn stomped on Xedford's foot and elbowed him in the gut, but he hardly flinched. She kicked and struggled, but it was as if he were made of stone.

"Look here, I'll make you a deal," he whispered in her ear. "If you beat me in a fight, I'll imbue you and let you go." He shoved the hilt of the blade into her grasp as he pushed her from his captive embrace. He took a step back and drew a second sword.

Syn looked down at the weapon in her hand. She knew it was a ploy to keep her from trying to aid her friends against the Scalers. It was silly to think she stood any chance against him in a duel. But she knew if she didn't play along, he might just detain her and make her watch her friends be eaten by the Scalers while he used her body as an incubator for a second Hal'point. At least this way she could fight and die on her feet.

She redoubled her grip in the sword. The hot poison of betrayal pulsed through her veins and urged her to draw the blade across Xedford's throat.

"Let's see what you got." Xedford circled her.

The haunting reached out to touch Xedford's features, transforming him into a vision of horror unlike any Syn had ever seen. His face became a skeletal cluster made of jutting bones and exposed sinew that shifted with every twitch of his face. Her darkened mind begged her to run and hide. She flicked her gaze over her shoulder where she saw the beasts lunge in and meet the attack of her friend's swords.

Drekton screamed, "This is for Rem!" and slashed at the Scaler towering above him.

Syn turned back to Xedford and raised her weapon. She fought back against the part of her that begged her to flee. Bruised, bleeding, suffering from her haunting, it didn't matter. Her friends were in danger, perhaps the only real friends she ever had.

"No more running, it's time to fight," she said to herself and raised her sword for trial number four.

54
DEAL

Syn slashed out at Xedford. He parried the blow with an easy swipe of his sword.

"You know, I wasn't lying the whole time," he said.

Syn tried not to look at his face as she pirouetted and sliced toward him. He knocked her sword away with a lazy parry. Sharp bones sprouted out of his skin in all directions. The flesh of his face dangled with flaps of bloody entrails.

"Lies and deception are all you know." She cringed back and tried to look away from his distorted face.

"I wasn't lying about us." He brought his blade up and crossed it with Syn's, then grabbed her by the sleeve and pulled her in close. For a moment the illusion of his face disappeared, and Syn got a glimpse of his rugged features and roguish smile. "I know you felt it too, that night in the cave, I know you saw what we could be together."

Behind their cross of swords Syn could see his earnest expression untouched by her haunting. She couldn't deny the feelings she once held for him, as misguided as they were, the desire had burned within her unlike anything she had ever known... all the way up until his deception dwindled it to ash, and the memories of the boat matched her disgust at his haunting-twisted face.

"You used me." Syn elbowed him in the face, and he let go of her sleeve. His bandana fell off and his face turned back to the mutilated nightmare of his true form.

"We could still do it, you know. Me and you can gather our crew. Together, we'd be unstoppable." He blocked another of Syn's attacks.

Syn said nothing as she tried her best to get inside his defense, but she realized he was hardly trying. He could have parried her attacks with his eyes closed and killed her a hundred times over, but he didn't deliver any strikes of his own. How long would he try to convince her before he gave up and killed her?

A screech turned her attention to Drekton and Relia as they fought the Scalers. One of the beasts knocked Drekton off his feet. He flew backward with the force of the hit and skidded along the floor, crashing into a stone pillar.

Syn retreated to put herself in a position between Drekton and the Scaler. Xedford followed her, but this time he attacked with heavy blows that vibrated all the way down the bones of her arm when she blocked.

The Scaler snapped its jaws and clawed at the ground. Syn shuffled away from Xedford's attack to get into the path of the beast. The Scaler raced for Drekton but had to scramble around the dueling pair, buying Drekton enough time to find his feet and ready his defense before it reached him.

Xedford did not relent in his assault. Syn had to turn her attention away from Drekton to meet Xedford's slashes. She blocked a blow with the metal of her three-barreled wrist. His sword clanked off the barrels, but he did not relent. She ducked and parried as he danced her away from the Scalers.

"Real clever, Syn. But enough interference. That's their fight."

Relia screamed, mocking the Scaler's shrieks as she fought.

"You don't understand, do you?" Xedford said. "You don't see justice's been done here tonight. Revvor had all but handed the raid over to Redd the Collector."

"Justice? Don't talk to me about justice. This is a massacre." The clang of their blades echoed off the domed roof.

"I had no choice. Redd is evil incarnate. I had to save the crew—"

"Save them? You just executed them all! Don't pretend you're some misunderstood hero, Xedford. You would murder your entire raid just to advance yourself."

Xedford shook his head. "Your friends won't last long."

The truth of his words bludgeoned her to the core. She turned her head so her single working eye could glimpse the fight. They fought bravely, but it typically took a team of ten Legionites to bring down an adult Scaler. Drekton and Relia didn't stand a chance. Soon they would tire and wouldn't be able to move out of the way of the beasts claws and teeth fast enough.

"Come with me and let's be done with all this," Xedford spoke in a soft tone. "You see, Nighterrians are of a higher calling. I know you don't understand just yet, but once you're one of us, you'll see the world like I do."

"I thought you needed me to prove myself worthy of your raid"—Syn lunged forward with a jab—"by fighting you."

He blocked her weak attack. "I just need you to make your choice. I need you to show your loyalty to me"—he nodded toward Relia and Drekton— "not them."

There it was, the real reason for this "trial" of his. She crossed her blade with his and slid the edge of it down to the pommel as she leaned in. "If I choose you, will you let them live?"

Xedford's gruesome face contorted, but Syn thought she might have read hurt in his expression. He pushed her away and lunged in to redouble his attack. Syn nearly caught a blow to her neck, but he pulled the strike at the last moment and left only a shallow cut.

His eyes spoke disappointment as he said, "If that's what it takes."

Was this enough to pass his test? "Let them go and I'm yours," she said with false bravado. "Imbue me so I can become what you want, so I can see through your eyes."

Xedford let out a dark chuckle and the tattered jowls of his torn-up face trembled as he laughed. He pointed his blade at Syn. "If you're fixing up a ploy, think again. The imbuing is a long and painful process. It will cripple you for hours. So don't think you'll be able to turn around and kill me with your newfound strength."

Syn's anxiety rose like bile up through her throat. That was exactly what she had planned if he didn't follow through with letting her friends go. She found herself just barely able to keep hold of the dam that stopped the fear from letting the haunting flood over her senses.

Too late to back out now; she would have to take her chances. "Deal." She dropped her sword and stepped toward him. "I surrender."

Xedford leveled his Hal'point loaded three-barrel at her chest. The bones of his face rippled, and Syn felt deception permeate the air. She knew he could be lying, that he might do what he wanted in the end, but this was the final play she had. Relia and Drekton were nearly out of time.

She stepped forward and let the hard row of metal barrels press against her chest. She glanced down at the weapon. The cure, the answer to all she ever wanted, lay loaded within the barrel. Her parent's redemption, the reinstatement of her soul, and the end of her haunting remained only a trigger pull away.

But none of that mattered anymore. All she truly desired was safety for her family and friends.

"One small amendment, if I might be so bold to add." Xedford's red eyes sparkled with wicked delight. He clicked the trigger into his palm. "I'll let the boy go, but I want the girl for my crew. She's got a certain... enticing fire to her." He smiled and licked his lips with the hungry desire of a bear in heat. "And I'd like to have a taste of that flame before she becomes my incubator."

In that instant, Syn understood she had failed his test by sacrificing herself to save her friends. But the realization had come too late.

Xedford pulled the trigger.

No! Her haunting seized control of her body. Darkness rushed in to surround her. Without conscious thought, and with speed and strength completely outside her abilities, she threw herself out of the way of the incoming shot from the three-barrel.

Adrenaline made time seem to slow. The Hal'point flew from the barrel and sailed past her. It shot through the air. Its trajectory carried it toward the portal. She watched it pierce through the shimmering surface to be lost forever in the chaos of the other side.

The appearance of suspended time ended. Syn stood in dumbfounded shock. How had she moved to quickly? She just had time to register the look of pure rage cross over the bones of Xedford's mutated face before an ear-splitting scream yanked her attention to the rear of the Hall.

She glimpsed green scales slip past a set of columns and

fall off the edge of the tier. The Scaler shrieked on the way down as Drekton stood at the edge of the cliff watching it fall.

Legion incarnate, he did it! He killed a Scaler!

Relia looked over from her battle with the remaining Scaler to delight in the victory. A deadly mistake. The split second of distraction was all it took for the beast to seize the opportunity.

"Relia!" But the warning left Syn's mouth too late. By the time her voice echoed off the stone, the Scaler had clamped its jaws over Relia's shoulder and dug its venomous teeth deep into her flesh.

Syn didn't see what happened next. Her vision stayed focused on the look of horror on Relia's face, but she felt Xedford's fist connected with the side of her head. The world tilted and she hit the ground with a smack.

55
SHADOWS

Syn recovered from the blow to the head and blinked awake to find the Hall swirling with demonic shadows. *No... Relia.* She clamped her eye closed as her body shook with terror. She wanted nothing more than to hide away from the horror unfolding around her. The haunting had reached its zenith, and she always kept her eyes closed for this part, but she had to look.

Syn sat up from the stone floor and fought past the coalescing shadows that reached out to strangle her. Lighting struck her vision with searing bright pulses that erupted through the darkness. Beneath the illusions, she could feel the portal beside her. In front of her, Relia laid convulsing on the floor.

Syn crawled over to her. Xedford must have placed her there so Syn could watch her change. Relia's eyes overflowed with fear. Tears fell down her face as she gasped and struggled against the effects of the Scaler's venom.

"Relia, I—"

Syn looked up at the sound of screams. Through the

whirling shadows, she could just make out Drekton battling Relia's Scaler.

A sob racked Syn's body as she sat helpless and unable to halt the arrival of death for either of her friends. Blood covered the floor where Relia laid, and scales already grew up through her skin. Soon the Hall would have another deadly beast.

Syn pulled Relia on to her lap and stroked her wild hair out of her face. Relia choked and shuddered as her body trembled with the coming change.

"It's alright," Syn lied as she sobbed. "You'll be fine, I'm right here—"

"I wish I could say it didn't hurt that you'd rather die than join me." Syn peered up through the tempest of ghosts at Xedford looming above her. His face appeared more deteriorated. The scraps of hanging flesh fell off his face to further expose a mess of jutting bones. "You're lucky I got a wealth of Hal'points waiting to be harvested on the other side of that portal."

"You've lied to me from the beginning. You were never going to make me anything more than a stepping stone on your path to corruption!"

Xedford offered her a sad, gruesome smile. "That's where you're wrong. I'd have made you my weapon."

Syn grasped a new understanding of the words he once whispered in her ear. *Everything is a weapon if given the right... incentive.* With his Hal'point now lost to the portal, all deals were off. So why hadn't he killed her yet?

"What do you want from me?" Tears burned the swollen socket of her left eye and sprinted down her face. She didn't want to see Drekton lose his battle with the Scaler, she didn't want to watch Relia become the very thing she hated most in the world. Did he keep her alive just so she could witness it all?

Xedford walked around her in a slow circle. "Oh, Syn, what we could've been... But I see now where your loyalties lie."

"You would have used me as your incubator the second I stopped being what you wanted!"

"You ought to know that what we shared was real, in a sense. I didn't want it to be that way, but I found myself longing for you."

Syn's pulse pounded in her head and threatened to cripple her, but she made herself look at her destroyer. When she stared past his distorted face, she found his eyes spoke the truth of his soul. He *had* truly wanted her at his side, but maybe he needed to be sure she was worthy of his diabolical company. All that nonsense about the convert, had he only been trying to see if she would sully her hands for him?

"I hate to see you go to waste. You had so much potential, Syn. I don't know what you done to me, but even now I want you." Sadness entered his tone only to be replaced by anger. "But I can't have you, no, not anymore."

Syn couldn't fathom what that meant. He did really, in some twisted way, come to love her? She didn't have a mind for his games. She held Relia in her arms and watched scales sprout from her skin. She didn't have much time.

Xedford continued, "It's a right shame to see you meet your end in such an undignified way. I was rooting for you, honestly. I wanted you to get your cure and overcome..." he motioned toward her weeping on the floor. "Whatever this is."

Syn snapped her single-eyed stare up at him. "So, what then? You love me or something? I don't believe it! Someone like you could never love another living thing other than yourself."

"I wouldn't call it love. Perhaps an infatuation of sorts. Either way, I feel I owe it to you to give you something."

"And what's that?"

"I want to fix you. I aim to offer you a shot at redemption." He kicked something with his foot, and it slid across the floor to Syn. Elaine. Her broken dagger spun across the ground before coming to a rest beside her. "Do what you couldn't before, kill her." He nodded toward Relia.

"What?"

"Your Chief told me what you did back at your village. That sacrifice you couldn't perform, and the mercy you couldn't offer some little boy. Redeem yourself by killing the girl and I'll let you live. I'll even let that one go free." He nodded toward where Drekton fought his losing battle with the beast. "I can use one of the remaining apprentices as my incubator. Afterall, you did save my life, that day in the woods. And for all the moments we shared, I'll spare your life."

Another trick? Syn could hardly wrap her mind around his words. She held Relia's convulsing body tight. The storm of her haunting made it hard to think. She felt the ghosts pounding at her skull, begging to be let free.

She fought against the shadows to stare at Xedford. He no longer wore his typical bandana around his head and, if she focused, she could catch glimpses of his real face. A deep scar extended across his forehead and a memory seized her: She was chained to the wall in the brig after her severing. A face with a familiar voice and a scar across his forehead whispered, *"So much wasted potential."*

"You're lying!" she screamed through the tears. "Why would I trust you? You were there after my severing. You traded me to Magoila and left me for dead."

Regret crossed his eyes. "But you found your way back to me. You proved the Fates got something in store for us."

The Fates, not the Legion. More compound lies. She recalled the rest of the Nighterrian crew Xedford had hidden away to protect his deception: the one with the burn scars and the one with the blue eyes. Xedford had sworn the imbuing would cure all, yet he wore a scar of his own.

"I've been so blind…" She stared down at Relia writhing in agony. She couldn't let her turn.

"I was telling the truth that day when we first met. You remember?" Xedford didn't wait for a response. "I said I saw myself in you. I too, used to be weak, until I learned how to turn off the part that made me fragile. I want to show you the same thing. It'll change you… fix you. You ought to see what it's like."

"I won't fall for your false promises again. You'll just kill us all in the end."

"Pick up the knife, Syn. Can't you see she's suffering? The boy will die right quick unless I call my Scaler off. Kill her and I'll do just that."

Another lie. Another deception. But what choice did she have? She looked to Drekton covered in a blood, bleeding from too many wounds and beginning to slow. Xedford could be lying, but Syn couldn't deny the truth of the situation. Drekton had put up a good fight, perhaps better than any mortal she had ever seen, but it was not enough. If Xedford didn't call the beast back, Drekton would die or meet the same fate as Relia.

Relia. Syn looked back down and shed more tears. The transformation continued, and the panic in her eyes spread as the growth of scales increased. Utterly helpless, Syn felt at Rem's coin in her pocket. *I can't lose them all.*

Syn picked up her broken dagger.

"Sometimes killing is mercy." Xedford loomed over her with his ghastly features. "It'll unlock something in you that will harden your heart. It'll fix you, even without the imbuing."

Relia's body seized and trembled with the change. Her mouth bobbed open and close as if she were trying to say something but couldn't get the words out over the torture. Her face began to elongate. Her nails grew and hardened into curved claws. The beast had nearly emerged.

Syn placed Elaine at Relia's throat.

Hesitation made her seek Drekton through the shadows. Syn gasped as she watched Drekton get knocked to the ground. He bled from clawed slash marks that tore his skin to tatters. He tried to get up, but he could hardly lift his sword. The Scaler licked the air and prowled toward him, choosing to savor the victory before it fed.

Syn glanced at the three-barrel still strapped to her wrist. If only she had the ammunition to use it. Useless. Helpless. A memory assaulted her as if brought on by the haunting.

In a forest of saplings, you are an ancient oak.

Xedford stood over her with his twisted bones for a face. "You're running out of time. Do it now, redeem yourself."

You must embrace the shadows cast by your branches.

The blade shook in her hand as she held it to Relia's neck. Out the corner of her eye, Syn could see the beast close in for the kill. Relia's face morphed. The bones of her limbs began to extend. Syn watched her eyes beg for an end. In her memory, Syn saw flashes of Lektra's imploring gray eyes and Rem's terrified brown eyes. She held mercy at the end of a blade. She had been here before, too many times before. But this time things had changed. Syn had changed.

"You're broken, Syn," Xedford said. "And you'll always be broken unless you do what it takes to seize your cure."

Syn stared down at her reflection in the side of Elaine— Elaine, her broken friend that had accomplished so much blood.

"You once told me everything is a weapon." Syn twisted her head up at Xedford. "I might be broken. But the thing about broken things is, in the right hands, they can still be... *deadly*" —Elaine clattered to the stone floor.

In one swift motion Syn yanked Rem's coin from her pocket and jammed it into her three-barrel. She let go of the strangle hold she held on her haunting and allowed the ghosts to rush forth and take control of her body. Aided by her curse, she hardly thought to aim as she thrust her weapon into the swirling shadows. The darkness clicked the trigger into her hand. She pointed her fist in Drekton's direction and fired.

The coin shot through the air and the shadows parted to reveal the Scaler closing its jaws around Drekton's head. The coin blasted through the tunnel of shadows and struck home through the Scaler's eye. The beast toppled to the floor.

Without pause, Syn snatched Elaine up off the floor and leapt at Xedford. The phantom shadows powered her through the air as she drove the broken edge of the blade down into Xedford's gut in the exact area of his weakness. They fell to the ground, knocked over by the supernatural strength Syn commandeered from the depths of her shattered mind. As they fell, she embraced the darkness of her ghosts and seized control of the hands emerging from the shadows.

In a split second of mind-shattering realization, she discovered they were *her* hands. Hundreds of them, all belonging to her from every iteration of her past lives. They bowed to her, just as her lungs swore fealty to her breath and her heart vowed allegiance to her life. She welcomed them home like long lost children as she reached out and willed them to grab hold of Xedford's limbs and arrest him to the ground.

"What..." Xedford stammered, unable to see the invisible hands of Syn's haunting.

With the precision of a butcher, Syn carried Elaine deeper into his stomach—exactly two fingers width above his navel. She brought the blade down as she screamed.

"I"—stab—"AM"—stab—"NOT"—stab—"WEAK!"   Blue

blood splattered her face with each descending arch of her knife.

With one last stab, she aimed for Xedford's chest and buried Elaine up to her hilt. She shoved her hand into the hole she made in his gut and watched his eyes widen in terror. He screamed in pain while Syn screamed alongside him, letting lose the fear and torment pent up over years of shame and self-hatred.

Dark silhouettes hugged her in an embrace of ghostly hands and lent her the navigating strength to dig around inside Xedford's stomach as he struggled. Amongst the slippery slosh of blood and organs, she found his spine and felt the pointed edge of a protruding object. She grasped it with slick fingers and ripped it free.

Syn didn't waste time to watch Xedford die. She jumped over to kneel beside Relia's contorting body. Scales covered almost every inch of her skin and her face appeared fully reptilian. Syn picked up her clawed arm and found a spot on her wrist that still contained human flesh.

No time to bother with the three-barrel, Syn said a silent prayer to the Legion, then jammed the freshly harvested Hallowed Point into Relia's forearm.

56
NOTHING

The added strength of the ghostly hands helped Syn slam the Hal'point all the way into Relia's bone. Relia jolted. Her mouth went wide with a silent scream as her back arched off the floor. She then thumped back down on the ground and laid still—too still.

"Please let this work," Syn pleaded. "Wake up! Relia, wake up!"

Syn waited. Relia didn't move.

Syn surveyed the scales covering Relia's immobile body. They didn't shed or disappear. The claws didn't fall off, and the bones of her limbs didn't shrink. Syn leaned over her and felt for a pulse or a breath.

Nothing.

"Please..." She knew it was foolish to think the Hal'point would cure her. The healing abilities of the imbuing process were transformative and powerful, but they had their limits. She thought of the hidden scar on Xedford's forehead and the Nighterrian with the burned face. Perhaps the imbuing did not heal certain wounds.

With the corners of her vision still dark with haunted shadows, Syn felt despair rise and threaten to crush her. She grabbed hold of Relia's shoulders and shook her. "Relia!"

No response.

The wave of grief crashed over her. She collapsed over Relia's body and wept. She cried and implored the Legion to restore her friend but still, Relia remained breathless.

The whirl of fusing shadows shrank while Syn mourned over Relia. They abated with gradual stillness until Syn was left alone on the cold, stone floor of reality. The haunting passed, but the horror remained.

A moan and a rustle of movement yanked Syn from her grief. She looked up and immediately felt a stab of guilt. *Drekton.* She jumped to her feet and ran over to where the dead Scaler collapsed with a hole through its eye. With a heave, she rolled the carcass away to uncover Drekton.

Drekton coughed and rolled onto his side. Still covered in blood from head to toe, he stared up at her with a look of delirium as if he were still emersed in the fight for his life.

"It's over. Don't worry, it's over." She helped extract him from beneath the body of the beast.

Drekton sucked in a gasp of pain as he rolled free. Claw marks and deep gashes split his skin into a bloody mess. Bruises blackened his face and one of his eyes was so swollen he could hardly open it.

He groaned between clenched teeth as he asked, "What happened?"

"The Scalers are dead." She put her arm around him to help him sit up. "So is Xedford."

She glanced over to where she had left his body and her heart stuttered in alarm. Instead of finding him dead, a pool of blue blood smeared a short trail leading to the portal.

Syn shoved the fear aside. Good. Let him die on the other

side with his precious beasts. She assured herself he could never survive the gaping hole she made in his gut without a Hal'point. Her only regret was that she had left Elaine stabbed through his chest.

"How did you do it?" Drekton asked, which yanked Syn's attention back to helping him. "One minute I was about to be eaten. Then..." His vision wandered over the dead Scaler and a bloody spot on the floor beside them. Rem's coin sat imbedded in the stone where it struck after passing through the beast's eye. Drekton reached out a shaking hand and retrieved the mangled coin.

Syn kept her arm around him. In his weakened state, he could hardly hold himself upright. "I'm sorry. It was the only thing small enough to fit in the three-barrel," she explained. She decided to leave out the part where she seized control of the shadows of her haunting.

He looked at her with eyes wide in amazement. "Don't be sorry. You... you saved me."

You saved me too, she wanted to say as her mind strayed inevitably toward that night in the woods ten years ago. Instead, she said, "We should get you patched up before you lose any more blood."

Drekton nodded and let Syn go to work tearing off strips of his tattered tunic to bind the worst of his wounds. She wished she had needle and thread, but she supposed the makeshift bandages would have to do for now.

Drekton's sights wandered around the Hall. He went rigid and Syn knew his gaze had fallen on Relia. "Is she..."

Syn couldn't bring herself to look back at her friend. She knew she laid there half monstrous, and still without breath. "Yes." Syn wiped her eye as she continued to work. "I tried using Xedford's Hal'point to imbue her, but it didn't work. I guess she was too far gone."

"I'm sorry."

"I am too."

First Rem, then Lektra, now Relia. Every time she let someone in, they were taken from her. Was this what it meant to have friends? To do everything to try and keep them, yet at the end you must mourn them anyway?

Syn shook off the bitterness and bit her lip to force herself to look back at Relia. Tears warped her vision in her right eye. Yes, she decided. Friendship would always be worth the torture of loss.

She finished doing her best to staunch the flow of blood from Drekton's wounds and together they sat in grief-filled silence. It would be best to leave the Hall before any surviving crew emerged from the portal, but Syn couldn't bring herself to move just yet. She continued to throw glances toward Relia's body, hoping in vain to see her twitch or gasp a breath.

Still nothing.

Drekton's vitality grew as he recovered from the tremors of the fight. Syn no longer had to hold him up, though she continued to remain latched onto him. She felt as if she needed something to hold onto or she might drown in the emptiness. The adrenaline from the fight replaced itself with hollowness, like a vast chasm opened inside her.

Drekton didn't move to free himself from her embrace. Perhaps he felt the same.

"I shouldn't have come to the trials," he said, breaking the silence. "I shouldn't have left my mother alone to go on this foolhardy mission. I've been selfish and-and," he sighed, "and I shouldn't have sought the Law of Retribution." He looked at her with his brown eyes flowing with shame and regret. His naked vulnerability caught Syn off guard.

"I don't blame you for what you did, you had every right. You were mourning Rem's death."

"That's no excuse."

"It is." Syn looked back over to Relia's distorted shape. She couldn't help but also see Rem's ruined body lying in the snow. "We were both mourning his death in coming here."

She looked back at Drekton's swollen, bloody face. His eyes held so much pain. Drekton stared down at the mangled coin in his hand as a pair of tears leaked from each eye and traced clean lines through the blood covering his face.

"It wasn't your fault... what happened to Rem," he said.

Syn resisted the urge to reach out and wipe his tears. This version of him reminded her of her childhood best friend. She shook her head to find her way out of the reverie. "I wish I could have saved him."

Drekton looked away from the coin. His eyes slid over the stitched-up X across her face. "You loved him like he was your own brother. In a way you've lost just as much as I have, but you've paid so much more." He reached his hand up, it hovered over Syn's severed eye as if he were going to take her face in his hands. He hesitated, then dropped his hand to his side.

Syn held his stare for a long moment. What she wouldn't give to hear him say the words, *I forgive you*, but he didn't speak. Amidst their shared grief, an unspoken truce passed between their eyes. For the moment, it was enough.

"I think I can walk now." Drekton wiped the forbidden tears from his eyes.

"Right. We should go." Syn helped him find his feet. Together they shuffled to where Relia lay.

The sight of her body felt like an icicle stabbed through the chest.

Syn knelt beside her. "I'm sorry, Relia."

At least she didn't reach full transformation. Syn wasn't sure what Relia's "Fates" said about death, but in the Legionite faith it was believed that her soul would go on, and she would soon be reborn. This gave Syn only a shred of comfort. On the verge of saying, *I'll see you in another life,* Syn touched the severed cut across her face and returned to silent reverence.

"I didn't know her much," Drekton said, "But I did feel like I got to know her a bit while I was trailing you two during the first week of the trials."

Syn remembered how he used Relia's insanity tactic to gain advantage while fighting the apprentices. She gave a fleeting smile and let the tears flow.

"She was... unique, that's for sure," Drekton continued.

Syn gave a sad chuckle. "To say the least."

"Brave too," he added. "Fighting beside her just moments ago, I wasn't sure which was more threatening, the Scaler, or the feral look on Relia's war face."

Syn now smiled in earnest. She would miss her wild, capricious friend and her ridiculous curses, and the way she went about life being unapologetically herself.

Drekton said a Legionite prayer that offered little comfort.

When their goodbyes were said, Syn took a final look around the Hall. She didn't know what to make of the shadows she espoused to achieve her vengeance. Did she truly take control of her haunting and use it to perform her bidding? She needed a clearer head to think things through. Right now, she felt far too exhausted and grief stricken as she came to accept that Relia would not rise. She and Drekton needed to make their escape before the inevitable arrival of enemies from the other side of the portal.

Syn unstrapped the three-barrel from her wrist. She wished she could give Relia a proper ceremony, but they had no way to get her down from the tier. All she could do was place Lektra's three-barrel over Relia's chest in an offering to the dead.

"I..." Syn began, but something was different about Relia's

body. Her features looked less serpentine, and the spread of scales appeared fewer. "Drekton."

"What?"

"It's Relia!"

Drekton crouched over Syn's shoulder as she checked again for a pulse or breath.

Nothing.

"What is it?" Drekton asked.

"Does she look more... human?" She tried to stifle the rising hope, but it bubbled up despite her best effort.

"Um, not really."

"But she has less scales than she did a moment ago. And look! Her claws are shorter."

"I... don't see a difference."

Syn ignored him. She stared at Relia and held her breath.

Nothing happened. She could feel Drekton's doubt and the contagion of it led Syn to think her broken mind had reached its distorting lens into her everyday senses. *Perhaps I've truly gone mad.*

Syn gasped. A single scale on Relia's cheek retracted into her skin. Syn clapped her hands over her mouth as Drekton cursed in surprise. Another scale disappeared into her skin and then another and another.

They watched her bones begin to shrink. More scales burrowed themselves back into her flesh to leave behind soft human skin. The claws sank back into her nailbeds and blonde ringlets sprang from her scalp once more.

Tears of rapture spilled from Syn's face as the miraculous transition continued. Relia's body began to take on the familiar shape of a girl with a filthy mouth and a knack for gambling. Finally, Relia—in all her humanness—laid before them. No wounds, scrapes, or bruises marred her skin. Syn felt at her neck for a pulse.

"Anything?" Drekton asked.

"No, still... wait—"

Relia gasped and shot upright. She looked around the room and met Syn's tear-filled expression. A moment of wild fear crossed her eyes before confusion settled in—as if she had just woken from a nightmare.

Relia gulped a handful of ragged breaths before breaking the silent suspension of disbelief to ask, "What in the fucking shit just happened?"

57
RETRIBUTION

After a grueling journey through the crags, Syn's tired and shaky legs finally came to a halt beneath Relia's weight. She and Drekton had half-carried Relia along as she stumbled through the treacherous rocks. The three of them looked on in relief at the vast desert spread out below them.

"Finally," Syn breathed. One last push down the steep decline and they would be back on flat ground.

Drekton surveyed the Outpost in the distance. "We can't grow complacent now. There could still be outlaws lurking around corners." He slipped out from where he held Relia up on her right side. "I'll go scout the way."

"Be careful," Syn said. Drekton nodded and she watched him run off at a limping jog.

"Well, he seems chipper," Relia bristled, and Syn knew it was all in good humor.

Relia's recovery came slow but with steady improvement. She could nearly walk on her own now. Syn smiled and tried to help her sit down on a nearby boulder, but Relia brushed her arm away. Instead, Syn took a seat beside her as they waited for Drekton to return.

During the journey through the crags, Syn had explained everything, even the assistance aided to her by her haunting. Drekton had raised a cautious eyebrow at this, but Relia embraced it as Syn's "magical gift of insanity."

Syn didn't feel magical. She bled from countless wounds and every bend of her joints screamed with tired protest. The left side of her face had gone numb at some point during her fight with Xedford, but now she felt it begin to throb with a searing ache that kept time with every beat of her heart. Yet, the pain remained merely physical. The joy of Relia's recovery helped keep the raw agony manageable.

She sat beside Relia and soaked in the night. Thoughts of her haunting pulsed through her mind like a sore she couldn't help but prod. The way she embraced the power of the hands clawing at her from the dark was something altogether unheard of. It both frightened and thrilled her. Was it a one-time ability granted to her at the edge of death, or was it an atrophied muscle she should have been exercising all along?

Either way, it changed everything. She surprised herself to find she no longer had the desperate desire to leave her haunting behind. The weight was hers to bear. And although the burden remained heavy—she could still feel the mass of her ghosts dragging down her soul—she found Relia and Drekton's presence made it bearable.

Relia turned the three-barrel Syn had given her around in her hands. The metallic barrels caught the light of the stars and stole Syn's attention. She noticed Relia hadn't put the weapon on yet. Perhaps disbelief stayed her hand.

"It feels mighty strange to be holding this," Relia said.

"You earned it."

"Thanks to you." She elbowed Syn in the side with gratitude.

Syn grunted and smiled. "I'm glad you're alive."

"Hah! Me too!"

Syn hesitated for a moment, knowing what she wanted to say but the words were buried beneath exhaustion. "Relia," she began, growing serious. "Back at the Hall... I didn't get to tell you I'm sorry." She held Relia's stare hoping she understood her sincerity. "I never should have turned my back on you. I should have known you wouldn't betray me. I hope you can forgive me."

Relia nodded and sighed. "I wish I could say, 'how dare you!' But truth is, I doubted you too. I apologize for not believing you back at the last trial. I feel like a real sorry ass for leaving you behind."

Syn offered a regretful smile. "Call it a truce?"

Relia held up the three-barrel in her hands and chuckled. "You saved my life, *and* you got me imbued. I'll take those odds any day of the week."

"You would have done the same for me."

"Would I?" Relia teased with a nudge to Syn's side again.

"Yes," Syn said with absolute surety. She could tell Relia's strength was growing by the ferocity of her nudges.

The two sat together in content silence as they waited. Syn glanced back at the night sky. She would be happy to see daylight again. Had it really only been a matter of weeks since she saw the sun? The brutal nature of the trials and the unrelenting night made Syn feel like she had aged years. Perhaps that was the nature of survival in the realm of darkness. In a place where you either learn to survive or you meet a swift end, anyone toiling beneath the shadows became hardened survivors. Was it the darkness that turned the people of Interterra into ruthless killers?

Or maybe the darkness was merely a cloak of obscurity to hide behind. Her thoughts turned to Xedford, and she felt her insides clench. She shoved the memory of the boat and the cave into the darkest corner of her mind and vowed to never think of it again.

Drekton came hobbling back up to meet them. "All clear." He moved to help Relia to her feet, but she smacked his hand away and stood on her own.

Syn nodded her thanks to Drekton as she stood to make the final trek down the crags. Relia's stubborn insistence on walking on her own made their progress slow, but they eventually made it down the last grade of hill and onto flat land.

Dusty, iron-colored dirt surrounded them. In the distance, the square corners of the Outpost jutted up from the flat span of desert. The crater leading down to the portal sat quiet and unimposing just ahead.

"What do we do now?" Relia asked.

"Now we go home," Drekton said.

The mention of home made Syn's hand fly to the throbbing cut across her face. As happy as she was to have Relia and Drekton alive and by her side, she still felt dread and shame creep up at the prospect of returning home a Severed woman.

She stowed her self-pity as Relia began to wander toward the Outpost, as if she were drawn to the land of drunken debauchery and cutthroat gambling. Syn grabbed her by the back of her tattered vest and reeled her in.

Relia turned around. "What?"

Syn nodded to the hole in the ground where Garon lay just on the other side. "Drekton and I have to return to Garon. I would like it if you came with us."

"To that frozen wasteland where you ain't got ale or cards?" Relia said with mock appall.

"You're forgetting the human sacrifices," Drekton added.

"And the villagers, every last one of which hate my guts," Syn said.

Relia threw her hands in the air. "Sounds like a lovely place!"

"But the Legionites worship Nighterrians," Syn said.

A wolfen smile crawled over Relia's face. "I suppose I'm overdue for some worshiping."

"Better put on that three-barrel then." Syn nodded to unloaded weapon clutched in Relia's hands.

Relia regarded the three-barrel for a moment as if she were uncertain. Then, with a shrug, she began to strap it on.

The three of them walked the short distance to the crater. Syn felt the usual pull of the portal before she saw the dark hole glittering like the water of the black sea. It sat with the promise of daylight on the other side. They shuffled down the slope to the bottom and stared into portal's surface.

She didn't know what to expect on the other side, but she knew she had to go—as much as she dreaded it. Her family needed her. She had to return to see her parents taken care of, even if that meant spending the rest of her days hunting for food and searching for dry firewood.

Relia spat into her hands and rubbed them together to wipe her face. She sat down in the dirt and bowed before the portal. With her lips nearly kissing the dirt, she mumbled something that sounded like a prayer.

Drekton gave Syn a confused look.

"She considers the portals her gods," Syn explained. Relia stood and hawked a massive glop of spit into the portal. "I think," Syn added.

Relia finished her strange ceremony. Drekton eyed her wearily. "Ready?" he asked.

The three of them took a collective deep breath.

"Let's go," Syn said with more bravery than she felt.

With her jaw set in determination, Syn took a single step and led them through toward whatever retribution lay on the other side.

PART SIX
LOST AND FOUND

<h1 style="text-align:center">58</h1>

<h2 style="text-align:center">TANOK</h2>

Tanok threw surreptitious glances at the alehouse as he worked oil into the cracked skin of another grunt. From the window, he could see the men inside laughing and drinking—as if they hadn't just murdered a young plumb-blood and sentenced an innocent girl to death.

Lektra, you brave little idiot! Tanok cursed and bent back to his work as he tried to come up with a plan. Xedford and the Graver had already left through the portal with Lektra, and he was running out of time.

His original plan included waiting until he earned his Hallowed Point. He would then expose the corruption from the inside, but he knew his opportunity to carry out that strategy died the moment he saw Lektra on the back of that wagon. Nervous sweat broke out over his body.

I need to act now. He knew he wouldn't get another opportunity. After Xedford left, the rest of the posse had taken advantage of his absence to seek inebriation. He could simply run away—make for the portal and save Lektra—but he knew better than to test his mortal strength against that of a

Nighterrian. And with one as barbaric as Xedford, he didn't stand a chance.

The creak and smack of the alehouse door yanked Tanok out of his plotting. He jumped and looked over his shoulder. The Skully stumbled onto the porch.

"Is something wrong?" Tanok asked.

"Privy. Where's it at?" The man did not look well. His eyes seemed dark and hollow, sweat drenched his face like he had a fever.

"It's around back." Tanok took in the way the Skully leaned against the post to hold himself up. "Here, I'll take you there." He wiped his oily hands on his trousers and placed his weight beneath the man's arm to help him walk.

"I don't need your help, light-dweller." He pushed Tanok away but stumbled, nearly falling as he tried to walk down the steps of the porch. Tanok swooped in and caught him. The man grumbled and cursed but let Tanok help walk him down the two steps. Tanok smelled ale on the man.

This is my chance.

The orange starlight shinned off the man's bald head as they walked around the back of the building. If the stories about Redd's men were to be believed, the Skullies got their nickname because each one of them had their Hal'point imbedded in their skulls. Whereas most Nighterrians kept their Hal'point location secret, Redd's men relied on their boss' fearful reputation. No one messed with Redd the Collector's Skullies—unless you desired a torturous death.

But the bold statement was not without risk. A risk Tanok hoped to take advantage of. His heart struck like a blacksmith's hammer in his chest. He glanced down at the Skully's left arm and recognized the Dracman three-barrel strapped to his wrist.

Could it really be this easy? Tanok did his best to stow his panic while he sorted through options for his next steps. Lava pits dotted the flat landscape as they reached the backside of the row of shops. The heat radiated the smell of sulfur, tickling the inside of his nostrils and rousing an idea.

With his right hand, Tanok reached to his belt for the blade he spent night after night sharpening for a moment such as this. He steered the man toward a large lava pit.

The Skully stopped as they reached the pit. "Where... This ain't the priv—"

Tanok yanked his blade free, spun out from under the Skully's arm, and sliced the back of the man's ankles. The Skully's dropped to his knees beside the pit and—before he could get out a scream—Tanok shoved the man's head into burning lava. The heat was unbearable, but Tanok continued to sit on his back and hold his head into the scorching pool until the man's legs ceased to kick.

He pulled the body out and nearly vomited. After all the massacres he had witnessed as an apprentice to Revvor's raid, he didn't expect to blanch at this killing, but the head was now just a gruesome stump that reeked of burning flesh. With an effort, he buried his disgust and swallowed back the bile climbing into his throat as he pulled out a small dagger.

He cut into the man's left thigh. Tanok didn't have the calm dexterity of the Graver and soon the man's leg was a tattered mess. He forced himself to think of Lektra. He pictured her pitiful blue lips of paralysis and the determination barely covering the fear in her eyes. He let the image of her grant his hands the stillness to squish through hot muscle until he felt along the slippery bone of the man's femur.

There! He paused, then clawed his way deeper into the man's thigh. He cut away the muscles from the bone and pried out a tiny, foreign object. He held the bloody Hal'point up to the light of the lava hole but didn't let himself marvel at it for long.

With trembling fingers, he ripped the three-barrel off the Skully's arm and shoved the rest of the body into the pit—hiding the evidence of his murder. The lava boiled with delight as it swallowed the body whole.

Tanok loaded the weapon with the Hal'point and pointed his fist to his throat. He had long ago abandoned speaking prayers to the Legion, but he mouthed a silent one to the orange stars above as he clicked the trigger into his palm.

He thought of Lektra and his home in Veldt as he pulled the trigger.

***

Tanok stumbled and ran through the frozen woods. The world seemed too bright, and he could hardly think straight.

Without time to let the imbuing take hold, he had forced himself through the portal and hoped for enough strength to take down Xedford. The Hal'point embedded in his throat radiated with pain and an odd tingling feeling.

The strange new sensations of the imbuing encumbered his progress through the woods. He ran in bursts of incredible strength followed by sudden bouts of crippling weakness that crumbled him to the snow as his body seized and trembled. He cut his arm on a branch and saw he still bled red. How long would it take to gain the strength of an imbued? He didn't know, but he begged the power to hasten its arrival.

I'm coming, Lektra. Tanok felt as if he had been running for hours, but he pressed on following the tracks in the snow and pushing his strength to the limit.

There, in the distance, he spotted three red-robed men. He pulled to a stop and braced himself against a tree. His stomach writhed like a den of snakes as he neared the cart parked behind the group of men. A breath of relief whooshed out of his chest at the sight of his sister's dark hair.

Tanok stepped as close as he dared and peeked out from behind the cover of a thick tree. With the Skully's stolen three-barrel on his wrist, he took aim at Xedford. His arm shook and his vision swam with the brightness of the snow reflecting the glaring sun.

He fired. The bullet clipped one of the Gravers, missing Xedford completely.

The force of the three-barrel's kick made him stumble. Tanok regained his balance and stepped out from the tree to take aim again. He knew a bullet wouldn't kill Xedford, but if he shot him in the eye, it could incapacitate him long enough for Tanok to part his head from his body.

Tanok fired again and missed. This time the recoil of the barrel knocked him backward into the snow.

"You!" Xedford clicked the trigger of his three-barrel into his hand. Betrayal raged across his features as he returned fire.

Tanok rolled away through the snow. "This is what you get, Xedford!" He hardly recognized his own voice. The Hal'-point embedded in his newly imbued throat pressed on his vocal cords, making his voice deep and rasping.

"What are you doing?" Xedford shot again.

Tanok ducked behind a tree to dodge the bullet. "I've come to give you what you deserve."

Tanok saw the Gravers run away with Lektra in the cart of bodies. He longed to chase after them, but he needed to eliminate the real threat first. Three Gravers would be no trouble to take down. It was Xedford he needed to handle first.

Another barrel blast grazed Tanok's shoulder. He gasped at the sting but was glad it was Xedford's third shot. Xedford would need to reload—but Tanok wouldn't give him the opportunity. He jumped out from behind the tree and fired his final shot at Xedford. It caught him in the gut.

Tanok pulled his sword free and ran in for attack. He expected Xedford to recover from the blow with ease, yet he stayed doubled over. Tanok took the chance to swing at his neck, but the weak swing only sliced the back of Xedford's head.

Xedford lashed out with his sword and grazed Tanok's chest. Tiny droplets of blood colored the snow red as he ducked away.

"How long you been a spy in our ranks?" Xedford slashed at Tanok again.

"Since I found out your trials were a sham." He swung at Xedford but missed. His eyes focused on the blue blood seeping from Xedford's gut. Tanok dodged behind a tree to avoid another deadly slice. He noticed Xedford attacked while still doubled over in pain. If he hadn't healed yet, that meant only one thing; he had a wound to the site of his Hal'point.

"I took you in, you were a part of our raid!" Xedford screamed.

Tanok delivered a stab to Xedford's stomach. He watched with satisfaction as more blue blood flowed from his wound. Xedford stumbled back and Tanok took the opportunity to thrust at him again. Tanok rained down strikes, cutting through his weakened defense and parting flesh. He searched for the right angle to dislodge the Hal'point and make Xedford vulnerable for a killing strike. He was almost there, he could see Xedford slowing. Another slice and—

Tanok hardly saw the flash of the blade Xedford yanked from his boot before it punctured through the center of his chest.

The stab stole Tanok's breath, and he staggered back. Instinct made him drop his guard and yank the knife from his sternum. Red, mortal blood spilled from his wound. The crimson blood proved his mistake. He hadn't allowed enough time for the imbuing to take hold.

"We could have taken Revvor down together," Xedford choked as he held his stomach with one hand and gripped his sword with the other. "We could have had it all..." His face contorted into a grimaced smile as he raised his sword. "But now... all you'll get... is this." He swept the blade down.

Unable to halt the arrival of death, Tanok watched the steel glint off the bright snow as it arced through the air. He took comfort in knowing he would at least die at home on the Surface instead of some ditch in the pit of the dark realm.

The strike reached him, and he just had time to think of his sister and pray for her survival before the blade severed his head from his body and all went dark.

59
A PROMISE

nip. Syn cringed as her mother cut the stitches from her face and pulled them out one by one. Vertah grumbled about the poor workmanship all the while applauding how the wound didn't draw infection.

Snip. Syn did her best to employ patience as she sat in the cramped room. The smell of animal fat and dried blood made her feel at ease. *I'm home.* It wasn't the longhouse she grew up in, but a tiny hut beyond the Outskirts.

In the days since her return to Garon, everything had changed. Syn recalled the day they emerged from the portal. After Relia used her newfound position to smooth things over with the Elders, Drekton had gone on his own to reunite with his mother while Syn and Relia went to search the whole of the Outskirts for Predon and Vertah. After a while, they found them in a rickety hut far removed from even the Outskirt citizens on the edge of the village.

"Is that them?" Relia had asked as they stood at a distance watching the pair chop firewood.

Syn couldn't get her legs to move. The sight of her parents

brought a flood of homecoming relief, but a bolt of sorrow pierced through her as she took in their patchy cloaks and pitiful home.

Then, perhaps sensing her presence, her mother turned around. Her hands immediately clapped around her mouth to truncate a silent scream. Predon turned around next. He stared with his mouth ajar as if he beheld a ghost.

Vertah took off sprinting through the snow. She rushed toward Syn, catching her in an embrace that nearly knocked her to the ground. The strangeness of her mother's affection stunned Syn for a moment, then she hugged her back. Vertah pulled back from the hug to regard her daughter with tears in her eyes.

Predon's lip trembled, and his face went blank with fear as he reached them. He lifted a slow hand and touched Syn's shoulder. The relief that sprawled across his expression told her he must have truly thought she was a mirage.

"You're here... you're-you're *alive!*" Predon said.

Vertah's joy turned to sadness as she traced the stitches of Syn's face. "You've been Severed!" she nearly sobbed the words. Tears threatened to spill from her eyes, but she didn't seem to care.

Tears? Syn didn't know her mother could produce tears. In her mind, Syn always imagined her parents complicit in the decision to deliver her to justice. But after seeing their reactions, she felt guilty for thinking they would serve her up to be maimed and damned.

Syn hadn't expected such joy at her return. Now, she glanced thankfully up at her mother and watched through the dim light of the cramped room as Vertah removed the stitches from Syn's face with steady hands and an unreadable expression.

Since her arrival back home, Syn had spent most of her

days helping her parents build out their hut and gather resources. They had devastatingly few possessions after being forced to trade them for food and supplies in other villages.

Relia proved an enormous help. Over the course of the past few weeks, the imbuing had taken hold and her strength and vitality increased tenfold. She tested out her newfound powers by helping to fell trees for the building of a workroom, but she mostly enjoyed hunting for meals which she chased down by foot.

Predon and Vertah took a liking to Relia immediately, though they sometimes lifted eyebrows at her strange and often crude behavior. However, as a Nighterrian, she could do no wrong in their eyes.

Relia stayed by Syn's side as often as her attention would allow, but Syn could tell she didn't like being cooped up in a little village full of people who worshiped her. Relia spent a good portion of her time exploring the woods and marveling at the wildlife, all the while constantly complaining about the cold. Syn knew Relia's destiny would take her far from Garon. She only wondered how long it would be until she left.

Syn saw very little of Drekton during the day. He spent most of his time with his mother. Although Relia and Drekton spent a good chunk of their day apart from Syn, they always found their way back to her tiny hut when night fell. The three of them shared something few others ever would. Nightmares seized them as they slept, and a deep unsettling befell them once darkness plunged them into night.

Syn and Relia quelled the fear by huddling around the hearth and drinking tea while waiting Drekton's arrival. Relia continued to grumble about the lack-luster tea and did her best to explain to Syn's parents what ale was and how to make it.

The two of them took turns telling Predon and Vertah the

tale of the trials in minute detail. Embarrassed, Syn left off the part where she fell for Xedford's seduction. But everything else she told without reserve.

Syn's parents remained shocked and disgusted by the corruption. They continued to ask questions about the scope of the exploitation, but Syn didn't know how many other raids of Nighterrians operated like Revvor's crew. Relia insisted not all Nighterrians were corrupt, but she had spent most of her life avoiding the law enforcers as she gambled her way from town to town.

Once Drekton arrived on these late nights, he tried to help fill in the gaps of their knowledge, but he too knew little of the extent to which the Nighterrians' tainted influence reached.

Syn felt continually grateful for the two of them. Their presence helped ease the acceptance of her harsh new reality. Tensions were taut as a bow string between Syn the rest of the Legionites, especially Drekton's mother Faylyn. Although Drekton did his best to explain that Syn shouldn't be held responsible for Rem's death, Syn only had to take one look at Faylyn to know the loss of her youngest son was still as fresh as powdered snow.

Despite Relia and Drekton's combined effort in pleading Syn's case to Chief Groth and the Nameless Elders, Syn and her family remained exiled, "Until a time in which the entirety of the village has forgiven them."

With Relia at her side to vouch for her honor, Syn could likely convince the village to forgive her despite their heavy resentment. However, there remained Faylyn who held tight to her grudge and Chief Groth who refused to let his punishment be undone. It would be a long time before either of the two forgave Syn. If they ever did. Eventually time might weather away the wounds, but for now Syn and her family remained stranded on the edge of the Outskirts, ignored and unwelcome.

"Ouch," Syn complained as Vertah ripped the last stitch from her face.

"Oh, quit your whining." Vertah dabbed a warm towel at Syn's eye before moving to smooth on a salve. A deep sorrow shadowed Vertah's face while she rubbed on the pungent salve. "You'll have a scar of course, but perhaps the pine rub will help." She leaned back to look at her work. "I'll give you the recipe. You'll have to apply it twice a day if you want the redness to go down."

"Thank you," Syn said, though she knew she would forgo the remedy.

A light scar or a big ugly scar, it didn't matter. Her soul would remain severed. She sometimes caught her refection in water cups or bowls of drained animal blood and gasped before recognizing her own face looking back at her. She could open her left eye now, but it remained sightless. She would stare at her reflection with her one good eye, grimacing at the destroyed eyeball and its milky iris.

"I should be getting back to my duties. I want to finish the workroom before nightfall." Syn hopped off the worktable with a grunt. Her other injuries were healing, but her body continued to ache.

"Wait just a minute, Relia and your father should be back soon. We have something for you."

As if on cue, Predon parted the elk skin door. He smiled his genuine smile and held an item wrapped in cloth. Relia skipped in behind him with her toothy grin in place. Vertah had taken to calling Relia "the wolf-child." To embrace the nickname, Relia had chosen to clothe herself in wolf pelts from the slew of gifts offered to her from the villagers.

"Did you get it?" Vertah asked.

"Sure did, thanks to Relia." Predon nodded his appreciation to Relia and walked over to his wife. Together they turned their backs on Syn and unwrapped the package like a pair of children hiding a mischievous deed.

"What is it?" Syn tried to peer around them, but their fur cloaks provided cover. She turned to Relia. "What did you help them get?"

"You'll see."

Predon and Vertah turned around and offered Syn what laid across their hands: The family sword. The sharp blade glittered in the fire light and the carved hilt stared with a hundred empty eyes sockets.

"What... how did you..." Syn knew they had traded it in another village when they ran out of supplies just before she returned.

"Relia helped me track down the man I traded it to. I'm sorry it took so long to retrieve, but here it is," Predon said.

"And we want you to have it." Vertah's brow creased as she looked at Syn's scarred face. "You've earned it."

Unbidden tears sprang from Syn's eyes as she picked up the sword by the white hilt. She missed Elaine terribly and felt naked without a silent friend at her side.

"I-I don't know what to say."

The carved antler hilt provided a comfortable grip. She remembered how heavy the sword weighed after her failed sacrifice, but now the weapon felt agile and deadly in her hands. She could see herself able to wield it against beasts and humans alike. Any who threatened her would meet the edge of her blade.

A giggle escaped her. Where did these ideas of grandeur come from? She sheathed the family heirloom in the leather scabbard at her belt before she could let herself get carried away by fantasies of heroism. She grabbed her parents up in a tight hug.

"Thank you," she said, her face crushed into the fur of her mother's yak pelt. "I know just what to name it."

"Syn names all her things," Relia explained to Predon and Vertah—as if they weren't aware of their own daughter's idiosyncrasies.

Syn released her parents from her hug and looked back down at the weapon hanging at her side. She remembered Rem's delighted face on the day her father handed it to her. She smiled at the memory of his unending questions.

Relia nodded to the sword. "Well, you gonna tell us what her name is or are you fixing to make us guess?"

"*His* name." Syn patted the hilt. "His name is Rem."

Relia smiled her understanding. "I figured I might name my three-barrel. Any ideas?"

Syn stared down at the shining weapon perched comfortably on Relia's wrist. The gray of the barrels reminded her of Lektra's eyes.

"How about Lektra?" It seemed fitting as the three-barrel was Lektra's parting gift to Syn in exchange for a promise.

"Lektra it is." Relia smiled.

"Which reminds me," Syn recalled the begging words spoken from Lektra's bloodied lips as she died. "I have a promise to keep."

60

TREASURE

"**A**nd you're sure this is where we'll pick up his trail?" Drekton looked over his shoulder at Syn as he marched through the snow.

"I never said I was sure. It's just a hunch," Syn said.

Relia shivered at Syn's side. "Syn's got magical powers, don't you doubt her."

Syn rolled her eyes and led the way through the woods. "I always knew something was off about Xedford's story about how he got injured. I saw his wounds. They were clearly stab wounds, not claw marks."

"What about Lektra's brother? What makes you think it was him?" Drekton asked.

"Lektra said Tanok had infiltrated a posse of corrupt Nighterrians and that Xedford was one of them. And Xedford himself mentioned an apprentice who betrayed him. I don't think it's a stretch to assume they were one in the same."

"Well let's hurry up and find him," Relia said. "I'm done freezing my tits off out here."

Syn patted Rem's hilt as she walked on with growing

uncertainty that she could prove her theory. They had already passed the place where she had met Xedford for the first time. She didn't know in what direction or how far he had come before she encountered him. And even if they did find where the battle had taken place, what then? Did she expect to find a bloody trail leading straight to Tanok's hideout?

She wandered on through the woods, unsure of what to look for. The gathering cold seemed unusually oppressive. Perhaps the few weeks in Interterra's sweltering heat had ruined her acclimation to the winter snow. She noticed Drekton squinting at the brightness of the overcast day and thought he might feel something similar.

It felt odd to be walking calmly beside him with nervous twitches in her fingers—as if she were once again the innocent, foolish girl she was before Rem's death. But she could not let herself get lost in fantasies of days past.

Everything had changed.

It had been weeks, and still Drekton's mother had not budged in her hatred for Syn, despite Drekton's attempts at explaining how she saved his live. Perhaps Faylyn would never forgive her. Syn commiserated as she trudged on through the snow. "Maybe we should turn back. I don't even know what to—"

"What is that?" Relia emerged from her shivering misery to point at a tree in the distance.

"A tree," Drekton said with an annoyed sigh.

"No, look!" Relia took off running.

Syn and Drekton exchanged a look, then raced after her. They reached the tree in question and huddled in to see Relia trace her gloved fingers over a circular hole in the trunk. An imbedded bullet was just visible at the center of the hole. Syn clapped Relia on the shoulder to congratulate her discovery before whipping around to survey the area.

"This is where it must have been." Syn spotted another tree with a chunk missing from the side as if a bullet had grazed it. "Over there!" She pointed and ran off.

She made her way toward the tree, but her foot caught something hidden beneath the snow and she tripped. Her head landed in a pile of snow, cushioning her fall. She opened her eye and gasped.

She laid face to face with a severed head.

Drekton helped her scramble to her feet. She knelt to peer down at the glassy, vacant eyes of the head. Syn exchanged a look with Drekton and Relia. Her fall had disturbed the blanket of snow covering the rest of the body.

"Is it him?" Relia leaned over and squinted.

"I don't know." Syn brushed away the frost to uncover more of the face.

Drekton and Relia wasted no time in diving down to begin unearthing the rest of the body. "He's wearing a three-barrel." Drekton broke the stiff left arm from the snow. "You think he's Nighterrian?"

Syn examined the lethal cut that separated the head from the body. "No, he bled red." She studied the features of the severed head and compared them to her memory of Lektra. She sighed and reverently brushed away more snow. "It's Tanok. He looks just like her."

Relia cursed and sat down beside her in defeat. Drekton joined Syn in dusting the snow off the body as a solemn silence clouded the air.

Syn didn't know what she had expected to find. She knew it was silly to hope they would find Tanok at all, but still a part of her had longed for another comrade in their midst. Perhaps she desired someone to tell her what to do next. She felt so lost and out of place since her return to Garon. She wanted justice for Lektra and all those who fell victim to the crew's deception, but she didn't know how to go about vengeance as a Severed one.

Drekton broke the despairing silence. "We should bring his body back to the village."

Syn nodded. Drekton moved to pick up the body, but Relia shoved him aside. "I got this!" Showing off her Nighterrian strength, she easily plucked up Tanok's frozen body. Drekton glared at her but said nothing.

Syn cradled Tanok's head and climbed to her feet. "Wait."

"What?" Relia stopped and looked over her shoulder.

Syn glanced back and forth between Tanok's head and his body. The truncated cut on his shoulders appeared dark and crumbling as one might expect of a body left to the elements for over a month. But the cut to Tanok's head was still red and fresh as a next day butchering.

"Does his head look... less decomposed than his body?" Syn asked.

"The snow keeps bodies preserved," Drekton said. "The head must have been buried deeper than the rest of him."

"Still..." Syn held Tanok's head up in front of her face to get a better look. His eyes were dim and his skin pallid, but otherwise he looked as if he had died mere hours ago. The decapitation had left most of his neck attached to his head. She turned his head around to get a better look at the lethal cut and paused when she spotted something strange.

What is that? Syn pulled off her gloves to work her fingers into the vertebrae of Tanok's neck. His flesh was too frozen, however, and she grabbed for her dagger.

"What are you doing?" Drekton stared back at Syn.

She pried away the frozen flesh and dug into the bone with her blade. "There's something..." She sheathed her dagger and grasped at the shimmer of blue she glimpsed against the white of the bone. With a pinch and a yank, a small, hard object fell into her hand.

Syn's jaw hinged open at the sight in her palm.

"Pissing Fates!" Relia nearly dropped Tanok's body. "Is that a Hal'point?"

"So he *was* a Nighterrian," Drekton stepped closer for a better look.

"Why would Xedford go and leave behind a perfectly intact Hal'point?" Relia asked.

Syn couldn't take her eyes off the sacred treasure in her hand as her mind shuttered to catch up with the implications. "Xedford must not have known he was imbued. The imbuing must have been too recent to show signs of change. Even his blood was still red."

Syn stared down at the blue aura the Hallowed Point cast on her palm. She held her breath at the incredulity, then she thrust it toward Drekton. "Here, take it."

"What? Me?" He pushed her hand away from his face.

"It was Rem's dream. You should honor his memory."

"I..." He stared down for a long moment as he considered. When he looked back up, his eyes glistened but remained resolute. "No."

"No?"

"No. I can't take it, it wouldn't work. I didn't finish the trials," he said.

"We all know the trials were a sham. The crew designed them to recruit only the most vile and immoral competitors so they wouldn't have to feel guilty when they murdered them. You're strong, I'm certain you would survive the imbuing."

"Even so, I don't want it. If I were to become Nighterrian, I would eventually have to return to Interterra to try and take down the corruption of the Nighterrians. I-I can't abandon my mother again. I'm all she has left."

"You wouldn't have to leave. You could stay as Garon's protector."

Drekton shook his head. "I want to help dispel the Nighterrian lies and expose the truth to other Legionites. I can't spread this truth if I am a Nighterrian myself."

He was right. As much as the Legionites worshiped Nighterrians, they were still seen as outsiders. They were not citizens and although they were always welcome in Garon and the surrounding villages, none ever stayed for long.

Drekton closed Syn's hand around the Hal'point. His touch sent zings of nervous energy through her fingers. "Take it and restore your soul."

"It won't undo the Severing." She thought of the scar on Xedford's forehead. Although the imbuing saved Relia from becoming a Scaler, it seemed the healing powers of the imbuing offered nothing for old wounds.

Drekton placed his other hand on her shoulder. "Then take it and return honor to your family."

"But your mother, she'll—"

"My mother will forgive the family of a Nighterrian. And so will the Chief. They must, they are Legionite after all."

She looked into his eyes. A warmth gathered in her chest and pushed back against the cold. "Thank you," she said.

"You'll do it?" Relia piped up with eager excitement.

"Yes," Syn agreed. She shook her head, still in disbelief. "But I don't want the imbuing to be performed in secret. It's time we open the eyes of our people and show them that the Nighterrians are not divine messengers of the Legion. They need to know the Nighterrians are people—people just as flawed as the rest of us."

61

A NEW PRECEDENT

I can't wait to fix you.

Syn shivered at the memory of Xedford's words as she stood atop a small stage at the base of the Ancestral Hill. When she first agreed to accept the Hal'point, she hadn't thought about how it would affect her haunting. Now, a headache pounded her skull as she tried to shove Xedford's voice from her mind.

She hadn't experienced an episode of her haunting since she returned, but she could feel the weight of one pressing its presence over her mind. The beat of drums didn't help. Would this be the last time she experienced her curse's oppressive company?

To her right and left stood Drekton and Relia staring their calm presence into the anxious crowd. Syn managed a half smile at them through the throbbing pain in her skull. Together, the three of them had lobbied the Elders to break with the tradition of keeping the ceremony of the Imbuing in Interterra. They refused at first, but the desire to see an

Imbuing performed in front of their eyes won them over in the end. Even Chief Groth couldn't deny his curiosity.

"This is how it should be," Syn said to Rem at her belt. Too many Nighterrian codes were cloaked in secrecy. If the Legionites knew exactly how and why the Nighterrians gained their powers, it might keep them from allowing ignorance and blind worship to take place.

Over the previous days, Drekton had spent many hours conversing with the Elders and the Prime citizens of the village about the true nature of the Nighterrians. He hadn't found much success. The belief that the warriors were the chosen soldiers of the Legion and blessed with divine power was embedded deep in the Legionite culture. Turning the tide of hundreds of years of tradition would take time and evidence to prove.

Syn hoped the day's spectacle would rid them of some of their misgivings. If only they could see the Nighterrians as still human, perhaps they could understand that power did not make you holy. If a Severed girl could become Nighterrian, it would prove that Nighterrians carried with them the human scruples and scars of their true self.

Syn felt a hand on her shoulder. She turned to offer a smile at her parents standing behind her on the platform. Predon gave an encouraging squeeze to her shoulder. Syn longed to bring them the honor they deserved. Once their daughter was imbued, her parents could finally be forgiven.

She turned back to the front. The crowd around them muttered with excitement and skepticism over the sound of drums and singing. Chief Groth headed the ceremony despite Syn's hatred for the man. She felt it would help quell her unsteady relationship with the village. With Groth's ego sore from being outranked by a young, filthy-mouthed Nighterrian,

Syn hoped asking him to conduct the ceremony would ease his displeasure. The prospect of being the first Legionite chief to ever reside over such a miracle was too exciting for him to resist, despite the grudge he held against her.

The music of drums ceased and Groth launched into a speech.

"You ready?" Relia asked.

"Ready as I'll ever be." Syn tried to rid herself of the thought that stalked her waking dreams: What if the whispers were true? What if the Imbuing would never take on a Severed one? The crowd all waited to witness either a miracle or a massacre. Looking out at their hungry, expectant faces, Syn realized they would be satisfied with either.

"Don't worry. It won't hurt for long," Relia said, as if that was what worried Syn.

Pain she could survive, a failed imbuing, she could not.

She felt for her sword at her hip. "Rem, give me strength."

Darkness spread at the corner of her vision and quickened her heartbeat. She fought to steady her breathing as she tried to imagine what would it be like to live without the haunting —without dragging around the weight of dread and fear that plagued her everyday of her life. Would it be peaceful? Would she become as happy and carefree as Relia? As Rem used to be?

Syn cringed as her haunting threw visions of shadows all around her. Of course. The most important day of her life and she would be plagued by her illness.

When Groth finished his speech, Relia held the Hal'point before the crowd. "Behold!" she began, and Syn nearly clapped her palm to her face in embarrassment as Relia launched into a speech of her own. "On this day we honor Syndrah Tri-Garon. The survivor of trials and savior of Nighterrians!" she boasted, enjoying the rally of the crowd. "She done saved my life many times over. For her bravery and sacrifice, she's earned this here reward. With this Hal'po—er, Hallowed Point, I hereby grant her the blessing of the Legion."

Relia loaded the Hal'point into her three-barrel which she had prepped with only a quarter the amount of blackpowder so the Hal'point wouldn't shoot clean through. The voices of the crowd resonated with a mixture of awed whispers and bitter scorn.

"Let it be known," Drekton said, and Syn balked at the pseudo bravado he adopted to match Relia's speech. "That this Hallowed Point will only grant mortal strength and abilities. It will not change her character. The time for more careful selection of Nighterrians is now. And who better than Syn to begin the dawn of this new era?"

A few hoorays of excitement went up, but most of the crowd remained skeptical. Someone shouted, "Sacrilege!" From the back, another yelled, "A Severed does not deserve the honor!"

Drekton sighed under his breath. Then added, "And what better village than the village of Garon to be the first Legionite community to witness an Imbuing of one of their own?" The crowd cheered at this.

"Way to eclipse me," Relia complained.

Syn looked to Drekton with a blush prickling her cheek. The stoic and serious boy from her childhood transformed before her eyes into a man who could conduct a crowd. The silly flutter of her stomach died as Relia held up her three-barrel.

Syn pulled down the fur of her collar and motioned to her shoulder. The drummers picked up with a war-like rhythm. She felt the cold of the barrel press against her skin. Shadows leapt into her vision as if to say goodbye.

A bizarre fear suddenly seized her. Would it be lonely

without her ghosts? They had been with her all her life. They were a part of her. Who would she be without them? The drums increased in tempo. With every mallet strike, doubt hammered the fear of loss into her conscience.

"Welcome to the club," Relia said with a wry smile.

Wait, I don't want to be without my ghosts! Syn opened her mouth, but too late.

Relia pulled the trigger.

The air went out of Syn's lungs, and she stumbled backward with the force of the shot. Her parents caught her and held her upright.

Searing pain sprang like daggers of ice through her veins. The shadows in her mind swirled and her head pounded with such violence she couldn't hear anything else. The world darkened as excruciating pain racked her body. She felt certain her skin was being flayed with a dull knife and her bones set on fire.

The torture came to a crescendo as her vision twisted with flitting horrors. Reality and nightmare collided and swirled into her sight as confusion and terror gripped her. The power of the Imbuing seemed to last for an eternity, and she still couldn't gasp a breath. She would have collapsed if it weren't for the hands that held her upright.

Syn looked down and noticed not all the hands were human. Some of them were made of shadows but they held her tight, and she could feel the pressure of their grip. Panic jolted through her terrorized body. *What is this?*

The ghosts of her visions solidified into faces, faces she recognized from her dreams. They flickered; with every blink of her eye, they disappeared only for her to blink again and find they reappeared in greater number.

With her lungs out of air, she felt as if she were drowning. Unable to find her breath, her chest burned, and she could feel unconsciousness on the other side of the dizzying whirlwind.

The visions of shadowed faces came closer. They converged and reached their hands toward her. They wanted something. They wanted *her*. She felt their desire, their raw need, and the hunger for something outside their grasp.

I can't breathe! They came closer. *"Help me!"* she begged and reached out to touch one of the hands.

The faces turned to smoke and evaporated into a brackish mist.

To her horror, she watched, stricken, as they poured into her. The darkness streamed in through the pores of her skin, her nose, her mouth. She could taste the emptiness of the shadows and the smell of her own fear as the black mist gushed in through her eyes and filled her senses. The swallowed shadows extinguished the pain.

She took a breath.

Sweet frozen air! She drank it in. Panting, gasping, her vision cleared. She looked around to see the bright snow; the faces of her friends; the concerned crease of her parents' foreheads; the crowd staring in rapture.

The pain slid away at a trickle. With it, the strength of her legs. She slumped against her parent's hands as fatigue took over her feverish body.

Syn spied Relia smile her toothy grin. Drekton nodded with encouragement. They mouthed words that she couldn't make out. She was soaked in complete exhaustion. Her shoulder ached like it had been torn from her body. She felt for it to make sure it was still there. Still intact.

Thoughts came slow. *I've been imbued.* Yet something was wrong.

Sound returned to her, and she heard the crowd cheering. She looked around the village and caught whisps of shadows ducking behind huts. Sinister faces popped up and disappeared through the crowd.

I've been imbued. Panic pounded her heart like a war drum as she watched her ghosts disappear only to materialize all around her. *But my haunting remains.*

Worse, it seemed to have taken on a life of its own.

62
ONWARD

The wind tickled the trinkets of Syn's hideout. Syn sat in her hammock listening to the chime of Jordan's beads clink against Tyler's broken pottery. It felt strange to be back in her hideout in Garon. Since her return from the trials, she was often too busy with her family to find much time to get away to the treetops.

Of course, she had showed Relia her secret place. Relia had laughed and touched each one of the trinkets as Syn introduced them.

"It's nice to meet you, Raymond, Dustin, Ryan." Relia had said, giving a pretend handshake to each of the boys.

Today, however, Syn found herself alone in the branches. She traced the scar across her eye, feeling at the raised edges as she watched her friends twist in the wind. The Imbuing had healed the cut, but a scar remained. Her left eye continued to see only darkness. Although the Imbuing could heal all immediate injuries, her theory that it left past scars untouched proved correct.

She felt at the heaviness of her soul, the only constant she ever knew. It was there as always, the weight of her past lives piled upon her shoulders. But they were different now. She didn't fear them like she once did.

"Let's give it another try," she said to Rem in his scabbard.

Syn closed her eyes and concentrated. She let her mind stretch out to the dark recess of her consciousness and invited the shadows to come forward. When she opened her eyes, she could see whisps of darkness beginning to coalesce.

She focused on the air in front of her and swallowed down the inkling of fear that burned her throat. She willed a single shadow into being. The mist of darkness gathered and fused together in the shape of a hand. The hand hovered beside the broken comb named Marcus.

"Touch the comb," she commanded.

Nothing happened.

Syn concentrated harder and held her own hand up into the air. "Move Marcus." She waved her fingers and the shadow hand followed suit. It ruffled the leather cord of the comb, sending Marcus twirling in a circle.

Syn smiled and made the shadow twist the cord again. Her body trembled as if she were lifting an immense weight, and her breath came in shallow whisps, but she did it. She summoned her haunting and wrestled it into submission.

"Shit of my ancestors!"

Syn gave a start and dropped her concentration. She looked down to see Relia climb up the last branch of the tree. "You silent thief!" Syn cursed and broke into a smile. "How long have you been there?"

Relia plopped into the hammock. "Not long. I'm surprised you didn't hear me coming."

"I was busy."

"I can see that." Relia motioned to the comb that slowly

lost its momentum but continued to twist on its cord. "You did it this time."

Syn offered a half smile as she sat back and flexed her fingers. In the few weeks following her Imbuing, Relia had encouraged her to practice the new avenues of her curse. They sat quietly watching Marcus slow and eventually come to a halt. He then moved only in tune with the wind. After Syn lost her focus, the shadows always slipped away. She hadn't suffered an episode since she became a Nighterrian, but she didn't think those days were past. She only waited to see what new form it would take.

Much had changed since her Imbuing. Syn's parents had moved back into their old home in the third ring and regained the title of Tri-Garon. Some villagers still held weary grudges, but many mornings Syn woke to find gifts littering their doorstep.

Although the village now embraced Syn as a deific warrior, Garon no longer felt like home. She didn't know if it ever had. She loved her family, but with their honor restored she felt as if she were no longer needed.

"I got something for you." Relia invaded Syn's downcast mood and dug into her wolf cloak.

"I think you've already given me enough."

Relia shrugged. "What are friends for?" She handed Syn a wrapped package.

Syn untied the leather chord binding the cloth around the mysterious object. The cloth fell away to reveal a familiar three-barrel.

"You're a Nighterrian now, you ought to have yourself a three-barrel," Relia said.

"But what about you?" Syn looked to the secondary weapon strapped Relia's wrist.

Relia shrugged. "I borrowed Tanok's. I don't think he'll

mind, considering he ain't using it." She pressed Lektra's three-barrel into Syn's hands. "But this one belonged to you from the start."

Syn's mind flashed with memories of Lektra. The imbued blood that now flowed through Syn's veins was all thanks to Lektra's bravery, along with her life. She owed her so much and more.

Before Syn could protest, Relia began strapping the weapon to Syn's wrist. In a matter of seconds, Syn wore the dangerous contraption on her left arm. She marveled at how light it felt with her Nighterrian reenforced strength.

"Thank you," she said in awe. Relia grinned but Syn sensed her bated breath and knew something weighed on her mind. "Is there something else?"

Relia shifted in the hammock and reached out to touch a broken utensil named Richard. "I gotta go back to Interterra."

"Oh." Syn knew this was coming. Relia longed for adventure, and she didn't belong in Garon. Syn shouldn't have been surprised, but it still caught her off guard.

"And I'd like for you come with me."

Syn hesitated. "What are you planning?"

Relia turned away from Richard and looked at Syn with her wild, red eyes. "We got unfinished business."

Syn nodded. "Some of Revvor's crew is still out there." Although most of them likely fell victim to Xedford's trap, Nighterrians were tenacious. Surely some of them escaped.

"And others. You said Xedford and Lektra revealed Revvor's crew was under the thumb of Redd the Collector. Who knows how many raids of Nighterrians have turned into crime lords and outlaws?"

"And how many more innocent teenagers will they take advantage of once word of the second imbuing spreads?"

"Exactly."

"But what are you proposing? We go track down the surviving crew, extract justice, then seek out other outlaw raids and topple their criminal enterprise?"

"With a little drinking and gambling in between," Relia added. "You know, to keep our spirits up."

Syn chuckled but apprehension tugged at the edge of her mind at the thought of returning to the endless night and the horrors that lurked in darkness.

Her thoughts traveled again to Lektra as she touched the steel of the barrels on her wrist. Lektra, the poor, brave girl with gray eyes and a dead brother. With her dying words, Lektra had encouraged Syn to seek justice. She put all her faith in Syn, but the world would never know of her sacrifice.

"So, what do you say?" Relia asked.

Syn finished running her fingers over each of the barrels and looked up at Relia's hopeful face. "When do we leave?"

THE GRUNT SNORTED AND GROANED AS IT TUGGED AT THE REIGNS IN Syn's hand. Syn rolled her eyes and dug her hand into a sack to feed the beast a chunk of raw meat.

"Filthy beast." It slobbered over her outstretched hand. She distrusted the grunts, but Relia, ever the performer, insisted on procuring them to make for a more dramatic exit.

Syn looked up at the daylight, bidding it goodbye. She didn't know how long it would be before she would glimpse the sun again. The portal shimmered behind them, spreading invitation with its presence.

Relia held her own grunt in tow as they stood at the top of the Ancestral Hill. Her intrepid expression stood out beneath the war paint. The village children had begged for the honor of painting the faces of the Nighterrians and Syn had grudgingly agreed. Relia wore it with regal pride. With a pinch of jealousy, Syn thought it made her look more intense and terrifying. Syn just felt silly.

Drekton stood beside Syn and her parents. Although Syn invited him to come along on the mission with them, he elected to stay behind. He felt he could do more in Garon and the surrounding Legionite villages than in Interterra. He had quickly taken to his new task of spreading word about the corruption of the Nighterrians. It would be a journey of diplomatic relations and reversing hundreds of years of ritual and belief. Syn did not envy him.

"Be careful in there," Drekton said to Syn. He turned to Relia and jutted his chin at Syn. "Don't let anything happen to her."

"Well, I ain't planning on feeding her to any monsters if that's what you mean," Relia laughed.

He ignored her and turned back to Syn. "If you need anything, you know where to find me." His brown eyes burrowed into her, making her feel giddy and nervous.

"Take care of them," she nodded to her parents as she tried to stifle her awkwardness. Why did she find it easier to talk to him in the midst of mortal danger?

"I will." Drekton gave her one of his rare smiles. Part of Syn wished she didn't have to leave. He dug in his pocket and pulled out a small object. "My mother wanted me to give you this." He placed a flat stone into her hands.

It was a whetstone. One side was flat and smooth while the other side contained five concentric rings carved into the stone to represent the village rings of Garon. A small hole burrowed into the top turned the round stone into a necklace. Syn examined the gift with wordless appreciation.

"She said to keep your blade sharp and kill as many Scalers as you can." Drekton placed the leather chord over her head, so the stone hung around her neck. "I suppose it's her way of saying she forgives you."

"I-I will. Tell her I'll kill them all." Gratitude formed a lump in her throat. "And tell her thank you."

"Be safe," he said, then he turned and retreated down the steps of the Hill, throwing one last look over his shoulder with a small smile playing at the corners of his lips.

Perhaps the one upside of the war paint was its ability to camouflage Syn's blush.

The grunts snorted as Predon walked up and hugged Syn with all his might. He didn't say anything, but he didn't need to. Syn and her father always had an unspoken understanding of each other. She knew how much his heart ached while saying goodbye. She felt it too and hugged him back. Once he let go, he moved on to clasp Relia in a similar embrace.

"Whoa there, papa bear!" Relia laughed.

Vertah approached Syn next and threw her arms around her. "I'm so proud of you." Tears spilled from Syn's eyes. Vertah held her for a long moment. When she let go, she blinked back tears and looked to Relia. "You two be careful."

Relia nodded, serious now. "We will."

"Bring them down," Vertah said with stern conviction. Her eyes hardened into the familiar woman Syn knew as she stepped back beside her husband.

Syn didn't bother wiping her tears away. She allowed them fall, letting the cold air freeze them onto her face. Together, she and Relia mounted their grunts and turned them toward the portal. Syn soaked in the brightness of the day and took one last look over her shoulder to offer her parents a courageous smile.

"Ready?" Relia asked.

Syn patted her sword at her hip and adjusted the three-barrel at her wrist. Armed with Rem and Lektra, she nodded. "Ready."

With a nudge to their spiked haunches, the grunts snorted into action. In two galloping steps, Syn and Relia plunged into the portal and hurtled onward toward the promise of danger and justice.

ACKNOWLEDGMENTS

First and foremost, I need to thank my husband, Joe. I'm not certain I would have continued writing if it weren't for your relentless pleas for "more book!" (At the same time, it's a wonder this book was ever written since you insist on trying to talk to me when I'm writing.) You'll always be my biggest fan. I love you.

I would like to thank my family for all the years of inspiration and encouragement. Jenna, your love for plots with a series of deadly tasks inspired the Nighterrian trials and the entire premise of this book! Thank you for being my alpha reader and my sounding board for all my weird story ideas.

A big thank you to my friend and writing partner, T.L. Humphrey. Your insight has been integral in whipping the manuscript into its final form. Also, I dub you the official leader of the Team Xedford fan club!

Thank you to my beta readers: William, Louise, and Caleb. Your feedback helped me refine the rough edges of this story.

Shout out to my, now, defunct writing group. Your input on the first few chapters helped me shape Syn's journey. I'll miss our chats over glasses of mead!

To Anna Stileski and the team at Bow's Bookshelf: Thank you for believing in my story and for bringing it to life!

And finally, thank you to my Street Team for spreading the word about Trials for the Haunted. And to all you Freaks from my Metalhead community and my Nerds from my Reader community: Your support in all my endeavors means the world to me. Y'all truly are the best bunch of nerdy weirdos the internet can find. Stay freaky.

ABOUT THE AUTHOR

As a fantasy, science-fiction, and horror author, J.J. Kīmmorist likes her music heavy and her fiction dark. A metalhead and an avid horror movie connoisseur, she hosts a YouTube channel discussing where music and storytelling meet. She lives in a cottage in the woods with her husband, nephew, daughter, and two greyhounds. Find out more at kimmorist.com.

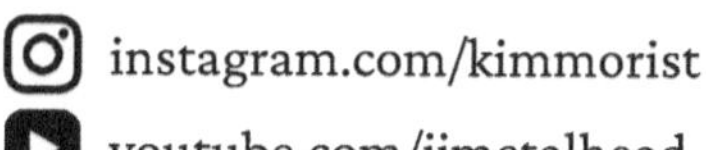

instagram.com/kimmorist

youtube.com/jjmetalhead

www.ingramcontent.com/pod-product-compliance
Lightning Source LLC
Chambersburg PA
CBHW022017300726
48970CB00003B/926